Sky Emblem

Christopher Hwang

Dragon Ink Publishing

ISBN: 0615688683
ISBN-13: 978-0615688688

ACKNOWLEDGMENTS

To my family, particularly my sister, for all her support.
A great thank you to Joey Huang, for your support too, and your concept art.
And a big thanks to Andrea Radeck for creating the marvelous cover art.

Chapter 1

A shadow passed overhead leaving a swath of swirling leaves in the forest below from its wake. A young boy was in the forest but paid the sudden darkness no mind, nor did he flinch when the airship above moved on and released the sunlight. They were a common sight in the entire continent of Valeria, and the boy had already seen three hover across the horizon earlier just today alone. There were a great variety of them: some were large, some were small, some were fast, and some were so heavily armed that one could see their vast array of cannons from the ground. But there was no time for the boy to even give the passing airship a sideways glance.

In Valeria, everyone is born with the talent to use magic. But there are a rare few who simply do not have the ability. In fact, they do not have the ability to interact with magic at all. The rest of the people of Valeria either consider them useless or dangerous as they not only cannot perform any work that any other "normal" person could do easier and quicker, but also because of their ability to disrupt the very flow of magic. The latter ability is particularly disruptive to a society that relies completely on magic, which is why all who are born without magic are exiled from every city.

Solah was one these exiles. He was young, no more than sixteen years of age, but his body was scrawny, a sad result of a life spent on thievery and hunting for whatever scraps of food he could find. His face wasn't as smooth as a boy his age should have been, and along with his hawkish features, made him appear much older than he really was. His light brown hair, however, was not as untidy as one would expect. It was only recently cut and ordered, deeply contrasting with the rest of him.

He was running through the vast expanse of greenery that surrounded the medium-sized but strategically important city of

1

Windsgate. He left a line of trampled leaves and twigs in his wake just as the airship above had left a trail of raining leaves.

His pursuers probably thought the thief that broke into a mansion after dispelling all its locks was an enchanter. Enchanters were, after all, the only mages that could enchant and disenchant objects. A very powerful enchanter he had to be too. He left no magical presence so that they couldn't even track him with their spells. One couldn't blame them for thinking such though; exiles were so rare that most people only read about them as some anomaly in academic books.

It was lucky for Solah, however, as both the city and its homes had no actual physical barriers to keep him out. Everybody's doors were sealed with magic that he could easily negate with a touch. Of course, the more wealthy residents had alarms that detected the presence of any intruder, but they were built to detect a person's indentation on the natural flow of magic, and exiles had none, which is the same reason why his pursuers had to resort to more mundane methods of tracking, methods that they were quite unskilled in. Solah had learned this long ago, and so his smuggling runs became more and more bountiful as he dared to steal from the richer more and more.

Solah had no qualms about stealing. After all, it was they who banished him into the wilds when he was young and defenseless. If he hadn't stumbled onto the solitary home of another exile, he surely would've died. Grandma Nama, as Solah came to call her, lived in that home that was in the middle of nowhere. She had gladly taken him in and treated him like a son. Nama was younger back then, though now she was late into her seventies. She had provided for him until she could no longer even leave the home to harvest fruits. Since then, Solah had provided for her in return for her kindness. At first, he would harvest the fruits and vegetables that grew near their home, but he took too much every time, and eventually they stopped growing. He had to venture further and further out to find any food, until one day he ventured so far out that he saw the city. Windsgate was only half a day's walk from their home, and he hadn't known it was there his entire life. Since that day, he went into the city and stole food for himself and Grandma. He grew more efficient too: very quickly he had made a large basket he could wear on his back. He learned to hide this basket outside the city in the forest so he could make quick trips back and forth to fill it with food and other supplies.

Then, instead of having to come back everyday to the city to gather food, he only needed to come once every two weeks.

Nama liked to read books too. She taught him how to read and sometimes he would manage to swipe one or two on one of his runs. Of course the old lady gave him an odd look the first time he gave her a new book, but she didn't ask about where he got it. He didn't know what Nama would've thought about stealing, but she never asked so he left the subject alone.

He had been seen breaking into a home very few times before. Usually, the person who saw him would scream out and scream out, "Thief!" or some other equivalent term. He'd flee, and nobody would follow. However, it was on this day that Solah's luck had finally given out. Several city guards were chasing after him after today's last smuggling run. Now he was regretting targeting one of the largest homes he had seen in his ventures in the city; it probably belonged to someone very rich or powerful.

Nevertheless, he was still lucky in other ways. Nobody saw his face, so he'd only have to change his clothes before coming back tomorrow. The airship that passed above him didn't seem like it was searching for him. It was a small worry that was in the back of his head, but his reason told him they wouldn't deploy an airship just to find a petty thief. Not only that, but also the airship's wake was shaking the weak autumn leaves out of the forest's trees and they were covering his tracks quite well.

But Solah didn't want to take any chances. He kept running for well over an hour while clutching a bag of oranges in one hand and a bag of potatoes in the other. He would've kept running for much longer too, if not for what happened next.

He jumped through a thicket into a small clearing and what he saw completely stopped him in his tracks. There was a giant mess: a thick glowing liquid appeared to have exploded and spread all around the surrounding trees and binded to them, stuck like glue. And at the center of the mess was the most peculiar thing: a silver dragon bound by the green liquid.

The dragon heard the noisy rustling and tilted his head as far as he could to direct his eyes to its source. A human! And a young one at that, from what he could tell. The boy stood there just staring at him with his mouth hanging open. His dumbfounded look, along with his ragged clothes and how he was carrying his two still swaying bags almost made him chuckle.

Of course, the dragon was in no position to judge another's appearance; he must've looked just as silly stuck there with that gooey fluid all around his body. At least his snout wasn't glued shut.

"Ah," the dragon started, "As you can see, I'm kind of, umm, stuck. Do you think you could, ah, dispel this mess, or fetch someone who can?"

Solah tried to collect himself to make a response. He had seen dragons before in Windsgate, though they were a rare sight. He had read in one of the first books he had stolen before that dragons usually kept to themselves in their great mountain city in the north. It made it especially surprising to find one in the middle of the woods covered in goop, though.

"What is it?" Solah managed to say. He started walking towards the dragon. There was a table with some empty bottles and vials on it, and a bag he didn't look into. He put down his own bags onto the table.

The dragon laughed as he recalled the experiment, seeing how silly the whole situation was.

He began explaining, "It was an alchemical experiment. Dragons don't use potions, but I wanted to learn. This was supposed to be a very basic potion. I was just supposed to compress ten gallons of water into a small vial, no larger than a fluid ounce. Now normally liquids are incompressible, well, I mean to say, enough to be considered such, but that's what this enchantment was supposed to allow. It looks as if I made it halfway through, but then the water's viscosity increased a hundred-fold before bursting dramatically-"

Solah stopped listening to the dragon halfway, not because he wasn't interested but because he couldn't understand what he was going on about. Instead he walked closer as the dragon jabbered on his scientific babble until he moved close enough to the dragon that he turned silent and stared at the boy.

But the dragon didn't keep his mouth shut for long. "Well, if you could do something, I'd appreciate if you did it quickly. I've been trapped like this for quite a number of hours. Actually, I was quite afraid I'd die here if nobody stumbled into this clearing."

Curiosity overrode Solah's fear of the sticky fluid. He wanted to touch the thing but was afraid he'd get his finger stuck to the glue too.

The dragon shivered as the boy moved closer. There was

something strange about him, and he was making no hand motion that usually preceded a spell cast by the humanoid races. He started to genuinely worry now: he'd be able to survive stuck here without food or water for a few weeks, but the boy wouldn't be able to last more than a week if he also became stuck. "Please," he said, "if you don't know what you're doing go find an enchanter that does. I don't want both of us to-"

Too late. The boy had touched the fluid softly with his index finger. But something happened that neither of them were expecting. The eerie green glow faded starting from the point of contact and quickly spread throughout the entirety of the mass. In a frightened reaction, Solah pulled his hand away. Yet, right as he pulled away the entire mass expanded and burst explosively back into water. The force of the transformation knocked him down to the ground.

After all the water had settled into the soil, the dragon laughed again.

"Well, being drenched in water is still an improvement over being trapped like a rat in a trap!" he hollered. "Say, thanks for saving me human! But now I'm intrigued, what did you do to turn the thing back into water?"

Solah looked up to see the silver dragon lying on his back with a large grin on his face. Without the glue covering him, Solah could see the dragon was no bigger than a large horse, though his wings, fully spread out on the floor, definitely made him appear much wider. Large white belly scales started from the bottom of his head and went down to the tip of his tail, which had a spade shape at the end of it. The table had also been knocked over, broken into two, and all the glass vials had shattered. Some of his oranges had rolled out of his bag, and the dragon's bag had some bottles filled with colorful liquid knocked out of it.

After forcing himself to sit up, he explained, "I don't really know. You said something about an enchantment, so I thought I could dispel it like any other magic."

The dragon's eyebrows shifted and he rolled over. With his belly and all four legs back on the ground, the dragon turned until his entire body faced the boy. He held his forearms to his head and gave the boy a most inquisitive expression before continuing, "So you're an enchanter then? Incredibly auspicious if that were the case, but there's something odd about you."

The boy was somewhat confused and didn't know how to respond. His kind were shunned by the rest of humanity and he didn't know how dragons felt about people like him. But he had just saved the dragon, and if he didn't like exiles the worst he'd do was leave, he hoped.

"No, I'm one of the exiles. I suppose you don't like my kind like everyone else?" he said.

"Exile? What do you mean?" the dragon asked.

Now Solah was really confused. He knew his kind was rare, but did dragons not even know of their existence? Maybe they were called something else, so he continued explaining, "An exile. Magic doesn't exist in me, and whatever I touch is dispelled. You must know us by another name."

The dragon craned his neck down and gave the boy a closer look. "Interesting, I have to say I've never heard of anyone with such a condition before," he said.

Now Solah was curious as he looked at the dragon, just noticing his twisting horns and the line of brown hair that emerged from his forehead and traveled down his spine until it tapered off halfway down his tail. He remembered dragons rarely traveled into human cities and the mages probably just never told the dragons about exiles. But then he started wondering and asked, "You mean there are no dragons that are like me?"

"Heavens no!" the dragon surprisingly loudly replied, "We dragons are attached to the flow of magic by nature. If we were not connected to magic at all, as you say you are, then we'd be dead, just as you'd be if you were cut off from the air." Then he looked upward as if in deep thought before jerking his head back down to the boy. "This might be interesting. I want you to touch me."

"What?" Solah said, "But you said the absence of magic would kill you!"

"Exactly, that's why I'm curious what will happen if you do touch me," he said.

"No, I don't want to kill you," Solah said, "Why would you even risk your life?"

"Why? The pursuit of knowledge is always a risky thing, my young friend. And I really doubt you'd kill me with a touch. Either way, you touch me or I poke you, same thing right?"

Solah could tell there was no persuading him. He did almost kill himself with some potion experiment after all.

"Alright, alright," Solah said. He hesitantly moved his hand to the dragon's claws and poked him as lightly as he could.

But that was all the dragon needed. The feeling was indescribable; he felt incredibly empowered and unfurled his wings with strength. Solah retreated his hand as soon as the dragon shuddered.

Then the dragon settled down and regained his wits. "Ah, again you surprise me, human. There is something about you. It's very difficult to explain."

Solah was happy nothing bad happened to the dragon, who he now considered a friend, something he had only read other people having in Nama's storybooks. Although, usually the stories only involved humans with human friends. But right now he was curious and wanted the dragon to tell him what he felt. "Please try," he said.

The silver dragon sat back on his haunches using his tail to balance himself so that he looked like he was standing up and used his forehands to tap the bottom of his snout. "Well," he began, "I suppose you could imagine the flow of magic like the flow of water in a river."

"Okay, go on," Solah said.

"Imagine then," he went on, "That you're like a rock in the middle of the river. You are not affected by the flow. But it's not just that, you make the flow around you turbulent. The flow becomes chaotic. It explains a couple of things, actually."

"Like what?"

"For one, humans, and elves for that matter, though they try to pretend they don't, manipulate the flow of magic by sheer force. It's quite symbolic really, they use their hands to cast spells. They try to control magic. When you touch something it's like the rock in the stream, the magic around whatever you are near becomes chaotic, so much so that any spell is broken. It can't be controlled when it's that chaotic."

That was definitely interesting to Solah, and the dragon managed to explain it in a way that he understood.

Seeing the satisfied look on Solah's face, the dragon continued, "And second, you actually invigorate me. Remember when I said dragons are magic by nature? The chaotic flow around you, I can actually use it. There is more power in it. As humans use their hands, we dragons use magic naturally as we breathe it. Though it's rare we ever have to use our breath weapons."

"Breath weapons? So it's true that dragons can breathe fire?"

"Fire, water, ice, acid, whatever. We can breathe whatever is needed. But we can't manipulate magic as humans and elves do. Magic powers our breath weapons and flight. We're also quite resistant to magical attacks."

"Well that's definitely good to know," Solah said, "So what will you do now?"

"Me? Well I suppose I'll head back to Windsgate and buy more alchemy supplies. Like I said, dragons don't manipulate magic, but alchemy is just mixing stuff together. The ingredients need to already be enchanted by a human though. I suspect a certain merchant sold me shoddily enchanted water. Ah, but where are my manners! My name's Rauliax Moonsilver, you can call me Raul if you'd prefer. And I owe you a life debt for helping me out of that *sticky* situation," Rauliax said with a small chuckle at his pun.

"Oh, well thank you. My name's Solah. I don't suppose you could take me back to Windsgate? The guards have probably given up looking for me, but I'd rather pretend I'm traveling with you if they're still out there."

"Guards? Why are guards chasing you?" Rauliax asked.

Solah realized he hadn't told the dragon what he was doing in the middle of the forest in the first place. He explained what happened to him and about his past and Grandma Nama. He told him truthfully and even said that he needed to go back to the city to find enough food for the both of them, and the dragon surprisingly didn't judge him as a no-good thief.

"Well, you don't have to worry about her anymore," Rauliax said, "I'm quite wealthy in Noriath, the dragon city. I'll commission someone in Windsgate to deliver supplies to your home every week so you won't have to steal anymore."

Solah was left in awe at Rauliax's generosity.

"Oh lift your jaw up, it's the least I could do for you after saving my life," Rauliax said, "But I do have one request. Can you come back with me to Noriath? I would love to research your abilities further."

Solah was already at the age when many young people become afflicted with wanderlust. Since Grandma was going to be taken care of, he agreed to go without much hesitation. Rauliax made Solah ride on top of him so they could travel faster, much to both their delights; the boy was enjoying the break from running and the dragon was energized by the boy's presence. The boy was surprised at how warm and soft the dragon's scales were; he had expected them to be hard and cold and asked him how dragon scales were supposed to be strong if they felt so soft.

"Punch me then," Rauliax said, "As hard as you can."

The boy shrugged his shoulders and pounded his fist down on the back of the dragon. The scales seemed to harden in response to the force, and he ended up bruising his own hand.

"Any more questions?" the dragon said with a smile.

Solah shook his head in response, a positive 'no.' He made a mental note to read that book about dragons he stole about a week ago to satisfy his curiosity without suffering any particular pains. Rauliax then picked up the potion bottles that had fallen out of his bag on the flipped table and put them back in. Then he did something Solah found most peculiar: he threw the entire bag into his mouth and swallowed it.

"Did you just eat a bag of glass?"

"What? Why would I ever want to give myself internal hemorrhages-oh! You don't know much about the outside world, right?"

"Only from what books I've obtained."

"I see. Well, I shall endeavor to act less aghast in reaction to your questions."

"Umm, thanks?"

The dragon chuckled. "You are most welcome my young friend. And to answer your question, I was not eating the bag. It's another magical talent that dragons possess. We can store a near infinite amount of objects by swallowing them."

"That's sort of different," Solah said. He felt the dragon's muscles flex as he started walking and sat silently while he wondered how such an ability would work.

After walking towards the direction of Windsgate for a few minutes, the silver dragon then suggested returning to Solah's home first so they could deliver the oranges and potatoes the boy already had to Nama and have him change clothes so nobody might recognize him in Windsgate. The boy agreed. Rauliax ran quickly; he dared not fly as he had no harness for the boy to safely stay attached to. Nevertheless, they arrived at his home under Solah's occasionally flawed direction in a little under two hours.

Chapter 2

The walk over was not at all unpleasant. The two of them made good company and curiosity fueled their topics of conversation. Particularly, Solah wished to know more about dragons in general, and Rauliax asked many questions about exiles, though after they passed Windsgate on their way to Solah's home, his questions became more directed towards the boy's own past.

"And how exactly did a single human girl like your Grandma manage to build a house in the middle of nowhere?" Rauliax inquired.

Solah had actually asked this very question to Nama herself. Her response was that she didn't actually know who built it. "Well she didn't build it herself," he said like it should've been obvious, "She told me that there was another exile that lived in there before she blundered in. He offered her shelter, just as she did for me. Beyond that, I don't know anything else."

"Intriguing. I can't help but imagine a petite, yet venerable, and somewhat eccentric lady living in a dilapidated hovel," the dragon said quite bombastically.

Solah, for his part, did not understand several of the words the dragon had just spoken. "Was that even Standard?" he questioned with a raised eyebrow.

The dragon chuckled softly, but loud enough for the confused boy to hear. "Of course, silly boy, I was only testing your aptitude for the language. You can't be blamed for being deficient in the art, I suppose," he added, "especially given your circumstances."

Now poor Solah was completely baffled. He couldn't tell if the dragon was insulting him or not, but another question quickly surfaced to his head and the somewhat unpleasant feeling of being inadequate faded away from his desire to know the answer. "Wait a minute," he began, "I know from my books that dragons are intelligent and sentient, but how do you know Standard? I thought that dragons would have their own language."

Rauliax's mouth frowned a little before he responded, "We did. It was Standard, only it wasn't called Standard before all you humans and elves realized what a superior language it was and adopted it as your own main language." He sighed and continued, "I suppose we should be flattered, but then you had to go all about claiming it was your own language *based* on Draconic. In my opinion, just changing the written form to look more gracious than claw marks doesn't make it your own language."

"Oh," the boy said innocently, "I'm sorry. I didn't know anything about that."

The dragon inverted his frown and tried to look unoffended before starting up again. "Oh my," he said with extreme politeness, "Do forgive me. It was nothing to do with you personally."

Solah only nodded at him. It was refreshing to have another companion to talk with: his entire life he had only known the sweet voice of his Grandma.

The two unlikely pair continued chatting all the way until they reached the boy's home.

"Well I must apologize for assuming you lived in a dirty old shack," Rauliax said as he looked at the house. And indeed, the home was quite an improvement from the roofless hovel he expected. It was built from a foundation of wood logs, decorated neatly with flowers and other various vegetation indicative of a feminine resident.

Solah, still completely unused to proper social etiquette, just nodded his head at the dragon. The dragon, of course, shrugged off his rude gesture, now completely understanding and tolerating his ignorance.

There was, of course, no door large enough for the dragon to fit into, so he stayed outside and waited for Solah to do his business. The boy needed to tell his appointed grandmother that he was leaving for a bit, and he was somewhat worried that she wouldn't allow it. Eventually he grew bored of waiting, so he trotted over to the biggest window on the log house and tried to peer inside, but a dark red curtain blocked his view. He could, however, hear the conversation Solah and his Grandma were having.

"What do you mean you're leaving," an elderly female voice said, "And how exactly did you manage to get somebody from outside to take care of me?"

"I told you Grandma," he heard Solah reply with a half lie, "I helped a wealthy traveling merchant out and he wants to repay the favor, and he wants to bring me along to help him his business. Besides, I do so want to go adventuring."

Well, it wasn't a lie, more like a deliberate hiding of certain facts, Rauliax thought. Then there was a deep sigh, so loud that he could hear it through the wooden wall.

"Alright, alright. Well if all my affairs will be attended to, but I'm still worried about you," Grandma Nama said. "Does he know about your," she paused before continuing, "Your special talents?"

"Yes Grandma, he does. And he assures me he'll keep it a secret and doesn't judge me any differently for it."

"Very well then, my dear Solah. Please come back often, I'll miss you quite so."

"As often as I can manage, Grandma!"

"But first, I must insist on meeting this generous man!" Nama shouted.

The eavesdropping dragon couldn't see it, but Solah's face scrunched up as he tried to come up with something that would keep Nama from meeting their benefactor.

After a short pause, he heard the boy say, "Okay, Nama, he's waiting for me outside. He doesn't wish to intrude by coming in and wants to leave as soon as I'm ready."

"Oh, such polite nonsense. I, at the very least, want to see his face before I let you off with him for more than a month."

"But Grandma, it's quite cold outside, are you sure you should be going outside?"

"Now Solah, I may be old but I'm not so old I can't even go outside for a short walk. Come on then, fetch me my walking stick."

Rauliax could hear the boy continue to protest, but his Grandma would have none of it. He decided it would be wiser not to keep any secrets and scurried off to the front lawn. The silver dragon reached into his mouth with a claw and grabbed out a folding table, a chair, and some refreshments.

Then the front door swung open. One would've expected an elderly woman to faint at the sight of a dragon on her lawn, but Grandma Nama actually smiled at the sight. In fact, Solah sported a more surprised face than she had.

"Well there's a sight!" Nama exclaimed, "A dragon sitting on my lawn serving tea, it seems!" She turned her sight to Solah's face and whispered to him, "So, this is the answer to all the protests then? I daresay if you told me before I still would've gone along with it, he seems quite a gentleman, though I haven't seen a dragon in the flesh before to tell."

"You must be Solah's grandmother, I presume?" Rauliax said politely after she stopped whispering. He was sitting on his haunches and was indeed pouring a cup of tea for her from a large kettle using his forehands.

She turned her head back towards the dragon and replied, "Not biologically of course, but as much a grandmother as any."

"Of course," the dragon said and gestured toward the chair on her side of the table, "Tea, if you'd please? Brewed in my land, not the greatest but it's all I have left." He was now pouring into his own cup, one with an extra large handle for his claws to grasp more easily. His forepaws were more like a hand, only scaled and larger, though his feet looked a lot more like talons.

"Well don't mind if I do," she said.

Solah hid himself back into the house under the pretense that he had to gather some more equipment and clothes before leaving. Now Grandma Nama and Rauliax were also quite a sight to see: an elderly lady having tea with quite a talkative dragon. And they talked for a long while too, so long that Solah had long finished packing and was now just waiting for them to finish before opening the front door again.

They talked quite a length about why Rauliax was interested in Solah, and the dragon explained how he had rescued him in the forest earlier that day and how he was interested in studying the exiles' power, and that he genuinely wanted to treat him for saving his life. Satisfied that he had no ulterior motive, Nama then asked about more personal subjects, and Rauliax added his own friendly questions afterward. They ended their discussion when they ran out of tea, and at last Solah opened the door.

He walked over and helped Nama back into the house, despite her protests that she could walk perfectly fine as long as she had her walking stick. Rauliax folded up the table and put everything back into his mouth before Solah came out again with a pack of items he had arranged in one of the baskets that he normally used on his thieving runs into Windsgate.

"Oh, hand me your pack," the dragon said, "It's no burden to me."

The boy let him have the basket, but didn't expect him to hurl it into his mouth.

"Hey, hey! That can't be clean, can it?" he yelled out.

"Oh, definitely so!" the dragon replied, "The table and chair we were using earlier was stored in the very same place."

Solah didn't realize that fact until the dragon told him. The table and chair were actually quite clean, now that he thought about it. Then his mind wandered to how exactly he stored objects he swallowed, but then he thought too long and the dragon had picked him up and set him on his back.

"Have you said your farewells?" Rauliax asked.

"Yes," his rider replied.

"She's actually quite energetic for a human of her age, you know. Hold on tight!" Before the boy could react, Rauliax started running with a surprising leap that almost knocked him off if not for his hand managing to clutch the tuft of hair that lined the dragon's back.

They traveled most of the way in quiet. Occasionally Solah would ask a question. Once he asked how the dragon's ability to store objects worked, he assumed they just stored a separate part of their stomach that didn't digest the items. Rauliax found that assumption quite silly and explained it to him in terms he could sort of understand. He said that food and drink can take one path down the mouth, and air another. For dragons, another path led to a pocket dimension, where they could store many things without encumbrance.

They made it back to Windsgate in a little less than an hour, much faster than what it would take Solah to travel alone. The city was not very large despite possessing several docking platforms for the airships that frequently stopped by since it was a central hub for the western side of Valeria, and it was not fortified by a wall. Instead, there were wards that defined the boundary of the city. The wards created a faint, almost otherworldly, line of light that repelled most small animals and warned the city guard of any other intrusion, but most of the city was more physically marked by the butt ends of the buildings that lined against the wards. At the main roads into the city, the wards cleared a way to allow passage, though at least two guards watched each road. Rauliax came up from the most commonly used road, which was freshly paved and even, and the guards recognized the dragon and let him in without further questioning. Luckily, they did not recognize the newly clothed boy that was on his back.

They entered the merchant district before Rauliax let Solah down and explained what he needed to do.

"Now, my first order of business here is to deal with the merchant who sold me the main ingredients I used in the little experiment in the forest. Stay behind me and out of sight until I signal you forward, okay? I've got a little plan that should get me what I paid for," the dragon whispered. "Try to follow along the conversation, and prepare to use your ability when appropriate," he added with a wink of his left eye.

A portly man noticed the dragon waltzing towards him. He felt a twinge of fear as he noticed the dragon's very unhappy frown, but he mustered his business acumen and chimed up before the dragon could call him out.

"Ah, Mr. Moonsilver," the merchant said, "What a pleasure to deal with you again! Perhaps I could interest you in-"

"Oh hush up you," the dragon curtly replied, "You know darn well you sold me poorly enchanted, shoddy alchemy ingredients! They darn near killed me, you know!"

The man stammered, quite taken aback. He hadn't expected to see the same dragon again since they were rarely seen to begin with.

"Now," Rauliax continued, "You'll hand me a refund, or else!"

The dragon definitely didn't need to add that last piece of intimidation, he already looked intimidating enough. Too much, perhaps, as the merchant lurched forward.

"Mr. Moonsilver, my good sir," he said, "I do hope you are not threatening me. It was made quite clear all sales are final. Please don't make me call for the guards."

He may have been ignorant in the art of alchemy, but the silver dragon was definitely no fool in the art of speech. He had prepared for this response and waved his claw to signal Solah, who was hiding behind him. The merchant hadn't noticed him until he moved to Rauliax's side.

Then the dragon gathered whatever etiquette he could muster and finally replied, "I would actually appreciate it if you did call the guards, my dear businessman. Then my friend here could show them exactly how shoddy your enchantments are by dispelling them with utmost ease."

The merchant let out a laugh, his large belly bobbing up and down with each expulsion of air. His enchantments were actually quite well forged, and he had only sold the dragon his defective materials since he didn't actually expect him to use them and discover their quality; most dragons weren't particularly interested in human magic after all. He composed himself and said, "You really expect this boy to have the experience to remove my enchantments? I dare you to try!" he said confidently, calling the two out on what he was sure was a bluff. He pulled out a lockbox and beckoned them to open the magic seal.

Rauliax and Solah looked at each other for a moment. The dragon nodded his head and his exile friend moved forward. He started waving his arms, pretending as best as he could to look like he was casting a spell. He was doing it quite well too, if only a little too dramatically. He ended the motions by raising his right hand up above his forehead before dropping it down slowly to touch the box with a gentle touch of his index finger. Then he took the box and opened it without effort, much to the merchant's chagrin.

"Well then?" the dragon asked with a satisfied grin.

The merchant, surprised as he was, now found himself outwitted and reluctantly handed Mr. Moonsilver another batch of the alchemical ingredients he had purchased several days earlier, except this time he made sure they were of the highest quality. He didn't want to see this shrewd dragon again, after all, and made a mental note to never try to rip off any other dragons in future transactions.

Rauliax happily took the bag of goods after inspecting it and accounted for everything. He leaned back onto his tail, standing as upright as he could, and gave a slight bow to the merchant before turning around and walked away. Still walking upright using his tail to balance himself, he hurled the bag into his open maw. Then he dropped down his forearms and returned to walking on all fours with Solah following aside him.

"Isn't it uncomfortable to walk like that?" the boy asked.

"Not really. It does feel somewhat awkward though, so I don't like to do it for too long," Rauliax replied.

Without warning, Solah dropped himself onto all fours and tried to crawl along like a dragon, but he uprighted himself only a moment later. "You're right, it does feel awkward."

Chapter 3

"Root of Iswald? No sir, you won't be finding any of that here."

That was the last ingredient on Rauliax's list of alchemical regents he wanted to purchase and had journeyed into human cities to find. Solah and Rauliax made an odd pair as they wandered about the city looking for everything on the dragon's long grocery list and had received many curious looks from other shoppers. The many merchants that they went to, however, didn't bat an eye as they were far more interested in profit.

Rauliax waited expectantly for the gaudy looking merchant to continue, but asked after an uncomfortable period of silence had passed, "And where do suppose I could find some?"

The merchant rubbed his chin a little before replying, "It's quite a rare item, sir, you'd probably have to head all the way over to Farrain. You might be able to find the odd trader that has some elsewhere, but the only place I can guarantee would have it in stock is the capital."

Farrain was the capital of the realm of Wesar, which consisted of nearly about three-fourths the western half of Valeria. A great mountain range separated the continent in two, and it was there that the border of Wesar was drawn against the border of Elemar, the country that filled the eastern side of the continent.

The two kingdoms had long been in a state of unsteady peace. The Ridgeback mountain range was impassable by foot. Many expeditionary teams had tried to find a safe passage, but all had failed. It was not until a century ago, when airships were invented, had some hostilities arisen. Yet always the two country's tension only culminated into small skirmishes along the immediate areas surrounding the Ridgeback Mountains, and neither side had ever actually downed an airship. Of course, sea ships had existed for much longer, but they had neither the speed nor the maneuverability of airships, and since they could only land on easily defendable harbors, neither kingdom ever tried to openly engage each other at sea. Indeed, the sea was practically the only venue for trade, which was deemed a high enough necessity for mutual benefit, between the two kingdoms, though all seafaring ships were directed to only certain specific harbors. Even so, both nations were constantly wary of each other, and this avenue of free trade also constantly exchanged spies to both sides.

Nevertheless, it can be said that hostilities had recently spiked within the last half decade, when the late King Arashal became lord of Elemar. Airship engagements along the western side of the mountains had increased tenfold, and now the Third Fleet of Wesar was constantly stationed nearby. Scout ships patrolled the entire length of the mountain range without much rest.

Windsgate was located well west of these hostilities, but the capital was still even further west.

"A days ride by airship," the merchant replied when Rauliax asked how far Farrain was. "Not sure how fast that is for a dragon though."

"Excellent, thank you for your time," the dragon said before gesturing to Solah, who was standing next to his tail. The cheaply dressed boy came up and gave the merchant a small tip for his information before they both left.

The outdoors bazaar was quite busy still, even as the day's light was fading. There were only a handful of shops that Rauliax couldn't fit through, for which he was grateful he had his exiled companion to help him with. He had found it best to pretend that his friend was a powerful enchanter, a prodigy at such a young age. It was easy enough to fool anyone who asked: the supposed prodigy had seen an actual enchanter dispelling a piece of armor in passing and was able to gracefully replicate the hand motions now, but of course the boy still tried to keep a low profile. Luckily, nobody had asked him to enchant anything, and in any case Rauliax kept the boy from interacting with anyone for too long. The dragon had given him a small bag of coins so that he would not have to continuously reach in and out of his mouth every time he wanted to buy something, and it was easier for the boy to handle the small coins anyway.

"Your money is so small," Rauliax had said, "In Noriath, the dragon realm, we just use gold bars, or silver bars, to trade with."

The boy had replied in kind, "Well maybe you could, but I

couldn't possibly lug around a couple of gold bars all day."

The dragon had shrugged his wings in silent agreement.

Now, with the rare root being the last and rarest object the dragon was looking for, he decided to start towards Farrain in the morning. But before he left the city, he bought a set of nicer clothes for the boy, compounding his earlier generosity when he had procured a supply-maid to service his grandmother's cottage in the forest. The search for a good supply-maid actually took the better part of the day. They settled with an older looking gentleman for the sole reason that he had asked no questions. And he wouldn't, he had said, "As long as the monthly dues kept coming in."

He had also purchased a custom made harness. It was relatively simple: the main belt looped around the dragon's neck, locked in place by the shoulder straps, and had another smaller loop intended to be wrapped around Solah's waist. The main belt also had two hand grips to hold onto during flight. The best part of it, to Rauliax, was that the entire thing could compress enough to fit into his mouth, and thus his internal extra-dimensional storage, so that he didn't have to wear it all the time.

There was no inn with a room, or doors for that matter, that would fit a dragon in Windsgate. Some innkeepers had offered use of their stables, but Rauliax, of course, would have none of that.

"It's not only undignifying to sleep next to filth-ridden horses, but it's also incredibly stupid that they expect me to pay for the privilege," the dragon said with great disgust.

"Then where shall we sleep for the night?" poor Solah asked.

"I'm going to sleep in the forest. And don't worry about me, I'll lay down a rug so it'll be quite comfortable." Then the dragon added, "If you want, I'll pay so you can stay in a room."

Solah didn't want anymore expense on his account. It was actually a strange feeling to him. He had wondered why he should feel guilty over spending the dragon's money. He was very wealthy, it seemed, and offered first, in any case. It wasn't like he was stealing from him. Yet now it felt painful to his conscience to continue accepting the dragon's generosity so willfully.

It was his face, he thought. Everyone he had stolen from were faceless, he didn't know them and didn't care about them. He cared only for himself. But now, this dragon was his friend, and despite his more dubious thoughts refused the dragon's offer.

"No," he said, "I couldn't possibly ask you to pay for more. And I suppose it would be odd if I went back home after just barely leaving?"

The dragon replied, "It'd be a nuisance, in my mind, to have had a day to get over the departure of a friend, only to have him come bustling through my home again before the day is even over."

"Then I suppose I'll sleep out with you," Solah said, "It shouldn't be too uncomfortable, you do have some sheets that I can cover myself with, right?"

"Of course." And so that was settled.

By sunset, the pair had finished setting up camp and Solah had a completely guilt-free dinner shared with his dragon companion. It had been quite a long time since he had eaten food that he hadn't stolen. Though he had long ago forced his conscious shut, the feeling was now quite nice to him.

The camp and cooking fire flickered brightly in the night sky, courtesy of Rauliax's fire breath. Solah had noticed that despite the dragon's sharp teeth, whose appearance was amplified by the harsh contrast of the fire and the night's darkness, he had eaten mostly fruits, and what little meat he did eat he had cooked a bit before consuming.

"I like their sweet taste more," he said when Solah asked him why he was eating more fruits than meat. "I like the oranges in particular, even more when they're juiced."

Afterwards, they rested on the thick carpet the dragon had unrolled. Solah laid down on it and thought it actually felt nicer than his bed at home.

The two then had a conversation, mostly of no great importance, to tire themselves into sleeping. They put out the fires which left only the moon to light the sky. It appeared to Solah that Rauliax was glowing slightly: the light of the moon seemed to reflect off his scales like they were crystal clear water that ebbed slowly in a lake.

Then there was a rumble in the ground, so strong that both of them could still feel it through the heavy rug. The moon suddenly disappeared as a great shadow swallowed it away, but then they could see it had illuminated the edges of a massive airship. Smaller shadows were also outlined; all in all about six small ones surrounding the centerpiece, and they could see the flashing white lights that lit in alignment under the shadows. They traveled due east at a steady pace, and eventually the ground settled.

"Interesting things," Rauliax said, referring to the airships. Then he added, "Humans, born without wings. Yet they seek the sky, where we have lived all our lives. Can't say I blame you guys though, I think I'd die if I couldn't fly anymore."

"I see them all time, and they all look different," Solah said.

"They weren't always there though. I remember it was only a century ago that humans started embracing technology, enhanced with magic."

"You remember?" Solah asked, now very confused, "You mean you were alive back then? How old are you?"

"One hundred and fifty-four, still rather young by dragon standards," he replied nonchalantly.

"Young? How long do dragons live?"

"Well, the current Eldest is around eight hundred years old. He's got about a hundred more, I'd say."

"Nine hundred years old!" Solah exclaimed wide-eyed, "That's ten or eleven lives of a man!"

"Yes, but it's not like we think we're better because of it. In the great scheme of things, the length of a human life is like the blink of an eye to the life of the universe. When you compare one blink to ten blinks, it really makes no difference." Then he added, "In any case, the Eldest just stays in his home all day. It seems very boring to me to be so old. Live life to the fullest, I say."

"Is that why you're out here in Wesar? To explore?"

"Partly. Like I said earlier, I do have a genuine interest in learning alchemy. I tried to learn to use magic like humans and elves use it, but it's just not possible for dragons. I mean I can replicate the hand motions with perfect precision, but it's impossible for me to control magic like you-" he paused for a moment as he caught his error, "Like they do."

Solah was intrigued again, both at the dragon's description of magic and at how it related to his own abilities.

"But you can learn alchemy?" he asked.

"Alchemy is different," the dragon said, "It's just mixing a bunch of ingredients together to make a potion. The effects are completely determined by the properties of the reagents. Reagents that may or may not be enchanted, but obviously I don't need to personally enchant them."

22

"Ah, I see," Solah said. "Do you think it would be possible for me to make a potion?"

"Possibly, if you never touched any of the enchanted reagents. Perhaps if you wore some gloves, or used some tongs and mixed with a long rod."

Now the boy's eyes glimmered with anticipation. Perhaps he wouldn't have to be completely separated from magic after all.

The dragon added, "But then you couldn't possibly use any potion that you had to drink. Perhaps we could try an explosive bomb. Those just need to be thrown with enough force to shatter the container."

Solah was now staring at him with growing desire to make such a potion.

He noticed the boy's growing eyes and said, "Later, perhaps. I have none with me, and I'll have to buy more ingredients for an exploding potion."

The boy slunk to the ground in disappointment. The dragon stayed silent as he stared up into the stars. He saw another airship, flying very low, with many lights glittering around it as it came in to land at Windsgate. It was only the combined weight of the two that kept the heavy carpet from flying away from the wake of the airship's twirling propellers.

"Most I've seen in such short a time," Rauliax said, "I wonder if something's going on."

Solah said, "I doubt it, they're always flying about. It looks to me like they go wherever aimlessly, but then again I don't even know how they could fly."

"Oh, in principle it's actually quite simple," the dragon started, "They're one of the first things I studied when I started traveling into human lands. Magic and solid engineering keep them afloat. You see, the more they invest in the technological science, the less magical exertion people have to use."

He paused for a moment trying to figure out how to explain the whole thing to someone who understood neither magic nor, as far as he could tell, technology. When he first studied the airships, he had a solid understanding of science since without magic of the convenient kind used by humans, dragon society had to value the study of science and mathematics quite highly. He was knocked out of his thoughts when Solah told him to go on.

So he said, "You probably don't know this, but when other humans cast spells, they physically exert themselves. It can get to the point where their brain bleeds out of their ears."

Solah nodded in understanding.

"I remember reading the first airships that went aloft could only stay in the sky for a very limited time, based on their size. It's because they almost completely depended on levimages, who make things float and hover. Of course, at the turn of the century, humans began embracing technology, which is how the concept of an airship came about in the first place. So eventually they started figuring all sorts of ideas, and nowadays they can fly solely with the propellers you can see on them. The propellers spin to create lift, and they have enchantments on them to further increase the generation of lift."

Solah stopped him with a raised hand and asked, "How do the propellers lift up the ships?"

"That is a subject that requires an understanding of fluid mechanics," the dragon sharply said, "And all you need to know is that they create lift by spinning faster than the eye can track. And they do that by using Pyrucium, a special substance that combusts to power their engines. But it's actually a quite brilliant system: the Pyrucium actually renews the enchantments on the propellers at the same time! So modern airships can fly themselves without any exertion from a mage. For the same reason, cannons were added to augment the elemental mages' offensive powers-"

Solah stopped the dragon again and said, "Raul, that's quite enough learning for tonight. I'm going to sleep now, good night."

He wrapped himself under Rauliax's sheets while he was saying, "Oh, alright. Good night then." He started lightly snoring less than a minute after.

Rauliax whispered to himself, "It wouldn't be the first time I lectured someone to sleep." He made a small chuckle and laid his own head down to join Solah in sleep.

Chapter 4

Solah woke up under the bright light of late morning. He sat up and saw Rauliax sitting beside a table musing over a book. He was deep in his study though, and didn't notice the boy stir.

"What are you reading?" he asked.

Rauliax craned his neck towards him and said, "Oh, finally awake are you? I woke up an hour or two before you did and started thinking."

"About?"

"About you and your abilities. I remember reading somewhere about a particular area in the Ridgeback Mountains and started looking for the book."

"And what do I have to do with mountains?"

Rauliax moved his head back towards the book and started flipping through pages, but he kept speaking. "Well, the area is special. It's supposed to be a place where magic is nullified. So, I've been thinking that perhaps its power is similar to yours. Dragons don't travel far enough from our homeland to be able to research it, but I think I might pay a visit sometime."

"An area that nullifies magic?" Solah asked with great interest. "Where is it?"

"I believe it's at the southern edge of the mountain ridge, right where it borders the sea. Like I said, too far from the dragon realm for any of us to have seen it." He flipped through a few more pages before closing the book and tossed it into his mouth. He coughed out another one and started scanning through this book too while saying, "I remember when I first read about it that it might kill me if I wandered into it, much like I thought you might've harmed me with your touch. So now I want to investigate it further, perhaps its power is the same as yours."

Solah sat in the same spot he woke up, still covered in his sheets, and didn't say a word. He wondered what the possible ramifications would be if this place existed, and his desire to find it grew the more he thought.

The dragon broke his thoughts. "If anything, it should prove that your existence is entirely natural and not some sort of vile detestable thing other humans make you out to be."

To be accepted, Solah thought, might be a wonderful thing. He hated being thought of as an unnatural nuisance, even though he had learned to pay other people no mind. Nama accepted him, and now so did Rauliax. He liked him even though he was supposed to be a freak of nature, something supposed to be scorned according to other humans. But he realized he didn't need to be accepted by everyone, they wouldn't be his friends anyway. The more he thought about it, the more he grew fonder of the dragon, as he was friendly since they had met, and he only became a better friend as the days went on.

Then he spurted out, "Raul, will you marry me?"

The dragon burst out laughing so hard it seemed as if the force of exerting the sound alone knocked him onto his back. Solah only sat bewildered.

"Boy, do you even know what a marriage is?" Rauliax managed to say between laughs.

"Grandma said that when two people like each other very much they can get married," Solah said, quite confused now.

That last comment had stopped any respite from laughter the dragon had, and he let out another series of humored howls. After a while he managed to recompose himself and said, "Stupid boy, that is a very lax definition meant for children far younger than you! Marriage is appropriate when a man and a woman love each other, so much so that they want to live together forever."

"Oh," Solah simply said. He considered the dragon's ridiculously long series of laughs and figured it must've been an incredibly silly thing to suggest.

The dragon, however, started thinking things through more seriously. He'd only known the boy a day, but he already felt quite attached to him. He was only a curious thing that he wanted to study when he met him. Then he learned more of his life, and became rather good friends considering their short time together. He had taught the boy more things than he would probably learn from him.

And now he realized that the poor boy would be completely alone after his Grandma passed on, in twenty years at best. And that was a fate he didn't want his friend to face.

And so Rauliax said, "But you know what we can do? When we get back to Noriath, I'll get you adopted as my brother."

Solah lifted his head up cheerily. "That sounds perfect!"

"Good, we should start flying to Farrain now, it's almost midday and I want to get there before nightfall," Rauliax replied.

They had a small brunch before the dragon pulled out his harness and put it on without much fuss. Solah hopped on, making sure all the straps were tight and secure, and they flew off into the west.

Flying was a strange sensation to the human. Rauliax was flying as straight and level as he could, but being off the ground kept the dragon's passenger's stomach unsettled. The smooth yet deafening wind was soothing, at least a little, and kept Solah from hurling his breakfast. He had to shout for the dragon to hear what he was saying, but the dragon's voice was mostly clear even though it sounded relatively calm compared to his necessarily hoarse screaming. Something about a Doppler effect, the dragon told him, but he didn't quite understand it.

Having the boy on his back was also a new feeling for Rauliax: his chaotic wake of magic made flight feel incredibly easier. Dragon wings alone didn't allow a dragon to fly, but their magical nature gifted them the necessary strength to provide the necessary lift. The exile's power strengthened this natural magic and instead of burdening the dragon, having Solah on his back actually made him feel half his weight. It took quite a bit of willpower to resist the urge to perform flashy aerobatics, but he needed to in order to preserve his friend's digestive juices. He did, at least, fly much faster than he usually could.

Eventually, sometime mid-afternoon, Solah finally got used to the feeling, and his stomach stopped fighting with him. Rauliax noticed he had stopped squirming and grasping his belly, so he asked him if he could perform some aerial maneuvers.

"Strictly for tactical purposes, of course. If, perhaps, some spiteful mage discovered your true nature, we may be forced into a hasty departure, possibly requiring us to dodge fireballs or ice bolts," the giddy dragon tried to calmly explain, but of course he knew he was lying. It was doubtful anyone would hate an exile so much as to seek to eradicate them; after all, they were banished from society instead of outright murdered at birth. He hoped, at least, that humans had evolved well past such a point of savagery.

Solah hesitated for a while. He barely managed to feel comfortable flying normally, and was quite afraid of what these maneuvers would entail. The dragon had craned his neck back so he was looking at him with one eye, however, and the force of persuasion from that eye made him acquiesce to the dragon's request.

They started with a simple and slow loop. It didn't make Solah feel any worse, so they kept at it until they were making small quick loops in rapid succession: after about the fifth loop in sequence Solah couldn't handle it and made the dragon stop.

Rauliax complied, but even after returning to straight and level flight, his rider still didn't feel well. He looked back again, and saw him pale as a ghost. He didn't want to push the human too far so quickly, and didn't want to see him so uncomfortable, so he landed in the empty plains they were over and let the boy back onto the ground.

Having his feet on the ground seemed to be the antidote for his awful sick feeling, Solah thought, and sat a little. His face became pink again, and Rauliax handed him some food for a late lunch.

"Don't close your eyes next time," the dragon said as he was munching down a clawful of oranges. "And look forward, look at where I'm flying, and try to keep the horizon in view. Even I start feeling sick if I close my eyes for a while."

"Okay, I'll try," Solah replied between bites of his apple.

After finishing their quick meal, they continued flying westward. Along the rest of the way, Rauliax performed several gentle maneuvers and even flew upside-down for a little while. Solah, for his part, got used to most of the unusual sensations, although being upside-down became incredibly nauseous after only half a minute.

The sun was still high above the horizon when they saw Farrain. Actually, they saw the airships hovering and docked over the capital first, at least a dozen airships floating casually. One of them was absolutely colossal and dwarfed all the rest of them: it looked as if it was the size of a quarter of the city.

Farrain, unlike Windsgate, did have stone walls built around it. Solah could see another smaller circular wall inside the city that was taller than the outer walls, and it seemed that many of the airships were parked along it.

Rauliax landed by the outskirts of the city on one of the smaller roads that linked to its eastern gate. He said to his rider, "It's still late afternoon, we arrived a lot earlier than I thought we would, despite the entertaining maneuvering. Much thanks to how you make flying so much easier!"

Solah nodded, and stayed on his back in the harness so the dragon could run much faster towards the city without worrying about accidentally flinging him off. He asked why they had landed instead of simply flying in, to which the dragon told him it was because of common courtesy, and how it would be disrespectful to Farrain's airspace, especially when they had so many airships over it at the moment.

Of course, he didn't quite understand such reasoning, but he pretended to anyway.

Upon reaching sight of the entrance, which was large enough for an entire convoy of carriages to fit through, Solah dismounted from the dragon. The dragon packed the harness and stored it away. They walked through together side-by-side and the city guards let them enter without a word. Dragons were more a common sight at the capital than at an arbitrary city like Windsgate. To dragons, Rauliax explained, traveling to Farrain was like a vacation-like sort of endeavor: they didn't visit all the time, but when they did they usually stayed for a while.

They passed through the eastern gate into a large courtyard square. The area was bustling with activity as people went to and fro, though most everyone parted away when the silver dragon walked forward towards the map in the middle of the square.

The map was a simple rectangular stone block set upon a hefty marble pedestal. There appeared to be nothing on it aside from a pulsing green dot. Rauliax walked up to it and placed a talon on the dot, and promptly lines of purple light drew themselves onto the polished stone surface.

The map etched itself on the stone like an invisible pen with glowing ink were scrabbling over it. Solah couldn't help but stare at it. He was intrigued by the intricacy and magical talent that was probably necessary to craft such a thing.

Rauliax noticed his friend's fascinated expression and explained, "The green dot is where we are. If I keep tapping our location, the map will zoom out. Quite a marvelous contraption, isn't it?"

Solah nodded in agreement.

"Now if only I could find where an herbalist might be," the dragon said. He tapped on the pedestal and a face with eyes closed appeared in front of the stone.

It appeared to be the head of an elderly gentleman, but there was no color in the illusion to tell if his hair had grayed yet. It began to say, "Good evening, what do you require assistance with?" Then, before Rauliax could reply, it opened its eyes and stumbled back against the rock when it saw its patron. It gathered itself before continuing, "Oh my, a dragon! Well I wasn't expecting one of you, but please forgive my startlement. You are quite welcome to ask for any directions. If it's an inn you are looking for, there are several in the city with dragon sized accommodations."

Rauliax replied, "Yes, that would be good, but first I'd like directions to an herbalist, one with Iswald Roots in stock, if you know."

The head rolled its eyes to the upper right as if trying to recall something, then looked back and said, "Hmm, I can't exactly tell you if anyone has them in stock, but I know Lady Mary's often carries rare herbs like that."

"Alright, can you give me directions?"

"Certainly, Lady Mary's is in the trade section of the Upper District. Just pass through the Lower and Middle districts through the Circle Road, south or north at your leisure, and it'll be in between a surgeon's office and a tailoring shop. Dr. Devone and The Golden Braid. And the closest accommodations are at the High Horse, it's right in the Tourist District, just walk half a mile west of Lady Mary's, it's along the same road that way."

The map was now fully zoomed out, with a red and blue dot glowing where the herbalist and the inn was located, respectively. Solah could see the city was oriented around a large circular road, though overall the city was in the shape of a rectangle with a smaller rectangular lump attached to the west of it. The Lower District was highlighted in yellow, Middle in white, Upper in green, Tourist in purple, and inside the circle of the map made by the road was another thick ring, which Solah assumed to represent the inner wall, outlined in blue labeled as the Airdock District. At the very center of the circle was labeled the Royal District, and was drawn in a lighter blue. The Middle and Lower districts met right at the midsection of the rectangle, where the eastern gate was oriented, and accordingly they were standing right between the two Districts. Without the map, however, Solah wouldn't have been able to tell, aside from the fact that the buildings lining the Lower District's side looked somewhat older or poorer.

"Thank you very much," Rauliax said to the disembodied head.

It replied, "You're very welcome, if you require any further assistance please feel free to use the maps located in the center of every main district and in the front of every main gate."

The head vanished as suddenly as it had appeared, and the map returned to the default pulsing green dot it was showing before.

To Rauliax's surprise, he heard Solah say, "Whoa, I want to try that!"

He saw the boy try to extend his hand to the map, but managed to shove his own forearm and wings in his way before he managed to make contact. He was worried for a moment since his own claws were touching the map, but he let out a sigh of relief as the map etched itself on the stone again in response to him touching the green dot.

The dragon deftly wrapped his tail around Solah's waist, and before he could react, he had pulled the boy far away from the map. Then he proceeded to scold him, "Solah! I must remind you to not touch anything you don't have to! That map is obviously a magical device, but you thought you'd be able to use it without destroying it?"

The poor boy looked down on the ground upon realizing his incredible stupidity. He stammered out, "I'm sorry. Curiosity killed the cat, apparently."

That remark unfurrowed the dragon's eye ridges and he said, "Hmm, yes. I can definitely relate. Come on then, I didn't mean to be so coarse, it's only I'd rather not have anyone asking questions. When we go to Noriath, you can poke at anything you want without worrying whether it'll break or collapse!"

The boy nodded, though he was still beating himself up on the inside for not realizing something so obvious.

Rauliax then suggested that he ride on him again, as the city was considered pretty large even by dragon standards.

So Solah hopped onto the dragon's back without the harness, and they walked on past the stone map at a leisurely pace, which was still about twice as fast as a human's casual pace. The dragon was now more used to the exile's invigorating touch, and managed to contain his excitement. They took about ten minutes to reach the Circle Road despite walking twice as fast as everyone else and having a clear way since all the pedestrians gave way when they saw the dragon lumbering towards them. As they approached the outer core of the city, the duo saw the airships parked at the Airdock District grow larger and larger until they could count the number of propellers on each one of them. At the center, floating over the Royal District a little higher than the others was the massive one they had seen when they had flown in.

Solah could see some of the ships were designed similarly, and deduced that there were several classifications for them. Rauliax nodded, and explained to him the several types: scouts, front-line tankers, artillery, frigates, battlecruisers, and the huge one was the Admiral's, the capital ship of Wesar's fleet.

The Circle Road was organized neatly with traffic flowing clockwise moving inside the inner half, and vice versa for the outer half. There were three wide lanes on each side, meant for carriages, the dragon told him, and the outermost one for parking. There was also a smaller lane for pedestrian traffic on the edges that allowed people to walk either way. Every thousand feet or so there was a crosswalk, and every mile there was a turnabout for carriages to use. Buildings surrounded the road like trees wrapped around a trail through the woods, but the road was wide enough to not feel claustrophobic. The buildings on the inner side of the Road had their backs built into the wall that surrounded the Airdock District, and there were small alleyways scattered about led through the inner wall, but once in a while they'd pass a more official looking entrance.

Traffic was light, so Rauliax elected to run a little faster in the passing lane. They passed a carriage that was being pulled by two horses who took the dragon's sprint as a challenge and tried to outrun him, encouraged by their handler since they must've been late to wherever they were going, but he, quite literally, left them in the dust as they ran across a section of the stone road that had been covered in a film of dirt from the wind.

Solah rode on in silence, taking in the sights and sounds of the city while holding tightly onto the dragon's back hair. It was quite overwhelming to him: since they had entered the two of them had done nothing but walk, and he felt they probably could've gone back and forth through Windsgate twice already. For a moment, he thought of sneaking out at night from their inn and go thieving about a while, but he thought better of it. He had no excuse for it now, and Rauliax would disapprove if he found out. And, of course, he'd probably get lost in this massive city, especially at night, unless he stayed close to the Circle.

They continued running, and Solah looked at the airships again. He could tell, by the nearest one, that they were locked into their docking platforms by huge cranes that wrapped around their hulls, and their propellers weren't spinning. He remembered the airships that landed at Windgate: they didn't get grappled like that and still hovered next to docking ramps under their own power. People were loading boxes into the dirigibles, and eventually his eyes wandered to the Admiral's ship, though it was always there in his peripheral vision.

He could see now that every section of the ship was lined with cannons. It was carried by at least fifteen propellers spinning inside a circular donut-like shell that contained them. The metal propeller ducts were a bright shining contrast to the wooden hull of the ship, and he wondered why the rest of the ship was not made of metal. The massive ship had several sails, though he couldn't see the upper deck of the ship since it was floating too high. He saw a word engraved near the ship's bow in shining silver, almost as bright as Rauliax's scales when they reflected the moonlight and much brighter than the propeller shells. It was the vessel's name: the *Corona*.

Chapter 5

"Thank you very much, you can pay for all of it with the bar if you want, or I can get you a bill," the cheerful little lady said.

Solah gave her the gold bar he was grasping and took the bag of Iswald roots. Lady Mary's was a relatively large store, certainly the biggest an exile like him would've seen. The owner, Lady Mary herself, was a rather energetic old lady, and her merry disposition reminded him of Grandma Nama.

Despite the size of the store, however, Rauliax still couldn't fit through the entrance without causing some damage so he sent Solah in to fetch the last alchemy regent, along with some extra herbs to be used for an explosive potion, that he was looking for. Solah had told the lady what he wanted and waited about ten minutes as she first ran through the aisles for the more common items and then went upstairs to find the root. There were only a handful of other customers in the store who were wandering about the aisles of plant-life, and the waiting made him edgy as he thought several of them were staring at him, and not in a good way. So to avoid staying longer than necessary, he gave her the gold bar as payment so he could leave immediately.

Rauliax took the bag and inspected its contents. He approved, and hurled it into his mouth before letting Solah back on. Despite their speedy travel, partly since they were afraid of the store being closed when they arrived, through the city, they had arrived at the shop near sunset, and when Solah came back out from the shop the last of twilight had faded.

The dragon then walked, a little slower than before, along the straight road to the Tourist District towards the High Horse inn as recommended by the map keeper. It was named so since most dragons and elves who visited stayed there, along with some traders and, suitably, tourists from Elemar. Notably, the Tourist District held a teleportation stone which allowed transport mages to warp in Elemarians from other teleportation stones located at trade harbors.

Rauliax elaborated on these stones to his intensely curious rider. "Usually, transport mages can only warp someone a mile, at most. The teleport stones allow them to do that across the continent, as long as there's another stone there, but they're incredibly rare."

"Transport mages? You mentioned levimages before too, does everyone only specialize in one area of magic?" Solah asked.

What the boy was lacking in social graces, he made up for with his astute observations. Rauliax replied, "Well, for humans, yes. Manipulating magic is tricky business, I hear, and it takes a lifetime of training in one thing to be proficient at it. So you have transport mages, levimages, elementalists, enchanters, signalers, naturalists, protectors, transmutators, and so on. On the other hand, elves live long enough to master several branches, so you'll find they're quite flexible."

"Oh, what do they each do?" Solah asked.

"Well, I just told you what transport mages do. Levimages, obviously, levitate things, although they also move them, they're called kineticists sometimes. You already know what enchanters do since you can so brilliantly fake being one." Rauliax smirked as he recalled how he had trapped the merchant that tried to con him, with Solah's help. "Elementalists are a tricky breed. Usually an elementalist only chooses one element to practice. Fire, ice, and lightning, I believe. Might be more, I forget. Obviously they mean 'element' in its traditional meaning since it has a very different one in the realm of science. And yes, any adolescent should be able to cast the easy cantrips of every school of magic, but, for example, a non-fire elementalist could light a candle easily enough but no way could they hurl a fireball that would burn anything. On the other hand, elementalists can also use related elements with ease. For example, an ice elementalist can also use water." He paused and craned his neck over to check Solah's face to see if he understood how ice and water were related. He knew Solah wasn't particularly well versed in science or vocabulary, but was relieved to see his education wasn't so neglected since he could tell from his expression that he understood the relation.

The pause was long enough for the boy to ask him if something was wrong, but he shifted his head back towards the road and went on. "No, nothing, just checking if you were comfortable."

"Oh don't worry about me, your back is as comfy as my bed. I always thought dragons were reptilian, but you feel very warm."

Rauliax shook up his head in contempt. "Hmph, a common misconception. Just because we look a little like lizards doesn't mean we are the same. No, we are quite warm-blooded, just like you are. I don't blame you for thinking that way though, a lot of regular non-exiled humans think the same, and they have access to books that would teach them otherwise!"

"I suppose I should take that as a compliment?"

The dragon laughed. "Moving on then, signalers are an interesting type of magician. They can send messages and visions to other people, although only signalers could reply until a just a dozen years ago. You see, the physical method by which signalers performed their work was unknown until twenty years ago, when radio waves were discovered to be what they manipulated with magic. Then eight years later, engineers were able to harness radio waves with technology, and now just about anyone with a transceiver can do the job of a signaler. Of course, they're still useful, since with magic radio waves can be enhanced to transmit across the entire world without static or degradation. Radio transmissions and frequencies can also be locked by them, which is important in battle since transmissions could otherwise be heard by the enemy. And technology can't replicate their ability to send visions, though last I've heard they're working on that."

Rauliax probably should've looked back then, because when he finished talking he heard the boy ask, "Umm, what are radio waves?"

"Oh dear," the dragon said. That was something he should've suspected the exile not to know. He explained them as invisible vibrations in the air that move at the speed of light, and compared them to the flow of magic. Solah didn't quite comprehend, but they had reached the border of the Tourist District by then. Unlike the border between the Lower District and the Middle District, the Upper, Tourist, and Airdock Districts all had a wall marking their boundaries. There was only one road and one entrance into the Tourist District, aside from the teleportation stone, and in front the gate were half a dozen guards blocking the way.

They came up to the gate and the leader of the guards, a middle-aged woman dressed in silver robes that presumably covered her armor, stepped forward. "Halt, by order of King Devran, the Tourist District is under lockdown. None may pass."

The dragon looked at her curiously and asked, "Is there some sort of trouble inside? We just need a place to stay for the night."

She replied sternly and with authority, "I'm sorry, I am not at liberty to say. If you are looking for room, there are several inns in the Middle District for you, dragon."

"Very well then," he said.

Rauliax turned around and they went to the map stone in the middle of the Upper District to ask for directions to an inn. He tried to ask the same illusionary advisor why the Tourist District was closed down, but the head didn't know.

"I'm sorry, but I was just notified the district was shut down a few minutes ago. They didn't tell me why, and it's not my job to ask," he said apologetically.

"Alright, thanks anyway. Are there any landmarks to help me find the Corona's Flare?" Rauliax asked, referring to the inn the head suggested.

"Oh, it'll be quite obvious. It's on the inner side of the Circle Road, and the sign has a light on it that alternates colors every five seconds. At a horse's pace, it'll be about a ten minute walk from here."

"Very good then, thank you for all the help."

"No need, only doing my job sir. If you need any further assistance, be advised that map guiders will be off work in about an hour and services will not resume until sunrise."

Rauliax bowed his head and the illusion dissipated into the night.

They found the inn easily: as the guide had said there was a very obvious alternating light that they saw a mile away. The doors were big enough for two dragons to walk through at a time, but Rauliax let his rider off before they went in.

"Remember, try not to touch anything that might seem magical," he told Solah.

"Yes, but I hope you'll forgive me if I don't recognize something as magical," the boy said.

"Of course, but do try to stay in my sight so I can warn you if you're about to," the silver dragon said. His scales shimmered from the light on top of the Corona's Flare's sign.

Solah nodded, and they went in.

There were a dozen or so patrons sitting in the main room where food and drinks were being served. Some of them looked up at Rauliax, but most of them were used to seeing a dragon in the Flare and didn't even bat an eye. Framed photos of the flagship *Corona* were all along the wall, and there was a large model of the ship hanging from the center of the room. The model looked very accurate to the pair as they had walked around one entire side of the ship the entire day, and Rauliax counted fifteen ducted fans under the wooden hull that was less texturized than its real life counterpart. Four more were at the aft of the model, and there were an uncountably high amount of cannons sticking out from all sides of the airship model. The two of them both muttered out an "Oh" when they realized the meaning behind the inn's name at the same time.

"Will it be a dragon's den and a room for your friend?" a rough, female voice called out.

They looked over towards the stairs and saw the innkeeper, a woman who looked a lot like the guard from the Tourist District.

"No, thank you, we'll share the den," Rauliax called back. He had kept his frugal nature restrained for a while, but mentally slapped himself for acting so rudely. Not for a friend, and certainly not for a future family member, he thought. Then he slipped his head down and whispered to Solah, "Unless you want your own room, of course."

There wasn't really a reason to be so quiet, but Solah whispered back, "No, your company is more enjoyable than a soft bed in my own room, I'd think."

He said it with such conviction that it made the dragon happy. Not a lot of dragons enjoyed his company, and Rauliax found most dragons his age to be incredibly immature. Not that Solah wasn't immature, but his was a kind made from understandable ignorance that could easily be fixed with knowledge. The kind of immaturity he couldn't tolerate was the type that controlled a person's thoughts and actions. In that sense, Solah was mature far beyond his years.

The woman moved down into the main room and said, "Oh, alright then. Do you guys want to order anything for dinner?"

"Yes, please," they said in unison.

She laughed genuinely at how cute two of them were acting and gestured them over to a table near the back. There was a beanbag on one side and she moved a chair over to the other side.

Solah sat down on the chair and noticed the wall their table was up against had portraits, protected under extravagant frames, lined down across. They all depicted a lone person with a professional smile wearing a hat embroidered with a sun at the front.

Rauliax looked at the beanbag for a moment, and then sat down on it. "Oh, very comfy."

"I'm glad you like it dear, I think its fun to sit on too! My name's Wendy, by the way, owner of this fine establishment." She put down two menus and noticed Solah glancing up and down at the portraits and said to him, "They're pictures of all the admirals of Wesar. All the way back fifty years, since the *Corona* was built. Can't believe she's still in service, but they keep retrofitting her so she's about as modern as a brand new ship. I heard they just finished adding another twenty cannons on her so she's got a whole two hundred now."

"Fascinating," Rauliax said, "But why do they need so many cannons on a single ship? It's not like there's a war that makes it necessary."

"No," the innkeeper admitted, "But it's always a nice way to instill some national pride, you know? Knowing our flagship's better than anything the easterners got. Besides, rumor has it that Elemar's going to try something soon, never hurts to be prepared right?"

"Agreeable, but it still feels like overkill to me." Then he chuckled a little. "Oh my, don't mind me, I'm just a traveling dragon after all. It's absolutely none of my business."

"Oh, no offense taken my scaly friend. Now what would you fellows like to drink?"

"Orange juice please!" Rauliax said with genuine desire.

"Just water for me," Solah said.

She jotted down the drinks in her head and said, "Alright, orange juice and water. Take as long as you want to look at the menu. Do you want your stay to be billed on the dinner receipt or would you rather pay tomorrow morning?"

"I'll just pay it all tonight," the dragon said.

"Very good then." She walked off to serve another table before getting them their drinks.

After the innkeeper brought back the drinks and went off to service the other patrons, Solah looked over the wall again. All the admirals had ten years of service, as he assumed the years under each portrait meant. Above the years, there were scrabbles of writing that he could barely make out as each admiral's signature. There was no picture of the newest one, however, as he scanned down the wall and none of them had listed the current year.

After Solah sat back down, Rauliax went on, "I've never actually seen any of them in person before. Important men and women, kept out of sight, like most of the royal family. The newest one, Admiral Lina, I believe, just took office two years ago."

"How do you know so much about human affairs?" the boy asked.

Rauliax took a sip of his orange juice and savored the taste. "Well, tell me you don't learn a lot after living a century. Okay, actually I tend to travel a lot, so naturally I learn a lot about the outside world. Other dragons don't usually go out enough to care. At all."

Then Solah wondered if humans often went to dragon territory. Even though he knew he'd be fine just with Rauliax, he didn't want to be the only human in Noriath. He asked the dragon, but then realized right after it shouldn't matter at all: he was an exile anyway. And everywhere he had been outside his home he was surrounded by nobody truly like him. Still, the feeling of being surrounded completely by a different species with no familiarity beside his friend still nagged at his heart.

"Yes, airships come in to trade quite often. Sometimes human engineers and other intellectuals pay a visit to our highly esteemed University," Rauliax said with a hint of pride. "We also hire some humans for construction: your deft hands are better for more delicate architecture."

"Oh, okay," Solah replied. He wouldn't feel completely out of place, or perhaps even unwanted, then.

Their waitress returned back a while later and they made their orders: steak for the both of them. Solah never had steak before since he never stole raw food, and people rarely left out such expensive cooked meat out in the open, so the dragon suggested trying it.

Solah cut a small bite and tried to put it into his mouth as elegantly as the dragon was eating his larger cut. He closed his lips around his fork and suckled on the steak's juices, and with his mouth full he blurted out, "Oh heavens, this is delicious!"

Rauliax paid his manners no mind and just agreed nonchalantly, "Mm, yes it's been cooked quite evenly."

They finished their dinner and Wendy led them to the dragon den, which really was just a large room laid with a specially soft carpet. The entire room was, in essence, a giant bed.

Solah stopped trying to walk in after a few steps, and just started rolling on the carpet since it was easier and not at all uncomfortable. Wendy giggled a bit at the boy's antics, and then Rauliax entered and suddenly the den felt half as small, but he didn't mind.

Wendy stayed standing before the extra-wide doorframe. "It's not too cold yet, but if you want to, feel free to use the fireplace, but make sure the *kid*," she said with extra emphasis as she kept her eyes on Solah who was still rolling around, "Stays near the open window. There's no chimney to ventilate and I don't want the fumes to choke him."

"Oh, don't worry I won't use it," Rauliax said, half to the innkeeper and half to assure Solah.

"Alrighty then." She stopped looking at Solah and turned his eyes to Rauliax, who had already found himself a comfortable place and curled himself so the tip of his nose touched the end of his tail. "Now, I hope you don't mind me asking, but a dragon and a boy of his age make quite an odd pair. Is he training to be a naturalist, or is he taking a break from his magic studies to study some engineering or something?"

It was true that such a pair were uncommon, but not so rare as to be overtly questionable. Naturalists, mages who had the power nature at their command and who were masters of herbology, often tried to study with elves or dragons, but elves were particularly disdainful of outsiders and dragons usually rarely left Noriath.

Rauliax paused a moment to think before answering. "Yes, he's a naturalist. I hired him to help me study the local plant life and gather some herbs," he said, only half-lying. I thought it'd be mutually beneficial to hire someone so young, since it was inexpensive for me and I thought we'd both learn quite a bit."

She found this answer satisfactory and replied, "Well, that's good and all, never thought a dragon would want to know about the local flora though." She let out a chuckle and continued, "Here's the keys for the den, and your lodging fees include a free breakfast in the morning. Thanks for staying at the Flare!" She tossed the keys to the dragon and left after closing the doors.

Keys, he thought, this particular inn must have had plenty of draconic guests before. There was an actual physical lock on the door,

41

which was impossibly difficult to find unless it was imported from Noriath, and he mused that the innkeeper knew dragons couldn't manipulate magic, not even enough to mentally flip a lock enchantment on a door. He touched the lock and felt a current of power in it: it had been bound with another spell that made it just as powerful as a normal door enchantment. The lock was really just a conduit between the physical and magical realms, and the key was just used to flip the door into the lock position in place of a normal human's will.

Of course, it was a good thing Solah hadn't touched the door. He stored the keys away after he used it, and afterwards warned the boy not to roll, or even move near, the door.

Rauliax spent the rest of the evening filling the large gaps in Solah's knowledge. An hour of vocabulary, an hour of math, and another hour of practical science; it turned midnight before they knew it, and they turned in for the night.

Chapter 6

Solah awoke to find the room he was sleeping in felt much larger than he remembered it. Then he sat up and realized his dragon companion wasn't in the room anymore. There was an odd amount of light in the room, so he looked out the window and saw grey clouds had come in overnight and blanketed the entire sky. They were letting through enough light for him to realize it was long past morning already.

Then the door opened and Rauliax hurried through carrying a half-chewed through orange in one hand and an apple in the other.

"Here," the dragon frantically said. He tossed the apple over to Solah, who barely caught it before it hit him in the chest. Then he took another bite out of the orange and said, "We have to leave. Now."

Solah's faced scrounged up, absolutely perplexed. "What do you mean? Why?"

"I'll explain once we're in the air," Rauliax said. He pulled out a jacket from his mouth and gave it to the boy. "It's going to rain, wear this. It's a raincoat and it'll keep you warm." The dragon also handed him a pair of goggles, which he stuffed into one of the large pockets inside the coat.

The boy was now very concerned; not about the hygiene of the clothes, of course. Perhaps someone had discovered he was an exile? He didn't question the dragon, whose tail was swishing with nervous energy, and put on the raincoat. The outer surface of it felt strange, as if it were covered with oil, but the inside was nice and warm. He nodded, silently telling the dragon he was ready.

Rauliax led him out into the main room they had dined in the night before. Wendy was sitting behind a bar counter and caught sight of them.

"Hey, you two leaving already?" she asked. "I'm sure the news was wildly exaggerated, as these kinds of things always are."

Rauliax responded, "Yes, we should leave as soon as possible. You're no simpleton, Ms. Pearce, and as we discussed during breakfast, you agree that this kind of news can bring about a complicated political situation."

Wendy Pearce, the innkeeper, nodded her head. "I understand, Mr. Moonsilver. You've already told me of the closure of the Tourist District. And I can fathom how fear could make them lockdown the entire city."

"So you see why we must take our leave now," he said.

"Perfectly. Thanks for the generous tip," she added, "And I hope to see both of you again in the future!"

"You're very welcome, the steak was delicious. I'll be sure to recommend the Flare to my more outgoing companions," Rauliax said.

She bowed at the both of them and they left the inn through the extra large entrance designed for dragon customers.

The clouds made the Circle Road seem especially gloomy. There were very few people outside compared to yesterday's bustle of activity. The dragon, after he hooked on his harness, nudged Solah with the spaded end of his tail and he understood the meaning. He hopped onto Rauliax's back and locked himself in the harness. The dragon looked back to make sure his rider was safely harnessed, and upon his confirmation, leapt into the sky without delay, ignoring the courtesy of Farrain's airspace that he had so delicately followed the day before.

Solah looked behind him as they rose into the grey sky. He saw that several of the airships that were docked yesterday had departed, and the crew that he could see on the deck of many of the others scurried about frantically. He could've sworn he saw one of them on the closest airship staring at him, or at his dragon, though he couldn't be sure from this distance.

He remained silent until Rauliax had flown far enough to level off into normal cruising flight a little below the cloud deck. "Now will you tell me what's going on?" he asked.

"War's broken out," Rauliax bluntly said. "King Arashal has sent his entire airship fleet over the Ridgeback Mountains."

"What?" Solah said with confusion. "Isn't that a week's flight to the east? Why'd we have to leave so soon, and in this kind of weather?"

"War makes people irrational," the dragons said. His voice was clear, carried by the wind. "It's why they closed down the Tourist District. They might've closed the entire city if we stayed."

"The Tourist District? But that was last night!"

"Indeed. He invaded late in the evening, after the clouds had rolled in. Rumor has it that the Third Fleet of Wesar was decimated. They were scattered along the length of the mountain range and were hunted down from cloud cover."

Solah processed this information for a bit, and then realized Grandma Nama could be in danger. "Raul, we have to go back and rescue Nama!"

"That's where we're headed," the dragon said with conviction. "Don't worry though, there's no danger there yet. The Second Fleet has assembled at Imilune, a fort city at least two or three days east of Windsgate. I'm afraid Elemar still has the clouds in their advantage though now that the Second Fleet expects it, they have mages scanning the clouds for activity."

They flew on back to the east. It started raining shortly after their conversation, and its pattering drowned out any further verbal exchange. The raincoat was working quite well: Solah felt abnormally warm under it though his exposed face that the hood couldn't cover was nearly freezing cold. At least the goggles kept the rain from pelting his eyes. He leaned forward into the tuft of brown hair that lined the scruff of the dragon's neck and back. It proved very effective at insulating heat, and combined with the dragon's own radiating warmth, brought feeling back into his face. Solah's thoughts wandered to wondering how the dragon wasn't freezing to death in the cold wind and rain. Then, he realized that the dragon was always naked, and nobody, not even himself, found it strange in the least. He shrugged it off and decided it must've been magic that kept them warm, the natural magic that dragons possessed, so they didn't need clothes.

Solah lost track of the time as he laid his head down into Rauliax's hair. It was a strange juggle of warmth and vision: he had to keep his eyes looking forward through the goggles or he'd start feeling sick. He could see through the rain a strange bump in the cloud ceiling, an elongated round bump. It almost looked like the bottom of an airship.

And it was. Rauliax tried to fly a large distance around it, but it descended quickly down through the cloud cover, the clouds parting like dust to reveal the ship. It was small compared to most of the airships Solah had seen before, and was carried by only four propellers on the bottom, with another two on the rear attached around a small rudder. It was flying a green banner on a relatively short mast that Solah didn't recognize.

Even through the rain, Solah heard the frantically beating dragon yell, " It's an Elemarian ship! A scout, but I don't understand! It still couldn't have possibly gotten this far west so quickly even if it managed to avoid detection!"

The ship approached them with a burst of forward velocity as if it had suddenly gained a power boost. Rauliax couldn't outdistance it under the resistance of the rain, even with Solah's presence.

And then the dragon jerked back and stopped in mid-flight. If Solah wasn't harnessed, he would've flown straight off from the forward momentum.

Rauliax roared and screamed out, "This isn't good! How did they even see me? I should be invisible among the clouds!"

It was true, Solah thought, his silver coloration should've kept him camouflaged from sight, especially in the rain. And he wondered why an Elemarian ship would care about a lone dragon enough to chase him down. He tried to turn his head around to look at the ship and saw tendrils of vines extending straight from the forward section of its deck; a dozen of them, at least. He moved his head to try and see under Rauliax as much as he could, and he could see some of the vines had wrapped themselves tight over the dragon's limbs.

Rauliax was struggling against the binding vines, but only managed to gain altitude with his efforts. Gained altitude, but pulled closer to the ship.

"Solah!" the dragon called out with his head craned towards him, "If you could manage to touch it somehow, maybe if you unlatched, no that's too dangerous, but if you could twist-"

With Rauliax's head turned toward him, and Solah concentrated on the dragon's cry, neither of them noticed another ship was descending from the cloud ceiling that they were very close to touching now. There was no sound, no warning thanks to the deafening rain. The dragon just jolted forward as his binds were suddenly cut. He snapped his eyes forward and saw the new airship: a Wesarian scout ship. They were firing their cannons toward the vines and the foreign ship.

Solah watched the barely registerable black trails of the cannonballs fly toward the ship that tried to capture them. They looked like they impacted nothing as there appeared to be an invisible shield around the ship that rippled with white pulses as it absorbed the force of the cannonballs' impacts. The ship quickly rose back into the safe cover of the clouds after taking some hits.

Then the Wesarian airship started moving towards them. Its flag, blue with an outline of a tower shield, didn't flow with the wind and just hung limply at the top of the mast. As it flew closer, Solah noted its name. The *Reliant*. It was designed a little differently than the green bannered ship: it had two propellers attached on each side of the ship that were circumscribed in a donut enclosure made of white painted wood and faced upward, two propellers under the hull itself, and only one large fan on the rear side. The upper deck converged to form an empennage tail section that cut off to form a rudder above the rear spinner.

"Hmph, needed eight of them to tie me down. Let's greet our rescuers," Rauliax said. "We must look suspicious enough, might as well make a gesture of goodwill and not make them chase after us."

And so he flew towards the deck of the *Reliant*, with as much grace and dignity as a rain-pelted dragon could perform. But as he flew closer, similar vines he had just escaped from shot out to tug him down onto the deck.

Solah shouted, but he was silenced not just by the rain, but also by amazement at what he saw as they descended. There was an invisible barrier around the Wesarian ship too, and now that he was up close he could see the rain fall and splash around the protective sphere. Then, as they reached the border of the wall, it parted and rain fell through. After they passed, he saw it sealed again and stopped any more rain from flowing through.

Rauliax didn't try to resist. It would've been useless and considerably rude. Instead, he continued his own way down to the deck, letting the vines escort him instead of forcing him down. He landed within a circle of mages, naturalists based on the entangling vines they summoned, and bowed as far as the binds would allow.

Then a young gentleman wearing a feather tipped hat appeared in front of him. "Don't try to act innocent, dragon. We've received word that several people saw you and that boy leave Farrain in a hurry. Quite suspicious, don't you think?"

Another man wearing a dark red hat, edges lined with silver, appeared next to him, standing a little taller than the first man, and said, "Lieutenant, if these two were in league with Arashal, why would one of his own ships be trying to capture them?"

"Maybe it was an act, to fool us into trusting them," the lieutenant said. "In any case, they fled the capital right before lockdown. They cannot be trusted, captain."

And the captain said to his lieutenant, "Perhaps. We shall see." Then he turned his gaze to Rauliax's eyes, as if he were scanning them for treachery. "Well? Explain yourselves."

Rauliax met the captain's gaze with a disarming stare. "I'm afraid we were simply in the wrong place at the wrong time. I'm just a visitor, and the boy I had hired to work some magic for me."

The captain released his analytical gaze and locked it straight at Solah, who was still sitting in his harness. "Is that true, son? What is it you're doing for him?"

Solah stammered and paused as he tried to recall his false story. "Yes. I'm just helping him gather herbs, and advise him in their use," he managed to stammer nervously.

The lieutenant butted in, "So you're a naturalist? Summon a plant then, or something. Prove it."

"No need," the captain declared. Then he whispered to his lieutenant, "I can't read the dragon, but the boy is definitely lying."

"What shall we do with them then, sir?" the lieutenant said with a malicious smile.

Before its captain could respond, a volley of cannonballs and bolts of lightning shot from the clouds into the *Reliant's* magical barrier. The attack was unrelenting, and the captain barked out orders in reaction. "Keep the dragon bound, and make sure the boy stays in the harness." Then he shouted to the upper portion of the deck, "Helmsman! Get us moving, don't keep us here like a lame duck to be hunted!"

The ship lurched forward, and a juvenile voice called back, "Yes, captain! Very sorry, sir!"

The captain had no time to scold the trainee helmsman that took over while he and his lieutenant came down to interrogate the dragon and his rider. The *Reliant's* cannons fired blindly up into the clouds, and several elementalists had shown up on other parts of the deck.

Cannon fire roared with fireballs, lightning bolts, and ice shards in both directions, and sometimes fire would meet ice and cancel each other. Rarer still would a sharp enough piece of ice shatter a cannonball.

Despite his crew's efforts, however, the captain noticed the barrier around his ship gain a purple color and contort, and he pulled a black box out of his coat and ordered through it, "Warp Master, swap the upper barrier with the lower, and be ready to rotate through the others at my command."

"I'm on it," a voice from the little radio replied.

He sent another order through the radio, "Signals officer, send a transmission to the admiral: we've captured the suspicious boy and the silver dragon, and we're under attack from an Elemarian scout ship, one hour west of Windsgate!"

"Trying sir, the weather is making it difficult to concentrate," another voice called back through the black box.

"Do what you can," the captain replied. He watched overhead with fear and anticipation.

Cannonballs rained down from the sky in time with the falling rain droplets. There was no escape for the *Reliant*. "Captain, we have to get rid of their height advantage," the lieutenant said.

The captain nodded. "Agreed, it's dangerous and we might collide with them, but at this rate we'll be gone before we make a dent in their barrier." Instead of calling an order to the helmsman again, he ran back to the upper deck and took the controls himself.

Reliant rose rapidly, even against the current of downward force being applied to it from the hail, both literal and figurative, of fire coming from above. This risky move proved to be a good one as the direction of fire trailed off to the side: the enemy ship was moving away.

Now at the upper deck, the captain called the signals officer without his radio. "Donnovan, keep tracking them, and tell our battle crew where to aim!"

"Yes, captain!" the officer replied. Then he waved his arm into a sphere and yelled through it. "Direct all fire to heading one seven-niner, angle negative fifteen degrees." The voice boomed through the ship and even Rauliax and Solah heard it.

Much of the deck crew, mostly fire and lightning mages, shuffled to the starboard side of the airship and continued hurling their respective element. Some of them were overly excited and leaned dangerously over the gold-painted railings. However, the enemy's return fire still hit its mark, but the *Reliant's* magical shields were holding if only barely.

Signals officer Donnovan shouted, "Captain, they can detect us too, you know!"

The captain's face remained firm. "Of course I know that, and I'm sure as hell not going down without taking them with us. Tell the levimages to give me full forward power!"

Solah felt the ship surge forward and couldn't understand what they were meaning to do. Rauliax, however, did. "They mean to ram into them," he said softly.

"Are we going to die, then?" Solah asked with a twinge of fear in his voice.

Rauliax didn't answer, but he faced the lieutenant, who was still watching them. "You, you're the lieutenant of this fine ship yes? Please release us, if you let us go we can help you fight."

The lieutenant scoffed at him. "Right. Release you so you could escape, or even help them destroy us. Tell us your real story, dragon, and maybe I'll think about it."

Rauliax sighed. He was really tired of being stuck, first from the failed experiment in the forest, then from the Elemarian ship, and now at the hand of *Reliant's* naturalists. He whispered to Solah, "I have an idea. Unstrap yourself and get down."

Solah did so, and the lieutenant raised his arms to prepare to restrain the boy.

"Stay where you are," he said, "I am no naturalist, but I will freeze your legs if you take another step."

"Lieutenant," Rauliax said, "If we were truly your enemies, we would've easily escaped far sooner. We wouldn't have even come near your ship. Please release us, so we can save your lives."

The lieutenant barked a rough laugh, even this near to defeat. "Escape? You look in no position to escape, dragon. Maybe if we had only two or three to restrain you, but you can't escape six."

"Then allow me to demonstrate," Rauliax said in kind. "Solah, the vines."

The exile gave him a queer look, and then he smiled as he understood. He moved towards one of the vines that was entangling his friend's forearm.

"Stop! You have been warned!" the lieutenant yelled. Solah paid him no mind and walked casually closer to the vine.

The lieutenant's face contorted and he moved his hands in an elliptical motion using his index fingers to twirl around. The air around Solah's legs seemed to pulse and vibrate, but then nothing happened.

"Wha, what magic is this?" the lieutenant cried. "Naturalists, restrain him!"

One of the mages in the circle around Rauliax unwrapped the vine he had grappled around the dragon's wing and flung it towards Solah. It touched him, and withered into nothing.

The lieutenant started panicking and barked out, "Restrain him, restrain him! Forget the dragon!"

All of the mages released their vines to grab at Solah instead, and the boy hopped himself back onto Rauliax's back. All of them withered away into dust as they touched him.

"I've got a good hold," Solah shouted, "Go!"

The dragon didn't look back to check how secure his rider was, and leapt into the air before the mages could regain their composure.

Once they flew far enough up, the dragon stopped and gave Solah time to secure himself into the harness. After he was safely buckled in, he asked, "What should we do now?"

"I'm going to clear the way. Then you're going to poke some bubbles," the dragon replied.

"All magic gets dispelled when it comes near you, even those that are constantly willed. I needed to confirm it wasn't just enchantments," the dragon replied.

"You mean you weren't sure we were going to get away?"

The dragon sighed, a little ashamed of himself. "I know sometimes the risks I take are a little too great. But it worked out, yes?"

"I...I suppose. What now, then?"

"Think it through, Solah! We're going to fly as close as we can, and you're going to poke their shields."

Solah widened his mouth as he comprehended. But then he asked, "We're still going to help the *Reliant* after they took us prisoner?"

Rauliax replied, "To be fair, we do appear awfully suspicious. I'd rather keep good relations with Wesar. If we save them, it can only look good for us, yes?"

The boy thought about it for a second in the beating rain, then nodded.

"Alright, here we go!" Rauliax shouted. He flew with a surge of speed forward and he breathed. His chest expanded as he drew air into his lungs. He turned his head towards the area where the two ships would've been fighting and he released the air in a blast of wind that parted the clouds temporarily. The gust was great, and he kept it up for a whole minute as he breathed out wind. The rain even stopped where the clouds blew away. When he finished, the sky in that area was clear as ice, and they saw the two ships trading fire. The barrier around the *Reliant* was glowing a faint red, and he saw some cannonballs manage to pierce the failing shield and crash into the deck.

Rauliax dove through at full speed, no longer having to worry about the rain shredding Solah apart, and soon was ahead of the Elemarian ship. Nobody on board was paying attention to the pair since they were all focused on the *Reliant* behind them.

"And down we go! You touch, I'll burn!" Rauliax shouted gleefully, his excitement overriding any hesitation.

Solah only hoped they would stay unnoticed. Magic he could repel, and dragons could to some extent as well, but the cannons he wasn't sure of. Would a cannonball crush through dragon scales and injure his friend? Were the cannonballs forged from real metal, or conjured, like the grappling vines? He had no time to ask.

The dragon flapped forward, then turned his back to the ship and let inertia bring Solah to the forward barrier. They couldn't see it dissolve when it impacted his head, but they certainly felt the gush of wind that followed the dissipation of that power. Rauliax then flipped himself forward and let out a stream of flame from his mouth and fire quickly engulfed the bow of the airship.

Rauliax wasted no time to pause, and continued his way down under the ship. He flew right along the lower barrier and made a quick spin to make it meet Solah. As he spun, he shot out more flame at the lower hull and the wooden planks gave no resistance to the spreading fire. Once the lower barrier was dealt with, Rauliax flew on to the rear of the ship while continuing to spit fire at various parts of the under deck. Again, he flipped himself backwards and had his momentum ram Solah into the rear barrier which offered no resistance to being nullified. He dove right after he felt the power gush away and was safe from the exchange of fire.

The Elemarian scout had no clue what had happened, and the attacks from the *Reliant* flew straight into the hull of the ship. The impacts flung crewmembers overboard, and both Rauliax and Solah heard the terrified screams of those who were plummeting to their deaths.

Then Rauliax turned around and made another pass at the belly of the ship, this time aiming fire around the propellers. They passed to the front of the ship, and turned around to look at the fruits of their labor. The wood and metal around the propellers that held them in burned away and they spun out of their emplacements. The ship sank a little, and then hovered in place without movement.

Meanwhile, the rear of the ship was decimated as the *Reliant* flew closer, now a predator to the weakened airship. There was no further return fire as panic broke throughout the Elemarian ship. Cannonballs streaked through the ship and splintered wood flew everywhere, some large enough to impale the crew to death. Fireballs surged and consumed what remained. Their frost elementalists tried to contain the fires by summoning water but it wasn't enough: fire was burning in too many places.

After another minute, the ship started sinking again as if the hand that was holding it aloft had suddenly disappeared.

Rauliax flew away from the falling, burning wreckage towards the *Reliant*. "Either the fire got to the levimages, or a lucky cannonball hit their chambers," he mused.

The wreckage plummeted into the forest below and toppled any trees that stood in its way while the clouds reformed overhead. The rain returned shortly after and put out the fire before it had spread too far into the forest.

They had won. A dragon and an exile practically single-handedly brought down an airship. A scout, only, but it was still not to be expected. Solah thought he should have been happy, but he was unused to battle, to seeing death. It chilled his heart, and he understood why his kind were exiled. He could see why the fear people had for his kind was not entirely irrational. An exile with a dark soul could easily cause a lot of harm.

But he wasn't like that. He would fight against evil, and show them not to be afraid of him. Even if in the end they wouldn't, he'd still try.

And then Rauliax roared in pain as their battle high wore off. Solah, now focused back to normal as the adrenaline wore off, noticed something off in his peripheral vision. He shifted his eyes toward it, and saw a gash in the tip of the dragon's right wing: scale and skin had been torn off, exposing reddish bone. In the heat of combat, neither of them had noticed a stray cannonball had grazed Rauliax's wing.

Chapter 7

Instead of just waiting for the *Reliant* to fly over to them, Rauliax limply flew over to have them converge quicker while maximizing each glide per flap of his wings. The ship's red barrier was gone now, and the rain was freely pattering onto the deck.

Rauliax unceremoniously plopped himself down onto the clearing on the deck that the captain was gesturing to. The dragon then closed his eyes and said not a word while holding a claw onto the top of his head. Small droplets of blood were dripping from his wound, which washed away with the rainwater.

"Get down here," the captain ordered at Solah.

Without any guidance from his tired friend, the boy obeyed and began unlatching himself from the flight harness.

"Captain, shouldn't we keep the dragon tied up?" the lieutenant butted in. The feather in his cap had been replaced with a small wooden stake.

"Avery, the dragon's in no condition to fly away from the ship." The captain then pointed to the steaming rubble down in the forest. "And they kept us from turning into that. Now be a bit more polite, please, and if you can't, it's an order."

"Very well, captain," Lieutenant Avery said grudgingly.

Solah jumped down onto the deck, but the moment his body left the dragon, Rauliax let out a great whimper and his head fell crashing into the wooden floor.

"Keep...keep touch," he mumbled.

The boy quickly put his hand back on Rauliax's side. "Are you alright?" he asked.

There was a rumble in the dragon's throat. "Mm, yes. Just tired. Very tired. Keep a hold on me. I'll probably faint otherwise. I'm not too used to breathing fire, and certainly not so much at once. And the injury isn't helping either."

"Now, I ask you again, boy, what are you? No lies this time," Avery demanded.

The captain now glared at his lieutenant. "Polite, Avery. If you can't do it, quietly remove yourself from the deck, please."

The younger officer then bowed in apology. "Yes, sir, sorry sir."

"No more outbursts, now, go to the signals officer and bring back a report," the captain added. The lieutenant hobbled off to the upper deck and then the captain turned his gaze back toward Solah, who was vigilantly keeping a hand on the tired dragon. The good captain cleared his throat. "I'm very sorry for all the fuss. Captain Dillan, at your service."

"I'm Solah, and this is Rauliax," the boy replied.

The captain nodded, his eyes fixed on the boy's like before. "Very well, Solah. You've just helped us destroy an Elemarian airship. You are not an enemy, then. But, you must understand that I must ask what you are and why the two of you are here, rushing away from the capital in such weather."

The dragon rider suddenly started feeling cold under his raincoat. He hesitated to answer, and looked to Rauliax.

"Go ahead, the worst they'll do is exile you again," the dragon whispered.

So then Solah told the captain everything. From his home near Windsgate, leaving out the part where he stole to survive, to how he met the dragon not two days ago in the forest, from randomly exploring the area of course, he told him everything.

At the end, Captain Dillan nodded. "I thought your kind had died out, but then again if we send you into exile it's the point to not see you again, yes? All in all, it sounds like a highly improbable scenario, but I see only a little deception in your eyes. Most of it is true then as we've all personally seen your abilities, but you're leaving something out."

Rauliax shifted and said with his eyes still shut, "It is somewhat distasteful. But we'll tell you if you promise not to punish the boy for it. I'll gladly pay whatever restitution is necessary."

The captain contemplated a moment, and then said, "Very well, as long as it's not something horrific like murder."

The dragon's eyes opened wide at the very suggestion of the idea and he said, "Oh, nothing of the sort. Go ahead Solah."

And so the poor exile told his story again, including the thievery, and at the end the captain nodded.

"Very good, no deception this time. I can understand then, and since it is my opinion that it was not your fault that you were forced into such actions, I will vouch for both of your good characters if it becomes necessary."

"You are a good man," Rauliax said.

"I appreciate honesty," the captain replied.

They left it at that, and a few moments of silence passed before Lieutenant Avery hopped back down from the upper deck.

He took his hat off, pulled out the splinter and tossed it into the rain, and went on, "Sir, the *Lightsworn* should be here within ten minutes, they were only a little behind us when we left Windsgate."

The captain smiled. "Oh, a frigate? Good, they'll have a medical team or a healer at the least. We'll also swap a protector. This blasted rain is starting to feel quite annoying."

"Yes sir, they'll be escorting us back to the capital."

Captain Dillan nodded, and his two guests understood they were probably going to get entangled in unpleasant politics despite their attempt to escape earlier.

The lieutenant noticed the two staring at each other awkwardly and said with a disdainful tone, "No, no, neither of you are in any trouble. The admiral actually wants induct both of you into the aerial fleet. Bah! Your little stunt impressed more than my captain, you know." Then he added in a quieter voice, "And thanks for that, I guess."

The captain laughed. "Hah! Looks like you're more valuable as a military asset than as a feared unknown swept under a rug, boy. That's a good thing, by the way."

Rauliax opened his eyes at last. "You can't just force us to fight for you," he said calmly.

"Oh, definitely not," Avery acquiesced. "We can't force a dragon, and the boy is under your protection, as it seems, so the admiral and the king are both willing to strike a deal with the two of you. Which is more gracious than what I would've done." Of course, the last part he said so quietly that nobody heard him under the rainfall.

The captain took a step forward and said, "Now then, our orders are simply to take you back to Farain. As captain of this ship, I owe you for saving my ship and my life." He glared at his lieutenant and continued, "By my order, you will be treated as guests, so long as you remain mutually courteous."

Rauliax craned his neck down to represent a bow, and gestured Solah to do the same. The boy did so while keeping his hand on the tired dragon. After he finished, the dragon said, "Very well, then, Captain Dillan. We accept your splendid hospitality."

"Excellent," the captain replied. "Now if you'll excuse me, I have to finish inspecting the battle damage. I'll send an ensign down so you can tell him if you need anything." Then he gestured to his lieutenant. "Come on then, Avery. Go check on the warp master."

"Yes, sir," he said, and they both went separate ways. The lieutenant went under into the ship, while the captain went to the upper deck.

After they left, Rauliax wrapped his tail protectively around his friend and said, "I'm so sorry Solah. I've just dragged you into a war. I shouldn't have asked you to come with me, if I hadn't you'd be safe in your cottage right now. This is my fault."

Solah felt a little angry, but he didn't know why. It wasn't because he might be about to join a war, no. He wasn't angry at the poor dragon either. No, it was because he didn't like seeing his friend beat himself up over what was happening.

"Nonsense," the boy said, "I wanted to follow you in the first place. If you hadn't suggested it first, I might have asked. It's not your fault, who would've thought there'd be a war? Besides, if I had stayed in my home and you flew off to wherever, wouldn't I still be in danger, just like Grandma is right now?"

The dragon had to admit that was very true. And his Grandma was still in danger, especially now if an Elemarian ship had pierced itself so far into the west. Fatigue was seriously starting to wear in, so he just grunted in agreement.

Later he'd have to ask if the rumors he heard in the morning were true. He needed to know if the Third Fleet really was defeated or not. But he was too tired now and instead fell asleep, though before he did, he covered Solah from the rain with his good wing.

With the rain blocked away, the boy took off his goggles and put them into his inner coat pocket. Then he was left alone to ruminate upon his situation. War, he thought, was something he had only read about. People died in wars. It was a very unpleasant thing, and many times fought for petty reasons. What was this war for? What was so important that people were dying over? Land? Power? Those were the usual things in his books. They didn't seem that important to be worth killing for, though.

And so he kept on wondering, his thoughts continually swimming until the rhythmic soft sound of the rain hitting the membrane of the dragon's wings tired him out. He shifted so he sat leaning against the dragon's silver side in a position that would make it unlikely for him to lose contact with him. The dim light of the cloudy day still managed to seep through the wing's semi-transparent membrane, though that faded as Solah fell asleep to the mixed sound of rain dropping and the dragon's heartbeat.

When the boy awoke, the first thing he noticed was that it was dark. Dark, but with a faint light; the light of the moon. The dragon's wing amplified it, and through the wing the milky white light was brightest. He pressed a hand onto the dragon's side and lifted himself up, careful to keep his hand on him.

"Awake then, finally?" a low familiar voice asked.

"Yes, what time is it?" he replied in kind.

"A little past midnight. I didn't know you could sleep so much, I've been awake for about two hours already, but I didn't move since I didn't want to disturb you."

The boy chuckled a bit. "Oh sorry. But yes, there's usually not much to do at home, you know. So sleep is rather pleasant."

"Mm, yes. You can let go now."

The boy took his hand off the dragon with a bit of reluctance, and then he heard a large sigh before the wing lifted away, uncovering the night that barely illuminated the *Reliant*'s deck. The moonlight promptly faded away, leaving only the ship's enchanted fire posts lighting the deck. The clouds were still there, but there were patches of clearing now.

"You're feeling better now?" Solah asked.

"Yes. I need to practice my fire more. It really tires me out too quickly. Actually, that first gust should've left me...well breathless." The dragon chuckled at his pun, but continued when Solah didn't appear to understand the joke. "You're really something, the extra energy really kept me up. Water and light, those are my specialty. I can use those breath attacks for half an hour straight before I'd get that tired. The wound still hurts a little though. The doctor from the *Lightsworn* said the ball cut into the bone and even splintered it. He patched it up, but he didn't know enough about dragon physiology to do anything else."

The boy looked over to his right wing and saw the wound had been wrapped up with some cloth. It didn't bleed anymore, at least. He still felt a little phantom pain in his shoulder. Empathy hurt, sometimes. "Will it be okay?" he asked caringly.

"Luckily, I do know a little about dragon physiology," Rauliax said as if he shouldn't have. "Don't even worry a bit, this would only be considered a minor inconvenience. I'll be fine in a month, maybe two, tops. We can regrow an entire wing in a year, you know."

"An entire wing?" he asked. He was pretty sure he couldn't regrow his arm if he lost it.

"Yes, our natural magic at work." The dragon's voice became a little more boastful as he continued, "Human and elvish healers haven't been able to force magic to regrow an entire limb yet, for your information."

That was interesting to know, but Solah was just happy to know his friend would be fine.

Then his stomach rumbled and reminded him he hadn't eaten pretty much the entire day. It also reminded him that it was a good thing he had practiced maneuvering flight on the dragon before the battle, as he had not felt nauseous at all during the fight. Danger also helped keep that feeling away. Then he also realized the ship wasn't moving.

Rauliax heard the rumble and turned away before the hungry boy could speak. He faced the stairway to the upper deck and said, "Ensign Waters, wake up."

There was a little bit of grumbling from the corner of the bottom of the stairway before they saw a figure stand up.

"Oof, what's going on?" the supposed Ensign Waters said.

The dragon replied, "He's awake. Go fetch him some food, if you'd please."

"Oh! Of course, right away."

The figure moved away and seemed to meld into the ship as he went under the deck.

Then Rauliax continued speaking as if they had not ended their previous conversation. "Actually, I think I'll heal much faster if I stay in contact with you. Could be as short as a week."

"Then I'll try to stay with you constantly until then," the boy replied. Then he moved over and leaned against him while standing.

The dragon found it more difficult to resist quivering in his still somewhat weakened state as the energizing feeling came back to him. He managed though, and just said, "Thank you, Solah."

He nodded in response, and then asked the dragon, "By the way, where are we? It feels like we've stopped moving."

"We're parked in the Airdock District, back at Farrain. We arrived past nightfall, so they'll deal with us in the morning."

"Oh, alright then."

Ensign Waters came back up shortly after holding a plate full of food. Solah managed to briefly glimpse the ensign's appearance as he walked towards him and a little light illuminated him. Young; he looked even younger than himself.

The ensign handed him the plate full of food, and he gobbled it down with the included spork. He couldn't really tell what he was seeing since it was too dim where he was leaning against the dragon, but whatever it was it tasted good.

After he finished, the ensign took the plate back down and returned with two plastic cups. He handed one to Solah, and the other larger one with a straw he handed to the dragon. He took a sip; it was orange juice. Rauliax had probably asked for some earlier.

The dragon also drank some from the straw. He let out a satisfied grunt, took another sip, and then set the cup down.

Then the ensign looked at the dragon and said, "Now then, I've already introduced myself to you." He shifted his head to the exile. "And for you, Ensign Waters, at your service." He took a step back and said, "And my thanks to the both of you. The captain said you saved the ship, and our lives."

Solah stammered, "Umm, you're welcome, I guess."

"It's stupid, I think. The dragon's a nice fellow, and if he keeps you company you must be nice too. It's stupid. Instead of trying to understand you, they just banish you. Scared, that's why I think they do it. Scared stupid. Like long ago, they were scared of dragons too. They tried to make war with them, because they were scared of them. Turns out they were nicer than them."

Rauliax knew what the young ensign was talking about. He wasn't alive back then, no, but the old dragons remembered, and their history books definitely didn't forget. It was hundreds of years ago, far before he was born, when humans tried to fight against dragons.

Supposedly, they thought dragons were feral beasts. Ironically, they now spoke the same language the dragons used back then. It was ancient history to him though since dragon and human relations were quite civil now. Sure, there were some very old dragons who still remembered clearly enough to still hold a grudge, but their anger was pointed solely at humans who had died long ago.

Waters continued, "I think they'll accept you now, like the dragons. You've proven yourself useful, not a menace. At least, the captain does. If you're ever in trouble, call on any of the *Reliant's* crew."

"Uhh, thanks," the exile replied.

"But onto business," the ensign said. He took a few more steps back and said, "The captain says you're probably going to be inducted into the fleet. He told me to give you both a crash course in airship tactics and command. Ready to learn?"

"We *might* join the fleet," Rauliax said.

"Still," Solah said, "the topic sounds interesting. Can we hear it anyway?"

"You could help save a lot of people," Waters said. "Make them not stupid. But even if you choose not to, I'll still teach you the basics! Ready?"

"Sure," the duo said in unison.

The ensign held his hand out towards one of the flame posts, and the fire grew bright enough to illuminate most of the part of the deck they were on. "Great! Let's start with crew operations."

"Oh, you're a fire elementalist?" Rauliax asked.

"Yes. I know, my name makes it kind of ironic," Ensign Waters replied. "Still just an ensign though. The flame posts are already enchanted. I can just give the flame a little more oomph. Otherwise, I spend my time practicing my art. In battle, training fire and lightning elementalists like me stay on the gun decks and we run around sparking the powder used for firing the cannons."

"Not a bad gig," the dragon remarked.

"Not at all," Waters said. "But moving on, you've got the captain. Obviously he commands the ship, and he usually gives orders through the radio or the signals officer. Every ship has its own frequency, but the signals officer monitors every fleet frequency. The signals officer does a lot of other things too, like sending a visual image for a ship's transporters to use."

Solah, again, didn't really understand what radio waves were, but he figured it was some sort of magical way to convey information.

The ensign continued, "Speaking of transporters, every ship's got at least one: the warp master. He teleports people around the ship, to other ships, or to the ground, if we're close enough. But if a transporter doesn't know his ship well, or is teleporting outside the ship, he needs to see where he's sending someone off to and that's when the signals officer shows him. Never had a signaler beam a picture into my head, though. But anyway, usually the warp master stays at the highest point of a ship, a crow's nest if the ship has sails. And the signals officer at the next highest point. Ours stays on the upper deck."

Rauliax sucked up some more orange juice from his straw as he listened with interest.

"Oh, I forgot the lieutenant," Waters said. "He helps the captain out. Both of them can be any sort of mage, they just need to have command experience. Our lieutenant is kind of an ass, but the captain keeps him in line."

Solah grunted lowly to agree while Rauliax raised an eye ridge at the crewman's language.

"Next are the levimages. They usually don't do anything unless too many propellers are damaged. Then they're the most important part of the crew. They can also help make quick maneuvers, and increase the ship's speed if the captain needs it. Oh, speaking of the propellers, some of the crew are engineers and will be called to fix things when needed, but otherwise they do their magic thing. The not training elementalists obviously shoot fire, lightning, and ice at enemy ships. Fire's good at burning wood, lightning's good at draining shields, and ice is good at stopping propellers from spinning and putting out fires. Oh, speaking of shields, the barrier mages, protectors, well, they protect the ship. There are four on ours. One for the upper part, one for the lower, and two for the sides."

"Interesting, is it always that way even for bigger ships?" Rauliax asked.

"No, no. I've been told the *Corona* has sixteen since it's so huge! Four for each quadrant in the front and rear, then four surrounding the quadrants making up the two middle parts. Bigger ships might also have other mages too. We don't have a doctor, a transmutator, oh wait I forgot, we do have an enchanter. Scout ships don't usually have one, but ours insisted on staying on one. Something about avoiding combat, if the rumors are true. Of course, ever since we got him all our flame posts have stayed on, so it's been nice."

Ensign Waters kept the lecture going on the entire night, eventually delving into aerial tactics. Rauliax soaked everything in easily, but Solah had to stop the elementalist several times to clarify. Eventually, the clouds lit up and they knew sunrise had come as the morning light pierced through several of the holes in the cloud cover.

Waters had just started on about a certain Captain Pearce Maneuver when his own Captain Dillan interrupted him from the stairway with the usual throat clearing noise.

He said bluntly, "I'm to take the both of you to the admiral and the king immediately."

Chapter 8

Captain Dillan directed the duo off the *Reliant* into the Airdock District, which surrounded the Royal District, via a platform that connected to the ship's deck with a large metal board and led them to the King's palace. Solah, while walking away, saw the airship was parked with the clamps and there were already people repairing bits of the hull.

The palace, naturally, took up the center of the city. The structure gleamed as if it had been freshly painted white, and in the middle was a spire that was apparently the tallest point in the city, but it had been blocked from sight by the surrounding airships. The sun only illuminated the palace in the morning and evening hours as the *Corona* hovered directly over the spire and blocked out the sun for most of the day.

The entrance of the palace faced the south and composed of two massive doors more fitting for a dragon. Two guards stood at attention and they saluted Captain Dillan, who briefly saluted back, before allowing the three of them in.

The building was tall, definitely, but Solah had assumed it was because it had several levels, like the second floor of an inn. But no, the palace's main hall was just simply extremely tall, to the point that he felt like he had wandered into a giant's cave. The immense height even made Rauliax look dwarfish in comparison.

"These royal types are always so showy," Rauliax whispered to the boy.

He just nodded and continued walking, and the captain led them into the central chamber at the end of the hallway.

Two people were already sitting on one side of the long table, presumably having breakfast. On the left was a delicate looking woman wreathed in a heavy brown coat. Her hair, the top of which was covered by a feather-tipped hat similar to Lieutenant Avery's before it met an unfortunate fate, was neither pure white nor a faded grey indicative of old age, but instead shined an unnatural silver similar to Rauliax's scales. Her green eyes contributed to her overall uncanny appearance.

To the right of her sat a middle-aged man wearing a featureless golden crown. The crown had no design set upon it, and there was only a sapphire embedded in the front. He was slightly heavyset, undoubtedly a result of a life of luxury.

The king and the admiral, Solah thought. The admiral's eyes were a strangely bright shade of green, and they made her look otherworldly. Come to think of it, he hadn't ever seen anyone with green eyes before. Nama's and his own were an earthly brown, Rauliax's were blue, and as he recalled only Wendy the innkeeper had blue human eyes. He couldn't help but stare at her.

Then the captain directed them to sit on the opposite side, snapping Solah out of his entranced gaze. There was a velvety red beanbag for the dragon to set himself on, which he did with restrained glee.

"Thank you captain, you may leave now," the admiral said.

Captain Dillan bowed and left back out through the main hall.

The king cleared his throat. "Welcome, Rauliax Moonsilver and Solah-" He paused, then said, "I apologize, the good captain did not relay your last name."

The boy's eyes tried to look away from the king. "I have none," he stammered, "There is no need for one when you live with only one other person alone in banishment."

Then Rauliax said, "He will be a Moonsilver in any case, soon enough."

The lonely exile smiled at the thought, but the smile quickly went away as he was reminded that his Grandma was still in danger.

The king raised an eyebrow, but understood quickly enough. "Very well then, Solah Moonsilver. I am King Devran, and this is Admiral Lina."

The admiral nodded at them, but then said, "My lord, I suggest we dispense with the pleasantries. Time is of the essence."

The king nodded. "At your suggestion, then. Admiral, if you'd please, explain to them our situation."

The two guests listened as the admiral spoke. "The rumors you might have heard yesterday morning are true. The Third Fleet has been lost at Illum, and Arashal's fleet is headed posthaste to Windsgate."

Rauliax wondered how the admiral knew he had heard such rumors.

"The Second Fleet has assembled, but they cannot hold against this threat. He has gone completely insane, I say. He's practically emptied his lands into one gambit. When the storm came in, he sent his entire fleet over the mountains and took out several of the Third Fleet's ships from cloud cover, similar to how the *Reliant* was almost lost. Like hawks diving for worms. A cowardly move, cowardly but smart. I don't know how he passed over the mountains undetected either, the sensor wards placed along the mountains were enchanted with my own signals officer's oversight and they were checked just a week ago. The Third Fleet couldn't assemble quickly enough and only ten made it to Illum. That wasn't even a fight, gentlemen. His fleet of sixty against ten. We only took out three of them, plus the scout the *Reliant* took out, thanks to you, but we lost the entire Third Fleet.

"So he's moving fast. An all out assault, take all or fail forever, right?" Rauliax asked.

"Yes, we'd never suspect he'd be so daring. Our spies in Elemar have reported the only airships left in his country are a handful of scouts and whatever ships that couldn't fly undergoing repairs."

She sighed. "With the Third Fleet completely lost...gentlemen, I will be blunt. We cannot win this war, even on the defensive. The First and Second Fleet combined only make forty-two ships, and against such overwhelming numerical superiority I cannot even hold to hope for victory."

"Your cities have no defenses of their own?" the dragon asked.

"No, airships are *supposed* to be their defense. The only elementalists that can help from the ground are retired, and we've already called back as many as possible into service. They're not attacking the cities anyway, smart bastards. See, if they capture the capital, everyone will be forced to bow down without a fight."

"Well in any case, you can't possibly expect me and the boy to balance such odds," the dragon said.

"No, I've seen the captain's report. You were lucky they didn't consider you a threat, and I can see myself the random crossfire has broken your wing. We need help, gentlemen, outside help. And that's where you two come in. We need Noriath's assistance."

Rauliax shook his head. "That will be a difficult proposition. Even if I manage to get the Dragon Council's approval, our army is only a hundred and fifty volunteers, and only a hundred can be forced. You can expect no more than that, and we cannot be of much use if all it takes is one good cannon shot to take us down."

Admiral Lina nodded. "Yes, I understand. That is why we also need the elves to help us. We have sent an emissary, but he was denied entrance into the Sylvan Forest. But you two are not affiliated with Wesar, and I think you'd have better luck."

This time Solah spoke up. "So you want us to act as ambassadors? Why should we decide to help?"

She replied, "If King Arashal takes over Wesar, he will not stop until he has taken the entire continent. Our spies have reported that he has convinced his people that it is their right, their destiny, to rule the entire continent. He will move on to the dragon realm and the elvish forest, and without any airships of their own, he cannot be stopped."

Then the king added, "And if that's not enough, Solah Moonsilver, you will be pardoned of any crimes you might've committed in the past, and you and all exiles will be welcome in my kingdom from henceforth, as long as you keep the peace. And, as also noted in Captain Dillan's report, I shall send a ship to take your grandmother to safety away from Windsgate. You'll be sent off to Noriath first, on the *Reliant*, and may stop there yourself if you choose."

The dragon and the exile took a moment to stare at each other.

Rauliax said, "It's up to you, Solah. Whatever you choose, I'll follow. I don't want to feel even guiltier for dragging you into all this."

The boy thought for a while. "What do you think we should do, though?"

"Personally, I think we should help. It does make sense what they say, if King Arashal has truly gone insane. But really, it's up to you."

Solah nodded and kept thinking. It was a little difficult as he could feel the admiral judging his movements, and he dodged his sight away from her. A week ago, if he learned somehow that Wesar was at war, he probably wouldn't have cared. They banished him into the wilds, entirely alone. He might have even died if he hadn't stumbled upon the little cottage in the forest. But now he knew it was because they were afraid of him. Maybe rightfully so, but then he thought about the nice people he had met. He didn't want them hurt in this war, and if they lost, he didn't know what would happen. If the admiral was right, then not even Rauliax would be safe in his homeland. If he just showed them, and made them understand his powers instead of fearing them, then maybe they really would accept him. He thought about what Ensign Waters had said, and it helped assure him.

But he still had to ask. "Why are you trusting me when you were the ones that exiled me?"

The admiral nodded in sympathy. "The general public does fear you, or rather what you are. They're afraid that someone can, while they're sleeping safely, break into their homes, bypass their locks, walk straight through their wards, and step through every alarm without consequence, and then slit their throats. You wouldn't, of course, but that is the kind of fear that has rooted itself in humanity." She took a long blink and continued, "But members of the aerial fleet have interacted with enough technology to understand you really don't have to be feared. The problem is, the general public doesn't take kindly to technology and don't understand a simple chain lock on their doors could keep you out. Not that they'd need one anyway, there's only two of you and I don't think you or an old lady would do any harm."

King Devran coughed. "Only two that we know of, admiral."

She shook her head and answered the king. "For centuries all that we've exiled have never been heard of again. I don't believe there are any more, my lord. And if there are, we'll deal with that when the time comes."

Solah understood, but still took a moment to think. At last, he turned back to the king. "Then I guess we'll accept your offer."

Color seemed to rush back into the king's face, and he sighed with great relief. The admiral made no reaction. She sat as stoic as ever, but her eerily green eyes now appeared less analytical and more friendly.

King Devran broke the silence with a clap of his hands, and he called for a servant. "Excellent, excellent! The *Reliant* will leave as soon as her crew is ready. Now, have a hearty breakfast before we send you off."

A servant came running out of one of the side halls carrying a plate of tea, cups, and other ingredients and set it down on the long table.

"Very good," the king said, "The usual for me."

The servant nodded, and then took the admiral's order. Then he asked Rauliax and Solah for what they wanted.

The dragon asked for just a basket of randomly assorted fruits and the boy asked for a steak, which everyone else considered unusual for a breakfast, but nobody made a remark about it.

After the servant left with the orders, the admiral poured a cup of tea for the king, and then poured one for himself.

Then she looked across the table. "How do you like your tea, gentlemen?" she asked.

The dragon said, "Earl Grey, lots of milk and a spoonful of sugar. And hot. Please, allow me to serve myself." He reached into his mouth and pulled out his tea cup, which was specially crafted to be better suited for dragon claws.

The admiral gave him a packet, and he stirred the liquid mixture with a claw. Then he lifted the cup and blew a gentle flame under it before taking a sip.

"And you?" the admiral said, looking at Solah.

The boy recalled the first time he tried tea way back when Nama could still walk outside. She would bring back some leafy things, grind them, and mix them with water. It didn't taste too good, in his opinion. "Oh, uhh, I don't drink tea, thanks. I'll just have some of the milk."

Both the king and the admiral raised an eyebrow, but Lina poured a cupful of milk for him anyway.

Then the dragon set down his cup and cleared his throat. "So, here's a question I hope you can answer, admiral. Do you know why there was an Elemarian scout so far west, far ahead of its own fleet?"

She frowned. "No, we don't. The logs were destroyed even before the ship burned. You were under considerable suspicion, dragon. The only explanation we can come up with is standard reconnaissance, but I don't know why they wanted to capture you."

Rauliax nodded. "They were prepared with a formidable number of naturalists for such a task. How did the *Reliant* manage to track us anyway?"

"The *Reliant's* signal officer detected a considerable pulse of magic coming from your direction, even through the chaotic current of the storm. Naturally, they were surprised to visually sight the Elemarian ship. Captain Dillan reported that the exile doesn't negate your powers like he does for us, does he?"

"Yes, he bolsters my strength. That probably made my magic imprint strong enough for your signals officer to detect, then."

"That's what I assumed too." She closed her eyes and gently knocked the table. "Damn it. I have no answers for why that ship was there. At least I know there can be no more, the clouds have finally broken up. I'm trusting you don't either, your actions have proven both my captains' faith."

Now Rauliax raised an eye ridge. "Both?"

"Yes, Captain Dillan and Captain Wendy Pearce."

Solah and Rauliax stared at each other in confusion. Surely she didn't mean *that* Wendy Pearce?

The admiral noted their mutual glance. "Yes, Captain Pearce, she had retired to work at her inn, but we called her back to duty only an hour after you were reported departing Farrain."

So Wendy wasn't just obsessed with airships, or the *Corona*, they thought. Her inn was her legacy.

Lina continued, "Naturally, she was briefed on our current situation after she took the day to consider returning to the service. By the time she did, you were already captured, and the moment she heard about it she marched straight to me and attested to your good characters and told me why you had left in such a hurry."

"Oh my," Rauliax said, "I will recommend the *Corona's Flare* and no other inn to all my adventurous friends then." And leave a large tip every time he stays there, he thought.

Solah agreed. "That was awful nice of her. Can we thank her before we leave?"

Admiral Lina shook her head. "Sorry, but she's already been sent off on assignment. Busy getting reacquainted with a new crew. I'll send you her regards though."

He looked down in disappointment, but the dragon's snout nudged at him.

"Don't worry," he said, "We'll see her again, eventually."

And so the servant returned with several others, each carrying a silver platter covered under a golden lid. They set down the platters and lifted off the lids in unison.

The king had scrambled eggs, French toast, and liberal amounts of maple syrup over his plate. The admiral simply had a stack of pancakes, with syrup on the side, and topped with a cut of butter. Rauliax received his fruit basket, and Solah salivated at the smell of his steak.

"I am very sorry sir. The morning chef is not familiar dealing with such a meal. Please forgive him if it is not to your standards, sir," the servant next to the boy said.

He didn't even realize the servant was speaking to him as he was far too busy scarfing down the bit of meat he had already cut when he started speaking. Only after he swallowed did he notice that everyone was staring at him, and that was when the words reached his brain. It was true, though. The beef wasn't as good as the one from Wendy's inn.

But of course he remained polite. "Oh, it's not a problem," he said. "It's quite fine, actually."

The servant bowed, and the rest of them followed suit. Then they left them to finish their meals.

After they finished, King Devran rose up and said, "Alright then. Rauliax and Solah Moonsilver, I hereby declare you emissaries of Wesar, but only for the benefit of my subjects. You are neutral ambassadors and not bound to my land. Your mission is clear and is done to protect all the peoples west of the mountains. Gain the aid of our neighbors. The admiral will buy you as much time as she can."

"I can give you a week, at most," she said. "The Third Fleet will make our last stand over Windsgate, and hopefully the Second Fleet will delay them at Imilune long enough to give you that much."

"Then we should leave as soon as possible," Rauliax said.

"Yes, the signals officer of the *Reliant* just confirmed they're ready to depart now. Go make haste."

"How did you-" Solah started to ask.

The dragon cut him off. "Magic, silly boy. Signalers are masters of communication, remember? Now off we go!"

Rauliax picked him up and put him on his back and then looked at the admiral expecting instructions. She just pointed to the main entrance. At first nothing happened, but then there felt like a gush of air. Then the massive doors swung open, and the guards outside peered in as if they were confused too.

Rauliax put a paw under his chin. "Hmm, kineticist, I assume?"

The admiral's expression remained fixed, and she kept her finger aimed at the exit.

"Right, right, we're off. Keep evil at bay and whatnot!"

He pranced off out of the palace with Solah on top. Once they were out of the palace, Lina let a smile creep onto her face. The guards shut the tower door behind the dragon, and they were greeted again by Captain Dillan.

"Looks like we're off on an adventure, huh?" he said. Then his tone became a bit more serious. "The *Reliant* is at your service, emissaries."

Rauliax grinned. "Excellent. My first request is that you and your crew lighten up. Especially that Avery fellow."

He barked out a laugh. "Done. And don't worry about Avery, he's just stubborn."

"Okay then," the dragon replied. "Solah, shall we go get your grandmother now?"

"Yes, let's hurry," he said.

He nodded. "Captain Dillan, we'll be making a short detour to the outskirts of Windsgate. Where we were heading before we were so rudely attacked. There's another exile we'll be picking up."

"Not a problem, I was told to expect as much. Let's get to it then!"

Captain Dillan led them back to the *Reliant*, which was fixed up already in the short time they were gone. Floorboards that were previously smashed were already replaced, and there was no evidence the ship had been in a battle yesterday.

The captain took them to the upper deck, and stopped in front of his cabin. The cabin's door looked out of place: it was much larger than needed for a person to walk through, and was off color from the brown of the surrounding wall.

"You're getting my quarters, it's the only part of the ship a dragon can fit in," Dillan said. "They just replaced the door and smashed out a bigger opening to fit in this one." He looked up at Solah. "All of my stuff's already been moved out, so feel free to touch anything. The door doesn't have a lock, but nobody will intrude."

Rauliax said, "Well, thank you very much captain. You know the deadline, yes?"

"Aye, a week. We'd best get going then."

He moved towards one of the two stairways that was on both sides of the captain's cabin. They heard him shout some orders above them, and the airship undocked soon after.

73

Solah looked forward to seeing Nama again by evening. It had only been a few days, but he did miss her already.

Rauliax went inside the captain's quarters, now theirs, and set up his folding tea table again. The room was a bit short, and if he stretched up his neck all the way, his twisted horns could accidentally drill into the roof so he tried to keep his head unnecessarily low. It made him look somewhat like a hunchback, if a quadruped animal could have a hunched back. Solah followed in after and took off his raincoat, which the dragon put into storage, and set himself onto the wooden floor.

Then it occurred to the dragon: when he adopts Solah as his brother, Nama would become his Grandmother too. It was a rather strange idea since she was half his age, after all, but not one he objected to.

Chapter 9

The captain had let himself in to his former quarters to ask for the exact location of Solah's grandmother's log house. Rauliax had made a mental note of its approximate location and marked the location down on a map. The captain rolled up the map afterwards and tucked it inside his coat. Solah was laying down in a makeshift bed that was hastily moved in and was reading a book on basic algebra.

They were traveling at optimal maximum cruise speed, Captain Dillan had explained, which meant that they were traveling at the maximum speed the airship was mechanically capable of in addition to the speed added by being pushed along by the ship's levimages at a rate that they could continue indefinitely. The *Reliant* was actually flying a little faster than that since the ship's normal compliment of levimages was tripled, and they each switched shifts whenever they felt exerted.

"The First Fleet has nowhere to go," Captain Dillan said, "So they shipped us over some more levimages. They won't do much good staying in Farrain, anyway. It's a good thing too, we're flying at twice our normal cruise speed now, so we should reach the outskirts of Windsgate in about two and a half hours."

"Very good then," Rauliax replied. "How long to Noriath then?"

"By tomorrow morning, a little after sunrise."

The dragon nodded. "Excellent. It'll take a bit of muscle to hasten the Dragon Council to action. My father is a member, so I should have them assembled by afternoon, and hopefully a decision by the next day."

"Really now? That should make things easier then. We do still have to get the elves to help after and time is short. How does the Dragon Council work, exactly?"

Solah perked his ears to listen. He still pretended to be reading his book.

"Well, the Council is made of eleven members. They're usually descended from former Council members, but if the general public dislikes one enough they can vote to have someone replace him or her. It takes a simple majority vote to agree on anything, and this includes going to war. My father will side with us, I'm sure, and he's close enough to two other members to guarantee their vote."

"So none of them have a stronger voice than another?" the captain asked.

"Well no, though the Eldest, that is, the oldest member of the Dragon Council, his voice carries influential weight. If he speaks out strongly about something, it's almost guaranteed the rest of the Council will follow."

"So if we can convince him to go to war, the others will follow through?"

"Probably. But it can go the other way too. If he outright rejects the idea, my dad might even be forced to change his vote."

"I see. Is there anything else we can do?"

"Not really. The Eldest is very old, and very wise. I'm sure he can see our side fairly. The only problem is that he's sick."

"Sick?"

"Yes, he's been ill for a month now. Besides sating my curiosity, that's the other reason I've been out collecting herbs. I need to find a potion that might help him. He could barely leave his cave last I saw him right before I left."

"Alright, so the Eldest is incapacitated. What ramifications could there be?"

"The Council might reach a tie vote. That...wouldn't be a majority. But at least he can't speak against us, though if I do find a potion I'm sure he'd be more easily swayed to our side."

The captain sighed. "Politics. I'm no good at it. And this Council business is even more complicated, I prefer the King just telling us what to do. I hope you can deal with the Council, Mr. Moonsilver."

"Of course, and yes that is one of the benefits of a monarchy. They do things faster. But they're not always right."

He nodded. "A benevolent monarchy has worked just fine for Wesar for more than a century, but you're right with kings like Arashal."

"Yes, and democratic oligarchies have their flaws too. But anyway I digress, would you like some tea?"

"No, thanks for the offer. I have to give the map to my helmsman now. Perhaps later?"

"That would be splendid."

The captain started walking out the makeshift door and paused. Then he turned around. "By the way, a couple of my ensigns have asked me if they could visit you. Curious bunch, those kids. Would you mind?"

Rauliax grinned. "Oh no, not at all. I wouldn't mind more company."

"Very well then. Feel free to kick them out when they become too annoying," the captain said before he left.

Then Solah put down his textbook. "So your father is on this Council thing? Does that make you royalty or something?"

"I suppose it does make me next in line to take his spot. I don't consider it *royalty* to be exact, but my dad is the source of most of my wealth."

"Wait, that means you're like a dragon prince. Oh, will I be a prince too, then?"

Rauliax laughed heartily. "Hah, if you want to consider it that way, sure. I don't consider myself a prince."

"Why not?"

"There's a difference between enlightened despotism and a democratic oligarchy."

Solah furrowed his brows at him. "Uhh, what?"

The dragon chuckled a little under his breath and said, "There's a difference between being a prince and being a future member of a group of people with ruling power that can be changed by the people at any time."

"Oh. Why didn't you just say that instead?"

Rauliax laughed again, but this time there was a snorting sound under it. "Because, dear boy, you need to study more vocabulary after you're done with that Algebra 1 textbook."

He drooped his head down and flipped through a few pages of the textbook lazily. "Alright, alright."

Of course, less than five minutes later he poked his head up again and asked, "Do you think you can find a potion that'll help the Eldest?"

"Boy, you eavesdrop too much. But I do believe so. In reality, I just went out to find ingredients. The actual possible potions that might work was already sorted out by a-" He took short pause before continuing, "A colleague. I could've assembled such a list myself if I wanted to, though."

"A colleague? Who? I thought most dragons didn't care much for magic."

Well, Rauliax thought, there was no point in hiding who it was. They were going to meet her eventually anyway. "The Eldest's daughter. Her name is Priscilla, and quite possibly the most vain, argumentative, and pretentious creature you'll ever meet."

Solah raised an eyebrow. "Uhh, okay? She sounds kind of unpleasant."

"Oh, unpleasant is a nice way of describing her. But she's smart, very smart."

"Is she smarter than you?"

Oh dear. Solah was far too observant sometimes.

"No, no, not at all. Okay, maybe only a little more in matters of alchemy, but I assure you we are equal in all fields of study. And she only started learning it since she couldn't tolerate me knowing something that she does not."

And the boy was observant enough to notice the hint of jealousy in the dragon's voice. He didn't push it though. "Umm, okay then. But if we get on her good side, she can help convince the Eldest to help us, right?"

The dragon's face showed a little relief as the subject changed. "Yes, assuming one of the potions work."

"Okay, so then the fastest way to get the Council to support us would be to help Priscilla cure her father, it's a win-win situation, yes? The Eldest gets cured and we get his support. And you already have all the ingredients, right?"

That was why Rauliax liked the boy. He wasn't book smart, but he sure was logically smart. "That's the plan. There's a whole list of possibly helpful potions though, and it might take an entire day to get through all of them. Priscilla will work as fast as she can. It *is* her father after all."

With the boy's curiosity satisfied for now, he slunk back into his textbook. Solving quadratic equations was difficult, but it'd probably make the two hours pass by quicker at least. Rauliax had sort of taken the role of a teacher and gave him a bit of homework to do while the dragon scribbled down notes trying to think of how best to approach the Dragon Council.

He only managed to finish part of his assignment though. After about an hour or so, a half-dozen boys, all of whom looked younger than him, came in to visit. They were led by Ensign Waters, who had sat down next to Rauliax at his tea table, but the rest of them stayed close to the doorway.

"See? Told you he's a nice guy. Come on, a random guy living in the wilds has the guts to fly on him, and you soldiers of the aerial fleet can't even move near him?" There was a satisfied smirk on Waters' mouth.

The boy standing furthest in frowned and sat down at the table across from Rauliax. His hair was light brown, similar in shade to Solah's, but looked frizzled and frayed. He introduced himself as Ensign Frazer. "And I'm not afraid of him, he just looks different is all," he said. Most the others also decided he was not threatening at all and crept up to sit on the floor in various spots.

The dragon poured himself a cup of tea and asked, "So what do you kids want to know?"

Frazer snapped. "I'm not a kid, Mr. Dragon."

His only reaction was to let out a laugh. "First, I'll stop calling you a kid when you're the same age as me, a hundred and fifty. Second, it's Mr. Moonsilver."

The young shipman rolled his eyes. "Alright, Mr. *Moonsilver.*" His tone then became a bit friendlier. "My dad works in Noriath. He says they have a lot of use for lightning elementalists. Besides the air service, there's really not much work for us in Wesar, but he doesn't explain what he does there."

Rauliax thought for a moment. "Oh, right. He probably makes supplemental electricity for our city. Practically nothing in our city is enchanted, so we use electrical energy to power many mechanical devices. Burning Pyrucium provides most of the power we need, but it only grows so much up north and our city's needs keep growing faster."

"How does that work? How does electricity make things work?" Frazer asked.

"Oh, it's somewhat complicated. Let me think, ah I know. I'll show you." Then Rauliax reached into his mouth and pulled out a bulbous apparatus made of translucent glass. There was a metal disc at the bottom that attached to thin wires inside the glass. Then he

79

handed it to Ensign Frazer. "Give it a small constant spark on the metal part, if it's not too difficult."

He took the bulb and said, "I'm better than most lightning elementalists my age, *sir*, I think I can do something as simple as that." The young mage held the bulb by its base between three fingers and the air started sizzling about his hand.

And then the wires brightened, and the bulb started shining brightly.

"Can one of you close the door?" Rauliax asked.

The closest crewman in-training got up and shut the door, but the light from the bulb kept the room lit.

"And you don't need a continuous enchantment for it," the dragon said. "Our streets are lit up at night with them, kind of like the *Reliant's* flame posts."

There was a collective "Whoa" as if the dragon had performed his own kind of magic. Even Frazer admitted it was pretty cool.

"So wait," one of the kids sitting a corner said, "There are lots of other humans in Noriath?"

The dragon replied, "Yes. We're not xenophobic, that is, we don't dislike outsiders like the elves do. We just don't like leaving our home very often. But we have no problem having humans in our city. We hire them a lot for work. Architecture, for instance, has applications where more nimble human hands are useful for such things as the finer sculpting of details. And lightning elementalists are another common sight, as I just explained. Some humans even study at our prestigious University."

"Oh, tell us about this University," Ensign Waters said.

Rauliax looked up, careful to avoid trapping his horns in the roof. "Mm, yes. The University of Noriath. A place where sappy, bright-eyed young minds go to try and pry knowledge from older professors who love to hoard their knowledge and research."

"That doesn't sound very pleasant," Frazer said.

"Oh, I'm just exaggerating of course. I'm just bitter because they never pay me for any research. And they don't like me either since I'm one of the youngest professors there." But those jerks didn't have a problem with Priscilla, he thought, and she was the same age as him. He still couldn't believe they let her be a professor too.

"Wait, you're a professor?" Solah asked.

The dragon shook his head. "Yes, though I don't really feel like one."

"Well, that explains why you carry around textbooks in your dimension thing."

He snorted. "And why I gave you homework! Don't stop just because we have guests, Solah!"

"He's the exile, isn't he?" Frazer asked. "Can I try some magic on you? I want to see if you're true." He opened the door again and stopped feeding power to the light bulb.

Solah paused a moment, taken somewhat aback by his question. He'd practically asked if he could try to hurt him. "Umm, sure, I guess?"

"Cool," Frazer said, "Here, Mr. *Moonsilver.*" He handed the light bulb back to the dragon, who tossed it back into his mouth, and raised his hand toward the exile.

Frazer started swirling his hands in alternating motions until a small bolt of lightning shot out from his palms toward the exile. Solah raised his hand out of instinct, but the lightning dispersed the moment it touched his skin.

"Didn't feel a thing," the exile said.

"That's…unnatural," Frazer said.

Rauliax set a forepaw on the table and leaned his head onto his paw. "I beg to differ," he added, "The fact that he is alive and breathing means he is perfectly natural, since he is a product of nature, yes?"

"It's still *wrong,*" he said.

Ensign Waters stepped up. "I beg your pardon sir, I'm sure he'll turn around eventually. Come on then everybody. Let's not disturb the captain's guests, the King's *emissaries,* any further. Let's go."

Frazer acquiesced, and the rest followed the two older crewmen out, their curiosity satisfied simply from seeing the dragon up close and seeing the exile's abilities demonstrated so clearly.

Right after they left, someone else popped in the doorway. Lieutenant Avery came in, and Solah pretended not to notice him.

"Hey," he said, "I'm just here to apologize. I mean, I know I did before, but this time I mean it. Sorry about being an ass and all."

Solah didn't look up from his textbook. "Apology accepted, sir."

The lieutenant tipped his two-feathered hat, a new one which replaced the one that bore a hole in it from the splinter wound it had suffered in the battle yesterday, and left without another word.

"Funny how everyone gets friendly when you turn out to be their only hope against destruction," Rauliax remarked.

The boy just shrugged his shoulders and managed to finish his assignment before they arrived at his home.

He sensed the ship stop, and shortly after Captain Dillan poked his head in and informed them that they had arrived at the lodge.

He said, "It was a bit difficult to find under the brush, but there was smoke from a chimney that gave it away."

"Ah, excellent," Rauliax said. "Erm, how shall he get to the ground? I still can't risk flying yet, my wing hasn't healed enough and I don't think your transporters can warp him."

"Oh dear," Captain Dillan said, "I'll go see." He ran out and asked the warp master if he could teleport Solah down to the earth just in case.

"No can do sir. There's like a void where he is. Don't sense him at all, I can't wrap any power around him. I can sense the dragon though, and if you didn't tell me otherwise I'd think he'd be the only one in your cabin," the warp master said.

"Hmm, alright, it's as I expected," Dillan replied. He ran around the deck looking for anything that could drop the boy down. Some ropes, maybe. "Oh, of course!"

The captain ran back into his former cabin and asked Rauliax for the harness that he wore for Solah. The dragon gave it to him with an inquisitive look, but the captain said first, "Yes, this will do." He ran back out again without giving either the dragon or the boy any time to respond.

He came back a few minutes later with the harness, except now the harness was attached to another belt loop via three short ropes that allowed it to hold two people.

"Here you go," the captain said as he handed the harness back to Solah, "It'll hold two people now. We'll wrap it around some ropes so we can pull you up and down. Back one might twist and fly up a little, but it'll still come back down on the dragon. But for now, we're using it to hoist you down so you can pick up your grandmother. Put her in the front one, I think it'll be more secure for a lady her age."

"Umm, okay," Solah said.

"Great, let's get to it then." He turned his attention to Rauliax. "Do you think you could help out? Pulling up two people isn't an easy task."

The dragon agreed, and then they all went out onto the ship's deck. Solah secured himself in the harness, which was then tied with three long ropes. The captain then ordered the ship to hover close to the ground, as close to the tree-line as possible, and then had several deckhands help lower two of the ropes as Rauliax held the middle rope.

Slipping him down onto the ground was relatively easy. He unstrapped himself and went inside the cabin while the captain looked over the ship's railings to wait for him to come back out.

About thirty minutes passed before the captain grew weary of leaning over and waiting. He was contemplating sending another person down, but then he saw Solah finally come back out with the elderly woman. The boy was actually using one of the basket pole tools he used to have for carrying stolen items back from Windsgate.

Even so, he helped Nama strap herself into the front harness, and then he strapped himself into the rear one. He tugged the rope, and then they started to ascend. Captain Dillan had rigged the harness with ropes in threes for redundancy, but his overly cautious construction was unnecessary, and the two of them were pulled back onto the deck without incident aside from Rauliax complaining that it felt like he was pulling most of the weight.

Once they were on deck, Solah dropped the baskets and went over to help Nama out of the harness. He helped her up and picked up her walking stick for her.

"What took you so long?" Dillan asked.

Solah was about to reply, but then Grandma Nama piped up before he could say anything. "Oh don't blame my dear boy. You come with your big airship, start hovering over my house and scare the living daylights out of me, and then you expect me to leave without any time at all? By the heavens, I hadn't even time to pack anything but my favorite clothes! If Solah hadn't insisted on the danger I was in, I wouldn't have gone at all!"

Captain Dillan recoiled as he was completely not expecting such a reaction from such a delicate old lady like her. "Oh dear, I'm very sorry ma'am, but we are on a tight schedule. Now that you're on board, perhaps Solah and Mr. Moonsilver can detail you on our current situation?"

Rauliax cleared his throat and tried to diffuse the old lady's anger. "Grandma Nama, it's good to see you again. We can discuss the situation in my quarters, yes? I have tea and biscuits all ready."

"Oh, well that sounds fantastic," she said. "I do hope you have a very good explanation for this. I'm far too old to be going places, and all Solah would tell me was that I was in terrible danger and that I had to leave quickly."

"It really is rather complicated," the boy said.

"Yes yes, so you insist, my dear," she said.

They went back to the captain's cabin after Captain Dillan cut the ropes and gave Rauliax back the now double-seated harness. Once back inside their cabin, the dragon explained everything to Nama's satisfaction. The tea certainly helped.

"And now we're going to the dragon city? Oh my, I didn't think I'd ever feel this excited in my life again," she said.

"You can stay there if you want, or you can come back. I'm adopting Solah as my brother, and you'll become my grandmother too," the dragon said.

"Well, that's certainly unorthodox," she said. "I'll see. I can bring my stuff over, yes?"

"Oh definitely, after my wing heals we can go anywhere you'd like. Assuming the cottage doesn't get destroyed in the war, of course."

"Everything is turning far too exciting far too quickly," she said. "I'm too old for this."

And so their conversation turned to the usual topics born from curiosity about Noriath.

Chapter 10

The rest of the flight was uneventful aside from the *Reliant* passing by a frigate on its way back to Farrain. The frigate was commissioned by a merchant's guild, the captain had explained, and that most airships were used for other purposes during peace time. Most often, scouts like the *Reliant* were used for private transport. Scout class airships were small and only had enough space for one or two spare rooms. Since scouts traveled the fastest, they were usually preferred by lavishly rich passengers. Frigates and larger ships were often used to carry cargo, often commissioned by one of the many merchant guilds in Wesar, and more than one of the guilds traded with Noriath on a regular basis.

After Solah had finished his math studies, Rauliax gave him an explosive potion contained in glass that he had brewed with some cannon powder he borrowed from the ship. It was a very small one so he had the boy throw it at him. It worked to everyone's surprise, and it was a small enough explosion not to hurt the dragon through his scaly hide at all.

Rauliax woke up early the next morning and went out to see the sunrise. The mountain on which Noriath was built on was readily visible as he looked off into the horizon. It was an odd thing, he thought, that he had such a desire to leave his home so often. No other dragons ever wanted to leave, and if they did they never did for long unless it was for business. He had to admit he was odd, but it didn't matter much to him.

Despite his lack of concern about what other people, or rather dragons, thought of his attitude, he still worried about his physical appearance enough to at least not be considered a rebellious child of a Council member. His claws were starting to bother him now. They were far too sharp for him to walk about the city without looking like a derelict, so he pulled out a claw dulling tool from his dimensional storage and started rubbing it over his claws as he watched the sun rise.

Since he learned the origin of the boy's name, he couldn't help but be reminded of him as light flooded the grassy plains that lay ahead of them. "Solah," he whispered, "Cute name." He chuckled lightly as he kept rubbing his claws dull.

Then a voice called out. "What are you doing?"

It was Solah's. The dragon craned his neck around and looked at him. "Oh, good morning, dear boy. Nothing really, just watching the sunrise. What are you doing up so early? You usually wake up much later."

"I couldn't sleep," he said, "I feel way too excited. I heard you get up and go outside, so I decided to follow. What are you doing with your claws?"

"Hmm? Oh, I'm just dulling them so I don't look like a savage when we get to Noriath. Unfortunately, evolution hasn't decided that they're more of a nuisance now that we don't really hunt for food."

"Oh," was all Solah said. Then he sat down next to the dragon and stared off into the horizon with him.

It was a funny thing, Rauliax thought, as a consequence of humans' relatively short lifespan, they tended to forget things quickly as the generations moved on. Sometimes they forgot important things, and learning from past mistakes was difficult if one didn't remember them. But there was one thing they did remember, and it's still present in their fairy tales: the ferocity of the ancient dragons that did not possess a lick of intelligence. Rampaging and destruction was all those ancient dragons knew, and that was what humans remembered. Unfortunately, that was why the people of Wesar tried to wage war against the dragons of Noriath so long ago without realizing they had evolved far beyond such a simplistic existence.

His thoughts were interrupted when Solah asked, "Does the mountain have a name, or is it called Noriath too?"

"Oh, it does actually. A very straightforward name too. The Homespire. See, Noriath isn't just built *around* the mountain, but it also includes the inside. Long ago, before we learned to build things, we lived inside the mountain in a huge network of caves. Of course, as our population grew, the mountain alone could no longer shelter all of us, so we did learn how to construct shelters outside along the mountain. And now the exterior is just as complicated as the interior."

"Is there a reason why you guys won't expand and make settlements in other places?"

"It's just our nature. Some sort of base instinct that wants us to stay near our homeland." He smiled. "I seem to lack that instinct, for some reason."

"I'm glad you do," the boy said, "Otherwise I would've never met you." Then he wrapped an arm around the dragon's shoulders, and they watched as the light started to reveal the large details of the dragon city.

An hour later, the Homespire looked almost in arms reach, an illusion created simply by how large the mountain was. Nama and the crew had woken up, and everyone was having their breakfast before they landed.

Rauliax had a glass, or rather three glasses, of orange juice this morning instead of tea, though Nama still had him brew a cup of tea for her. Solah had the standard toast and eggs instead of asking for something like steak again.

Afterwards, Nama tried to go outside to see the dragon realm for herself. She nearly tripped while limping towards the cabin's door where her walking stick was, but Rauliax managed to catch her before she hit the ground. He let out a yelp and shivered as he had nearly forgotten she was an exile herself with the same power that Solah had. But there was something else, some strange feeling he realized he had only felt the first time Solah had touched him. He couldn't figure out what it was though, and left it in the back of his mind.

All three of them set themselves on the front of the ship and watched the city grow larger. Solah could see the spiraling road that rose up around the mountain like a vortex, and at several points the road widened in a massive expanse of buildings made of white stone. Rauliax asked for another glass of orange juice from a nearby ensign, and he rushed off to fetch some.

And so they sat there for a while staring at the city. Eventually though, Lieutenant Avery returned with Rauliax's orange juice, and he handed it to him cautiously with a roll of his eyes. Then he turned around and said, "You know, it's really getting annoying. You've had four this morning, and the ensigns keep pestering me to chill each glass."

"Oh," the dragon said, "Isn't there another ice elementalist that can keep my juice cold?"

"No, I'm the only damn one on this ship," the lieutenant said. "We traded all of our elementalists for levimages, and now I have to go refrost the perishable food stores every couple of hours, and then chill everyone's drinks when they ask. And that damn enchanter of ours refuses to help me permafrost enchant the food stores. Damn loony, that one."

"Well I'm very sorry," the dragon said, "But now that I know, I'll ask for my drinks warm."

"Thanks, I suppose," Avery said grudgingly. He left without turning back for an acknowledgement.

Then the three of them saw a pair of dragons in the distance. They were easily seen as their dark blue and red hides made them stand out in front of the white stones of Noriath.

They flew up to the *Reliant*, circled it, and then landed at the upper deck after receiving a signal from Captain Dillan.

"What's that about?" Solah asked.

"Greeters," Rauliax replied. "They're just here to ask what we're doing here, and then they'll direct us to the best place to land."

"Very organized," Nama remarked. She didn't turn her head away from the mountain.

"I should go meet them," the dragon said.

"I'll come too!" Solah shouted.

"Alright," the dragon said. He put a paw on Nama's shoulders and asked her, "I hope you don't mind if we leave you here a while?" He didn't jolt from the influx of power this time, but he did notice that the first initially odd feeling didn't manifest itself.

She started sniffling when she felt the dragon's hand. The other two then noticed tears were slowly flowing down her eyes.

"Oh my, are you alright, dear grandmother?" Rauliax asked. Calling her grandmother didn't feel as odd as he expected it should have been.

She closed her eyes. "Yes, yes. I'm sorry, I'll be fine. It's just-" She paused as she tried to find a way to convey her feelings. "It's just that I have so little time left. I haven't ever seen the ocean, did you know? I've read about how beautiful it's supposed to be, and now I have barely any time to see. There's so much I want to do now that I can leave that cottage, but now I'm too old."

"Nama, Raul will take us anywhere you want, just you ask!" Solah said. "We'll fly everywhere, and you can see every place you've ever wanted to," he said.

"After this war is over, of course," the dragon nodded. "Don't you fret one bit, dear grandmother. And if you're uncomfortable with flying on my back, I'm sure I can hire a ship to take us anywhere, maybe even the *Reliant* would, since we're already so well acquainted. And as a matter of fact, the ocean can be seen behind the mountain on a clear day."

All she could say was, "Thank you." Then she managed to open her eyes again. "You two should get up to the deck now."

"We'll be right back," they said in unison.

They waltzed up to the upper deck where the two dragons were already talking with Captain Dillan.

"Ah yes," the red one said, "We received your message detailing your mission."

"And I see Professor Moonsilver is on board," the blue one said with a nod in his direction. His glance took a pause at the silver's bandaged wing.

"Very good then," the other dragon said, "The landing platform at the University has been cleared for you, just follow our lead."

"We will follow," Dillan said.

"And professor," the blue dragon said to Rauliax again, "Are you able to fly? Your father wanted to meet you as soon as possible, but I shall inform him of your injury if you cannot."

"I would not dare for more than a minute," Rauliax replied, "I'll take the road down from the University to our home and we shall meet an hour after landing."

"I shall inform him, then," the blue said.

Then they took off and flew towards the mountain at the speed of the *Reliant*.

Solah and Rauliax returned to Nama shortly after, and none of them spoke a word until the ship had reached cannon fire distance to the Homespire. Then Rauliax explained that the University was the second highest point of interest on the road up the mountain. The very top ended in a cave where the Dragon Council met and had their official quarters. Normally though, members lived elsewhere and only used their official quarters for business.

The University of Noriath was fashioned as a massive building constructed of pearly white stone. It was shaped like a box, but it was connected to the mountain and melded itself into it. The corner edges on the outside were rounded off with tower structures that had platforms for landing dragons on every level, and there were cranes attached to the towers that looked similar to the ones on the docking platforms at Windsgate and Farrain. The part of the structure that faced outward from the mountain was dotted with evenly spaced windows. The top of the building that jutted out of the mountain was mostly featureless, and the *Reliant* had more than enough space to dock.

"The University actually extends into a network of caves inside the Homespire," Rauliax said. "And the caves above it are the Dragon Council's."

"That's a really big place to learn things," Solah said.

"Indeed, the part outside the mountain is mostly just the library since it can get sunlight most of the day."

Then their ship docked on the landing platform, and two cranes from the towers moved over to hold it over the top of the building. The sounds of the engines died down to a smooth idle, and then the two leading dragons then flew away after they had finished docking. Rauliax noted the blue one flew down the road in the direction of his home.

Captain Dillan then came over to the front and said, "Alright, we'll stay put and wait for news." He handed the dragon a small device. "It's a radio, ship's frequency is 125.5. It's enchanted so it has enough range to call Farrain without fade or static, so don't let the boy touch it!"

"Of course," the dragon said. He tossed it down his mouth and smiled at Solah. "Very rudimentary design, but magic makes it better than ours. I'll get you one you can use though."

"Okay," was all the boy said. He still wasn't very sure how radios worked.

"Do hurry," the captain said. Then he bowed lightly and went down into the ship again.

"Now, first things first. Priscilla should be up already. She likes working in her lab early before students can knock on her door and pester her with incessant questions, so let's go ruin her quiet morning, shall we?"

"Uhh, okay," he said.

"Would you mind staying with her while I deal with my father?

90

She can study your powers for a bit while I do that."

"Sure, I don't see why not," he said.

"And dear Nama, stay on the ship for now. I'll come back and we'll go to my father's house after I deliver to my colleague her herbs."

"I've waited more than half a century to see the outside world. I think I can wait a little more," she said.

"Off we go then!" the dragon said. He picked Solah up and set him on his back before strolling off the ship into one of the towers.

Inside the tower was a massive spiraling staircase. The steps were built large enough that Solah thought he could take three steps on each one before reaching the next one, but they were of a very comfortable size for dragon feet.

They only moved down one level and walked into a long hallway. Rauliax walked at a very leisurely pace, and they passed several open doorways along the way until another dragon poked himself out of one of the doorways they passed through and called out to them.

"Oh, Professor Moonsilver! Professor!" he called out.

The silver dragon stopped and turned around. "Before you speak, may you answer me one question? Is Professor Ferae in her laboratory?"

Then Solah looked and saw this dragon was smaller than Rauliax, probably younger. His scales were light blue, and he had a white cloth draped over him hanging between his wings.

"Yes," he said, "She always gets here early before any of the students even wake up, and then she locks herself in her lab."

Rauliax understood why she did that, of course. It often became difficult to deal with incessant questions from curious students.

"Very good then. What did you need?" Rauliax said.

"Well, it's funny you're back almost right after Professor Reynolds decides to leave. Can you help me with some drag modeling?" the younger dragon asked.

"Drag modeling? Of what? And why would an old fellow like Reynolds decide to leave Noriath for any reason?"

"Some human business, I don't know what exactly. But anyway, I'm trying to use the property of similitude to calculate the drag on an airship, but the professor didn't leave the scale-ratio of the model in his notes."

"Just measure your model and compare it to its real-life

equivalent," Rauliax replied.

"But where do I-"

"Here," the silver dragon said. He pulled out a book from his mouth and tossed it at the student. "You really should check the library more often."

"Oh!" the blue dragon yelped. "I never thought of that."

"Yes, you should think outside the classroom once in a while. Now if you'll excuse me, I have to pay a visit to Professor Ferae."

"Ah, of course! Terribly sorry, sir. I'll try to remember that!"

The blue dragon retreated into his lab room and Rauliax continued off down the hall.

"What was that all about?" Solah asked.

"Of all the teachers here," the dragon replied, "Reynolds is one of the few that justifies keeping some information from his students. He wants them to discover things on their own sometimes. But I don't think he believed asking another professor is a legitimate way to find information by oneself."

"Oh. And the others just hoard their knowledge for their own sake, you said before?"

"Yes. A shame, really, but that's not our concern right now."

They kept on heading down the hall. Eventually, Solah could see that the white stone of the building turned dark and ragged as the hall seemed to turn from rectangular to circular. It was, he presumed, where the building merged into the mountain and the hall led into the inner caves.

However, they stopped before crossing that boundary in front of a door.

This door was especially odd as there was a note taped on it that said, "Do not disturb." The boy had noticed that only this one room had a door, but all the other rooms were open without any at all and he could peer inside and usually see messy tables and writing on green walls.

Rauliax let the boy off in front of the dragon-sized door and said, "Before we go in, I want to warn you about Priscilla. She and I might appear to be enemies, but let me assure you once more our relation is that of friendly rivalry."

"Rivalry? Will you be fighting?"

"Perhaps, just try not to say anything until the topic turns about you. And whatever she says, she is *not* smarter than I am."

"So you're smarter than she is?"

He snorted, and then said, "Bah. I will admit that I consider her an equal, though she may be a tad, only a tad bit better at alchemy."

Then the silver dragon tried to open the door, but there was a chain lock on the other side that he could see through the open crack.

A voice called out, "Can't you read the sign? Come on now, I expect anyone in the University to be able to read at a first grade level."

Then Rauliax tried to deepen his voice so he sounded older. "Delivery for Mrs. Ferae. Urgent."

"Oh very well," the voice said again. The chain was let down and the door pulled in.

Priscilla's scales bore a shade of light purple. It was a pleasant color, like that of a rare twilight, and she was about the same size as Rauliax. The larger scales that ran down her neck and belly were the same light white color as his, and she had stringy snowy white hair that did not flow down the entirety of the back of her neck. Her horns were lightly curved and did not twist at all like Rauliax's.

She looked at him and paid no attention to Solah. "Well, look who decided to show up! I can't believe you decided to just disappear without letting anyone know where the blazes you were going."

"Well, I'm sorry but you were the one who said it was urgent that someone got those herbs you wanted quickly."

She smirked and said, "Oh please, Raully. You must've left because you couldn't stand living under the shadow of my superior intellect! You're always off and about because you can't stand feeling inferior, of course! And who's this little human you've hitched up?"

"Hardly, Prissy. I've brought back the herbs and other ingredients we needed, and I found this boy in the forest. He has quite a particularly interesting power."

"Oh Raully, I told you to stop calling me that."

"Only if you stop calling me Raully."

"Psh, you're just jealous you can't compete with a mind like mine's."

"Please, I'm not the one who's researching how a variety of manure affects crop yield. Honestly, I don't understand why the University gives you grants for your ridiculous research." He said "research" while flexing two of his claws.

"Well, some of us don't have a rich parent on the council that spoils us by showering us with gold, you know. And it's all about presentation, when you've got charms and brains you can convince anyone to give you money!"

"Charms? Oh my, I can't possibly fathom why anyone would find you so endearing, Prissy. And it's not my fault your father won't share his riches."

"My father is the Eldest, and he's wise enough to know not to spoil children or else they'll never grow up! I've had to work hard for my funds. And the problem with your requests for research grants is that you have neither charisma nor brains!"

"Hey, I've worked too! And if you're referring to the one single time I made a minor error in my presentation on a faster method in calculating beam displacement-"

"Forgetting to add the constant of integration isn't a minor error, it's a stupid mistake!"

"Well, I was working on that presentation through the entire night, I bet you would've made a stupid mistake too!"

"Sure, and I assume that one time you thought twenty-one was a prime number was also a minor error?"

"What?! That was a hundred and forty years ago, how can you possibly still remember that?"

"As if I would forget any mistakes you've made!"

"That was all the way back in grade school! You can't possibly judge me from then. And can we please move on to more important things?"

"Right, more important things. Like your newest attempt at getting a grant? I never thought I'd see half the committee fall asleep during a presentation." she said sharply.

"Hey! It's not my fault they don't find atomic decomposition interesting!"

"Like I said, it's all about presentation! Besides, there's no practical application for it."

"No practical application? Were you even listening to my presentation? If we could discover a way to split an atom, the energy to be harnessed could power all the lights in Noriath and replace all our non-renewable sources of energy!"

"See what I mean? An absolute bore. You should've twisted it and explained how powerful a bomb it could make."

Rauliax furrowed his eye ridges, shocked at her implication. "Have you gone mad? You can't possibly even suggest such a thing! I know *you* understood how much power could be released! Such a bomb wouldn't discriminate between its target and innocents! Everything would be destroyed! Buildings, wildlife, everything! We are scientists second, living beings bound by morals and ethics first!"

Priscilla took a step back. She had crossed a very fine line and she knew it. "Yes yes, you're absolutely right for once, I'm sorry for even suggesting it. But the fact remains, you need to work on your charisma. Don't you see what I just did? If you had that kind of enthusiasm in your presentations, perhaps less of the board would fall asleep! Now can we please move on to what's important at hand?"

Solah, of course, watched the conversation with great interest. He didn't understand much of what they were arguing about, but he'd never seen Rauliax so riled up before.

Rauliax shuffled himself together after stifling another snappy remark and said, "Very well then, which potion do you want to try first?"

"I've already made a list of them, they're ordered in descending possibility of being effective. We'll make the Saint's Blessing first and try it out on my father."

She started listing the necessary ingredients, and Rauliax pulled out the bags he remembered they were in and handed the regents to her. She'd dump them in a bottle without much care, to Rauliax's distaste.

Then she mashed the ingredients until they were a sufficiently mixed and put the bottle over a fire to melt its contents into a mushy blue fluid. Rauliax hated to admit it, but she was much better at handling potions than he was. She claimed her rough handling was 'efficiency,' and since the potions she made always worked as intended, he couldn't complain.

But that didn't mean he wouldn't. "Must you hack at the tea leaves so barbarically?"

"Must you always question my methods? Which work more often than yours?"

"At least I never animated my lunch! That sure must've been embarrassing, yes?"

She snarled. "You know, I've actually been waiting for you to refer to that noodle incident. I know somebody snuck in a lifestone into that heating potion, and I know the only person that would've known what it would have done is *you.*"

"What? How could you possibly think that I would tamper with your potion? Honestly, such immaturity! Now, can we get back to this one we're working on? How long until it's done?" That, of course, was what the silver dragon said, but inside his head there was another voice that he tried to ignore. That little voice said, "Damn, she's good."

"Ten minutes at boil," she said, "And what about this human boy?"

"My name is Solah," he butted in.

Before she could say anything, Rauliax said, "Solah's not a normal human. His power has made him an exile from the rest of his kind. For good reason, I understand, though still quite wrong, in my opinion."

"That's an odd name. And what is his special little power?" she said rather demeaningly.

The boy said, "It's not an odd name, my Grandma Nama gave it to me. She said it sounded like the word "solar," which was fitting since I made her life brighter, like the sun." There was not a single hint of embarrassment in his voice.

Rauliax nodded and said, "Yes, anyways he seems to negate magic by touch. I haven't had time to study it thoroughly, but it's like he forces the flow around him to become chaotic."

She studied the boy with wandering eyes, and then she said, "Interesting. I take it that since you're not dead from his touch, it doesn't affect dragons?"

"No, the chaos is actually quite empowering to us, if my experience is representative of all dragons."

"Well, as much as I want to try myself, there are scientific methods to go through." She furrowed her eye ridges. "You're far too reckless, you know that? Have you performed any observations?"

Rauliax flicked a paw at her derogatory remark. "Scientific observations? Heavens no, we've had no spare time for that."

"Right, you're sure you weren't just too lazy?"

"What? Don't be ridiculous! I can tell you this: his ability works through clothing, and gloves, but sufficient distance or a buffer material seems to block it since the airship we came on didn't fall out of the sky and a potion in a glass bottle was unaffected by his proximity. A dragon's body also blocks it from transferring to something else, apparently." He went on to explain how he discovered these facts, such as the incident with the map stone in Farrain, and he detailed how they had flown to Noriath on the *Reliant*.

"Of course, those weren't scientific observations at all. So many questions you didn't answer. Like how thick or thin clothing will allow negation? Or what kinds of materials do or do not allow it to pass?"

"Yes, yes, I'm sure you'll perform the necessary procedures for analysis. Just don't do anything that might hurt him." Solah raised an eyebrow at that last remark.

"Of course you brute, what do you think I am? Some sort of savage?"

"No, but I think you're only slightly better. Very slightly."

She snorted, "Pah, you're just jealous of my overwhelming intelligence and wisdom." She didn't give him any time to respond and went on, "Hand me some cheap enchanted items and I'll start my analysis after I give the potion to my father. I know you have some in there." She pointed at his belly, though they both knew perfectly well their storage dimensions were not in their stomachs.

Rauliax took the insinuation with great insult. "I am *not* fat, you rude little brat. Honestly, so juvenile!"

She waved him off with a paw. "Items, please!"

He rolled his eyes and took out a small variety of objects from his mouth. Some glowing iron balls, some small lockboxes, and some other seemingly inert trinkets.

"Quite a bit junk in the trunk, it seems," she said with slitted eyes. Then her face became more serious. "You said you came with him on an airship, right? And it's still docked here?"

"Yes, the *Reliant*, why?"

"First, does the *Reliant* have an enchanter on board?"

"Yes."

"Go get more cheap and easy enchantments, the more experiments and observations I can make, the better. Second, tell me how you met Solah and tell me what happened to your wing."

Rauliax's face also hardened and he said, "Not now, Priscilla. There's Dragon Council business to be done."

She nodded. "Long story short?" she asked.

"There's a war to be fought. Ask Solah for the details, he's not as clueless as he looks. I have to see my father now."

"Okay then, but don't forget those enchantments when you come back, you oaf."

"Of course, princess."

Rauliax left into the hallway and shut the door behind him. Priscilla went over and locked the door again.

Then Priscilla glanced up and down the human boy before matching his eyes and asked, "So tell me about this war. Actually, start at the beginning. How did you and Raully meet?"

"Well, I was running through a forest near a city and stumbled upon him, uhh, entangled by a failed magical potion."

She smirked. "Of course. That reckless, asinine, fool of a dragon is always finding himself in trouble. I swear, he has no regard for his own safety, and he behaves as if nobody would care if he were hurt." Her tone had changed near the end, but she quickly added after turning her head away, "Like his parents, you know? He is their only child."

She was acting very strangely, Solah thought. "Would you care too?"

"Care about what?"

"If Raul were hurt?"

She faced him again, but averted her eyes from his. Rauliax was right about the boy: he wasn't as clueless as he looked. "Don't be ridiculous, of course it would be tragic for such a brilliant mind to go to waste. Well, relatively brilliant, I mean."

She was stammering out her words, but Solah couldn't figure why.

There was a brief pause, and then she said, "Now, put on some gloves and let's start with some preliminary research, you can tell me the rest of the story later."

"Umm, Raul has all my stuff," the boy said.

She sighed. "Right, then we'll just start with pure physical contact."

She took one of the enchanted trinkets Rauliax had dropped off and put it on a table. "Hold on, I need to grab a notebook." She ran off into a smaller room in the back of the laboratory.

Solah wondered how long before his soon to be brother would come back.

Chapter 11

Rauliax trotted down the road down to the first major settlement below the University with Nama riding on his back. When he went to fetch her from the *Reliant*, she had walked over to him without her cane, and though she waived it off by calling it energy derived from excitement, he couldn't help but notice a change in her style of movement.

In any case, he had gently helped her onto his back and then they started down the path to his father.

"I really miss flying," he said. "Running down this road is so agonizingly slow. It's true what they say. You don't appreciate what you have until you lose it."

"Well, luckily I've never had wings so I can't say I completely understand what you're feeling," she said, "But I understand what it is like to lose the ability to do things."

"Age affects us all, eventually," he said.

"You'll take good care of him when I'm gone, I hope?"

"Yes, and you shouldn't worry so much. Solah's a bright boy, he could've taken care of himself even without my help. But pray let's not talk of such dreary things now, grandmother."

She hummed and said, "You're right. How long until we're there?"

"About ten minutes at this pace," he said. "Wish I could run faster, but I might slip off the road if I'm not careful."

Nama nodded, and they continued down.

Noriath consisted of several major populated areas connected by a main spiraling road around the mountain. They were medium-sized cities in their own sense and each settlement had their own fanciful name, but they were still considered a part of the whole city of Noriath. The road was not just maintained for dragons like himself that were wounded and unable to fly, but also for the many humans and rarer elves that inhabited the dragon realm. Dragons were not xenophobic, in fact they welcomed other races into their city, but since they didn't like to leave they were mistakenly described as such sometimes. Elves, on the other hand, truly did not allow outsiders into their forests, though the younger ones had no problem with leaving to explore the continent.

In fact, elves were very uptight in their tradition. If any individual elf were to think in a manner that opposed their tradition, he would be thought of as an outsider and forced out of the Sylvan Forest as any human or dragon would. Those individual elves often found their way to Noriath.

The Council's Grove was what the highest city in the "city" was called. It was named that way since most of the Council members had their private homes there because of its proximity to the peak of the Homespire. It had no great walls or obvious boundaries and the buildings simply became more densely packed as they entered the city, and there were soon other dragons passing them by along the main road through the city.

They stopped in front of a building with a large arch built as the entrance. Above the arch, carved into the wall, were five stars in glittering gold.

"Here we are," Rauliax said. He was about to help her off his back, but instead was surprised when he felt her absence and saw that she had already hopped off onto the ground herself and was standing steadily without any aid.

She saw his expression and said, "I don't know either. I just feel so energized, and my legs don't hurt anymore."

It could just be the adrenaline high from experiencing a new world, the dragon thought, but it didn't *feel* right.

"Nevertheless, stay close to me. I don't want you suddenly falling down and getting hurt," Rauliax said.

She took a step closer to the dragon. "Okay."

He walked up to the archway and knocked on the wall with a fisted forepaw. A moment later, the wall parted ways and revealed itself to be a pair of sliding doors. The dragon who opened the way was silver, like Rauliax, but her scales were brighter and she was larger than him. She had the same spiraling horns that he had.

Her eyes glimmered as she saw who was at her front door. "Raul!

You're home!" She leapt up onto her two rear legs and gave him a hug.

He started to say, "Hi mom, I-"

"You need to stop leaving without a whisper," she said, "And this time you've dragged yourself into so much trouble!" She made a quick glance at his wing, and her eyes added on to that last sentence, "In more ways than one."

Rauliax did feel somewhat guilty for that. He always left without telling anyone, especially his mother, since he knew she'd voice her disapproval and he couldn't bear to hear it. "I'm sorry mom, but you know-"

"It's alright Raul. Dad's waiting for you in his study." Then Rauliax's mother glanced at Nama and said, "A friend? She looks old for a human."

"A human boy saved my life," Rauliax explained, "And I want to adopt him as my brother once dad approves. He's staying with Priscilla for some...research. This is his grandmother."

"Oh, that would mean she'd become my honorary mother!" She bowed at the elderly woman and said, "Please, come in and make yourself comfortable. I'll go fix some brunch." Then she looked back at Rauliax. "Don't keep your father waiting!"

"Thanks mom," he said.

Rauliax's mother led Nama into the kitchen, and he set himself off for the study. He stopped in front of another wall and knocked on it.

A voice called through the wall, "Enter. It's not locked."

He leaned back onto his haunches and used his paws to part the sliding door and saw his father sitting on his haunches behind a hefty desk. He was more grey than silver, and his scales shone much duller than his son's. His horns were sharply swept back straight, but he had the same colored hair lining his back as his son.

"It's good to have you home again, son, though I wish it were under happier circumstances," the larger dragon said. "King Devran has already forwarded most of the details. Disturbing things have been set in motion, but I can't discuss that now."

"What do you mean, dad?"

"The Dragon Council has already convened, and they're waiting for your testimony. We needed to be up there an hour ago, but I'm sure they'll understand. I received Mr. Yolun's message," he said, referring to the dragon that greeted him earlier, "and have forwarded it to the Council so they expect you'll be late, but let's not delay any further. They already know about the war what has been communicated to us by radio, but I've only managed to guarantee two other votes in our favor."

"Well, alright then," Rauliax said, "But how am I supposed to get up there without flying?"

"Taken care of, there's a stretcher waiting outside."

"Oh dear, how embarrassing."

"Endure it, we have to go now."

The two of them went outside again, and indeed once outside there were two dragons carrying a stretcher for Rauliax to lie down on.

They nodded at him as he set himself down on the stretcher and only said a formal, "Sir."

Once he was securely strapped in, Rauliax's father said, "Alright, to the Council Chambers. Follow my lead."

The stretcher was built to be carried by two long poles that extended out laterally under the bedding, and the dragon in front first lifted the pole over his shoulder before the rear dragon followed suit. Then they flapped their wings in unison and started flying to the peak of the Homespire with Rauliax's father in the lead.

Once at the top, they helped Rauliax off the stretcher. "Good day, sirs," was all they said before they flew away down the mountain.

"Come, let's go," his father said.

They entered the cave, though Rauliax felt a little anxious. He had seen the Council Chamber many times since his father's official quarters were deeper in the caves, but this was the first time he would see the Chambers in use.

The cave was brightly lit with enchanted torches. The mountain peak was too high and isolated to bother installing long electrical wires up to, so they made do with imported magic instead. They walked a little through the caves until they at last reached the widened opening where the Council sat in a circle of debate.

The Council members were already arguing with each other before he entered, but Rauliax couldn't discern much from the echoing effect created by the large room.

There was some muttering as they entered, but that quickly gave way to silence as Rauliax's father raised his paw.

"Forgive us for our tardiness," he said, "I hope you all received my message and you can now judge for yourself the veracity of his injury."

Several of them looked at Rauliax's wing and saw the long dried blood that bled through the patch and nodded.

There was a dragon sitting near the direct opposite side of the entrance to the chamber. He was sitting a little to the right though, from Rauliax's perspective, and there appeared to be enough room for two dragons to sit on the left of him. He was red, with random stripes of black running along his back, and he looked at Rauliax with unfriendly brown eyes.

That red dragon said, "Very well. Wyrst, take your place on the Council and we can begin today's agenda in earnest."

"Thank you, Malyfar," Rauliax's father said.

Wryst Moonsilver's son, however, noticed a suspicious look his father was giving the red dragon.

Rauliax's father said nothing else, however, and he sat down two places left of Malyfar, leaving only the center empty.

The Eldest is too ill to take part, Rauliax thought, his sickness must be getting worse. He hoped Priscilla would find a treatment for her father. He disliked her, sure, but that didn't mean he wished ill on her. He knew Malyfar was the next oldest council member, so he would be acting as the leading voice today. It was unfortunate that his father was younger than him by only a year. He wondered what would happen if the vote was split fifty-fifty as there were ten members present.

And so the red dragon spoke. He cleared his throat and announced, "Today we will vote upon Wesar's request for assistance. This matter is of utmost importance, and a vote must be reached before we disassemble. Sir Moonsilver?"

Rauliax's father replied. "Representatives of the people, I present to you Rauliax Moonsilver, my son, who has been appointed ambassador by King Devran. Son, give us a report on the status of this war."

And Rauliax did. He told them everything about the sudden attack and how Wesar would be soundly defeated without their help.

After he finished, the debate started.

"I believe we should help," Rauliax's father said, "Wesar has long been our trade partner, and we have developed a good long-term relationship with them."

"True," Malyfar said, "But humans have fought wars amongst each other all the time. We have never bothered to interfere, and they have never bothered us since nearly the last millennia after they drug themselves out of incivility. Why should we care now? If Arashal defeats Devran, we have the time to develop a trade relationship with him."

There was a lot of murmuring, and then Malyfar added, "And if the situation is so dire as Wyrst's son says it is, why not start a good relationship with Arashal now by pledging to him our plans to not interfere?"

Rauliax had to respond. "Sir, I don't believe you understand. King Arashal has no intention of stopping at Wesar. He wants the entire continent, including Noriath, and will not stop until he has the Homespire as his throne in the north."

"So the ambassador of King Devran says," Malyfar replied. "Your views are skewed even if you are a dragon, young one, and it is up to us to see this in a balanced light."

The dark blue dragon next to Rauliax's father spoke up. "However, we cannot deny the fact that Arashal has made a sudden and aggressive move against our relatively peaceful neighbor. This does not speak kindly to his overall ambitions."

"Indeed. Thank you Marissa," Rauliax's father, who sat next to her, said.

"Yet, I believe we should at least try to contact Elemar and get their side of the story," a green dragon on Rauliax's right side said.

"We cannot afford to wait for a response that may never come," Rauliax replied, "Wesar will be lost if we choose to be patient."

"And yet Delvic is also correct," Malyfar said, "A little patience may save the lives of many of our soldiers from being needlessly squandered in a human war."

"A human war that may turn into a dragon-human war," Wyrst said. "If the battle comes to Noriath, the army will not be able to stop an entire fleet of human airships."

"I agree with the General," the light green dragon next to Marissa said. "We risk much by doing nothing, and we have much to gain by helping."

Rauliax had nearly forgotten his father was the General of the army. He had come into that position before he was even born, and his status was what the five stars over their home meant. There hadn't been any use for the army since he was born, so he had thought little of his father's involvement despite the fact that he had spent a little time himself in the army.

"I think you place too much faith in the humans' newfound aerial strength, Sirio," Malyfar said. "It took ten humans to take one of us down the last time we had a war."

"But," Wyrst replied, "They have embraced technology now. We can't shrug off cannonfire like we can fireballs."

"Or so you claim," Malyfar responded, "Yet I have not seen these supposed weapons that you say can strike us down so easily."

Rauliax tapped his claw onto the solid ground. It made a light noise that echoed through the chamber. He almost wanted to slap the older dragon for his ignorance, but he managed to restrain himself. It was understandable that other dragons, especially Council members, would not have any reason to witness a cannon in action, but the blatant rejection of physics irked him. He would have to use his title as leverage. "As a professor of the University, I can attest to the power of these cannons."

And to this Malyfar said, "You may have chosen the path of knowledge at a young enough age to earn your professorship so early in life, Professor Moonsilver, but you are still young, naive, and inexperienced with humanity. On this subject, I must question your expertise."

Now they were questioning his intelligence, Rauliax thought. He really hated politics. It didn't help that most of the Council were wise, but not book smart. Not a single one of them had chosen to attend the University, probably a product of laziness since they didn't have to do anything to make money aside from being a Council member. His own father didn't understand much engineering, and he had to explain to him several times the amount of power that could be transferred with a cannon before he understood dragon scales couldn't protect against a well-placed shot. Again, it didn't help that practically no dragon other than himself had ever seen an airship in battle.

So the debate went on into the late afternoon until at last even Rauliax's father grew weary.

"Enough, let us cast our votes," Wyrst said at last. "Yea, if you support helping Wesar with our army. Nay, if you do not."

The Council shuffled a bit before silencing themselves. Then they started voting clockwise.

There was a yea from the first dragon, then a nay and another yea from the light green dragon. Marissa gave a yea, and so did Wyrst. Of course, Malyfar gave a nay, and so did Delvic next to him. The next dragon gave a yea, upping the yea total to five, and Rauliax hoped for another from one of the remaining two dragons.

But neither did. It was a tie vote.

"A split vote," Rauliax said, "Splendid."

"This vote is far too important to leave the Eldest out of," Wyrst said, "We must have his decision accounted for."

"He is too incapacitated to even speak," Malyfar said, "And if you will lean upon his final vote to pass this notion, then you may have to wait until he is better, and I trust the war will be over by then and we will be trading with Elemar."

"Then we shall wait," Marissa replied.

Malyfar shifted his eyes. "Very well. This vote is deadlocked, and the Council may now disassemble until the Eldest calls for us to convene to announce his vote."

Rauliax let out a long sigh. The entire day was wasted then, unless Priscilla managed to find a potion to help her father.

The Dragon Council shuffled again as everyone started leaving, tired from the long day, and Rauliax went up to his father.

"I'm sorry son," Wyrst said, "I got us the two other votes I promised, but it wasn't enough."

"That's alright. I'll try to help Priscilla find something that'll help the Eldest."

"Ah yes, Priscilla," his father said with a grin. "When are you two going to hook up and have children?"

"*What!?*"

"Oh come on son, she's the only girl you talk to. When's it going to be?"

"Dad! You're insane! I absolutely loathe her! I can't believe you'd possibly think there was something going on between us!"

"If you say so," his father replied. His grin grew wider.

The idea of him and Priscilla being romantically involved revolted him. Or rather, it should have, but, to his own surprise, there was only faint-hearted rejection of the idea. He quickly shook his head to rattle the thought out of his head.

Then his father's face swiftly turned back to the serious grim he had worn the entire day. Rauliax had only rarely seen his father act this solemn before for extremely serious Council matters: usually he was quite fond of silly humor and that little remark was the only lighthearted thing he had done all day.

"We must return home now," Wyrst said. "I've called for the stretcher already."

The younger dragon shook his head. "Dad, I seriously need to go help Priscilla, it's our best chance to get the final vote we need."

"That's exactly the issue. You'll see. It concerns Malyfar."

"He was really adamant against us," Rauliax said, "In fact, he seemed like he really wanted to help Elemar defeat Wesar."

His father nodded. "Exactly. And I believe his behavior confirms what I have to show you. Let's go."

Rauliax acquiesced, and so he flew back down to their home on the same stretcher with the same dragons that carried him up. Again, they left with only a nod and a formal, "Sir."

He followed his father into the house. Nama was taking a nap, and his mother had gone shopping. He followed him through another pair of sliding doors into the guest room.

Inside was a dragon and an elf. The dragon was colored sky blue and smaller than Rauliax, and his body was much more slender. The elf wore a light brown tunic with green accents, and the dragon had his left forearm sleeved with a nicely knit cloth.

He can't be older than a hundred years, Rauliax thought, and the elf he couldn't tell, but he appeared like a boy Solah's age so the elf must've been around eighty or so years old. The elf's clothing was well kept, and the kind of sleeve cloth the dragon wore indicated he was a servant of a someone high class.

"Allow me to introduce Ozzari, the dragon, and Siwan, the elf," Rauliax's father said. "They were Malyfar's servants." Then he presented his son to the pair.

"*Were?*" Rauliax asked.

"Yes," Ozzari replied, "We *were* his loyal servants."

Siwan added in, "He's *changed*, he has us doing things that make us feel uncomfortable."

"Our most recent order was to deliver a shipment," Ozzari said. "It was to Elemar."

Siwan shook his head. "Ozzari didn't want to go so far away, you know how dragons are."

The sky blue dragon nodded. "But it's more troubling than that. The admiral of the Elemarian air fleet met us and took the shipment. They were design plans that would boost the lift power of their propellers without relying on Pyrucium."

Rauliax scrunched his face trying to figure out why Malyfar would do such a thing, and what use did Elemar have for better engines anyway?

"But," Siwan continued, "Malyfar had us stay a month to ensure the plans were adapted into their fleet without issue. Then Admiral Morit had us direct his fleet through a place he called Evoscar. When we entered, I realized something was terribly wrong there. I couldn't muster a cantrip in that place."

Ozzari widened his eyes. "I, on the other hand, felt overwhelmingly empowered. It was a very unusual thing."

That sounded very familiar, Rauliax thought. Apparently, the null zone he had discussed with Solah did exist and did share his ability. But then he realized that meant Elemar was using the upgraded engines to fly through it undetected by Wesar's sensors!

And then Siwan spoke in a somber voice, "That was when we realized they were going to invade Wesar through the anti-magic area."

"We couldn't let them," Ozzari said, "Malyfar made a deal with King Arashal for those plans, we think, but we couldn't let them just destroy Wesar and Siwan's home."

The elf nodded. "So we fled. We flew as fast as Ozzari could. A scout ship chased after us. Even with my magic, they managed to keep up with us. We were lucky it was cloudy, and we finally managed to lose them somewhere in the west."

And there was the answer to the question Admiral Lina couldn't answer, Rauliax figured. That scout ship that tried to tangle Solah and him was chasing after a dragon and a rider, but they had ensnared the wrong pair.

"And then we came to hide here," the blue dragon said, "We thought General Moonsilver should know."

"Aye, you were good to come to me," Wyrst said. He faced his son. "It appears that Malyfar knows far more about technology than he pretends to."

"This is traitorous," Rauliax replied. "He must be questioned. I believe these two, their story answers an anomaly in my own."

"Yet, it's not that easy son. Remember the number one rule in politics?"

Rauliax rolled his eyes out of disappointment. "Everyone lies."

His father nodded with a sad smile. "Indeed. Clearly Malyfar is lying and hiding some important information. Yet if we raise this charge against him without solid physical proof, we will be the ones accused of lying to try and nullify Malyfar's vote to create a majority vote for us."

The vote would become five to four, true. But Rauliax understood that it would be impossible to convict the red dragon based solely on testimony that could easily be seen as a great forgery.

"What must I do, dad?" Rauliax asked.

"Tomorrow, the Council will convene again for some other issues, but I'll put the situation up on the agenda and we'll try and break the deadlock. I don't think anyone will change their mind. You know how dragons are, but during the time we're gone I need you to sneak into Malyfar's home and search for anything incriminating."

Roguery? The thought felt most distasteful Rauliax, but he knew it was necessary just like when Solah had to resort to it to survive. "I see. How will I get in?"

"We've both got a set of keys," the elf said. "We'll help you. Malyfar was a gentle dragon when he first took us in off the streets, but he's changed. His behavior hasn't been *right* for over a year."

"He always yells at us now," Ozzari said, "I hoped that by going to Elemar he'd go back to his old self."

"So that's that, then," Rauliax's father said. "These two will stay the night here. Go on now, you have the rest of the day to *mess around* with Priscilla."

The young silver dragon recoiled. "*Dad!*"

"Sorry son, your mom and I just can't wait to have a grandchild!"

Rauliax couldn't bear to have the two guests even in his peripheral vision. He turned his back and shouted "*Honestly!*"

"Goodbye son, have *fun!*" he heard his dad call.

It irked him to no end, but it was a nice respite from the severely somber mood his father was in all day. But then he remembered something and had to face him again, and to his dismay he saw the two guests snickering.

Nevertheless, he managed to ignore them and focused on his father. "Dad. I met a human friend while I was gone. He saved my life, and I owe him. May I have your permission to adopt him as my brother?"

His father opened his mouth as if to say something, shut it, and then opened it again. "Yes, after this all blows over. Bring him along on your search too, the more trustworthy help we have the better. I don't know how long the meeting will last, but most of them are very weary after today's long debate."

"I understand," Rauliax replied. Then he jittered out of the house as quickly as possible and started running up the road to the university, but he was stopped when he heard Siwan calling at him.

"Wait, wait! I almost forgot!"

"Forgot what?" Rauliax turned around and asked.

The elf ran up to him and said, "Your wing, sir. Let me help you with that."

The silver dragon shuffled his right wing. "Eh? What do you mean?"

"Bring it down, I can probably heal it," the elf replied.

He shrugged his head and brought his wing down so that the elf could touch it.

He unwrapped the bandage and let it fall to the ground. "Oh good, it's only a few days from being fully healed anyway. Here, this should fix it now," the elf said. He hovered his hand above the bandage and started moving them like he were knitting a sweater.

There was a light glow, and then the tender scales grew hard and sealed themselves over the dragon's injury.

"There we go, you should be good to fly now," the elf said.

There was one type of magic humans couldn't use that elves could: healing magic. But even then, only a rare few could work the intricate spellweaving, and it was supposed to be even more difficult when trying to mend other species.

So that was why Rauliax asked how he managed to do heal his wing.

"I'm not too great at using magic," Siwan said, "But healing magic is the one thing I think I'm okay at. Ozzy, err Ozzari, used to get hurt all the time, so that's how I managed to learn to heal dragons."

Rauliax flexed his wing out. No pain at all, he thought. "Thanks!" he said to the elf.

The elf bowed. "Not at all, sir. Just promise me you'll find out what happened to Malyfar. Ozzy and I were street rats before he took us in, you know, so this is just, it's just. I don't know."

The dragon took a long blink. "I'll try."

"That's all I can ask for," the elf said. "I'll see you tomorrow." Then he went back into the house.

First things first, Rauliax thought, he needed to enchant some random stuff or Priscilla would throw a fit if he came back empty-handed.

So he went to a nearby general store and bought a bunch of cheap plastic sticks. He also purchased a radio: it had nowhere near as much range as the enchanted one Captain Dillan gave him, but he figured Solah might find it useful in the future. Then he headed up to the University with his newly healed wings to find the *Reliant's* enchanter.

Chapter 12

"You want to see the ship's enchanter?" Lieutenant Avery asked. "Why? He doesn't like to be bothered."

"I just need him to make a few enchantments," Rauliax answered. "A little test for the exile."

Avery shifted his eyes upward. "Alright, I'll go ask if he'd be willing to come up deck."

He went down into the ship and returned a few minutes later.

"I can't believe it," he said, "He agreed. Give him a minute."

And almost exactly a minute later an older man scrounged himself out up to the deck and waived at Rauliax.

"You are in need of my services?" he asked.

"Yes, just a bunch of easy enchantments will do. It won't take much of your time or energy," the dragon said.

"I will do what you need," the enchanter said, "But I will not do it out here. Let us go into your cabin."

Avery stood wide mouthed as he heard the enchanter. "What? Are you kidding me old man? You'll help this dragon, but you won't even help me make something as simple as permafrost?"

The enchanter only repeated his request. "To your cabin, please."

"Okay," Rauliax said. He went into the former captain's cabin and the old enchanter followed him in. The enchanter then shut the door tight and locked it with a spell, leaving Lieutenant Avery to his muffled profanities outside.

"Dragon, the fates are swirling about you and the *Spellbreaker*."

Rauliax raised an eye ridge. "Spellbreaker? I assume you mean Solah, but I don't get-"

"Yes, the boy," the enchanter interrupted. "The exile, whatever you wish to call him."

"Solah, then," Rauliax replied.

"Very well. Know this. You and Solah's actions will affect the fates of many. Stay true to your hearts, and all will end as it should."

The dragon never stopped raising his eye ridge. "Are you alright, sir? I don't understand-"

"No," the enchanter said, "It is too soon to say. Just stay true to who you are, and the path shall lead you where it must."

"Uhh, okay. I don't plan not to be myself, in any case."

"Soon, you may not be so sure."

"Look, ah, I'm sorry I never asked for your name." The dragon emulated a bow by lowering his head and said, "Rauliax, sir. May I ask yours?"

"Uracel, if you wish."

"Alright. Look, Uracel, I don't understand why you're speaking in riddles, but I'm just here so you can help me enchant some items."

"You will understand in time. But for now, yes I will help you."

Avery was right, Rauliax thought, a real loony. But as long as his craft was fine, he had no issue with it and tried to be polite.

And the enchanter worked quickly and quietly. Uracel even bothered to make the sticks glow with different colors instead of just making them all the same.

Before he knew it, Rauliax was walking down the hall that led to Priscilla's laboratory.

Again, he passed by several open labs, and there were many students working in the evening. He passed by one room that made him pause and take a look back.

Inside the room, he recognized a couple of the ensigns from the *Reliant*, particularly Frazer and Waters. There was a dragon too, one he recognized as one of the oldest professors of the university.

"Ah," Rauliax called out, "Professor Faraday. Good evening, sir. And to you, crewmen."

Waters waved back at him while Frazer turned around and said with a grin, "Well, good evening to you, Mr. *Moonsilver.*"

The other dragon, Professor Faraday, bore scales that were blue, but paled with age. He also tilted his head at Rauliax. "Good evening to you too, young Professor Moonsilver."

Rauliax lowered his head in respect and asked, "May I ask what you're doing with these human mages?"

"I'm testing a theory about electric fields. The lightning mages working in Noriath are always at the city's generators, so naturally I jumped at the chance to offer these young crewmen some work. Would you like a quick demonstration?"

"Sure, make it quick though, Professor Ferae is waiting for me."

"Ah yes, it's best not to keep the young lady waiting. Don't worry, this won't take long."

The old dragon directed his attention to Waters and Frazer, who stood face-to-face as if they were dueling. "Now then, my young gentlemen. A bit of fire, please, constant stream."

Waters spread his arms wide as if he were going to hug the lightning elementalist, but then fire spread in a nicely contained jet between his hands.

Then Professor Faraday said, "And now electricity. Channel it through the bracelet like last time, but with a little more force if you will."

Then Rauliax noticed the little metal bracelet wrapped around Ensign Frazer's right wrist. Some sort of stabilizer, he assumed. Sparks flew around it as the young lightning mage waved his left hand around it. He pointed his right fist directly at the jet of fire and then small bolts of lightning spread like a fan from the bracelet through his fist towards the flame.

Unexpected even to Rauliax, the fire shrunk before it completely faded away.

"No way," Waters muttered.

"I put it out entirely this time," Frazer added. The other crewmembers in the room also murmured in surprise.

But Faraday only bobbed his head up and down. "I knew it'd work! I just had to adjust the bracelet's output a little, see!"

"Fascinating," Rauliax said, "You managed to use an electric field to suppress a fire?"

"Exactly, my young friend."

"This is awesome," Frazer said, "I could never have thought lightning could beat fire!"

"I would love to learn the mechanics behind it," the silver dragon said, "But I'm sure it's a long explanation. Next time we meet, Professor?"

"Oh indeed, young Professor. But before you fly off, let me tell you one more thing. Remember your presentation five months ago?

The one where you proposed a weapon based on magnetic force?"

"Yes," Rauliax replied, "I recall you were one of the few who weren't asleep."

"Indeed I was not," the old dragon said, "No, I took your concept to heart. Your idea intrigued me so I funded my own attempt to create one based on your design. I actually finished a prototype a month ago and meant to show it to you, but you had vanished already."

The silver dragon lowered his head in disappointment. "Ah yes. Sorry about that. I would very much like to see it later though, perhaps tomorrow?"

The older professor shook his head. "Alas, I cannot. Professor Reynolds took it with him when he left for Wesar. I do not know when he will return."

"Just another reason why I must help King Devran save his country, then."

Faraday scoffed back, "Hum, indeed. Professor Ferae didn't stop talking about another imminent war the humans are fumbling with yet again during our lunch time. Most of us dragons do not care about this war that happens outside our borders, professor, but in this case I would not like to see our invention destroyed."

The young professor replied, "You misunderstand, Professor Faraday. The war will come to our borders if our ally should fall."

"You are still young, Professor Moonsilver. I have seen this happen many times. They'll just beat each other and then be too tired to bother fighting anyone else. They might try to attack us, sure, but they've never had the strength to do any real harm."

"But you must realize that the humans have the power to actually be a threat now."

"Perhaps. Their airships look impressive, but I've never seen them in battle."

"Believe me, they're strong enough. But enough, I must be off now."

Faraday nodded and said, "Yes, very well then. Good luck to you."

"Thank you," Rauliax said. He focused his eyes on the crewmen. "Play nice, now. Goodbye!"

The silver dragon then ran down the hall until he stood before Priscilla's locked lab door again. He knocked while balancing himself on three limbs and called out, "Shall you let me in, or will I have to guess the password?"

The door promptly opened up and Priscilla stood upright in front of it chewing out of a melon. She swallowed a bite and said, "About time you got back. Get in."

He did so, and then she shut the door and locked it behind him.

Solah sat up from the floor and greeted him. "Hi Raul!"

"Hello dear boy, sorry about taking all day. Council business took as long as expected. Priscilla treated you well, I hope?"

The purple magenta dragon squinted at him. "Of course I did, who do you think I am? Some cullion that has no notion of hospitality?"

"Oh, she was very nice," Solah said. "She brought me lunch and let me stay in the library when she went off to see her father."

Rauliax gave him a puzzled look and said, "Are you sure that was Priscilla and not some other purple dragon?"

"Umm, yes?" Solah said in earnest.

"Enough, please," Priscilla said, "I'm not in the mood right now. None of the first ten potions on my list helped at all. From the time, I take it your meeting with the Council didn't end well either." She glanced at Rauliax's now unbandaged wing. "And your wing is all healed already? Tell me what happened."

So then Rauliax summarized what had happened during his day. He told them everything; from what occurred in the Council meeting, to his father's suspicions, and to Malyfar's two servants.

At the end of it, Solah said, "It sounds like a bunch of fairy tales I used to read. Malyfar sounds like one of those crazy second-in-command types that are always trying to vie for more power." He paused and wrapped his hands under his arms. "You don't suppose he might be poisoning the Eldest?"

Rauliax and Priscilla's mouths went wide at the accusation.

They let a moment pass before the thought could really sink in.

"Impossible," the silver dragon said. "That's just impossible."

"But come to think of it," Priscilla added, "Malyfar has been constantly sending get-well gifts. And they've all been chocolate or teas. Edible things."

Rauliax closed his eyes in frustration. "Still, this is absolutely unfathomable. But you must take pre-caution. Reject further gifts. We're going to raid his home tomorrow and get to the bottom of this."

She shook her head. "No, I will *not* reject them. But I will take them and *analyze* their contents. But if what the boy suggests is true, then there is one potion that I believe may help."

"What?"

"The very last one on my probability list. Blausius's Lifespel. It counteracts Deathknell. Deathknell's the only poison that would cause my father's sort of symptoms. It's meant to take a long time to kill so it can hide its presence. I put it at less than one percent chance on the list only because he might have accidentally had contact with it."

"Lucky us, then. What do we need to make it?"

She started listing off some common ingredients. "And lastly, Root of Iswald."

"You're blasted lucky I decided to bother getting that thing," Rauliax said.

"No time for chatting, Raully."

"Okay, Prissy."

The two professors brewed the potion while Solah sat and watched them work. The two dragons didn't seem to be hindered at all by walking on two legs while handling small ingredients. It was odd, but they managed to be quiet the whole time.

They finished five minutes later and Priscilla announced, "Finished. Let's get this up to my father."

The other dragon nodded. "Up onto my back," he said to Solah. "Think you'd be willing to fly without the harness now? You've been riding fine enough to not worry now, I think, as long as I fly normally."

"Your hair is a fine enough handle," the boy replied, "And you can catch me if I fall, right?"

"Please don't," the dragon said. "But if I must, I will."

"Okay, I'll be fine."

Then Rauliax looked back at the other dragon in the room. "Did you want those enchanted items put somewhere first?"

"You can hold onto them for now. Let's go," Priscilla said.

They left the lab and ran up the hall at a brisk pace. They ran straight off the balcony at the end of the tower exit and flew up the mountain with Priscilla at the lead, and the boy no longer had to contend with fear while keeping himself attached to Rauliax.

The evening twilight was beautiful up in the sky, and Solah looked all around him. Up, and he saw the sky illuminated by the stars and the moon, as usual, but down he saw little lights all around the mountain. Many of them clumped into bright spots in what he assumed were the cities.

He asked the dragon, "Those are all from those light containing things you showed off before? There's so many of them!"

"Yes," the silver dragon called back, "And they come in a bunch of sizes too. Beautiful, isn't it?"

"It's like magic!"

Rauliax chuckled at the irony. "No magic, dear boy, only physics! If you think that's pretty, wait until tomorrow! I'll show you the view from the north side of the mountain. It's too dark to see them now, but the shimmering oceans are truly magnificent."

"I think Nama would like to see that too."

The dragon hummed to himself, then said to the boy, "She had no problem riding on ground so I'm sure she'll be fine in the air, at least for a short bit."

"That'd be great!"

They flew on upwards, and then Rauliax darted forward a little until he was flying right next to Priscilla.

"He's been staying in his official quarters?" the silver dragon asked.

"Yes, more assistance up there than in our private home," Priscilla replied. "He was at work the day he became too ill to fly back down, anyway."

The silver dragon nodded and they flew on.

"I should give the elf a gift for helping you," Solah said.

"The greatest gift," Rauliax replied, "Would be to help find out what is happening with his master."

"It's a good thing I'm good at sneaking then!"

The dragon under him chuckled as he watched the lights below turn smaller and smaller.

The boy didn't even realize they had reached the entrance to the Council's caves until he felt the dragon suddenly stabilize at the touch of the ground.

Twilight had faded by then, and the silver dragon's scales glowed lightly as they basked under the moon. They didn't dally and went into the caves, still lit by the flame posts, at a brisk pace. They hurried through the main Council chamber into one of the rear openings that led deeper into each council member's official quarters.

After a couple of turns and passing through one of many smaller caves, Solah lost track of the way to get out again. It was an uncomfortable feeling that led him to reflexively clench his fists harder around the dragon's hair.

At last, they passed through an opening that had several runic carvings engraved over the top of the mouth and found the Eldest's Council quarters.

The room inside was large, a bit larger than the captain's cabin on the *Reliant*, and far taller. Fully shelved bookcases stood against the side walls and a desk was pushed aside to part way for a bed that was like a smaller version of the carpet in the dragon's den of the Corona's Flare.

Lying atop the bed was Priscilla's father. The Eldest laid asleep, his scales a sickly grey shade of blue. His breathing sounded labored, and he only stirred when Priscilla shook his forearm.

"Daddy, wake up please. I've got another one that I need to try on you."

The Eldest half opened his eyes and mumbled incoherently but opened his mouth.

Priscilla uncorked the potion. "Blausius took six bloody years to make this formula," she said, "And that's a long time for a human. It had better work if he really has been poisoned." She laid down next to her father and helped pour it down his mouth extremely slowly.

"Raise your claw if I'm pouring it too fast," she said, "This one has a very rare ingredient so I can't have you coughing it out like the last one."

The sick dragon made no acknowledgement so Priscilla kept pouring until he had drunk it all.

"There," she said at last, "It's going to be at least half an hour before we see if it worked or not." She kept her eyes fixed on her father's the entire time.

Rauliax nodded, and then he asked her, "Prissy, if we're going to wait here, can you tell me what you learned from observing Solah today?"

She sniffled, and then slowly craned her neck around to face the other dragon and the human.

There was water streaming down her eyes. She lifted a hand to try and wipe and hide the tears, but they still saw.

"Are you okay?" Solah asked.

"Priscilla," Rauliax added, "If you want us to leave, just say so."

Her ears perked when he said her actual name. "No, it's nothing," she said. She managed to stop sniffling. "I'm alright. Don't you dare think otherwise, Raully." Then she managed a weak smile. "As for the boy, your original theory was on the right track."

Her smile grew wider, and her voice returned to its usual form. "But it was still *wrong*. He doesn't disturb the flow of magic, but rather he restores the natural flow. Think about it. When he touches an enchanted object, the manipulated magical energy returns to its proper unenchanted state."

She let the other two have a moment to think before she continued, "And since dragons are naturally magical, his touch actually restores our flow to what it was like when we were young hatchlings. That's why it makes us feel potent and strong again. Unfortunately, our bodies, since they are aged, can't keep the stronger current flowing and it quickly returns to normal in his absence."

"Hum," Rauliax said, "I never thought of it that way."

The boy added in, "She also said other people shouldn't be afraid of me. They can stop me if they really thought it through."

"Correct," Priscilla said, "Take, for example, a kineticist. One can hurl a stone at the boy and he can touch the stone, but the laws of motion still apply. Sure, the kineticist will cease to be able to manipulate the stone's trajectory any further, but the stone will still keep its momentum and continue flying at him at a lethal speed. His ability does not negate basic physical laws."

The other dragon tapped a claw at his chin. "Interesting. But the elements from a mage don't harm him, how do you explain that?"

She sighed. "You dolt, have you forgotten how human magic works? Elementalists summon fire, ice, or whatever, but those things are *summoned*, meaning their existence is entirely based in magic. An ice mage hurling a block of ice at him will completely dissipate when he touches it and will transfer no real energy. Not like the kineticist that throws a *real* object."

The silver dragon shook his head. "Ah, I see. That makes sense."

Then Solah said, "Do you think it'd help if I touched him?"

Priscilla shifted her head back to look at her father. "Maybe. Try."

The boy glanced at Rauliax, who nodded at him, and then he

stepped towards the Eldest.

He gently tapped the weakened dragon's forepaw. The Eldest's eyes shot wide open as the strength of youth returned to him.

The pale dragon coughed, and then he stammered out, "What magic is this?"

Priscilla screamed, "Dad, you can talk again!" Then she calmed herself and spoke quietly, "Don't strain yourself."

The Eldest took a long blink and color seemed to infuse itself back into his scales. He coughed again and then said, "I feel like a hundred years old again. Aside from the pain. What did you do, human?"

"Uhh, I don't know how to say it sir," Solah said, "I think your daughter could explain it better."

He shifted his head toward Priscilla and gave her a curious expression.

"It's a long story," she started saying, "See, Professor Moonsilver here found the boy-"

Rauliax interrupted her. "I hear someone coming down the hall."

Priscilla's eyes widened and she whispered, "I'm sorry dad, but we have to keep this under wraps right now. It will feel unpleasant."

The blue dragon nodded and put his head back down onto the bed. "I understand. Go ahead."

Solah took his hand off the dragon. The Eldest grunted, and his color faded again.

Rauliax poked his head out of the entrance and then came back in. "It's Malyfar. Act normal."

Everyone nodded at him and Solah went back to his side.

Moments later, Malyfar entered the cavern.

He took a sweeping look across the room. "Ah, I see Eldest Ferae has company tonight. I hope I'm not intruding, I've only come to bring some more gifts for the Eldest."

"No, you are not," Priscilla said, "Thank you for all your generosity."

Malyfar bowed. "I am as concerned for the Eldest's health as you are, my Lady." He pulled some boxes out of his mouth and stacked them up. "Green tea, grown only by elves. It's supposed to be very good for one's health."

"I appreciate it very much. Thank you again," Priscilla said. She started stacking the boxes onto the desk when Malyfar directed his attention to the other two in the room.

"Professor Moonsilver, I see you are here to pay your respects as well. You should see now that the Eldest is in no position to submit a vote, and it would be prudent to return to your home and let this war pass along as we dragons have always done with human affairs."

"You continue to neglect the strength of Arashal's fleet," Rauliax replied.

"And," Solah added, "His resolve."

Malyfar's eyes shifted towards the human. "Ah, and this is the other emissary we were informed of. What makes you eligible to claim to be a neutral party, human?"

Before the boy could respond, Rauliax moved between them. "He was born and raised alone in a forest, Malyfar, and has no affiliation with any country. If that does not satisfy you, then he is also my brother, and even you cannot question that claim."

"Hmph, very well," the red and black dragon said, "I was merely curious. A trait you and I share, yes?"

"Indeed," Rauliax retorted, "If by curious you mean you wish to know nothing about modern science."

Malyfar turned around and started leaving. "Do yourself a favor professor, and go home. Tell your father to give up on this nonsense."

"As if," the silver dragon whispered.

Malyfar left the room with his tail swishing in almost a mocking manner and said one last farewell. "Have a good night, my Lady. I pray your father gets well soon."

They stayed quiet until Rauliax made sure Malyfar had left the hall.

"I got all sorts of bad vibes from him," Solah said.

"If there's one thing I can't tolerate," Rauliax said, "It's willful ignorance. That blasted fool."

"At least," Priscilla remarked, "I have a bunch of tea leaves to analyze now."

The Eldest grumbled something, but they couldn't understand what he was saying. Solah went back to him and held his forearm again.

Life returned to him again, and then he said, "Priscilla, the pain, it has lessened. I think your potion is working."

Priscilla lit up and she moved over to wrap a wing around her father. "Daddy, I'm so glad. But it's a mixed thing."

"What do you mean, dear?"

"It means you've been poisoned."

"What? By who?"

"Probably Malyfar." Priscilla tiled her head down and looked at Solah. "I'm afraid to say you were right, little human."

"That is impossible," the Eldest replied, "That is unimaginable."

"No, it isn't apparently," she said. "But everyone will think just like you, daddy. We have to find irrefutable proof. Even if I test the tea leaves and find them contaminated, he can just claim the elves put it in, or some nonsense like that. No dragon has harmed another in millennia."

"I still do not believe it," her father replied.

"We'll find enough evidence so you do," she said.

"Enough so everyone will," Rauliax added.

Eldest Ferae coughed again, and then he made a quick glance at the silver dragon. "Professor Moonsilver. My daughter says a lot about you. I approve."

"What do you mean?" the silver dragon asked.

"Daddy! Not now, please," Priscilla said. Her cheek scales had flushed slightly pink, though it was difficult to tell under her normal magenta coloring.. Nevertheless, she quickly changed the subject. "Solah, I think if you stay in contact with my father, he can get better sooner. Do you mind staying the night?"

The boy nodded. "Not at all, if it's alright with Raul."

"Of course, I'll stay here tonight too in case Malyfar decides to show up again and cause some trouble." He went over to one of the bookshelves and pulled out a book.

Priscilla said, "Thank you, Solah." She was about to say something to her father, but he had already fallen asleep. So instead she said, "And you too, Raully."

The silver dragon froze as he heard her, but then he replied with a simple, "You're welcome." Then he opened his book and began reading.

Chapter 13

The rest of the night passed uneventfully. Priscilla was especially happy that her father had not coughed himself awake as he had done for the past week, though she herself woke up several times during the night to readjust her father's blanket.

In the morning, Rauliax woke Solah up. "We need to go down to my home now," he said, "Siwan and Ozzari will be waiting for us."

Priscilla had heard him, however, and was roused from her sleep. "I'm coming too," she said.

Rauliax recoiled his head. "What? No, you'd do better staying here with your father. Besides, didn't you need to analyze those tea leaves?"

"Oh no, I *will* be going with you," she replied, "I don't need to test those leaves. I already know they're poisoned. My father's gotten better already, which means that Blausius's Lifespell worked. Which means Solah was right, he is being poisoned. Did you see the way he looked at my father last night?"

"Malyfar?" Rauliax questioned, "What about him?"

She groaned in reply. "Psh, men. They never notice people's emotions. I saw, Raully. I saw how his eyes looked as he stared at my father. They were full of greed. Lust. I know he's doing it, and by the gods I *will* find out what he's trying to do. Didn't you see? Even my father didn't believe he could've done it. We'd need overwhelming evidence to prove it without a shadow of a doubt to the Council, and I *will* find that evidence. He's given something to Arashal, and I *will* know what he's getting in return."

Rauliax stared at her for a while, and then nodded. "Okay. We should go now. Can you tell the Eldest that Solah has to let go now?"

Priscilla rubbed her father's forearm until he stirred. "Daddy, we

124

have to go. I'll be back later, okay? The human has to come with us."

The Eldest shifted his head up and down slowly, then rest it down onto the bed. Solah let go and hopped himself onto Rauliax's back.

The old dragon grumbled, and then said, "I feel better now, even without the human, and can speak again without him."

"The potion really worked very well then," Priscilla said. "Keep resting, daddy, and don't eat anything until I get back."

He had another light cough but managed to say, "Okay, dear."

Moments later, the old dragon was snoozing again. Priscilla followed out a little after the other two to make sure her father was comfortable. The morning was early enough that nobody was in the council chamber except for the General of the Dragon Army.

"Son!" the older silver dragon called out, "You need to get home. Hurry, Siwan needs to see you." He noticed the boy sitting on his son's back and added, "And you are Solah, correct? Consider yourself already adopted into the Moonsilver family."

"We're on our way dad," Rauliax replied.

"It's an honor to meet you," Solah said, "You look a lot like Raul. I don't think I'd be able to tell you two apart if it weren't for the horns."

Wyrst laughed and said, "Yep, he has his mother's licorice horns. I'll get the official documentation done after this war business is over, but you can call yourself a Moonsilver now."

"Thank you, uhh, father-in-law?"

"No need to be formal, just 'dad' will do!"

"Alright, uhh, thanks dad!"

"You are most welcome. If Raul likes you enough to even consider adopting you then I think you'll fit right in with us."

"Oh, he will," Rauliax said.

Then Priscilla appeared from behind them.

The General saw her and bowed. "Lady Ferae, a pleasure to see you. Is your father doing well?"

She replied with a bow in return and wore a genuine smile. "Yes, quite so."

"Were you going somewhere with my sons?"

She twisted her head slightly in confusion, and then understood. "Yes, Raul has told me of your suspicions. I believe them. And I will help find enough evidence to prove them."

"I know that look," Rauliax's father said, "I'm not going to try to stop you. Go then, all of you, and good luck. The meeting will start in about one or two hours, and I'll try to keep it as long as possible."

With that, the three of them flew down to Rauliax's home as fast as it was safe for Solah to ride without a harness.

Rauliax knocked on the sliding door entrance and it opened almost immediately. Siwan stood in front with a frantic expression.

"Ozzy's gone," he said, "He snuck out sometime during the night. He left a note saying he was going to ask Malyfar what was going on. He hasn't come back."

"That's not good," Rauliax said, "He might know our plan now."

"No way," the elf replied, "Ozzy would never tell him anything unless we both agreed to. I think he might be in trouble."

The silver dragon thought for a moment. "Then we should head off as soon as the Council convenes." There was a rumble from his belly, and then he said, "Which means we have time for breakfast first. Are my mother and the elderly lady awake?"

"No, not yet. Your mother stayed up late last night and the elderly lady has been sound asleep since yesterday evening."

"Very well, let's head somewhere for breakfast then. We have about an hour before the meeting starts anyway. Everyone in agreement?"

Nods came from all around so they went off to some restaurant that had been a favorite of Rauliax's.

Siwan bore an unhappy smile the entire way and seemed to always be looking away at something distant.

The dragon restaurant didn't have tables, but rather the entire floor was a soft cushion like the dragon's den at the Corona's Flare. There were no tables, rather there were hard boards where food and drink were placed upon. There were a few other dragons having breakfast already, and they ate while lying down on their bellies.

It was a natural position for dragons, Solah noted, though it was a little odd for humanoids. It wasn't uncomfortable to lay down like that, however, and he had eaten like that before when he was sick and had to have Nama send him food to his bed.

A grey dragon with a much darker shade than Rauliax led them to their floorboard and took a quick drink order from everyone.

At the breakfast table board, Rauliax laid down across from Priscilla, and Solah across from Siwan. The elf, who sat cross-legged instead of laying down on his stomach, hadn't even acknowledged the boy's presence until he tried to start a conversation.

"So," Solah said, "Raul told me about you and Ozzari. How did you two meet? It wasn't like how I met Raul, I bet."

The elf's eyes seemed to focus back to reality. "Maybe. How about you tell me how you two met first?"

So he did. The elf was a little amused as he explained how the dragon had entangled himself.

"And I don't approve," Priscilla added, "You need to be more cautious, Raully."

The silver dragon bobbed his head mockingly. "Uh huh, I sure will."

"I swear, you'll get yourself killed one day if you don't stop rushing into things headfirst."

"And you're worried about that?"

One of Priscilla's eyes twitched. "Me? Absolutely not! But your friends will. Your family too. Stop thinking of only yourself all the time."

She was right, of course, and he had to admit it. "I suppose you're right. I'll try to take better care of myself, then."

All she said in response was, "Good. I still can't believe you were so impatient that you just had to stir up some potions alone in some forest."

He ignored her, and then Solah explained how he helped Rauliax out of his failed potion experiment.

That was when Siwan finally stopped looking so distant and became genuinely interested in the human. "You mean you can dispel anything, not just enchantments, but also spells that are being cast? With just a touch?"

"He's like the Null-Magic Zone," Rauliax said, "I wonder if you'll feel the same as you did when you were in it if he touches you?"

"I'd rather not try," the elf said, "It was wholly unpleasant."

"Probably," Rauliax replied, "Since Ozzari said being in that area empowered him, and that is how I feel when the boy touches me."

"I would like to see how a direct touch to a mage would affect them though," Priscilla said.

"The elf said it feels unpleasant, don't force it on him," Rauliax said.

"I wasn't suggesting it, stupid. That would be ridiculously uncivil and rude."

"I thought that's what uncivil and rude people do, especially to guests!"

She was about to say something, but clamped down her muzzle and stopped herself. "I'm not going to continue this childish conversation."

The other dragon only grinned.

Then Siwan cleared his throat and said, "I met Ozzy in sort of the same way, I guess. I was banished from the Sylvan Forest for my lack of talent. Elves my age should be able to master an art of magic already, but I was terribly behind."

Solah was confused. "You were banished because you weren't good enough at magic?"

"Well, not entirely, no. I was also rather outspoken about our leadership. That is a long story for another time. In any case, I was sent off to wander the continent. I found myself here, in Noriath, and though there were many kind dragons, I didn't really have any valuable skills to be put to use here and found myself impoverished. And eventually I had to resort to desperate ways to, umm, live."

"This sounds familiar," Rauliax said.

Siwan ignored him and continued, "One day I was running from a particularly mean dragon. And I didn't even steal from him either, he stole from me. I did some labor for him but he refused to pay, so I swiped my own payment and ran like the wind."

Solah smiled and said, "Let me guess, you ran into Ozzari?"

The elf chuckled. "Literally. Ran right into him. He was a poor fellow living in the slums like I was. I was out of breath and clinging to a bag of gold and he helped me up. Apparently he knew what a deadbeat the other dragon was and lifted me up as soon as he saw him bearing down on us. I dazzled the dragon with a bit of flashing light and then we flew right out of there. After that, we became best of friends. We made a great team and did good work, enough to buy ourselves out of the slums after a decade without stealing anything."

The grey-scaled waiter came back and distributed their drinks. She carried the plate of glasses with her tail wrapped through a hook under it, oddly enough, and curled it in front of her chest before putting the drinks onto the table. She took everyone's order then: Rauliax had waffles, Priscilla some toast with syrup, Siwan a simple salad, and Solah a steak again, though the waiter didn't act surprised at his order. She did confound the boy by asking how he wanted his beef cooked, but Rauliax answered medium for him. She whipped away afterwards and everyone took a sip out of their glasses except for Rauliax, who kept a constant flow of orange juice through his straw from his dragon-sized glass, and Siwan continued his story, causing Solah to forget to ask about what Rauliax meant by medium, after drinking down a gulpful of milk.

"Eventually, Malyfar took us in. He said he liked how we had stuck ourselves out of poverty with good honest work, and offered us a nice job as his servants. We agreed, and since then we've been paid well and did rather relatively easy work. He's always been nice to us, and always forgave us for any screw-ups we made."

The elf took another gulp from his glass of milk. "But recently, particularly right before he sent us off to Elemar, he was getting snappy at us. Last time Ozzy dropped a tea cup, he actually *slapped* him."

The two dragons gasped. "Physical violence?" Rauliax said, "What has he devolved into?"

"This is ridiculous," Priscilla said, "I've known the red dragon nearly my entire life. He's practically always kissing up to my father. I *know* he's always wanted to become the Eldest, but why would he suddenly decide to poison my father now? He's waited this long, surely he can wait another few hundred years and let nature make him the Eldest."

Rauliax waved his wings in a way that looked like a shrug. "Well, assuming he *is* poisoning him, he must have some sort of other plan. We'll find it out."

"The sooner the better. If he finds that I found the cure for my father, I don't know what he might do next."

The silver dragon nodded. "We'll find out today. I won't leave until I find something."

"Nor will I," she added.

"Ozzy and I will help," the elf said. "Once I find him. I hope he just stayed the night at Malyfar's home and is just waiting for us."

"We'll leave no stone unturned," Rauliax said.

The food came without utensils, and Solah was a bit confused at how he was supposed to eat his steak. Rauliax was cutting through his pancake easily enough even with his dulled claws, but he noticed the boy staring at his meal and helped him cut it into bite-sized pieces.

"Just use your hands, sorry," the silver dragon said.

Siwan added, "We're too high up the mountain. They're not used to serving humans or elves up here."

"Oh, that's fine. I'm not entirely unused to it. It's not like I use a knife and fork to eat an apple after all." Solah ate the little cuts of steak with his fingers, and he found the juicy meat good enough to not complain about at all.

The group had a hearty breakfast and left the restaurant exactly an hour later after leaving a payment of two silver bars, and giving a nice bronze bar tip for the waiter. Siwan led them to Malyfar's home, which was in the Homespire's cave network at the top of the Council's Grove. It was a long way in the mountain, and even inside there was a spiraling staircase to climb.

Rauliax was rather full from the meal and climbed the dragon-sized stairway slowly. He followed behind Solah, who was right behind Siwan and in front of Priscilla. Both the human and the elf had to stop a couple of times to let the dragons catch up to them.

"I told you not to eat the entire plate! It was your *third* full plate of waffles slathered with ludicrous amounts of syrup, you corpulent slug," Priscilla said, "Now move it!"

"I was hungry," Rauliax replied, "And I am moving!"

The purple dragon frowned. "Damn you, move faster then!"

"Well," he said, "You should've specified earlier then."

"Ugh, just let me go first, you asinine slowpoke."

"Whatever you say, dear."

"Do *not* call me dear."

"Okay, dearest."

"No past, future, or any alternative forms of dear either! My god, you're acting like such a hatchling!"

"Only because it annoys you, *darling*."

Siwan watched this argument with a wide smile and whispered to his human companion, "The way they go on, it sounds like they're a married couple."

"I don't get it," Solah whispered back, "I thought married people like each other?"

The elf let out a very audible laugh and said back, "Sure they do."

"Then why would they argue?" the boy asked.

"You're still too young to understand, I suppose."

The silver dragon gave way to let the other dragon go first, and Priscilla leapt up and caught up to the pair of humanoids in no time at all.

"Lead the way," she said. She took a quick glance at the other dragon. "He can catch up when we get there."

"It's not very far now," the elf said, "Once we reach the top of the stairs it'll be right before our eyes."

"Oh, see?" Rauliax called up, "We're almost there anyway, you impatient purple beast!"

Priscilla barked out in laughter. "Beast? Oh, the irony!"

Before they knew it, the elf announced that they had arrived.

At the end of the stairway, there was a large ornate wall decorated with various runes and symbols. Near the center were three circles painted black with small holes in the middle of each one. Siwan reached into his pocket and pulled out a three-pronged key that fit neatly into the three holes.

Then the elf took a step back and said, "Blade Aquarium."

The carvings on the wall lit a purple glow, deeper than Priscilla's shade, and parted way to show the great entrance hall of Malyfar's home.

Siwan explained before anyone had a chance to ask anything. "It's double locked with a physical and magical component. I had to put in the key and say the password to unlock the door."

"A tad bit overzealous in security, I think," Rauliax said. "He lives in the Council's Grove, not the slums."

"He's always been the paranoid type," the elf replied.

"Often," Priscilla said, "Paranoid people are afraid of others doing to them what they deep down really want to do to others. We shall see."

"Indeed," the silver dragon remarked. "My, this house is huge!"

"It is," Siwan said, "And Malyfar lives all alone in it, except for when he calls his servants over. He has us live elsewhere in the Grove other times. Sometimes he holds small parties though."

The entrance hall was massive, Solah thought, and it seemed comparable in length to the *Reliant's* deck length. There was a fanning stair at the end of the hall that lead to the second floor. The second floor's railings wrapped around the hall to the edge of the main door and were fashioned in shining gold.

"Let's split up," Rauliax said.

"That's the most brilliant thing you've said all day," Priscilla said, "Who with who?"

"Obviously not me and you," the silver dragon said.

"Can I go with Professor Moonsilver?" Siwan asked.

"Sure," the silver dragon said, "Solah, do you mind going with Priscilla?"

"Not at all," the boy replied, "Like I said before, she was quite pleasant in the lab yesterday."

"And I still think you were hallucinating," Rauliax said. He glanced at his archrival. "You didn't give him any drugs, did you?"

Priscilla snorted. "You wouldn't know good manners if they hit you on the head."

The other dragon let out a sarcastic laugh and said, "Uh huh. Let's go, then."

Priscilla and Solah went up the extravagant stairs and started searching every room from the left corner clockwise.

Rauliax and Siwan started downstairs with the room on the opposite side near the right corner and rotated through counter-clockwise.

The first room the dragon and the elf entered was a massive library. There was a musty smell in the rustic room from the hand carved wooden bookshelves and they started skimming through the books.

The elf grew eventually grew tired of looking up and down the bookshelves and went to the long table in the center of the room. He started peering through the stacks of papers that had notes scrawled all over.

Meanwhile, Rauliax paused as he scanned down one row of books. He pulled out a book he recognized titled *Applications of Fluid Mechanics in Modern Human Airships* by Professor Reynolds. He put it back and thumbed his claw down a couple more books in the same row and pulled out another one titled *Integration of Magic and Science in Airship Design* by someone he didn't recognize named Tresca. It was probably a human engineer, he thought, since dragons only resorted to applying magic in design when many attempts with regular materials and techniques failed. It was a sort of prideful thing dragons often did to try to compensate for their relative magical ineptitude.

The silver dragon flipped through the book quickly and put it back on the shelf before pulling out another one titled *Explosives, Projectiles, and Their Modern and Future Applications*. He flipped through this book a little slower and saw pictures and diagrams of various explosive powders, catapults and cannons. Near the end of the book he saw several pictures of weapons he had always imagined as theoretically possible: miniature hand-held cannons that fired millimeter sized projectiles. Such a weapon would, he thought, be incredibly useful for someone like Solah.

"It seems Malyfar does know far more about modern weaponry than he lets on," Rauliax said. "My father was right. So we've uncovered one lie."

"I can't make heads or tails of these scrabbles," Siwan said, "It's like they're written in moonspeak or something."

"Well, I am a *Moon*silver," the dragon joked. "Maybe I can read it."

He went over to the table and browsed through the notes.

"Integrals, theorems, formulas, derivations of said formulas, hmm." The dragon shuffled the papers in silence for a while. "Looks like a prototype propeller design. Here's a diagram."

The elf glanced the picture over. "That looks like the picture of what we gave to Admiral Morit, only with a lot of incomprehensible gibberish written all around it. What we gave were pictures and instructions written in plain Standard."

The dragon shrugged his wings. "Well, they probably weren't interested in knowing how these propellers worked, only how to make them, I suppose."

"Understandable," the elf replied. "Can we go to the guest room? If Ozzy came here, he'd be in there, probably."

"Of course, there doesn't look like there's anything else to find in his library."

The guest room was the next room up, but it was empty.

"Curse it," Siwan said, "If he didn't come back last night and he's not here, where else could he have gone?"

"You said Malyfar's servants live elsewhere in the Grove, right? Maybe he went back to your normal home?"

"He wouldn't just ditch me like that," the elf said with conviction, "Trust me, Ozzy and I are bonded by more than just common friendship."

The dragon thought about his own developing brother-like bond with Solah. He wouldn't leave the boy and vanish without a compelling reason, and he was sure the boy would do the same for him. "I understand," he said.

"Besides, he would have come already if he had gone back to our home. He wants to find out what's wrong with Malyfar as much as anyone. That was the whole reason he left in the first place!"

"Maybe he overslept, then?"

The elf let out a weak chuckle. "I hope so, he does like to sleep a lot."

The two of them moved on and continued searching through the home. Four hours had passed and they had finished searching the last room on the left side of the entrance hall. There was nothing else suspicious in any of the rooms, and Rauliax let out a disappointed sigh as the last one, the living room, had nothing either.

"I hope the other two upstairs had better luck," the dragon said.

"There's only one room left downstairs," Siwan said. "The basement. Over here."

He moved to the farthest corner of the room and pushed his palms onto the wall. They parted and revealed the way down into the basement.

"The basement is right next to the living room?" Rauliax asked.

"Yeah, it was the only place they could make the stone give way for another room back when this place was built," the elf replied.

"Right then, let's get down there then." The dragon peered down the stairs and saw only darkness. "Are there lights?"

The elf shook his head. "No, I don't go down there without Ozzy. I can conjure some light, but I'd rather not."

"Why? Not your area of expertise?"

"No. Remember when I said I escaped from that mean old dragon that kept my payment? I blinded him with light. Probably for days. Ozzy was looking away and was blinded for a few minutes. Power is not why I was not considered a good mage by other elves, sir. Control is what I have a problem with. If I lit up the basement, we'd probably both not be able to see for a few days."

Rauliax craned his neck back. "Okay then. Not a problem, I was just curious is all. Light breath is my specialty."

The dragon took a step down the large-stepped stairs and was almost immediately repulsed by the repugnant smell.

He craned his head around and asked the elf, "Ugh, what does he keep down here? Smells like rotten plants or something?"

"It's probably the rat feces," Siwan said, "We try to exterminate them all the time, but they just keep coming back."

The dragon grunted in disgust, but continued treading down into the dark basement until he reached the floor. Beyond that, the light from the living room did not penetrate.

The elf followed down and grappled his nose shut as he reached the floor. "Smells worse than usual," he said.

Rauliax grunted and said, "Well then, let's see what's down here." He opened his mouth and a gentle glow started emanating from it.

The white light grew and expanded until it illuminated the entire basement, but neither Siwan nor Rauliax wanted to see what the light revealed.

It was Ozzari. The blue dragon laid in a small pool of crimson, and deep scars adorned his entire body. His wings were missing as if they were torn from his back, and there was a trail of dried blood that flowed from where they were cut. His eyes were shut, and the right one had a long bloody scar cut across its width.

Siwan was too shocked to speak or move and Rauliax had closed his jaws a little when he saw the poor tortured dragon. The light dimmed a little, but it was still enough to see the wounds and the blood.

Rauliax tried to overcome the initial feeling of revulsion. He could still be alive, he thought, and dragons could regrow their wings so he would be alright. He had to be alive.

The silver dragon moved closer with trepidation, but also renewed resolve.

He touched the other dragon's arm, and felt cold. No pulse. No magic. He was dead.

For a moment, Rauliax felt nauseated from touching a corpse. But that disgust gave way to anger. Deep, bubbling fury rose in his chest and a fiery heat enveloped his mind and body.

"I'll kill him for this, I'll kill him, I swear!"

Small sparks of electricity flowed around his snout, and steam hissed from his nostrils. The gentle light was replaced by arcs of lightning, but their dance was still enough to see what Malyfar had done.

Chapter 14

Priscilla sighed as she entered the last room on the left side of the entrance hall. "This is another bedroom? This is already the third one on this side. What the devil does he do with them?"

Solah shrugged. "Maybe he likes sleeping in a different one every night?"

"Absurd amounts of money often make people act strange, so that's actually not totally out of the question." Rauliax's adventures out into the rest of the world came to mind as she thought about it.

"Though I think it's sort of odd how clean and organized they all are. He probably doesn't sleep in them, I think."

"True, they don't look like they've been used at all. And he doesn't have any personal belongings in them, just empty dressers and tables."

Nevertheless, they did search through every drawer to make sure they were completely empty. They found nothing, so they went back out onto the second floor balcony-like hall and moved toward the great heavy wooden doors that stood right in front of the stairs.

"This is the ballroom," Priscilla said, "I've never seen it, but my father, the other council members, and other rich folk often come when Malyfar hosts his parties."

She opened them by wrapping her wings around the specially designed golden handles. The doors opened and revealed a massive room even larger than the entrance hall, and nearly twice as tall. There were banquet tables covered neatly in white cloth that stood along the edges of the ballroom. There were also several of the hard boards that were arranged like in the dragon restaurant, except these boards were made of shiny silver.

"There's probably nothing in here," Priscilla said, "It's far too public to hide anything. Let's just do a quick walk-through and move on."

Solah nodded and they took opposite sides. They moved down the ballroom while pulling up each tablecloth to see if anything was under them.

Yet again they found nothing, so they moved on to the next room. It turned out to be the public restroom, complete with walled off stalls, for partygoers they assumed, so again they just did a quick scan and moved on, though Solah did take a short moment to wonder how exactly dragons used the stalls.

The next door opened up into a workshop. The floors were grey and cold, practical for what the room was used for, but very unlike the rest of the home. Wooden planks, metal plates, and various tools lay scattered around heavy work tables. In the middle was some sort of construct.

"Looks like a motor of some sort," Priscilla said, "This whole place looks like some absent-minded professor's laboratory. Disorganized and disheveled. Look around, but be careful!"

Solah nodded and wandered around the workshop. He only moved things that weren't metal or sharp and looked around with utmost caution.

Professor Ferae, on the other hand, fiddled with the motor device and tried to get it to work. She leaned upright over the table and tried searching for buttons, but found none. There were holes in various places, and she looked and pushed some metal rods through where she thought they might do something.

While she was tinkering with the device, Solah kept on looking around the workshop, but also chatted with her all the while.

"Why don't you like Raul?" the boy asked.

Priscilla grinned. "That's a silly question, silly human. I don't dislike him at all. He's the only dragon near my age with any brains, really."

"Then why do you two argue all the time?"

"Pah, that. It's always been like that, ever since we were hatchlings. Let's just say I tolerate everybody else less."

"But I don't get it. Your tone is completely different when you're talking to me."

She dropped a bolt and dropped down on all fours to pick it up. "Well, I think you're alright. For a human, at least."

"You mean it?"

"I do."

So the boy went on looking with a cheery smile while Priscilla kept on messing with the device. She became nearly obsessively focused on it until Solah's voice snapped her out of it.

"Hey," the boy said, "I haven't found anything. Did you figure out what that thing does?"

"No," she said, "And I won't waste anymore time on it. Let's continue our search."

They took another hour and browsed through two more rooms before reaching the master bedroom.

The bed was just like the one the Eldest lay on, and was embroidered with silvery designs of various plants and vines. It was obviously used, and Malyfar had neglected to tidy up the pillows before leaving for the meeting.

This time they looked through all the drawers and they were actually full of personal stuff, but they found nothing particularly incriminating.

Priscilla was rummaging through a wardrobe and stuck her paw into every winter wrapping that had a pocket. There weren't many wrappings since dragons only wore covers during winter or, in the case of researchers in the University, for safety.

"Try to find a journal or something," she said.

Solah walked over to a table next to the bed pad, but tripped over the purple dragon's tail.

His forehead hit the bottom of the table and he shut his eyes out of instinct. "Oww," he said, "Sorry, didn't see your tail."

"Uh huh," was all she said in response. She was far too deep in the wardrobe to notice much or to give a proper reply.

When the boy reopened his eyes, he saw something shine under the table. He instinctively reached for it. It felt like a box, and when he touched it a gentle wind flowed around and faded.

He pulled it out into the open and asked, "What's a box like this doing under a table?"

Priscilla dug her head out of the wardrobe and turned her body around to look at it. "Hiding something now, it seems. Let me see."

Solah handed her the box. She tried to open it and to her surprise it opened without effort.

"That's odd," she said, "It opened without a problem. Maybe not a terrible secret?"

"I think there was an enchantment around it," Solah said, "When I touched it I felt a gush of air that seems to happen when I touch a strong spell like when I broke the shield of an airship."

She peered at him and said, "A powerful lock enchantment, then? Just like his front door."

"Probably."

She looked back down into the box and saw a rustic old scroll rolled up all neatly. She took it out and put the box back onto the floor.

"What is it?" the boy asked.

"It looks like it would be a magic scroll," she replied. "Let's see what it says."

She unfurled the scroll and read it.

Solah saw her eyes travel down the paper and he saw her face grow more and more grim the further down her eyes wandered.

When she finished reading the entire scroll, she rolled it back up and put it back into the box. Then she stuck the box down her throat into what Solah presumed was her own internal dimensional storage.

"What did it say?" he asked.

She didn't look back at him, but stared aimlessly as if in a trance. "It's what we needed. It explains everything. You were right, Solah. Completely right. Malyfar's made a deal with King Arashal. In return for the design plans that would let his ships pass the magic nullification zone, Arashal promised him absolute rule of Noriath as a vassal of his lordship."

Solah sat down onto pad and let this sink into his mind. The entire Elemarian fleet passing through the Evoscar did explain why Wesar had no warning from Admiral Lina's wards, so that made sense. "You're sure of this?" he asked. "Is this contract finally enough to stop Malyfar?"

"He can't deny it's his. The contract is written in a mixture of human and dragon blood, from the smell, and the signature is irrefutably his, probably signed in his own blood, as is the king's."

"Then we need to take this down to Raul right away and get this to the Council."

She nodded. "Agreed, let's move."

They waltzed out onto back into the entrance hall. From behind the railings, they saw Rauliax at the foot of the stairs and another shadowy shape that looked like a dragon standing in front of the entrance door.

Chapter 15

Siwan repeatedly whispered Ozzari's name as he laid over his body. He cried, and for nearly half an hour Rauliax watched the elf use his magic to heal and seal the blue dragon's scars. It was a futile effort, but the elf refused to stop trying to bring the dragon back to life.

Rauliax's anger had abated enough to restore logic by then, and he had to go up to him and try to pull him away. He placed a paw over the elf's shoulder and tried to comfort him.

"Repairing his body will not bring his soul back," Rauliax said. "We have to bring Malyfar to justice. Let's get out and get to the authorities."

The elf nodded weakly, but tears still flowed freely down his face and down Ozzari's lifeless side.

"Ozzy," he stammered, "Remember that promise we made so long ago? I'd wait for you in whatever afterlife awaits us. I'm an elf, and you a dragon, but we are brothers nonetheless. It shouldn't have happened this way, but wait for me Ozzy. Wait for me."

Siwan forced himself to stand, and Rauliax helped him up the stairs back into the living room.

Rauliax broke the deadening silence. "Let's find the other two and get out of here. Ozzari's murder is enough for the Council to act against Malyfar."

"Okay," was all the elf managed to whisper.

The elf followed Rauliax out into the entrance hall, but there they found the main entrance closed and blocked. Before it stood an all too familiar red and black dragon.

The rage that Rauliax had managed to suppress flared back to life. Malyfar had murdered another dragon, he thought, and the worst punishment the Council could give was permanent banishment. That was, in his anger addled mind, not justice.

Rauliax whispered to the elf, "Is there another way out?"

"Yes, a more secret way," he replied.

"Go upstairs, find the other two, and take them out. I'll keep him occupied."

The elf nodded, and then started scurrying up the stairs while Rauliax walked in front of the stairway and faced Malyfar.

"So," the red and black dragon said after he glanced at the living room door, "It seems you've found something unsavory. I should have thought the foolish whelp would've gone to Wyrst for help."

"You *bastard*," Rauliax said, "You'll pay for what you've done. The Council will find out what you did."

Malyfar's eyes tracked over to the elf, who had paused as he listened to their words, and then he spoke in a louder voice. "You know, Siwan, Ozzari wouldn't tell me where you were. Even through the torture and the agony, he wouldn't speak. How noble and loyal of him. *Precious*. Unfortunate he had to die."

The elf ducked and cowered back behind the railings and let the shadows conceal him. The red dragon's words stung him deep and hurt him more than any physical pain he had ever felt.

Malyfar shouted in a louder and more commanding voice, "It's no use hiding, dear Siwan. I'll deal with you after I finish my business with this meddling dragon here."

Rauliax hoped the other dragon would not see Solah or Priscilla. He had to take all his attention and hope the others could escape unnoticed. "You'll hurt nobody else," he said. "The Council will banish you from the dragon realm forever."

The other dragon laughed and cackled. "The Council won't find out if nobody tells them. I'm afraid you'll be joining Ozzari, Professor Moonsilver."

"You're insane! People will notice I've gone missing!"

"People will simply assume you've left without a word, like you always do."

"My father knows I'm here, Malyfar! He'll know!"

The red and black dragon grinned most maliciously. "By the time your annoying father gathers enough proof, the Council will be bending before *me*!"

"What are you talking about?"

He barked out a hoarse laugh. "With Arashal's gift, I will become a god!"

Rauliax stared at him intensely. The former noble councilmember had indeed gone mad. "Arashal? So you've been conspiring with Elemar this entire time!"

"Quite," Malyfar said, "You're not the only dragon, you know, that has traveled much. I did so quite a bit in my youth, but you were not yet born to know. And I have gone farther than you have, beyond the mountains to the east. Unfortunately, you will never see that side of the continent now, professor."

Rauliax took what he said with a twinge of fear. His father, being the general of the dragon army, had forced him to learn a little bit of fighting, and he had sparred with other dragons a bit in his life. It was that sort of training that took time away from his studies, and that was how he, though reluctant to admit it, fell behind Priscilla in certain disciplines of science. That training was going to be the difference between life and death. "I won't be dying without a fight," he said.

"Oh indeed. I hope you'll provide more fun than the foolish blue dragon. On guard!"

Malyfar took a deep breath and then fire erupted from his throat. Rauliax leapt out of the way just in time and the fanning stairway took the entire blow. It was apparently made of some sort of fire resistant material since the whole thing didn't catch on fire, but it was still scorched black where the fire struck.

Rauliax wasted no time and retaliated with his own attack. A concentrated beam of burning silver light shot out of his mouth, but Malyfar was quicker. The black dragon switched element and fired out a blue smoke towards the advancing beam. Upon contact with the light, the smoke solidified into solid ice. The beam tried to cut through the ice, but it regenerated itself too quickly and they were soon locked in a standstill.

Rauliax stopped his attack and took a breath while Malyfar did the same.

"You are young and strong," the black dragon said, "But in your youth you are yet unskilled. You may have more power than I do, but I know how to use my power better."

Then the black dragon released another torrent of fire. This time, Rauliax didn't jump out of the way, but instead he fought the inferno with a stream of water. But light was Rauliax's favorite element, and the others he had less experience with, fire and wind being his least practiced ones.

Water, luckily, was his next favorite after light, but it wasn't enough. Fire appeared to be Malyfar's strongest element, and soon the stream of fire started winning ground and inched slowly past the steaming stream of water towards the silver dragon.

Solah and Priscilla watched the battle from the balcony. They stayed near the walls and the pre-occupied dragons didn't notice their presence. Siwan saw them from his corner, and his face regained some complexion.

The elf still had tears running lightly down his face, but he remembered his orders from Rauliax and signaled them to move towards him. They did so all while hugging the wall, and stayed out of sight.

"We have to help Raul," Solah whispered.

"I can't do anything," Siwan whispered, "Dragonscale is far too resistant for a single mage to pierce through. And I'm not anywhere near strong enough." The elf was also afraid that if he lost control he'd cause the entire cave to collapse around the home.

"I'm a scientist, not a fighter," Priscilla said. "If we get out, maybe we can find help before Raully gets overpowered."

"I know another way out," Siwan said, "Follow me."

The other two nodded. They went into the public bathroom, which was right next to them, luckily. The creak of the door was lost in the sound of elements clashing.

"Over here," Siwan said, "It's a passageway for party guests that want to leave, but not be seen leaving."

The elf entered the last stall and pushed against the wall. It slid open upon a hinge, and revealed a dark path.

Siwan went in and Priscilla followed, but Solah paused.

"Come on, Solah!" the purple dragon said.

"I can't," the boy said, "I have to help him. You two go run!"

She gasped and said, "Are you mad? You can't dispel dragon magic, boy."

"I know, but I have to figure out something! I can't just leave him here alone," he said. "You two go find help, I'll do what I can to buy more time."

Priscilla didn't move for a moment, but then craned her neck down. "Alright. We'll hurry. Don't let Raully get hurt, please."

"I wont, I promise."

She nodded at him and went down the secret passageway with the elf.

Meanwhile, Rauliax had to leap out of the way as the black dragon's fire completely overpowered his jet of water. The flames managed to lick his tail, however, and burned it slightly.

Malyfar scoffed at him. "See? Even with fire's natural enemy you cannot win. Your water breath is good for such a young dragon like yourself, but it's still unfocused. Strong, but not concentrated enough."

The silver dragon responded with another attack. Wind was not an element he was well trained in, but he could do one thing with air manipulation that wouldn't drain all his strength. He took a deep breath and started singing a deep note with massive vibrato as if he were a master of opera.

The oscillating waves from the sound blasted the area in front of him with sonic strikes. The floor beneath him cracked from the wave propagation, but before the cracks grew to where Malyfar stood, the black dragon had already puffed out another screen of blue mist.

The mist solidified into a massive wall of ice before the devastating sonic attack reached him. The sound hit the wall, then bounced back and the cracks in the floor took a double-take and ripped back towards the original source of the sound.

Rauliax stopped singing as he realized what the black dragon had done, but it was too late. The echoes were enough to spread the cracks back under him. He plugged his ears and shut his eyes as the pulsating sonic blast hit him, but it wasn't enough. After the vibrations ended, he took his claws out of his ears and small trickles of blood dripped out. He opened his eyes, and luckily his vision wasn't as damaged as much as he had expected, though his normally blue eyes became partially red.

He saw that Malyfar was saying something to him, but he could barely make it out as he was partially deafened by his own attack.

"A nice little trick with wind," the black dragon said, "But I've read of it before. Wouldn't have thought an academic like you would know how to sing. Too bad I've always been terrible at it. Not that I'll need any tricks, you seem almost out of steam. Death by fire, or by ice? I think ice will be easier to clean up."

Then Malyfar shot out a stream of water out of his mouth. Halfway along the stream, the water froze into solid ice and flew at the weakened dragon.

Rauliax mustered whatever strength he had left, combined it with his anger, and responded with a another beam of light.

The two elements slammed into each other and fought for dominance, but despite light being Rauliax's best element, he still started losing. The block of ice grew faster than the light could melt it.

The ice crept closer and closer, and Rauliax's eyes drooped as he prepared to die. He only hoped he had bought the others enough time to escape.

But Solah hadn't run away. He was still up on the second floor looking for a way to help his foster-brother as he looked down at the doomed battle.

The boy couldn't think of anything, but he had to do something. He ran down the burnt stairs and tried to jump towards Rauliax from the side so he could push him away, but he fell short and rolled onto his tail.

That was all Rauliax needed. He felt as if someone had poured power into him, and his eyes shot wide open as he concentrated it into his breath weapon. The light surged brighter and grew hotter as it turned pure pulsing white. Malyfar's eyes widened as he saw the beam evaporate his ice before it even impacted it: the radiating heat alone was enough to vaporize the water into steam.

Too stunned to move, the black dragon's head was engulfed in the blazing light.

Rauliax knew his attack was not pure light since it moved several times slower than the true speed of light, but instead it was more like a liquid form of pure heat. Rather, dragon-light was more like light completely in its particle phase when used as an offensive weapon instead of just a light source. And like a flowing liquid, it managed to transfer enough force to force Malyfar's body back against the main entrance door.

When the silver dragon stopped his attack, he saw the blast had completely melted Malyfar's head off and burned a hole through the door.

It was a terrible sight. The red and black dragon's body lay slumped against the door with his tail splayed out between his back legs. His entire head had been vaporized, and at his neck there was still molten flesh and bone. The liquified mixture, still glowing hotly red, dribbled down his scaly body and sizzled as it cooled and hardened.

He almost felt like hurling the contents of his stomach, but then he heard a familiar voice call out to him.

"Raul, are you okay?"

Rauliax replied, though his voice was shaky. "Yes, dear boy, I'm quite alright thanks to you. You've saved my life again. That was a smart thing you did."

The boy tried to get up and look around the dragon. "It was entirely by accident, I didn't know I could give you *that* much power. What happened?"

Rauliax unfolded his wings so the boy couldn't see. "Don't look. It's an ugly sight. We're okay. Malyfar's dead."

"Okay, I won't. What now?"

Rauliax sighed and collapsed. He had made a risky gamble and shoved all his strength, including all of the extra power the boy's touch gave him, into that final attack. If it had failed, he would've lost. And Solah would've perished too, once Malyfar figured out he was there.

"Now we wait and rest," he said. "Under my wing, don't look. Stay against me, please."

"Will do," the boy said. Rauliax shuffled around and covered him with a wing, and under it the boy sat leaning against his brother. "You have a nice singing voice, by the way. I'd love to hear you sing when you're not blasting things apart with your voice."

The dragon chuckled and set his head down on the shattered floor. "Later, perhaps. Rest now."

Chapter 16

"Son, wake up."

Rauliax felt something poking at his snout and grudgingly opened his right eye. He saw his father jabbing him with a finger claw.

"Oww," Rauliax said, "Stop that!"

"Get up," his father said, "Get up, both of you."

He looked up and saw two other Council member near his father. Marissa, the dark blue dragon, and Delvic, the green dragon as he recalled. Marissa was just finishing up wrapping Malyfar's body in a black bag.

Then he lifted his wing and let Solah see what was going on.

"Keep holding on," Rauliax said, "I still don't feel too great."

"Okay," was all the boy said.

He rubbed one of his ears and looked at his claw and saw it had been stained from his still not quite dried blood. He groaned and looked at his father again. "What's going to happen, dad?"

His father's eyes looked tired. "Priscilla and Siwan told the Council everything," he said, "Delvic has Ozzari noted down, and the rest of the Council has already seen the contract."

"What contract?"

"The contract that Priscilla and I found," Solah said.

"That's news to me," Rauliax said. "What was it about?"

Marissa moved up and explained. "It was quite cut and clear. Malyfar conspired with King Arashal to take rule of Noriath after Elemar's conquered the continent."

"Now Marissa," the green dragon said, "It's only clear that Malyfar had some dealing with the king for the sole reason of usurping the Council, and there was no wording to suggest the king would invade the entire continent. And for that, the traitor has been duly punished. In a rather uncivilized manner, I might add."

"It's already quite clear," Wyrst said, "My son acted in self-defense. There were several witnesses including the Eldest's daughter, and we've already gone over this so stop complaining."

The green dragon turned his nose away with reluctant agreement.

"A shame," Marissa said, "Our kin has not slain one another in millenia. I'm sorry that burden was forced on you, professor."

"In any case," Wyrst said, "The Eldest has gotten a lot better, and according to Priscilla you used a cure for poison. Poison from Malyfar. She's also detailed the specifics to us, and the whole conspiracy has been unmasked. Now, son, I believe you have business elsewhere?"

"We have to go see the elves," Rauliax said. "They must help Wesar. Has the Eldest voiced his opinion?"

"Not yet, no," his father replied. "He wants to see the two emissaries first. My *sons*."

Solah looked up at the older dragon with a smile.

"Time is short," Rauliax said, "We should go as soon as possible."

"Of course," Wyrst said. "And I'm sorry I couldn't keep the meeting long enough to prevent Malyfar from coming back so soon."

"It's okay," the younger dragon said, "I know you tried your best, and I'm alright now."

His father nodded slowly. "Godspeed, my sons."

Rauliax took Solah and flew, noticeably slower than usual, up to the Council's cave. It was still early in the afternoon, and they flew with an out of place sense of serenity.

But Rauliax hadn't forgotten what he had seen in the basement. He could still see Ozzari, alive and breathing, in his head. It was only the day before he had seen him, but now he could see the poor young dragon's lifeless body superimposed over his living one. The effect was haunting and he tried to shake it out of his mind, but the memory made his blood hot again with anger and disgust.

His mind raced as he thought about the contract. King Arashal was the cause for this. Without his influence, Malyfar, esteemed and second oldest member of the Dragon Council, would've never acted in such a murderous manner. The war had become personal, and he would not allow the mad king to live without justice.

Solah broke him out of his thoughts. "Are you okay? Are you still tired? You're really quiet."

"No, I'm alright," he said, "Just disturbed. Ozzari is dead. Murdered by Malyfar."

"That's what your dad meant? I, I don't know what to say."

"There's nothing to say. Malyfar has been punished for his crime."

"He almost killed you too."

"That he did."

Solah leaned down on the dragon's back and wrapped his arms as much as he could around the dragon's lower neck. "I don't want you to get hurt, *brother*. I don't want to see you die."

The dragon didn't know how to respond. A hole grew in his heart as he thought about it. No matter what happened, he would have to see Solah pass on as he grew old and fell to the merciless poison of time. It was nearly a guarantee that he would have to see *his* brother die if they made it out of battle unscathed. He shook his head to try and dispel those thoughts, and he tried not to think of it. There was still plenty of time to enjoy after all, and he would try to make the most of it.

So Rauliax left the conversation at that, leaving only his gentle wing beats the only sound in the air. Solah never let his arms part from around him until they reached the peak of the Homespire; there he sat up but kept a firm grip on the dragon's hair.

They found the Council chambers empty save for a messenger. The dullish yellow dragon greeted them with a wave and told them that the Council had disbanded for the day and that everyone had gone off to their offices. He directed them to the Eldest's chambers and said that he was waiting for them before heading back out to the main chamber.

There, near the entrance to the Eldest's official quarters, Solah hopped off and walked along his brother as they entered.

Priscilla was there, her wings wrapped around her father, and he was still resting on the pad that could have been his deathbed. Siwan was also there with his hands glowing and hovering below the Eldest's neck, his eyes closed and his face contorted in a mix of concentration and sorrow.

The Eldest did not react to them, but his daughter saw them enter and rose up to greet them.

Rauliax and Solah stood in silence as she strode over to the silver dragon.

"You stupid, asinine, reckless, insufferable, and selfless *saint* of a dragon," she cried. She moved up closer and closer to Rauliax's shocked and confused face until she was nearly right up against him and said, "You've saved our lives, my father's and exposed Malyfar's treachery."

Then she did something nobody in the room would've expected her capable of doing: she pressed the tip of her muzzle against Rauliax's in the draconic equivalent of a kiss.

Rauliax was completely stunned by her behavior, and Solah felt a little embarrassed to look, but he still took a peek and saw the silver dragon's cheeks flush with bright red, amplified by his light color.

A long moment later, she pulled her head away and stared at Rauliax straight into his eyes. "And don't you dare pull that kind of hero act again! I care, Raully. I care about what happens to you."

The silver dragon stumbled for words, but only managed to stammer out, "I, umm, alright. Does this mean that we're...?"

Priscilla pulled him in for a hug and said, "Yes, Raully, yes. I'm not afraid to admit it now."

Rauliax kept stuttering out his words. "I, err, I'll always protect you, and I, uhh-"

"Shh, no need for cliched speeches," she said, "I know. You need to protect yourself more than me, anyway." She shook her head gently. "It's been such a long time that we've pretended, hasn't it?"

He nodded.

"You," she paused. She backed away a little and looked at both Rauliax and Solah. "You both still have work to do."

Solah only stared at his brother who closed his eyes and nodded for the both of them.

Priscilla walked towards the silver dragon's side, between the two brothers. She craned down her neck to the human. "Don't let him get hurt, Solah. If you do, I'll," she paused. What would she do to him? "I'll never forgive you." The boy grappled at his heart. That would truly be a fate worse than death.

"I won't lose him," the boy said back to her.

She looked a little relieved, and then another voice spoke out.

"Nor will I." They all turned around and saw Siwan staring back at them, his face full of conviction. "I'm going with you two," he said. "I won't forgive Arashal for poisoning Malyfar's mind enough to murder Ozzari. I'm going to fight with you."

Rauliax already felt guilty about getting Solah stuck in this war.

"Absolutely not," he said, "I will not endanger another friend for this madness."

"I will go to Elemar myself if you will not take me," the elf said. "And besides, you will need my help to deal with the elves."

Rauliax had to admit he had a point. He hadn't the slightest clue how to deal with the elvish kingdom and was quite sure Solah didn't either. Diplomacy would be difficult without knowing the inner workings of their kind: their political philosophy, their leadership model, and even their cultural differences would be knowledge he needed but lacked. It was all knowledge that Siwan could help provide.

"Very well," he said. "You may come with us."

Siwan nodded, and then went back to treating Eldest Ferae.

They let him work a little while longer until the old dragon at last opened his eyes and focused them upon Rauliax and Solah. "I feel quite fine now, thank you," he said to Siwan. The elf backed off, set himself on the other side of Rauliax, and listened.

"I have heard the Council's story," Eldest Ferae said, "And I have heard my daughter's. Now tell me yours."

Rauliax stepped forward and began summarizing everything that had happened since a week ago. He spared no detail aside from the potion incident which he swore he would never let Priscilla know. He spoke for nearly an hour, Solah periodically correcting him or offering further detail, and everybody else listened intently.

When at last he finished detailing the result of his duel with Malyfar, he heard the Eldest stir and adjust himself on his floor pad. "Enough," the old dragon said, "Very good. Now, I wish everyone to leave except the boy."

"Just me?" Solah asked.

Rauliax stepped back in front of the boy. "Why?"

The Eldest's throat rumbled, and then he said, "I want to hear his story from *his* mouth."

The two dragons looked at each other for a quiet moment, and then Rauliax nodded. He started turning around and gestured at Priscilla and Siwan to follow him out of the Eldest's chamber.

Once the three's steps' echoes was no longer audible, Priscilla's father craned his neck down to observe Solah. "Tell me," he said, "you have been abandoned by your race and left to die in the wilds. Why do you wish to fight for them? Why do you seek to help them?"

Solah paused to think. The question was a blunt and forceful one, but he was able to answer it. "Because I don't believe they all hate me. Lieutenant Avery looked upon me with scorn until I saved his life, and now we're, well, friends. Maybe I just want to help other people understand that I'm just another person."

"So you want to prove yourself an ally? What if it doesn't work and the king of Wesar's command is not enough to stop people from giving you dirty looks? Do you fight just for the possibility of being accepted? You are already accepted here, why not stay here and out of trouble, Solah Moonsilver?"

Solah took another moment to think and shook his head. "It's not just for acceptance." His eyes focused onto the old dragon's eyes and did not look away. "There are a lot of good people in Wesar, and many of them are my friends now. The lady that ran the inn we stayed at, Wendy, I remember how cheery she was and how nice she was to Rauliax and me. And she even helped us out later after she learned of my ability. If I don't help, I might never see her smile again. Captain Dillan, Lieutenant Avery, Ensign Waters, they're all my friends. And if I stay here and hide, they'll die."

Eldest Ferae's eyes moved ever so slightly over the boy as if he were analyzing some invisible aura around him, but he said nothing.

Solah became uncomfortable with the silence and said, "If they don't get help from the Dragon Council or the elves, their chances of surviving are low. If Admiral Lina is right about the Elemarian king's desire, then there will be no safe place to hide in Valeria when his ships come. Isn't Malyfar's dealings with him proof enough of this possibility? Please, sir, I've already lost a friend today and almost another. Whether it was Malyfar's intent or not, you must understand that the guiding hand behind his madness was King Arashal's. Will you send help?"

Solah had kept his eyes locked on the Eldest's even when his wandered. The old dragon matched his eyes again and let out another deep rumble in his chest. "Go to the elves," he finally said, "and I shall think in the meantime."

"But sir, you know there's little time to waste!"

"That will be all, Solah Moonsilver. Go with the elf and your foster-brother to the Sylvan Forest. You also have little time."

Solah wanted to stay and argue, but he thought better of it. Debating with the old dragon would've been unwise if he were still balancing a decision in his head, so Solah decided it would've been best to do as he was told. The boy closed his eyes and shut the connection to the Eldest's, and then he bowed and turned around to leave. He half expected the dragon to say something before he left, but only the echoes of his footsteps followed.

When he strolled back to the main chamber, Rauliax, Priscilla, and Siwan stared at him to hear the news.

Priscilla got the first word. "Well, what did he say?"

Solah's head was drooping when he said, "He'd think about it. Otherwise, he just told us to go to the elves."

Priscilla shook her head and patted a forepaw onto the top of her muzzle. "Father," she muttered.

"Unthinkable," Siwan said. His voice started to stutter as he said, "Two dragons are dead, one a Council member, and the Eldest does nothing."

"If it is his command," Rauliax said, "then so be it. We can't waste any more time here, let's move out. Priscilla, if you could..."

"I'll do whatever I can," she said.

"Thank you." The silver dragon flapped his wings once and let the stale chamber air flow. He started to turn around and then paused. "Priscilla, before I forget," he said as he started reaching into his mouth. He took out the little black box that Captain Dillan had given him and handed it to the purple dragon. "It's an enchanted radio, supposed to have enough range to call all the way to the human's capital city. I've an unenchanted one, but we should be able to talk to each other if needed. Call us on frequency 125.5 if there's anything important, alright?"

Priscilla took the radio into her forepaws and nodded at him. Then she put it on the ground. "And before I forget, let me give you Malyfar's contract. The Council has already made copies, and I surmise that King Devran would be interested in seeing it." She reached into her mouth and pulled out the very box that Solah found and handed it to the other dragon, and he promptly stashed it away. She picked up the radio again and gave him a slight nod.

Rauliax smiled weakly and returned the nod before directing his attention back to his party. "Come on then, let's go."

The dragon turned around to leave, and Siwan and Solah followed in silence. The yellow scaled messenger in front of the Council chamber noticed their dreary mood and spoke no words as the trio passed him.

Priscilla watched them until they took a turn in the passage out and left her sight. After they were gone, she put the radio into storage and turned back towards the way to her father's chambers and whispered, "Don't die, Raully."

When they exited the cave, the sun was beginning to lower close to evening. Rauliax stood at the highest ledge on the Homespire and peered down below to look at the roads and towns that spiraled along the mountain. He took a deep breath and then gestured, with his tail, for Solah and Siwan to climb onto him.

The boy went hopped on, causing Rauliax's spine to shiver a bit at the influx of energy, but Siwan was a little more reluctant. Flying on the dragon's back was a sharp reminder of Ozzy, and he paused enough for Solah to prod him.

"It's quite safe really, just come on up and hold onto his hair. Rauliax won't be performing loops and rolls while we're on him."

The dragon added, "But if you'd like, I could put on the harness for you."

The elf mentally shook his head; that wasn't the issue at all. He didn't want to talk about it, however, and just said, "That's alright, I don't want to be an extra burden."

"It's no trouble, but it would be quicker if I didn't."

"Then I'll just jump on!" Siwan leapt up onto the dragon's back, but he landed too far and had to grapple onto Solah to prevent himself from falling. The elf gasped as he felt his connection to the flow of magic blank out and threw himself off the spellbreaker, but he managed to stay on the dragon by some manner of luck.

"Are you okay?" Solah asked.

"Yeah, just a misstep," the elf replied. "And sorry, I was just a little bit surprised by your power."

Rauliax arched his neck around and turned his head as far as he could make it go. "You'll get used to it," he said.

"I don't think so. It's like being choked to me, even a bit worse than that dreadful Evoscar."

"Oh, well that's *very* different from what I feel."

"That much is obvious. If I had wings and touched him I think I would crash to the ground from shock. No offense, Solah."

"None taken," the boy said.

"In any case," Siwan continued, "I'll just sit a little behind you. It's like you're a heated rock, if I stay far enough away the heat won't really affect me." He clutched onto the dragon's brown hair on his back. "Okay, I'm ready."

Rauliax nodded and said, "Priscilla would be fascinated to hear that. Anyway, we're headed to my place first. I just need to grab a couple of things and we're off."

Then the silver dragon leapt off the ledge and took flight. He descended at a moderately gentle pace and Siwan did not complain.

"You know," Rauliax said, "it's a very odd thing. There's two people on my back and I feel pretty light. Why, a couple of months ago I had to carry up a telescope that couldn't fit in my mouth strapped onto my back and it was definitely much heavier."

"I'm glad I don't inconvenience you," the lightly weighted elf said.

Rauliax smiled as he flew down to the Council's Grove. "Not in the least."

Although the elf tried to cover his reluctance, Solah had figured that flying was a reminder of his departed friend, but he went along with his initial presumption so as not to aggravate the still fresh wound.

Back home, Rauliax found his mother brewing dinner. The smell of cooked meat and sauteed vegetables permeated through the house, and she insisted on them staying for a meal before leaving.

"Your father hasn't returned from today's Council business yet," she said. "But we could have dinner in just a few minutes, would that be fine?"

"I don't know if we have the time," Rauliax said. "Let me give Captain Dillan a call." He took out the regular radio he had bought yesterday and tuned it to the *Reliant's* frequency. After a short chat with the captain, who said that he'd been trying to call him during the day when the dragon was knocked out, Rauliax agreed to stay since they figured they wouldn't make it to the Sylvan Forest by morning anyway.

"Excellent," Rauliax's mother said, "dinner will be ready in ten or so minutes."

"Don't cook too much mom! Humans eat a lot less than we do, and elves even less."

"Yes yes, I know. I'll leave some for your father anyway." She started turning away but then twitched back and added, "By the way, I'm not so keen on human appearances, but it seems to me that the boy's - our grandmother, looks very different. She's as confused about it as I am."

"Is that so? I'll take a look."

Rauliax took Solah to see Nama in the guest room while Siwan went into the kitchen to help cook despite Rauliax's mother insisting he not exert himself as a guest in their home. The two were rather taken aback when they saw Nama. She was sitting cross-legged on a dragon mattress pad, but her hair seemed like it was regaining streaks of black. Her face seemed smoother, and she no longer looked as much a fragile old lady as she had a few days ago.

"I'm no expert on humans," Rauliax said, "but it looks like your growing younger, dear grandmother!"

"What happened?" Solah asked.

Nama, with an even stronger voice than she had before, replied, "I don't know. I just felt like I was getting younger, and then when I looked at myself in a mirror this morning, well, there I was."

Rauliax looked her over curiously, and then he said, "Fascinating. I wish there was more time to figure this out, but I believe it might have something to do with dealing with dragons."

The boy still couldn't believe his eyes. "What do you mean, Raul?"

Rauliax shrugged his wings. "I could only guess now, but we should wait until after we get back to test my theory. In the meantime, if Priscilla, she's a purple little beast, ever comes over while we're gone, ask her to run some preliminary tests if that's alright with you."

"She's a nice friend," the boy added.

"A purple one," Nama said, "okay. Are you two leaving tonight?"

"Yes," Rauliax replied, "and we won't be back until the war is concluded."

The now not-so old lady smiled as if she had completely ignored the possibility that neither of them might return at all. "Bring back a souvenir from the elves for me!"

The dragon couldn't help but smile in return and said, "We will."

They left Nama to herself after telling her dinner would be ready soon. Rauliax took Solah into his room after.

"So I've been thinking of weapons you could use to protect yourself with."

"Oh? Like what?"

"Well, humans usually use enchanted swords to fight after they've exhausted themselves with magic, but obviously you couldn't use

157

them. I've been trying to think of something with more oomph than a rock slinger, of course."

"Have you come up with anything?"

"I've thought of the cannons on human airships and thought about miniaturizing them. The idea was actually in a book and I can imagine how it would look, but there's no time to fully design and build a hand-cannon now. Hmm, perhaps I could use my magnetic rail method for projectile propulsion."

"What?"

"Never mind, point is you need a weapon or I won't feel you're safe."

The dragon wandered his room a bit before he started rummaging through a drawer. Solah watched him pull something out of the lowest drawer.

"This is for you, Solah."

"What is it?"

"It's one of my baby teeth. I had it fashioned into a dagger since I thought it would look appealing, but it's far too small for me to use. I think I could sell it to an elf when I was little or something and never did, but now I'd rather you have it. This way, even when I'm far away, you'll always have me there protecting you."

He marveled at the dagger for a while. "Thank you, Raul. I don't know what to say. I only wish I could give you a part of me."

The dragon smiled. "There's no need, dear boy. You've already saved my life *twice*, remember?" He watched the boy gaze at the dagger before realizing he needed to give him the sheath, so he reached deeper into the drawer to pull it out. "Almost forgot! Here, tuck it in, wrap the strap around, and then just clip it to your waist."

Solah did so, and then he crouched as he thought of himself as a daring rogue.

They smiled at each other before hearing Rauliax's mother call them for dinner.

When Rauliax, Solah, and Siwan returned to the *Reliant*, the sun was near sunset. Once aboard, Rauliax noticed the ship's enchanter, Uracel, on the deck with his hand over an empty flame post. He waved over it, and then fire burned over it once more. Then he noticed the trio and stumbled over to them.

"Uracel," Rauliax said as he saw him approach. He gestured to his companions and called out, "This you know is Solah, and this is Siwan."

"Ah, I finally meet the spellbreaker. Uracel, ship's enchanter, at your service. And greetings to you as well, elf."

The two of them bowed before the enchanter. Then Uracel noticed that Captain Dillan was coming down from the upper deck, so he started towards the stairs down into the ship.

"I'd like to meet you all in your cabin tonight, if it's not too much trouble," he added before descending down the stairs.

"Not at all," Rauliax replied.

The captain came down and greeted the trio with a smile. "Rauliax, Solah, and who is this?"

"Siwan," the dragon said. "He's going to help us get the elves' support." The elf bowed at his introduction.

"Very good, very good," Captain Dillan said while looking over the elf, his eyes pausing over his sharp ears. "While you were away, the Dragon Council sent a messenger to fill us in on what happened. At least an answer of maybe is better than no, but it is good that we will enter the elven kingdom with some sort of knowledge of their business."

"I am sorry," Rauliax said, "that we weren't able to get the Eldest's approval. Perhaps if the elves were swayed, the Dragon Council will commit."

"That is a hope I am holding on to," the captain replied.

"We will get the elves to help us," Siwan said. "If we don't, then you will have one dragon and one elf no matter what."

"And one spellbreaker," Solah added.

"Spellbreaker?" the captain asked.

"It's what the ship's enchanter called me."

"Sounds better. And I appreciate your gestures, gentlemen." Captain Dillan turned around and began to return to the upper deck. "We'll arrive at the edge of the Sylvan Forest late tomorrow morning, so I wish you all a good night's rest."

"Thank you, captain," Rauliax said.

Shortly after the good captain returned to the upper deck, the cranes holding the ship lifted away and the sound of the engines increased while Siwan held onto a railing to keep himself steady since he was unused to flight on an airship.

As they departed the dragon realm, they saw the sunset; fitting as they had seen the sunrise on their arrival, except now the third member of their party was swapped. Solah tried not to stare, but he was sure there was water gleaming around his elven companion's eyes from the sun's last light.

Chapter 17

A middle-aged gentleman, his hair swept back with gel and face full of creases that belonged on a man at least two decades older than he was, walked into his prince's cabin. The room, lavishly decorated with golden drapes hugging the ceilings and purple tapestry hanging off the walls, was flooded with the deep orange light made shortly after sunset from the opened door as the admiral entered.

The admiral gave a bow and then stood at attention. Prince Rauleigh, son of King Arashal, hopped off the edge of his bed as soon as the light entered his room and lifted his hand to gesture at Admiral Morit. "I've told you a hundred times Will, you don't have to bow to me."

"It is a matter of civility," Will said. A small smile crept onto his aged face. "Just because I practically raised you like a little brother doesn't mean I should treat you like one!"

"But," Prince Rauleigh argued, "there is no reason you should act like a commoner before me either." Will had raised him when he was little since his father was too busy running the country to spend much time with him and his mother, the last queen of Elemar, had died shortly after he was born.

"I act in such a manner as to serve you, my prince, and to do so requires, by honor, me to respect you in a way befitting of a servant to his lord."

"Sometimes I miss how you used to scold me, you know?"

"The prince is an adult now, or very nearly enough one even if he does not like to act like one, so that such treatment is no longer permissible."

Rauleigh chuckled a bit as he remembered how he'd wander around Lokin, far out of the influence of the king's subjects, and get in the most bizarre sorts of trouble. Admiral Morit, then just Knight

Captain, always kept a watch on him and saved his hindquarters from asinine ruffians more than once, but afterward he would usually get a good lecture. He was actually saddened by the passing of his eighteenth birthday since he could no longer sneak around the crevices of the capital anymore, and he was confined to the wealthy areas of Lokin. Will never dared to scold him after again, and the lack of restraint, or rather the lack of ability to defy such restraint, bored him into becoming the princely icon he was meant to be. Still, he supposed he would have to face responsibility eventually. Battle was upon him, and he had to act like a king whether he wanted to or not. He said in response to the admiral, "Well, I can't argue with that." The prince changed the subject. "I don't suppose you've come without news?"

"Of course not! The bulk of the Wesarian fleet has assembled over the major port city Windsgate, about three days west. The *Eclipse* and the full might of the Elemarian fleet is ready. A smaller fleet is orbiting around Imilune, and we will move to claim the city in the morning as soon as we're done patching up the ships that were damaged at Illum."

The prince let out a deep sigh and sat back down onto the edge of his bed.

"What's the matter?" the admiral asked. He knew something had been troubling the prince ever since his father's deployment of the fleet.

The prince gestured for his old mentor and babysitter to sit by him. The admiral slowly sank himself down onto the edge of the bed as if it were dangerous to disturb such a sacred place, and then he listened.

The prince asked him, "What is the point of all of this?"

"All of what, Rauleigh?"

"Will, you're smarter than that. I mean all of *this*. What's the point of this war?"

"To claim the land that is rightfully ours."

"That is what the great kings and queens of the past have always repeated. Does this continent truly belong entirely to Elemar?"

"Yes?"

"Then why is it separated by such a savagely impassable barrier? The Ridgeback did not allow ground passage before, and it is only with the relatively recent advent of the age of airships did it become possible."

The admiral looked up to ponder a moment and then looked back down. "That is true, I suppose. But it is not my place to decide. If the lords of Elemar want me to fight for land then I will obey."

"Obey," the prince snided. "That, I think, is the only thing Elemarians know how to do."

"Well, free thought is something you can encourage when you become king. It's certainly something you've warmed me up to."

"Will, you're in a unique position of power. You have a greater ability to think for yourself than anyone but my father and I. You're a smart man, you have to be to become admiral of the fleet. Tell me, Will, do you think we should be doing this?"

Admiral Morit took an exhausted breath and settled himself deeper into the prince's bed. "Truthfully, I do not. We're going to lose a lot of good men fighting for something I personally don't really care about." He let out a light chuckle and added, "Not to mention the fact that I'll have to manage more than I can already barely handle."

"Managing a fleet stretched across the entire continent, dealing with the inevitable bouts of insurrection, and all while trying to please my father. It's a full plate, to be sure, but that's just the logistical objections. I want to know, Will, does this feel right to you? It's war, I know, but I can't get over the fact that we're *killing* other people. It's different from the minor border incidents."

The admiral's eyes shifted and his brows lowered. "I-it doesn't matter what I feel on the matter. I will do what the king commands."

"Then I will command differently when my time comes."

"You will give up control of Wesar after you become king?"

"After all this to gain control? I do not think to waste all these lives, but, like you said, I believe it would be less a logistical nightmare if I gave them sovereignty over their own lands while they pay tariff to us."

"A smarter move than your father's, I think. Ruling with an iron fist is not always the best idea, even if it is a most pleasing thought." The admiral rose up from the bed and walked towards the door. "We'll meet the Wesarian fleet in about three days. After they're dealt with, we fly straight for the capital."

"Thank you, Will."

The admiral stopped himself before he stepped completely out of the cabin door. He turned back and fumbled through a pocket under his leather jacket and pulled out a bottle of blue fluid. He walked back to Rauleigh and set the bottle into his hand. "Almost forgot. It's from your father. An emergency transportation potion. It'll take you back to the capital as soon as you're done chugging it."

The prince looked up to his old teacher and guardian. "Will I need it?"

"If only I knew."

Prince Rauleigh sighed again when the admiral left. Will had always been more a father to him than the king was, and he would've liked nothing else other than to take a smaller airship and travel the world with him, away from conflict and battle. He tucked the glass of blue fluid away into a drawer and prayed he would not need it.

Chapter 18

Admiral Lina stood at the edge of the structure on top of the *Corona's* deck in front of the colossal airship's bridge. Her wiry silver hair flowed with the wind as she stared off onto the horizon on the opposite side of the sunrise, knowing that the Elemarian fleet would be in her sight in just a few days. The *Corona* and the Third Fleet had moved to Windsgate and were as prepared for battle as they could be, but there was no way to prepare for an engagement of such an inordinate size. Border skirmishes amounted to nothing compared to what was coming, but at least the enemy had just as little clue as to how to fight such a huge battle as she and her captains did.

The Second Fleet would meet with the Elemarian fleet soon, but they were just there to buy time. The bulk of the fleet would retreat and join with the Third Fleet while ships mounted with artillery would provide covering fire in a delaying hit-and-run tactic.

The admiral only hoped she was buying time for something: she had received news from Captain Dillan about the situation at Noriath and the Dragon Council, and it was definitely not encouraging. Still, it was their only chance, and if help did not come then they would fall to such an overwhelming force no matter what she did.

An older gentleman with dulled and greying hair that gave the admiral's silver hair an even more uncanny appearance came up onto the balcony-like area and leaned over the railings next to her.

"Benson," the admiral said, "you've been serving in the Aerial Service longer than anyone. You were an admiral once, too, before I even joined the Fleet."

"Aye," he said.

"Tell me, what do you think of all this?"

"I don't know what to tell you," Benson said. "In all my years, I've never thought that the entire might of the two most powerful

165

countries on the continent would meet in open battle."

Admiral Lina took a deep breath but said nothing. Benson was old and wise, and he should've retired a long time ago. But he stayed and served as the warp master of the *Corona*, and his knowledge of the ship's interior was second-to-none. Only he and his apprentice, Lieutenant Warp Master Ryson, knew the ship well enough to teleport people inside the ship without needing a signaler to show them a vision of the location they were in, though the old man was the only one that complained whenever the king wanted to retrofit the flagship. Moving rooms and corridors around required him to relearn that part of the ship, and it was something he was loathed to do.

"But I will say this," the old warp master said. "You're young, smart, and one of the more talented admirals I've seen command this ship. That includes the ones before me, too, and I think you'll do a better job than anyone else could."

She stared out at the horizon again, and the light of day grew brighter. "Thank you, Benson."

"Nothing of it," he said. "Anyway, just came up to tell you some ensign dropped Pyrucium all over the sixth quadrant's shield circle. Not that I'll need it, mind you, but if I'm busy warping other people around then the other transporters might not get it right."

Admiral Lina smiled. A little problem like that was enough to take her mind off the coming battle, and she welcomed the reprieve. The shield circles were etched around various places around the airship and were the best places to position each barrier mage, and they were mildly enchanted so that they gave off a very obvious location beacon ripple in the flow of magic. Transporters not as well acquainted with the ship as Benson could feel the beacons and rotate the barrier mages around to where they were needed without waiting for a signaler to beam them a visual of their location, and it was a moderately important thing to fix if the enchantment was smudged with Pyrucium. The idea was generally the same for the engines: the propellers were ducted not just for the aerodynamic benefits, but also because the shell of the fans provided a physical entrapment for protectors to latch their barriers around in case they could no longer extend a shield around the ship. Or rather, in the case of a massive ship like the *Corona*, around a quadrant of the ship. "I'll send an enchanter to work right on it," Lina said.

"Thank you ma'am." Only a man as bold and experienced as he was could get away with calling the admiral that, and he was a good friend since he had mentored her quite a bit when she was a mere elementalist assigned to train on the *Corona*, so she didn't mind his casual manner. Benson bowed and left away into a little stairway down into the structure while she thought back to her time as a mere ensign, and how excited she was when she was assigned to the flagship of the Wesarian fleet.

Benson was the Lieutenant Warp Master back then, and most of the senior crew liked to converse with her since she was practically destined to gain command of the fleet because of her magic specialty. One thing that irked her to no end was Benson's refusal to change his philosophy on the placement of the warp mages during battle. She always told him not to put all his eggs in one basket in reference to his preference of taking himself and all the best transporters onto the crow's nest instead of spreading them out on the high sections of the ship, but he always said that having the best meant they would never allow the barriers protecting them fail. Even as admiral, she severely questioned his confidence in such philosophy, but she dared not change the venerably old transporter's habits through an order.

Back then, even though everyone knew why she had her silver hair and eerily green eyes, most of the regular crew avoided talking with her. She didn't have a problem with it since there was much to learn from the senior crew, but she was always saddened that her appearance drove people away. Her magic was rare, so rare that it guaranteed her admiralty, and perhaps it was that difference that helped convince her so easily in Solah's goodwill. A light chuckle escaped her as she thought about how Rauliax had mistaken her for a kineticist.

It had become even less easy to talk to her regular crew since she became admiral because the title added an aura of authority around her that most of the crew seemed to fear, and again her appearance definitely did not help. Benson had once told her that when he looked at her eyes, he couldn't help but feel them penetrating into his thoughts and chilling his heart, but of course he had long since told her he had gotten used to it.

She looked out again, this time towards the fleet assembled below the *Corona*. There was a dreadnought in front hovering just under the *Corona* which was blocking most of Windsgate from view, and she wondered whether they had their own little problems to deal with. Despite the name of the class of the ship, the dreadnought was only half the size of the *Corona*, but they were a match one-for-one to Elemar's dreadnoughts. In fact, only the *Eclipse* could dare to rival the *Corona* in size, but the rest of the fleet was too few for her flagship to handle their fleet just by itself.

She recognized the red trim around the railings of the dreadnought and knew it as the *Firestorm*, run by Captain Fourier. He was a clever fellow, older than her, but refused admiralty ten years before her appointment. He was also a master fire elementalist, and if Wesar was going to win without any outside help, a dim hope, then the reason would be because of the ingenuity of men like him. Or herself, really; the plan to send the exile as a neutral representative was a rather extraordinary one, she had to admit, but it was unconventional, and they would lose at conventional warfare.

Her thoughts drifted to that of Solah, Rauliax, and the *Reliant's* mission. The news from Noriath was disappointing, but there was still hope. There was always hope. A dragon engineer had come to finish their most recent unified project since the king's initial request for aid, but one extra airship, no matter how powerful it seemed to be, could not turn the tide of battle. Still, the gesture suggested that the dragons might change their minds before it was too late. Captain Pearce definitely reassured her too, and her faith in the originally suspicious exile and dragon was clearly not misplaced, so she prayed her faith in the dragons beyond Rauliax would bear equally good fruit.

Then there were still the elves. She wasn't sure how Solah or Rauliax were supposed to even gain an audience when all their messengers were denied entrance to even the edge of the elven forest, but Captain Dillan's report of an elf helping them was encouraging. If the dragons did not help, the battle might still be won if enough elves came.

If. There were many ifs in her plan, and there was nothing to it but a risky gamble. Tough decisions for difficult battles usually ended up as such. Nobody had a better plan, anyway.

She watched a scout pass by between the two massive ships, dwarfed by their immensity, and mused on its design. They were too small to do anything significant beyond surgical strikes, she thought, and that was only if the enemy was dumb enough not to target them. Then again, they weren't high-priority targets, and she wondered how long they could take the Elemarian fleet's barrier mages by surprise with Solah's dangerous, but now incredibly useful, power. It would be too dangerous to send the boy with his dragon against anything bigger than a frigate, but if they could dispel enough barriers, then even a scout could destroy one by itself. If they destroyed enough enemy scouts and frigates, it might lay off enough pressure on their ships to proceed against the battlecruisers and dreadnoughts.

But then there was also the *Eclipse* to deal with. In a sense, both the *Eclipse* and the *Corona* fought a war of attrition. Since they were both command ships, they would not join the battle unless one side saw need for it. That meant that the first flagship to enter the fray was practically admitting to the other side that they were losing. Admiral Lina would have to wait, think, and weigh the benefits of timing her entrance into battle: there was the potential morale boost of keeping the *Corona* out of battle, the strategic advantage of keeping the *Eclipse* out of battle, and the strategy of having her ship join the fray first and go in guns blazing to do as much damage as it could before the other side could react was plausible too.

The scout passed by, its small sail drooped against the gentle wind, and she could've sworn she could saw the captain of the little airship look at her from the quarterdeck. But when her eyes darted down to check, the man's head had noticeably twitched to the other direction, and she couldn't help but think that her eyes had a magical power themselves; one that drove looks away.

The scout didn't have any housing structures on it, and there was no bridge. Newer scout ships did have some structure, usually, and the *Reliant* was lucky enough to have a captain's cabin above deck that could fit a dragon though it, along with every scout ship, had no dedicated indoor bridge.

She had also briefly considered any possible advantage from landing the ships into a lake and holding there, but any serious strategy that could be formulated would've been useless anyway since only less than half the fleet was capable of landing in water: the *Corona* itself was too massive to float. Airship design hadn't changed much from sea ships, originally because of familiarity, but then around forty years ago human engineers that had studied at the University of Noriath had managed to find a way to allow the heavy airships to land in water and stay afloat without the aid of a levimage. In any case, she couldn't think of any way to turn it into a strategy when so few of her airships were capable of it and quickly abandoned the notion.

"No," she whispered to herself, "there's nothing for it. Either we win here, or King Arashal shall have his continent."

Chapter 19

Noriath remained visible for quite a while: the lights that dotted along all the little cities on the mountain lit up the Homespire like sparkling jewels wrapped around a dragon's horn. The night made them more visible, and arguably more beautifully so, but they too eventually disappeared once the *Reliant* flew far enough away. They saw another airship too, another mercantile frigate, and it flew south and away, and their navigation lights dimmed faster than the lights from Noriath did.

Once the Homespire faded into the blackness of the night, Rauliax, Solah, and Siwan made their way back into the captain's cabin and settled down. Before the dragon could finish rolling down the sleeping rugs, however, Uracel appeared in front of the entrance of their room and knocked on the open door.

"Come on in!" Rauliax said. "We're just settling in, so you'll have to stand until I'm finished."

"Oh," the enchanter said, "I don't want to be in the way. Go ahead and finish, I'll wait out here. The stars are quite bright now that we're away from all those other lights." True to his word, he stayed outside and stared up while waggling his finger as if he were connecting the constellations.

After the dragon finished setting down the rug and unfolded his portable table, he invited the enchanter to come back in. Uracel sat down on the rug, his legs crossed, and smiled at everyone.

"Tea?" Rauliax offered.

"Certainly," Uracel replied. His hands sifted through his inner coat pockets and pulled out a small packet. "My own, if you'd please."

"Of course." The dragon took the packet into a forepaw and used the other to take out a kettle from his mouth. He set the kettle down onto the table, took out a bottle of water, and poured it into the kettle. Once the kettle was full, he tossed the empty bottle back into his dimensional storage and pulled out a tea cup. Once he put the cup down and stuck the tea packet inside, he lifted the kettle and breathed a gentle flame under it until he could hear the water bubbling, and then he poured it into the cup. With his claw, he stirred the drink until he was satisfied with the color of the water.

When Uracel took a sip of it, he rumbled lowly to indicate that he was pleased. He took another sip and then set the cup down onto the rug next to him. "Thank you, that was very well made."

Rauliax smiled at the man. "You're quite welcome, now what was it you wanted to talk about?"

Solah and Siwan both set themselves down a respectable distance from the enchanter and listened to the man speak.

"You retrieved a scroll, did you not?"

Rauliax at first did not realize what he was referring to, but then he did and said, "What? The contract, how did you know?"

"I have ears," the man said, "and other methods that you might learn of tonight. May I see the contract?"

The dragon nodded, and then he took out the box that Solah had found in Malyfar's bedroom. He didn't know why the enchanter wanted to see it, but there was no reason for him to be rude and deny his polite request.

Uracel took the box and opened it. He handled the scroll as if it were a delicate petal, and unfurled it slowly before peering down the writing. He wore a frown that only grew harsher the lower his eyes wandered.

"It is as I feared," Uracel said. "This is a blood contract."

Rauliax nodded. "It is written in blood, that much we know. Probably King Arashal's and our own Dragon Council member, Malyfar's."

The enchanter shook his head. "No, this is a blood contract. A Blood Oath. As in fueled by blood magic."

Siwan was the only one in the room who visibly turned agitated when he said that. His ears seemed to perk, and his face hardened.

"What do you mean by blood magic?" Rauliax asked.

The man sighed, and then he took another sip of his tea. "Humans do not remember. Dragons never cared. But the elves remember. Blood magic is a foul thing that uses life energy to do what their users want. Blood, obviously, is the main catalyst for their spells. But the most dangerous part of it is that it has a method of imitating immortality."

"Impossible," Rauliax said. "If someone found the equivalent of the philosopher's stone, we dragons would've been all over it."

Uracel shook his head. "No, blood mages were driven to extinction before humans landed on Valeria. Elves, even across continents, keep in contact with each other, and that is how Valerian elves know." He glanced at Solah. "If it were not for the original spellbreakers, the blood hunters, then the strongest mages would've found the largest well of life energy in the known world, Noriath's dragons, and killed you all to fuel their thirst for power, to drain your lives and extend their own. But they were defeated, and nature finds balance so that the spellbreakers eventually died out too." He took another sip. "And now one has returned to balance the power that King Arashal has found."

Rauliax raised an eyebrow. "How do *you* know this?"

The enchanter held out the scroll. "This Blood Oath is bound by magic. If either party broke the contract, they would perish. I have seen it before in a vision."

Siwan's eyes seemed to become more analytical the more the enchanter spoke. His explanations involved more elvish knowledge than even he knew: blood mages were a topic he had very shortly studied at home and only knew by name.

Rauliax grew more and more suspicious of the enchanter. "What do you mean a vision? There are no real fortune-tellers, and I think you know all of this from some other source."

"No real fortune-tellers?" Uracel chuckled. "Perhaps not human ones, but there are elvish ones."

Siwan butted himself in, "Only the Keepers can truly see the future. And I doubt *you*, human, have ever seen one. Even I doubt that I have seen a true Keeper."

"Oh? Pray tell me, elf, who were the last three Keepers of the Sylvan Forest?"

"Easy. Keeper Inloc, who died at the ripe old age of five hundred and forty seven, Keeper Ellcadur, who vanished two hundred years ago at the age of one hundred fifty, and Keeper Nameron, Ellcadur's supposed brother, rules to this day."

"You are completely correct, young elf." Uracel stroked his chin thoughtfully. "Do you sense any perturbations in the flow of magic here?"

Siwan was slightly confused and glanced at Solah and Rauliax. "No? Unless you count the, umm, spellbreaker."

"Is that so?" The enchanter scooted himself closer the Solah, leaving his tea behind.

The boy, thinking he was just curious about his power, obliged him by staying put: he didn't want to be rude to the man anyway since he wanted to hear more about blood mages. It did sound like there were people like him, the spellbreakers, and they sounded like heroes of another time when he spoke of them as if in praise; highly unusual considering normal people seemed to think the opposite of him today.

Once he was within an arm's reach of the boy, Uracel stopped scooting. "I have become a master of the art of disguise, it seems. Not even an elf can see through my veil."

Siwan's eyebrows furrowed at the man as he tried to discern his game. "W-what are you talking about?"

The enchanter smiled. "I have worn this enchantment disguising me for so long that even I have forgotten what I look like." He reached out his hand to Solah. "Take my hand, spellbreaker, so that we all may see who I truly am."

Rauliax and Siwan looked at the man with intense curiosity, and Solah cautiously took hold of his hand. The change spread quickly from his hands up to his arms, and then to the rest of his body. What skin was not covered by clothing turned lighter, fairer, and smoother, but the most obvious change was on Uracel's face. His eyes became narrower, but their color changed to a blue darker than Rauliax's shade, and his hair grew longer and turned a light brown, a tad lighter than Solah's, and the tips of his ears sharpened like those of Siwan's. Green tattoos and markings unveiled themselves along the back of his hand and up his neck, and when the transformation was complete he simply glanced at Siwan with a grin.

The young elf quickly shifted himself so that he was performing a kneeling bow. When he rose again he asked, "Keeper Ellcadur, how?"

Uracel, now clearly an elf, sighed and said, "It's a long story." He released his hand from Solah's and used it to guide his cup of tea towards him. The cup hovered into the air and flowed gracefully into his hand before he took another sip. He set the cup down again and continued, "Two centuries ago, I started seeing visions of the future. One day, I would see the continent burn under the tyranny of an Elemarian king. Another day, I would see Valeria prosper as all its nations would be at peace with each other. I see possibilities for the future, many possibilities, but only one can be true." His eyes shifted towards Solah. "Through all of the visions, I saw you, Solah, as the weight that would tip the scale toward peace or ruin."

Before Rauliax or Solah could say anything, Siwan said, "Only the true Keepers can foresee the future."

"And I daresay Keeper Nameron has had none," Ellcadur said.

Siwan furrowed his eyebrows at him. "Is it true what the elder deniers say? Nameron was not your true brother?"

"No, he is my half-brother, but not a true Keeper."

"Then at least I was banished for good reason."

"You joined the deniers and spoke out against him?"

"Yes."

"A, hmm, rash decision. In any case, I also saw that he would try to take my place as Keeper, by force if it came down to it. I left before the situation would become that dire."

Siwan frowned. "You left your people because you were afraid to confront him?"

Ellcadur shook his head. "No. I left because I had to. Leaving Sylvanis in my half-brother's hands has delayed our eventual confrontation, but I had to do it because if nothing was done about King Arashal, it wouldn't matter who was Keeper." His head turned to Solah. "I left and wandered until the humans finally built this ship that I had seen so long ago, and then I stayed until I would find the spellbreaker because without guidance, I was sure he would fail and the vision of Valeria burning would come to pass. I can help you, Solah, but I can only do so much."

Solah was still flabbergasted by the fact that the ship's enchanter had been an elf in disguise, and a Keeper, which he presumed was a ruler of some sort, to boot! He asked to make sure, "Could you just show up and convince your people to fight with Wesar?"

"No," Ellcadur said. "Normally, it would be that easy, but I know my half-brother is a strict isolationist, and many elves will not believe that I am the true Keeper. I will have to face him, but you three must get us into Sylvanis first. It will be much better if we take Nameron by surprise. My revelation is a card I can only play once."

Rauliax nodded. "What do you think would give us the highest chance of entering the forest?"

"I do not know how the laws and rules have changed since Nameron became Keeper. Siwan, you are young and were raised under my brother's rule, what say you?"

The younger elf shrugged his shoulders. "I don't know, entry is pretty strict and the borders are well kept. Even elves that are thought to be too influenced by outside thinking are not allowed to return. Elves that are touched, such as myself. Along with other reasons."

"I understand," Ellcadur said. "If you cannot sneak or talk your way in, perhaps it would be wise to think upon the puzzle by a tree. The Sylvan's trees, I find, are most thought-invoking."

Siwan noticed that the older elf was grinning slightly, but he was not sure his confidence was deserved. "I will try to think up what I can," he said. "But I think just presenting you before the patrols would get us into Sylvanis."

"It is a risky business," Ellcadur said. "Try. If you cannot find a way then I shall go the last day we have. In the meantime, I shall return to my post as the *Reliant's* enchanter." He waved his hand, and then his elvish features shrank away until he looked like the middle-aged human he was before Solah broke his disguise. He finished his tea and handed the cup back to Rauliax. "Thank you. I wish you all luck. Don't forget the trees. They are quite pleasant to contemplate with."

After Ellcadur left, Rauliax said, "I suppose his mental facilities weren't as miswired as Lieutenant Avery and I thought."

Chapter 20

In the morning, the *Reliant* docked in Sator, a small settlement right outside of the north-eastern part of the Sylvan Forest. The forest there had a strange bubble inward and parted ways naturally for humans to build there, though the elves had always been rather uncomfortable with its existence right on their doorsteps. Nevertheless, the human settlers tried to appear as amicable as possible, and there was no wall, fence, or ward around the settlement. The settlement remained small and its buildings were both sparse in number and widely separated so that it would not intrude too much, and there was only a small platform for scout sized airships to dock and refuel on the locally abundant fields of Pyrucium.

Without any other idea on how to proceed, Rauliax, Solah, and Siwan decided to try to simply travel into the forest and rely on diplomacy to gain entrance to Sylvanis. There were no roads into the forest, so they just walked into it while Siwan guided them southwest to the heart of the elvish kingdom.

"Sylvan Forest is a rather redundant name, isn't it?" Rauliax asked while he carried the other two. He had no qualms about carrying them because it was a faster walk that way and the dragon did not mind since having Solah made him feel better than walking without any burden.

"What do you mean?" Solah asked.

"It reads like foresty forest."

Siwan laughed. "Names are silly, sometimes." He looked at Solah. "Not that it's anything to be judged, not at all."

"That's true," Rauliax said.

The trees of the forest did indeed seem more serene than the trees that the dragon or the human had ever seen. They spiraled up, many of them massive and larger than any in the forest near Windsgate, and there was an air of grandiose age about them. Rauliax could see how resting against one could make it feel like one were borrowing the wisdom of the ancient living nature around them, though he doubted there was anything he could come up with without Siwan's help.

They treaded no more than ten minutes into the forest before a group of elves descended from the canopy above. They surrounded the group and a taller elf stood forth in front of them. "You will go no further," he said. "Turn back and leave this land or we will force you out."

Siwan hopped off the dragon's back and took a step towards him, and some of the elves around the tall one raised their hands in a threatening manner. "We are here on a mission of peace and cooperation," the young elf said. "We must see Keeper Nameron."

"A mission? What business does a touched elf, a human, and a dragon have in Sylvanis?"

Rauliax took a step forward and the tall elf took a step back. "We're here representing King Devran and Wesar since you have so graciously rejected the king's messengers. War is coming, whether you want to believe it or not, and your forest is in danger."

"Not another step, dragon. There are more of us up in the trees, more than enough to break dragon scale."

"I told you, we are ambassadors and we are not here to threaten you at all."

The tall elf analyzed Rauliax for a moment, and then he said, "Amusing. The world outside must be bizarre if humans are sending dragons to represent them. But the answer is still no. We keep to ourselves, and our Keeper assures us that trouble will keep away from us. Nobody is allowed any further."

Rauliax frowned. "And there will be no way around your adamant refusal?"

"No."

The dragon whispered to Siwan, "Any ideas?"

"None," he whispered back.

Rauliax lifted his head and said, "Very well, we will turn back. For now."

The tall elf nodded. "Pray we do not meet again."

"A good morning to you too."

With that, the group of elves flashed away, presumably up into the trees above. Siwan set himself back on top of the dragon, and then Rauliax turned around and began walking slowly.

"Not even a slight bend in the rules," Siwan muttered.

"While their adherence to their Keeper's philosophy is admirable, blind obedience is not the best way to go about business when doom is looming." Rauliax sighed. "I think I will take Ellcadur's advice. These trees seem so very old, and they feel as if they have knowledge to share."

Siwan nodded. "They are old. The elders used to say that they used to be magical before the false Keeper came. It's been a long time since I've been back here. The elves do not patrol close to the edge of Sator, at least from what I remember. We can find a nice place to think there."

And indeed they did. They rode on Rauliax until they could see glimpses of Sator through the stripes of emptiness between the thick tree trunks and foliage and settled for a spot before a particularly dense tree.

Siwan stepped off the dragon first and lay against the trunk. Solah stepped off after, but he stood to look around. Rauliax pulled out a little picnic cloth and set it down onto the edge of the tree's base so that he could lie back against it. Deciding it was almost time for lunch, or at least close enough for a snack, he also took out a bag of oranges and other fruits like kiwis and bananas and offered some to both. Siwan took an orange, to Rauliax's dismay, and Solah took a banana.

The dragon chewed into his orange and suckled on it to try and get as much sweet juice as he could out of it while Siwan just ate his normally. Solah peeled his banana and kept looking around as if he were trying desperately to find some way to get into the forest. Perhaps Rauliax could just fly them in, but then he figured the elves in the trees would see and attack them. Taking the *Reliant* and fighting through would probably be a bad idea too; even if they made it he doubted there would be any elves willing to help afterward in spite of Ellcadur's authority.

Solah decided to sit down after eating half his banana and he sat on the cloth next to Rauliax. He leaned back against the tree, and he could've sworn a wind passed by.

The great tree's leaves audibly rustled louder, but the boy couldn't feel any increase or shift in the wind's velocity. He, along with Rauliax and Siwan, looked up and saw that not only were the leaves moving in waves, but also that the branches were swaying as if waking from inanimation.

Then there was a low rumble coming from inside the tree trunk that grew louder as it seemed to start to twist and move, and the trio stepped away from it. The rumbling seemed to form distinct noises, and then they heard words.

"Child of day, what magic have you done to awaken me?"

Solah looked at Rauliax for guidance. "The tree is talking, Raul, the tree is talking, is that supposed to happen?" The dragon provided no answer so he asked Siwan, "Is this elvish magic?"

Siwan's mouth seemed to be as wide agape as his was. "I don't," he stammered as he recalled. There was a smile as he finally understood. "I didn't understand what the elders really meant. They spoke like Keeper Ellcadur, remember when he said that he thought they were most thought-invoking? I thought they were all speaking metaphorically, but apparently not so!"

The low voice of the tree spoke again, "Child of night, your kin stopped communing with us a since over a hundred years ago. Why?"

"There was a law," Siwan said, half to the tree and half to his companions, "that was there before I was born. It forbid talking to trees, which I had always thought silly, but now I see what it was meant to truly mean. I have never known that the forest could speak."

The tree said, "The children of night stopped speaking to us, and then we had nobody to talk with. We forgot how, after a while, and slumbered like our neglected brethren in the land of the children of the sun."

"Humans?" Solah asked. "Are the children of the sun humans?"

"Like you," the tree said. "The presence of a son of twilight has not been felt here for many millennia, welcome."

Rauliax guessed that the tree was referring to him so he said, "Thank you."

The tree rumbled again, its echo bouncing off the trunk as if it were hollow. "I remember now the old magic you possess, son of day. It has been long since we have seen one of you. Why have you come?"

Solah had to wonder if the tree could help them. Ellcadur probably knew this would happen, and he had to believe that the forest itself would help them, so he said, "Do you know about blood magic?"

"From very long ago, yes, though it was called something else back then."

"Well, someone has found out how to use it again, and we need the elves, err, the children of the night to help fight against his army."

"We know the destruction they have wrought in lands far away from that time long ago." The tree seemed to slow in its movements. "We will not allow that destruction to come here."

"The children of night won't help us." Solah gestured for Siwan to explain.

The elf said, "A false Keeper rules us now. He won't even consider helping us fight against the blood mage. Our true Keeper seemed to think you might be able to help him take back his post."

"We know," the tree replied, "we remember the day your Keeper left. He told the Lordsap that he would return one day, but it has been too long and we did not believe anymore." The tree seemed to shake as if it was quivering. "We will help. We must help. I will wake my brethren, and you will go to Sylvanis. Where is the Keeper?"

"He's outside the forest," Siwan said. "We must find a clear way in for him, and he must be kept hidden until we face the false Keeper."

"That can be done. I must awaken the others. Come back after Mother Sun passes center of sky."

The three made their way back to the *Reliant*. They only told the captain that they might have found a diplomatic solution, but Solah and Siwan went inside the ship to find Ellcadur, still guised as the ship's enchanter, and told him about their encounter with the trees.

The Keeper was visibly saddened by the state of the Sylvan Forest's trees, but he was glad that he was right about Solah's ability to wake them. The trees, like dragons, were creatures of magic, but their connection had decayed as nobody spoke with them, and then they became silent just fifty years after his half-brother took rule.

Ellcadur acknowledged the forest's plan, and he taught Siwan a spell to signal him that they were in Sylvanis. Once he felt the signal, he would go into the forest and be taken to Sylvanis, and he would hide until Siwan gave another signal that meant the trio had either met with Keeper Nameron or the guards of Sylvanis. More probably the guards.

Then they'd have to play their hand.

They had a quick lunch and returned to the forest shortly after noon. The entire forest felt more alive, and sounds of rustling and movement became normal as they passed the trees. They found the tree that Solah had awakened and it asked them, "Are you ready to enter Sylvanis?"

"Yes," they all replied.

The big tree brought its branches down as if they were arms, and then they wrapped around Solah and Siwan's bodies. Thicker branches wrapped around Rauliax, reminding him of his encounter with both Wesar and Elemar's naturalists, and they lifted them up into the thick cluster of greenery above.

Chapter 21

The forest passed Solah, Siwan, and Rauliax along like hot potatoes, and they were handed off tree to tree by combinations of branches and vines. Solah was in the lead, which Rauliax guessed empowered the tree ahead of him since he was never dropped. Either that or nature was better than naturalists at restraining him, which was definitely not a bad thing in this situation.

Rauliax wondered where the elves dwelling in the treetops went, but only the image of the branches that handled him swatting the elves off of them came to mind. He hoped they hadn't harmed any of them, of course.

After a while, he noticed the amount of foliage grew less dense, and there were pockets of openings large enough to glimpse the small buildings inside the heart of the elvish kingdom. They were little shacks, as far as he could tell, but he could see there were lights coming from the holes of what tree trunks he could see. He had heard from the elves in Noriath that they lived inside hollowed out trees, but now he had to wonder if the trees they made habitable were alive or dead.

A few minutes later, he saw a clearing. If he didn't know better, he would've thought that the forest had carried them to another edge, but whatever lingering doubt he had was banished when he heard the deep voice of the tree that was holding him speak. "Careful now," it said, "I'm setting you down in the heart of the forest."

A batch of leaves parted ways in front of him, and he saw that his companions were already on their feet. He was carried through the opening and gently placed onto the ground, his legs a little shaky from the definitely *unique* form of transportation he just partook in.

Rauliax took a good look at their drop off zone. They were in a rather large clearing, but they were surrounded by a ring of trees that almost seemed artificially placed to appear evenly spaced. He supposed that if they could move, then it would definitely be possible for such an unnatural pattern to appear.

Solah and Siwan were both in front of the dragon, and they also looked at the clearing with some amount of wonder. The young elf's hands seemed to flash a small light, and then he said, "The Keeper's Rest," Siwan whispered. "I've never seen it before."

"And you will not see it for long," a voice from behind the group said.

An elf, similar in appearance to Ellcadur, appeared from between the space between the settling trees. He bore the very same marks and tattoos that Ellcadur possessed.

Siwan's eyes focused behind Rauliax and looked at the elf behind him. "Keeper Nameron."

Before anyone could say anything else, there were several bright flashes of inside the little clearing. Six elves appeared out of nowhere around them, and the tall one that had barred anyone from crossing the border appeared next to Nameron.

"Keeper!" the tall elf said. He kneeled and continued, "I am sorry, there was some blasted wind or something that kept us out of the treetops, and we could not guard the skies. It might have been dirty human magic, but it seemed as if the very trees kept us from our posts."

Nameron smiled. "Your teleportation speed is still admirable, Guardian Tybil. But I do not believe they flew in here on the dragon, and you are not to blame for this trespass." He glanced at the trees for a moment since he was an old enough elf to be aware of the possibility of their actions. He shrugged his shoulders, knowing that they would not be treacherous and that he would've known if his brother had tried to awaken them himself, and then turned to Siwan and frowned. "Touched elf, why are you here?"

One of the elves accompanying Tybil stepped forward. He looked just about as young as Siwan and said, "Keeper, I know him. He is Siwan Omicon, banished for his inability to control his magic and his corrupted mind."

"Well, thank you for the nice compliments, Percival," Siwan said. He had his hands tucked behind his back, and there he willed another small flash: the second signal.

Keeper Nameron's frown became harsher. "Why are you here?"

Rauliax spoke up and tried diplomacy. "There is a threat, master elf, coming from the east over the mountains. King Arashal's army of flying ships will come and face King Devran's army, and without your help the western lands will burn, including the Sylvan Forest."

"Is that why the king has been harassing me with a ridiculous amount of messengers? Has he become so desperate that he asks a dragon to represent him?"

"We desperately seek your aid, if that is what you are asking." He added in a little lie, "I am also here to represent my own realm. Rauliax Moonsilver, son of Wyrst Moonsilver, member of the Dragon Council, at your service." He gave a short bow and continued, "The dragons of Noriath understand the threat, master elf. If you pledge your forces, we will pledge ours."

"No. The elves will stay here as we always have, and we will persevere even if this King Arashal plans to attack us. We do not need any help, and we will not give any. This is your last warning, leave and do not come back, or we will be forced to escort your bodies out."

As if to further enforce the deathly seriousness of the Keeper's warning, several more elves flashed into the clearing with their hands poised and ready to cast.

Defeated, Solah and Siwan had no choice but to climb up onto Rauliax. However, before the dragon could unfurl his wings to depart, another elf jumped gracefully out of the tree that had originally put Rauliax down, and all eyes fell upon him.

"Ellcadur," Nameron whispered, low enough so that nobody could hear.

All of the elves in the clearing looked either Siwan's age or younger, and none recognized the old Keeper. The green tattoos on his skin, however, were unmistakably that of a Keeper's, and there were some gasps of surprise as he descended upon them.

Rauliax watched the old elf with keen intensity. This move was the most powerful and only remaining card in their hand, and if he didn't proceed well then things could get messy rather quickly.

"All of you here are young," Ellcadur said, "but your parents must have taught you about the past Keepers of the forest." There quiet murmurs of acknowledgement. "Then you all must know of how Keeper Ellcadur disappeared two hundred years ago. I have returned."

More silence followed. None of the young elves were sure what to make of his appearance. Nameron seized the confusion and said, "Lies, this is clearly some human or dragon trickery! Lay down your guise, imposter, and depart this forest or face the fury of its guardians."

The true Keeper of the Sylvan Forest was no fool, of course, and he was prepared. He pointed at the tree that dropped Rauliax before. "Lordsap, am I Keeper Ellcadur, who left this realm two centuries ago?"

There was a deep rumbling, characteristic now of the trees before they spoke, and then they heard. "You are, and long have we waited for your return."

Hearing the old wooden master of The Keeper's Rest caused some of the elves to drop their hands and turn their backs to the others.

"More trickery," Nameron said. "Tales your elders might have told you about talking trees are just that, tales and fantasy!"

As if ready for his falsifications, all of the trees surrounding them began to move and shake as they grouped closer towards Lordsap. "We are disappointed you would call us so," the great tree said.

Ellcadur seemed to grin as he continued playing the game, determined to win without bloodshed. "Indeed you must think all the guardians of the forest to be fools if you think they'd believe one human, two elves, and a dragon could animate a whole grove of nature."

Unfortunately for Nameron, curiosity caught his tongue and he said without thinking, "How did you awaken the trees without me knowing?"

Ellcadur restrained giving Solah a wink and just said, "There are things only a true Keeper would know."

With that remark, another handful of elves stepped over to side with Ellcadur, leaving the two contesting forces evenly matched. Nameron knew he couldn't let this battle of words continue, so he glared at Tybil and nearly screamed, "Guardian! What are you waiting for? Remove these imposters and control your troops!"

"Yes, Keeper!" The tall elf raised his hand and, along with the rest of the elves still under his command, began casting spells by waving their arms.

The elves that sided with Ellcadur stood flabbergasted at what

Nameron was about to allow to happen. Ellcadur noticed their confusion, reaffirmed their choice, and said, "Defend yourselves! If anything, this should only prove who the real imposter is."

Ellcadur's elves stood their ground and erected a barrier around their side much like the ones projected around airships. Pretty soon, a literal rainbow of colors erupted as Nameron's elves sent a barrage of flame, lightning, and ice shards. The very earth seemed to rise as some used naturalist magic to twist the grass before the barrier and grow them to an immense size, and then the blades sharpened as they slashed against the shield.

Nameron's side created no defense, but there was no opportunity for a counter-strike: their assault was simply too deadly to afford even a small weakness in defense. Ellcadur, meanwhile, casually stepped behind Rauliax and hid himself behind his wing, and when the dragon turned his head to ask what he was doing, he found that he had vanished.

Meanwhile, Siwan was trying to figure out what he could do to help. He could not aid in the generation of the barrier; with his lack of control he would not be able to synchronize with the other elves, and he might even cause enough a disturbance to break it altogether. He held back on attacking as well since he did not wish to harm the elves on the other side. Their ignorance was not their fault, though it greatly disturbed him that they would attack their fellow elves without even a hint of objection. He stared through, trying to peer through the crashing elements, and saw something that almost made him lose that restraint. Percival, who had been quite the bully to him before he was banished from the forest, was hurling fire from his hands with the widest smile he had ever seen on him, even wider than when he had successfully thrashed him when they were younger. The fire he summoned seemed to sharpen the lighting and shadows on his face, and he looked as if he were attacking his fellow elves with great glee.

Solah, meanwhile, was absolutely unsure on what he should've been doing. He thought to stand between them and hope they all target him instead, which would cancel all their attacks, but then if he stepped through the barrier it would be nullified too, and then everyone within would become vulnerable. His hand gripped around the handle of Rauliax's tooth-dagger, still tucked by his waist in its sheath, but he didn't draw it. He was too awestruck by the flourish of colors smashing outside, but then he managed to tear his eyes away from the magical explosions impacting the shield. He saw Siwan staring out, his eyes seeming like they were seething with rage. His hands were clenched, and steam seemed to be rising from them.

Rauliax was just as confused as the other two. He saw Ellcadur disappear, and he assumed that the old elf had some sort of plan. But of course he couldn't be sure, and he knew the old saying about assuming things. The dragon could wreak some havoc if he needed to, however distasteful it seemed to him, but he was hoping the real Keeper could resolve this somehow without resorting to combat. He peered through, looking as deeply as Siwan was through the barrier, and he noticed that he could not find Nameron anymore.

In the midst of the smokescreen of elements, nobody else had noticed that both of the Keepers had disappeared. The barrier was beginning to fail under the unrelenting assault, and it was turning a familiarly red tint. The elves under it knew it too, and just a few seconds later they ducked, jumped, and rolled out of the way of the crashing elements. Rauliax dodged the concentrated blast of twirling elements by hopping to the side, but a stray ray of ice aimed its way at Siwan. He raised his hand to raise a shield of his own, but Solah stepped in front of the frozen beam before he finished, and the entire stream of frozen water disappeared from existence. In the chaos, nobody else noticed.

Powering the barrier had caused many of the elves to start trailing blood out of their ears, and they had already expended what power they could safely use. Most all of them scurried away from the battlefield before Guardian Tybil and his troops could conjure another attack.

That just left Rauliax, Solah, and Siwan. The dragon knew they couldn't last long against so many, and he scurried to pick up the other two so they could fly away. The elves were quicker, however, and they threw another wave of spells against them, all of them having switched to fire attacks now. With that many mages in tandem, the blasts of flame were more than enough to melt dragon scale, and Rauliax was forced to side-step to dodge the attacks. Siwan was still standing behind Solah, and the spellbreaker's body broke whatever flame would've consumed him, and if Rauliax weren't busy avoiding the licks of flame himself he would've wondered how Solah's power could even cancel out the heat radiation. The dragon could feel the heat, but as long as he avoided direct contact with the flames he knew he would be fine.

The elves were visibly surprised too when they noticed that Solah and Siwan had not been turned into a pile of ash. They were beginning to tire as well, and some had some beads of blood dripping down their earlobes.

Siwan had seen Rauliax get targeted by the flames, and it roused an anger from inside him. He had his best friend die because he wasn't there to stop it. Ozzari died to protect him, to keep him hidden and safe. Rauliax took him under his wing after Ozzy and Malyfar were gone, and he would be damned if he just sat and watched and hoped that he could handle himself. With a vengeful ferocity, he stepped in front of Solah while the other elves recuperated, and then he unleashed his own brand of fire.

The only sort of control he forced upon the fire was to go forward, not back to Rauliax, and it was the bare minimum of direction. Fueled by Ozzari's memory, Siwan had his flames burn and consume everything in front of him, and Tybil's soldiers, unlike the elves that made their barrier, had no way to escape the unshackled fires.

But he couldn't stop them. The fires burned hotter and grew larger, and they started spreading to the trees. He clenched his eyes shut and tried to concentrate as hard as he could, but the fires were out of his control the moment he had conjured them and they had only grown more ravenous since. He silently cursed himself for allowing it to happen, but that self-hate only destroyed what little control he had, and the fires began spreading all around him, even towards Rauliax.

And then he felt a touch on his shoulder. It was cold, but it felt like a good cold. His fire disappeared, and then he looked at the hand. His eyes followed the arm up to meet Solah's earthly eyes.

"A-are you okay?" the spellbreaker asked.

Siwan rested his hand over the one on his shoulder, almost grasping it in gratitude. "I am. I almost burned down the Sylvan Forest again."

"You, uhh, well, there's nothing left but. Yeah."

Siwan turned his attention forward, and he saw what his friend was trying to say. There was nothing left of Guardian Tybil or his troops besides charred skeletons.

Almost as if he had sensed what he was thinking, Solah said, "Don't feel bad. They would've turned us into that if you hadn't done what you did."

Siwan sighed. "Percival, you damn fool." Then he looked back at Solah. "It's okay. I don't regret it."

"You're okay?"

"I'm okay."

"You're not tired out?"

"No."

"That seemed like a lot of magic you used though. Why aren't your brains leaking out?"

"Controlling a spell uses energy too. If I just unleash a spell without control, then it's almost as if I were manipulating the flow of magic naturally. I can maintain such a spell for almost as long as a human could, but then I destroy everything, and the technique doesn't work for more intricate spell work like enchanting or creating barriers. Elves can't do that normally since that usually ends up with burned down cities and forests. Part of why I was banished. Thanks for stopping me from lighting up Sylvanis, Solah."

The boy nodded. "That's good to know. I think we'll play together really well in a battle, don't you think?"

"If this one was any indication, definitely. I won't need to worry about control as long as you're nearby."

"I'll stay close."

"Thank you."

Chapter 22

Rauliax was tired. One of his wings had been slightly singed, but otherwise he was just tired from all the hopping and leaping he had to do, and the burnt remains across the charred clearing barely registered in his mind. However, he probably was the only one who noticed that Ellcadur and Nameron had disappeared, and he twirled around once to try and find them.

When he made a full revolution of his body, his eyes rested on Solah, whose arm was still holding on to Siwan's shoulder, and tried to form a difficult smile despite the circumstances. They were both alive and well, and though the loss of life was regrettable, there was no way that they could've averted it.

The ground was in smoky ruins, and there was a trail of smoke that ended at the Lordsap's base: the magic fire had almost burned to the trees, and that would've been most disastrous. There was a rustle, and then an elf leapt out of the old tree.

Ellcadur landed a little less gracefully than his first appearance, but it was still a good performance. He gestured his hand to bring something down, and Lordsap complied. Bound by vines and branches, Nameron appeared out of the brush and hung limply.

Ellcadur noticed skeletal remains on the ground, blackened beyond all recognition, and shook his head. "I did not hope for this to happen."

Siwan hung his head in shame. "I'm sorry."

The Keeper shook his head again, this time with more conviction. "No, it's better than the alternative. Solah would have lived, at least until they devised a way to restrain him, but you and the dragon would not have."

Siwan didn't reply, but Rauliax took a step up and asked, "What happened? I saw you disappear and then, well, *that.*"

191

"Easy. Veiled myself, and then went around and veiled him before hurling him towards the trees. They took care of the rest. Strong fellows, you know."

"Amazing that nobody noticed."

"Not really. I'm rather good at sneaking around."

Rauliax smiled. "Sounds like someone I know. What will happen now?"

"Now? You'll get an elvish army, as many as you can cram onto the *Reliant*. Then, I suppose we go to war."

Keeper Ellcadur had no difficulty returning to his role as leader of his people. The older elves rejoiced at his return since most had suspected Nameron of being a fake, and any worries about Ellcadur being another imposter was diffused when the forest itself defended his birthright. The young and impressionable were dazzled by the truth that Keeper Nameron had hidden from their lives, and they were amongst the first to answer Ellcadur's call to arms.

Nameron was locked away, and there was no animosity between the true Keeper and the families of the elves that were slain. It was a bad decision made by those individuals, and neither party would allow such foolishness to forge bad blood.

Captain Dillan and the crew of the *Reliant* were delighted to hear the good news, and they cleared out as much room as they could to accommodate the elves. It would be nearly a day's flight back to Windsgate, and they needed to arrive well fed and rested, so there was not much they could throw out that they had to replace with stocks of food and water anyway. Preparations went well into the night, and Ellcadur had assured them that they would be ready the next evening after sunset.

True to their Keeper's word, a trickle of elves emerged from the forest in the afternoon and walked into Sator to board the *Reliant*. The trickle turned into a stream, and by sunset the ship was, as Captain Dillan expected, crammed full to the brim.

"All in all, about a thousand of the best mages we elves have to offer," Ellcadur said to Captain Dillan on the quarterdeck when he finally boarded. "I pray it will be enough to tip the scales."

"Me too," the captain replied. He looked over the old elf's

shoulder at another officer standing by the helm. "Donnovan, have you located Uracel yet?"

"No, and I've no idea where he might've gone off too," the signals officer replied.

Ellcadur tried to withhold a grin, but he failed rather miserably. "Captain," he said, "I believe you are owed a little explanation."

"Explanation? I suppose I would like to know why you agreed to help us so easily. The dragon wouldn't tell me how he did it."

"I believe seeing would be quicker than explaining." Before the captain could respond to his vague statement, the Keeper motioned his hand, and then he was Uracel again.

The captain's eyes went wide, and he barked out a laugh. "Well, I'll be! An elf, the lord of the elves no less, has been part of my crew! Donnovan, you didn't sense anything different with him?"

"No sir," Donnovan said. "Feels human to me, nice trick, sir."

Captain Dillan forced out another laugh. "Nice trick indeed! I suppose you just walked in there and told them all to fight with us?"

Ellcadur's smile remained, though feigned now. "Just so, captain," he mildly lied.

The captain let out another laugh, and then he asked, "Are you ready to depart now, sir?"

"I am."

The captain nodded with a large grin and directed his attention to the helmsman. "Take us out."

"Aye, releasing docking clamps," the trainee helmsman said as he wrapped his hands around the levers and wheels that controlled the ship. "I'm not going to be flying the ship in battle, am I, sir?"

"No, do you think I'm a good captain or not? Leaving the ship in the hands of a trainee in a battle for our very survival, why I'd be a laughingstock of every other captain in the fleet!"

"Aye sir, thank you sir!"

The *Reliant* rose, its fans becoming visibly louder, and the last fickle light directly from the sun yet unblocked by the horizon shimmered along all the railings, fan ducts, and everything metal on the airship. Some of the elves figured out a way to weave more speed into the levimages' spells that were already boosting the cruise speed, and Captain Dillan expected they would arrive at Windsgate by early morning before noontime instead of a whole day.

Rauliax, Solah, and Siwan had to share the captain's cabin for the night with the original owner and Keeper Ellcadur. They didn't mind since there was still plenty of room, however, and Rauliax prepared a table of late night tea for when they retired to their room. When he reached into his mouth to grab a kettle, however, he remembered that he still had the radio and he pulled it out instead.

It was still tuned to the ship's frequency, 125.5, and he turned it on. He clicked the button to the side and said, "Priscilla, you there?"

He waited. About ten seconds later, there was another click from the radio, and then he heard her voice.

"Wow," she said. "I was going to call you when I got home, but I suppose now is as good a time as any other."

"Oh, you're not home? I can wait."

"No, I'm just walking out of the Council chamber right now. I have really good news."

The radio clicked again to signal the transmission ended, and Rauliax waited for her to continue. When she didn't, he clicked it and said, "Well?"

"What, you're not going to try and guess?"

"The Eldest voted in our favor?"

"Guess what?" The transmission ended again, and he assumed the woman was just playing games with him now.

He played along though and said back, "What?"

"For once in your life, you're actually right."

"You're kidding."

"No, I'm not, Raul."

"Oh. What convinced him?"

There was a strange sound from the radio, almost like a small laugh, and then he heard her say, "Well, I told daddy that if he didn't vote to send the army, then Raul would go off to battle all by himself, and if he were to die then I'd never ever forgive him for not sending help and I'd never dare love anyone else ever again and I'd never have any children, ever!"

"What."

When Rauliax unclicked the radio button, all he heard was roaring laughter. As Priscilla regained control of herself, she said, "I wish I could've seen your face. No, father voted for us because of Solah."

"Because of Solah?"

"What, is the reception bad? That's exactly what I said."

Rauliax snorted. "I know, come on Priscilla now's not the time."

"It is a woeful time we live in when I can't even tease you anymore. But yes, father said he saw something in Solah he has very rarely seen before. Conviction. Said the boy seemed to truly believe in what he was fighting for. I understand really, being a political leader of sort's means you see nothing but lies and veils all the time, so I guess that tipped him over."

"Well, I admit the boy has a certain naivety about him, but I couldn't have guessed it would've borne us so."

"Even the smallest things can have a great effect, Raul. You know that." Right after she released the radio, she clicked it again. "Hey, you called me first, what for?"

"Oh, right! The elves have joined us!"

"Really? That's excellent news! Are they all on your ship?"

"Yes, they're all on the *Reliant*, as many as we could cram."

"Do you have time to swing back to Noriath?"

"The admiral gave us a week, so we have another two days. I think we could spare one for a detour, why?"

"They're going to start outfitting the army with saddles tomorrow so mages could ride on them. Now that you have the elves, it would be much easier to outfit them and pair the dragons up, and they can have some time to get used to it."

"I see. Let me get the captain." Rauliax gestured to Solah and Siwan, who weren't really eavesdropping since it was impossible not to overhear their conversation in the room, and they rushed out the door to find the captain.

A few minutes later, Captain Dillan came running through the door, somewhat out of breath, with a mad look of happiness on his face. He looked right at Rauliax and asked, "You're serious?"

"Yes, captain!"

"Of course we'll divert to Noriath! I'll inform the admiral, my god I'll be giddy on this for a while! We have the dragons and the elves, no way we can lose now!"

Rauliax smiled. "Let's not be too hasty now," he said, "war's not won purely on force, after all."

The captain restrained his smile, but it was still quite clear he was happy as a clam. "Yes, of course. I'll send off orders now."

Chapter 23

The *Reliant* returned and docked at Noriath at the height of night, and again two dragons had come to escort them to the University with lights that had flashed red and green from their mouths. The yellow Council messenger had met them once the air settled around the ship, and he had explained that all one hundred and fifty dragons of the army were going to the fight.

"Never before has there been a battle such as this," he had said, "and you know how eager they might be to put the skills they've learned their entire lives to the test."

So it was that in the morning of the sixth day allotted by Admiral Lina, a hundred and fifty of Ellcadur's most elite of his best mages went down to the Council's Grove to pair with the hundred and fifty dragons from Noriath's army.

Hammer, anvil, and needle from both the native elves and dragonsmiths created the saddles and harnesses for the entire force, and General Moonsilver joined with Captain Dillan and Keeper Ellcadur on the quarterdeck of the *Reliant*. The triumvirate made up the three representatives of their respective races, at least until Admiral Lina took command for the human part.

Rauliax met his father on board while Ellcadur was down in the Council's Grove and Captain Dillan was under deck with Officer Donnovan communicating to the admiral. The young silver dragon smiled when he saw his darker father, and then they shared a hug.

"Dad! You're going to be fighting too?"

"I'm the General of the Dragon Army, what do you think I'm going to do?"

"Err, I suppose that's true."

The older dragon smiled though. "As I've been told by this fine vessel's captain, Ellcadur and I will be staying on the command ship so we can, well, issue commands."

"Oh! That's right, the *Corona* won't enter the battle unless the admiral deems it necessary."

"Yes. A strange policy, I think, but I suppose it does keep commands flowing uninterrupted."

"And you won't be in harm's way."

Wyrst seemed to look unhappy when he heard that. "You're worried about me?"

"Uhh, yes, of course I would be."

"Son, maybe I should go in and fight so you could finally understand how your mother and I feel about you always flying off to who knows where."

Rauliax backed his head away. He didn't want his father fighting, and he never realized how worried his old man would be, especially since it was rather likely he would be fighting with Solah on his back. He wanted to mentally slap himself again: he also just realized Solah was part of his family now, and it would've been devastating to Nama and his parents if they were to lose both the boy and himself. "Sorry, dad. I'm sorry. I know I've been, ah, ignorant of, well-"

"It's okay son. The captain tells me what a valuable asset you and Solah will be, so it's on me to figure out some way to keep you two safe."

"I hope you understand that a cloud of dragons around us would be horribly ineffective, right?"

Wyrst smiled. "Yes, but I'll figure something out."

"Thanks, dad."

"Just don't get yourself killed out there."

Rauliax gave a sharp nod, and then he walked back, since flying would've been rather showy over such a small distance for his tastes, to the captain's cabin. Inside, Solah and Siwan were sitting on his rug across from Priscilla.

"I have no empirical evidence," she was saying to Solah, "but I'm completely sure that she's becoming younger. I don't know why her age is reversing. I'll need more data, and I'll try and get it done before you come back." When she noticed Rauliax come in, she raised an eye ridge at him and said, "You're all going to come back." She coughed and stuttered as the other dragon approached her. "So you can hear my results."

"Priscilla," Rauliax said as he sat down onto his haunches mere inches away from her.

"Raul." Her tail seemed to slither beside them and tap onto his. Then she bumped her nose against the other dragon's snout and whispered, "Do you really have to go?"

"I do."

She closed her eyes and felt the other dragon's muzzle a little more before pulling away. "Okay. I promise I'll get you that grant for your study on atomic energy when you return."

"You mean it?"

She nodded.

"That's quite an incentive. I think with that offer along with, you know, the threat of death, I'll be quite sure to be careful."

She managed a weak smile. "Humor is an effective method of concealing stress, so fine. I'll take your word for it."

"It's also an effective method for subtly insulting people," he said, "and I suppose I'll promise to...to do it less often to you."

Priscilla dramatically wiped her forehead and flapped her wings so that she rose backwards onto two feet. "Oh good, I wouldn't be able to live without a daily dose of at least one of your snide remarks!"

"Humor helps conceal fear too."

Priscilla set herself back down on all fours, tucked down her wings, and looked away from him. She walked towards the exit and said, "I'll see you soon, Raul. Solah, don't forget your promise."

"Something will happen to me first before I'll let it happen to Raul," the boy said. While that was meant to assure Priscilla, the sentiment didn't comfort Rauliax at all.

Once she had departed, Rauliax lay down on the rug and started studying a book on airship tactics that Ensign Waters had given him on their way back to Noriath, and he called Solah and Siwan over so that he could show them the classes of ships that existed, their designs, and their weak points.

Afterwards, they devised a general plan of attack: Siwan and Solah would both be harnessed on Rauliax since the two of them gave him no extra burden. After Solah nullifies an enemy airship's shields, Rauliax would carve a opening in the hull with his intensified light beam attack, and then Siwan would unleash a furnace of fire and burn the ship's wooden hull away while spewing some into the opening to blast them inside and out.

It was a sound plan, assuming they could fly close enough without being shot down. Siwan didn't possess the power to control the intricate spellweaving necessary for a barrier that would hold against any more powerful than a punch, and there was no way a dragon could dodge cannon fire as dense as it would be in a battle of such proportions. They couldn't do it, sadly, despite how effective the maneuver appeared.

By the afternoon, some of dragons of the army began flying south to Windsgate. They left as soon as they were ready, and General Moonsilver had given the first one to leave, his second-in-command, an enchanted human radio so that they could keep in contact. They flew on ahead first, usually in pairs, and they had planned to group up a little north of Windsgate before continuing to join the Third Fleet.

The *Reliant* elected to depart late in the evening after most of the dragon army had flown off since they would catch up rather quickly with their levimages and elvish enhancements. The captain didn't waste that extra time, however, and he had hired several dragons to install further armaments onto the *Reliant*. Dragons had quickly filled the deck with extra cannons that drilled into the hull, and by the time they departed there were enough to rival the offensive power of a large frigate.

The dragon designed cannons, Rauliax noted, shined with a bright metallic gleam, the complete opposite of the plain black ones that humans used. They had a half-tube outside that bent spiraling upwards from the feeding opening, and on the half-tube they could load several cannonballs. There were pairs of hand grips further behind the cannons for more moment and leverage to aim them easier, and the ends of them curved sharply upwards to where a button could be pressed to fire the weapon. Even though they were sized larger to fit dragon hands, elves and humans could just as easily hold onto them.

The cannons were designed so that they could be fired rapidly in succession, unlike human cannons, and relied not on magic, but on the best engineering dragons had to offer: human cannons were usually fired by using a spark to ignite the powdered Pyrucium mix inside from, what Rauliax was told, trainee and ensign lightning and fire elementalists, though any mage could easily create the small spark if required. Dragon cannons, on the other hand, utilized a powder reservoir with a knockback hammer that rearmed itself with every shot. Another bunch of them, he had been told, were installed in

Farrain since the king's original request. One of the workers mentioned carrying one all the way to the capital to test on a new airship, but Rauliax thought nothing of it.

While Rauliax was watching the workers, who were mostly much stronger and more muscular than himself, he had finally learned what kind of mage Captain Dillan was. The dragons had lifted the cannons down onto the ship, and he had seen the captain help out by summoning tendrils of green vines to position their emplacements better before the workers let them drop into place. After he and the ship's other naturalists had finished positioning the cannons, the dragons came down to hammer the rather large nails on the bases of the cannons into the ship's wooden hull so that they would safely stay in place.

All in all, it was fascinating for Rauliax to watch. It amazed him what a huge divide there was in dragon intelligence: in the University, there were no other species that could dare to compare in matters of science, engineering, and mathematics. It was the University's engineers that designed these cannons, undoubtedly. At the base of the mountain, below the lower half of its height, the majority of dragons lived with only enough intelligence needed to live their daily lives, and they were often misinformed about a great many things. Most of the Dragon Council was like this too, but as he had learned, Malyfar was only obfuscating stupidity in his case. He doubted the worker dragons knew any more about the cannons besides the fact that they were weapons, and that they were to be bolted into the ship's deck. Then again, it was not prudent to assume, as he had learned from Malyfar, and it was just as possible that some of them had studied at least a short while in the University.

When evening came, all preparations were complete. The *Reliant* departed Noriath, and once more Solah, Siwan, and Rauliax watched the Homespire fade away into the distance, darkening as the sun fell but brightening as the city's lights flickered on. Their usual lookout spot had been partially obstructed by the new cannons, but they looked between them nevertheless. Either they would see it again, or this would be the last time they could view the majestic lights along the mountain.

Chapter 24

Admiral Lina had awoken early in the morning, so early that there was no sign of light yet besides the basking white glow from the moon. She stared out at the stars on the balcony in front of the bridge and almost wanted to dance in pure elation. She was happy when she had heard the elves would be joining their fight, but when Captain Dillan had told her the dragons were coming too, well, she nearly tossed her royally embroidered gold-trim hat off the ship in joy.

She knew she should've been sleeping, but the excitement kept her awake. Their numerical disadvantage had been patched up, but she had to incorporate the elves and dragons into her tactical overview so that they would be effective combat units. A thousand elves, fifteen percent of them on dragonback, would have to be distributed through the fleet to bolster their strength, and she still wasn't sure how to effectively strategize for such a massive battle. She doubted there was any way to prepare, and she knew she'd have to adapt quickly when the battle began.

They had lost radio contact, mundane and magical, with the Second Fleet since they engaged at Imilune, which was expected when the entire Elemarian fleet could devote their signalers to jamming all frequencies. To check on the Second Fleet, the admiral had sent several scout ships to fly back and forth between them, and by all reports the Elemarian fleet was advancing at a rate that assured the *Reliant* would arrive in time with the cavalry, exactly the amount of time she had promised to Rauliax and Solah. The last scout had reported in at midnight, and they guessed that the bulk of the Second Fleet would rejoin them approximately an hour after sunrise, and then the artillery ships would come in with Arashal's fleet on their tail. When that news had been heard, Benson managed to make her go to bed in relative peace. If she had to guess, she would've said that she had probably gotten five hours of rest before waking up and walking up to the bridge.

She should've stayed in bed, she knew it. Old Warp Master Benson had constantly nagged at her all night to get some sleep, but she was simply far too invigorated to fall asleep despite her attempt at counting sheep. She knew the old man was right, but she was simply restless. Besides, five hours was plenty enough rest to prevent completely crashing during the day, right?

Her high levels of energy also made her vision rather acute, and she kept counting the number of navigation and anti-collision lights on the airships that hovered in front of the *Corona* just to pass the time. She was lost in the rhythm of the *Firestorm*'s flashing red beacon light, but then she noticed another smaller but lighter red flash off the side of the ship towards the horizon.

She tried to see through the darkness, but she didn't see any other lights accompany the flash after. There was no hole of blackness around the flash to indicate that it was from an airship, and she didn't see it again. For some time she looked off curiously to the horizon, but she saw nothing for such a long time that she thought she had just started imagining things from her excitement.

But then it happened again. The flash was flaring red, almost as if it were an explosion. More followed, each at random intervals, and then she saw what she knew was an emergency flare.

She backed away from the edge of the platform's railing and ran into the bridge. She hadn't expected this to happen, especially not with the last scout's report, but in hindsight she should've expected the possibility. She descended down the *Corona*, as quickly as she safely could down the spiraling stairs, and practically flew into the senior crew quarters to awaken the ship's master signals officer.

The Third Fleet was at full combat readiness by the time the Second Fleet rejoined them over Windsgate. Admiral Lina had seen, after they had come closer, that the flashes were, in fact, explosions and fire. All in all, the artillery units in the Second Fleet did a fine enough job until the end: they had only lost two ships when they had been ambushed by cruisers that had shut off their navigation lights, but at least they were able to take down one of the Elemarian battlecruisers.

Their destruction, however, had caused the Second Fleet to lose considerable repellent fire, and they had to turn from guerilla warfare to flat out retreat. The admiral had sent a message to the *Reliant* to try and hasten their arrival. He was sure Captain Dillan would try his best, but it seemed that the battle was going to begin without him or his reinforcements. They would have to hold until their arrival.

And when they arrived, there had to be enough fight left in the fleet for reinforcements to matter.

Admiral Lina mimicked the enemy's tactic and had all of her ships turn off their lights. Without clear targets and fearing friendly fire, the Elemarian fleet stayed back as she expected they would do, and even old Benson said it was a clever move. Still, it would only buy them enough time until there was enough of the morning light to distinguish all of the airships, and that would be only a few more hours from now.

When she had contacted the *Reliant*, her lieutenant answered and fetched the captain who was, unlike herself, actually getting some rest. Captain Dillan would try to push his levimages and engines as hard as he could safely do, but the dragons could only fly at their own pace. The addition of a scout class ship wouldn't really upset the balance of power, but she hoped that she could at least utilize Solah's power to great benefit.

In any case, she had to keep the fleet in one piece until they arrived. In the bridge, she linked up the *Corona*'s many signalers with that of the rest of the fleet and issued orders so that the Second Fleet integrated themselves neatly into the Third Fleet to form the last defense against Elemar. Under the cover of darkness, she used the signalers' ability to detect and communicate with each other to order the fleet's ships, somewhat loosely for safety, to form up. Her dreadnoughts, eight of them, created their own orbit of airships around them and acted as the capital ships of the Wesarian fleet. They formed a staggered line in front of the *Corona* and held their position, waiting cautiously until the first light of dawn.

And when the light shone through the horizon, she saw them though the bridge's window. Fifty-five Elemarian ships, hovering in delta formation, densely packed around their seven dreadnoughts, and the *Eclipse* much farther behind. Her fleet of thirty eight stood at the ready, and then the entire Elemarian fleet began moving.

"Admiral," one of the bridge's signals officers said, "the fleet has secured frequencies 132.17, 118.5, and 121.5. *Corona*'s frequency 122.7 also secured."

"Excellent," Admiral Lina said. "Tell the fleet 132.17 for battle commands, 118.5 for general chatter, and 121.5 for emergencies."

"Aye sir."

The senior crew had already reported to their stations, yet Benson still remained on the bridge to offer his sage advice if needed, but the time for his skill was needed more now. "Warp Master," Admiral Lina said, "report to your station with your team."

"Will do, admiral," the old mage replied.

Once Benson and his transporters teleported themselves up to the highest crow's nest, Admiral Lina looked over to her second-in-command. "Fleet Lieutenant Holden, you have the bridge. Signaler Grayson, signaler Moreau, with me to the viewpoint."

The Fleet Lieutenant, otherwise called the *Corona's* captain when the admiral was not on board, nodded at her while the two signals officers she called for joined her and left the bridge to the platform balcony outside.

The two signalers were both ten years younger than the admiral, but she knew they were of the highest quality to serve on the flagship of the fleet. On the balcony, she looked out onto the battlefield and saw the entire Elemarian fleet stay in formation but steadily flow towards her fleet. There were too many to count, too many to make sense of, and doubt started to consume what little confidence she had. How was she supposed to come up with a plan for this incoherent mess?

But that was why she was the admiral. If she couldn't do it, it was most likely nobody else had any idea either. In fact, she wasn't sure if Admiral Morit on the *Eclipse* had any idea what he was doing either: their ships were organized, sure, but they were simply sent on a head-on attack. They'd definitely not be organized after they met, and she supposed that was when she truly had to think on her feet.

The *Corona* retreated to a safe distance as the *Eclipse* did not advance with its army, and then the battle began. Admiral Lina heard the first shots from the middle position, the head of the delta-wing striking against the forward battlecruiser guarding the dreadnought behind it. The two forces melded together after, and only the colors of their flying banners, blue and green, separated friend from foe.

On her right-most flank, she saw the red trimmed *Firestorm* get swarmed by a large force, and she guessed they were trying to destroy the fleet starting from one end of the line down.

"Grayson, battle command." In nearly an instant, the signaler had created a bubble that he grasped in the palm of his hand. She spoke towards the bubble, "*Firestorm,* I need you to move away from the capital ships, stay out of range and stay alive!"

Another voice that she recognized as Captain Fourier's replied, "Yes admiral, we'll maneuver as best as we can."

Sure enough, she saw the dreadnought back off and head towards the next capital ship up the line, the *Razor,* and their defending airships joined forces, although one frigate from the *Firestorm*'s group had already been destroyed by then when it was caught before it could escape with the group.

With two dreadnoughts holding the edge of the line, Admiral Lina was confident she could direct her attention elsewhere. Down in the middle, the battlecruiser that had taken the brunt of the spearhead attack was retreating, under the protection of two more battlecruisers and a frigate, but the capital ship was taking heavy fire. The enemy there ignored the limping battlecruiser and targeted the dreadnought, probably hoping to take it down first and break morale.

"*Ivan, June, Lightsworn,* stop helping the *Alexander,*" the admiral said, referring to the retreating battlecruiser, "they're not taking fire. Move to protect the *Oathshield,* prioritize their middle-class ships."

There wasn't an audible reply, but the ships did as she ordered. The rest of the battle was as chaotic as she had expected, and the booming of the cannons became inseparably indistinguishable: she could no longer hear the initial firings as they had just become one constant noise.

Spells flung everywhere, and shields rotated around and changed colors in a clockwork fashion. Occasionally, there would be a vessel that fell from the battle and crashed into the forests around Windsgate, and her heart would sink every time it was one of hers. Eventually, she became so disheartened with the course of the battle that the northern horizon took more of her attention than it should have. She realized this and instead thought of how to apply the *Reliant* to their current state instead of hoping its appearance would just instantly turn the tide.

"Grayson," she said, "Ask the *Reliant* if General Moonsilver could carry Keeper Ellcadur over on his back. Moreau, tell the *Thorn, Stoneholm, and Lightsworn* to link with you, most secure channel you can make, both of you."

Captain Dillan replied that the two commanders could definitely do what the admiral asked, and then she shared her plan with the four ships. "The *Reliant* will fly directly into battle," she said, "in arrowhead formation with the two battlecruisers, the *Thorn* and *Stoneholm,* and the frigate *Lightsworn* in front to guard. The right flank needs reinforcements, transfer two hundred elves to the *Firestorm* and two hundred to the *Razor,* as soon as you're in range. Then move on and distribute the elves where needed."

"Understood," Captain Dillan responded. "We're five minutes out, and the dragons will be about ten minutes behind us."

"Good to know." She saw another ship, basked in flames, descend uncontrollably to the ground, and she whispered, "Not a moment too soon."

Chapter 25

The *Thorn, Stoneholm, and Lightsworn* broke out of formation, and thankfully the Elemarian fleet didn't seem to mind them since they were more focused on the capital ships. They moved northward, towards Admiral Lina's left flank, and she was glad to see that the *Reliant's* captain was punctual enough to arrive when he said he would.

The little ship had been barely discernable from the distance until the last two minutes, at which point she saw some small gleaming from afar. It quickly came closer into view, however, undoubtedly bolstered by its speed enhancements, and formed up with the three airships she had sent to protect it. She also saw the grey shimmering of the dragon that had flown off the *Reliant*, and she could soon see the elf on his back as he approached.

"Raise the ship," Admiral Lina said to signals officer Moreau, "Incoming friendlies, do not fire."

The officer nodded, started circling his hands around an imaginary sphere, and dunked his head into it to convey the message. The voice of his words whisked from the platform down towards the entire ship, and everyone heard the undisturbed echo of his order.

The bridge's view platform wouldn't have comfortably fit all the people that would be on it, so she had Grayson tell Benson, who was now situated up in the boxed crow's nest with his warp team, to move her and her signalers to the forward deck, close the very edge of the *Corona*.

She saw the old warp master raise a hand and start twirling his other hand around his arm, and then ten seconds later she was there, her signalers standing in the same relative position near her. She raised a finger up to the sky and shot a little magical flare into the sky, and the dragon seemed to rock his wings in affirmation. They landed on the deck behind her, and the elf on his back hopped off with utmost grace and bowed to the admiral.

"A pleasure, admiral," Ellcadur said.

The dragon behind him added, "Wyrst Moonsilver, at your service. You're already acquainted with my sons, I'm told."

The admiral looked past the elf and marveled a bit at how similar the dragon looked like his son. "You have been told correctly, sir." She focused back to the old elf. "Thank you, both of you, for coming to our aid."

"Think nothing of it," Ellcadur said. "We understand the ramifications of what will happen if we lose here today."

She nodded and focused on the elf. "Captain Dillan told me how you helped us. An entertaining story, if I do say so myself. I'd like to hear why you were on the *Reliant* disguised as a human for all that time, but that's another conversation for another day."

The Keeper smiled. "And we shall live to see that day."

The three leaders looked on over the edge of the railings and saw the *Reliant's* formation drive on through to the right flank relatively unhindered. Some ships with free cannons took pot shots at them, but there was nothing particularly worrisome. They were moving as fast as the battlecruisers could go, but she saw that the *Firestorm* was starting to lose one of its upper quadrant barriers as it was glowing nearly as red as its trim color.

She turned her head to Ellcadur and asked, "Keeper, will your elves be able to teleport themselves over to my ships?"

"Most of them can. A shorter distance will be less tiresome, and if you can assist it would be most welcome."

"Very well, I'll tell the *Firestorm* and *Razor* to have their transporters ready to facilitate transport." She turned to her signalers and issued more orders, one to have the elves on the *Reliant* on deck so that the two dreadnoughts' transporters could see them, and secondly to have the two ships prepare to lower their least attacked shield area to allow the transport.

When she turned her head back, she saw that the last order didn't really apply to the *Firestorm*. One side of her upper shields had failed, and already fire was being flung at her sails.

Solah and Siwan were securely mounted on Rauliax's harness, and they were waiting for the most opportune time to join the battle. The captain suggested they fly while transferring over the elves since they would have to lower their shields, and that would prevent Solah from nullifying their own defenses. The intricate failure of a complex spell like a shield prevented another from forming in the area it was broken by Solah for a while, and any extended period without a barrier in place was deadly in a firefight like this.

Rauliax stood on the quarterdeck and waited for the transfer to occur. His nerves, along with Solah's power, drove energy through his veins, and he felt more confident than he should have been. There was more excitement than fear even though he knew he was going to fly right into the mess next to them, and for some time there would be no other dragons, but he knew he should have been afraid. If not for his own sake, then for the precious cargo he was carrying and the result of what would happen if he were to fall. He just didn't feel it, however, though some guilt did arise from his lack of overall fear.

Siwan appeared to look stoic but purposeful. He was here for the chance to avenge his friend, and he wouldn't let any other emotion get in his way.

Solah, on the other hand, felt sharp chills up his spine as he looked at the inferno they were flying by on their left side, and the rushing wind from the heavy propellers attached to the three ships guarding them didn't help. He clutched onto Rauliax's hair tighter, but he wouldn't give in to his fear. He was scared, yes, but he wouldn't let his friends down, and he wouldn't let anything happen to Rauliax, or, for that matter, Siwan.

"I can feel you trembling, Solah," the dragon said. "Are you sure you want to do this?"

"I'd be more afraid of what would happen if we don't help."

Rauliax nodded, though Solah could only see his head bobbing from behind. The boy was right, and if they didn't fight today then they would have to fight another day. And without a fleet of airships. At home.

When the *Reliant* approached the southern hot spot, they saw how the *Firestorm* had been pierced: there was a hole in the layer of friendly airships around it, on the upper starboard side, and an Elemarian ship, a rather large battlecruiser held aloft by no less than eight propellers, was just pummeling fireballs and cannon blasts through while taking much less fire itself.

The *Firestorm* did manage to rotate another protector there to reform the barrier, but the damage was done: its sails were flaring with fire, and the deck bore marks of destruction.

"Before we leave," Rauliax said, "take the radio, Solah." He reached into his mouth and pulled out the little black box, and then he twisted his arm around so that the boy could take it.

Captain Dillan, standing across them on the quarterdeck, saw the radio and came up to them. He said, "Fleet frequency is 132.17. Try calling the admiral."

Solah twisted the knobs until the numbers matched, and then he clicked the button as he had seen Rauliax do, and he unconsciously turned his head around to try and look at the *Corona*, but it was mostly obscured by the ships covering their rear. "Admiral Lina, this is Solah, do you hear me?"

It took her a moment, but she heard her voice call back, "I hear you, Solah. Thanks for calling, I know I can give you orders if necessary now."

"No problem, go ahead and direct us when you see us flying."

"Will do."

He tucked the radio into his inner coat pocket, and then he watched the *Reliant* approach the burning airship.

When its forward section was protected by the dreadnought, the ships around the *Reliant* moved over so they covered their aft sections, and then the elves standing on deck began to flash away, and Solah could see them reappear on the other ship's deck. Several of the elves joined the ship's ice elementalists to try and put out the fire before it spread to the hull, but progress seemed slow.

Then his hands felt lightly strained as Rauliax leapt into the air and flew towards the *Firestorm*. The ship's barriers were all at the very least lightly strained so their condition was clearly visible, and he quickly caught sight of the lower starboard section that was unprotected to allow the elves to teleport over. He dived through it and shot himself up near the top of the burning sails, and then he took a breath before hurling some water from his mouth.

Solah heard the admiral's muffled voice as Rauliax was helping to put out the fire, and then he pulled out the radio and heard her say his name, but not what she wanted him to do. He asked her to repeat herself, and she called back, "Don't waste Rauliax's strength on putting out that fire, Solah. It's taken care of. Go hunt down some scouts and frigates, they have few defenses from behind so it should be easy to sneak up on them."

He conveyed the order to Rauliax, who gave a thumb up in acknowledgement. He stopped huffing water down, but he did want to see how the ice elementalists were going to do any better without him. Still, he knew he had to do something more productive and went back out the opening before the elves were done warping over.

Once he was outside of the shield perimeter, Rauliax turned around and saw the gap sealed behind him as the elves had completed transporting over. He flapped his wings harder and flew up until he was over the ship, and he saw the elves were helping to return more fire to the Elemarian battlecruiser in the hole than the *Firestorm* was taking, and below the crew parted ways to allow one man under the still burning sails. He wore a hat designed like the admiral's, but its edges were lined with red and gold trim: Captain Fourier, he presumed.

The captain of the *Firestorm* drew his hands up, and then with a gush of will it seemed like the fires sunk into his hand like iron dust to a magnet, and there between his hands it coagulated, heavily compressed, and danced as the raging element tried to escape its prison. He looked up at the battlecruiser assailing his ship, and then he threw his hands toward it. The fire that was absorbed mingled, boosted, and turned nearly white-blue when he joined it with his own spell, and then he shot the fire out in a molten stream towards the Elemarian ship.

The white hot fire slammed into the opposing ship's lower shield, and Rauliax could've sworn he could feel the heat from where he was hovering. The blast slammed into the barrier, and it turned red faster than Rauliax could've flown over to break it with Solah, and then the fire burst through and consumed the bottom of the ship.

Watching from the *Corona*, Admiral Lina let out a restrained chuckle. "Truly one of the best fire elementalists of our time," she whispered to nobody in particular. A few more cannon blasts later and she saw the battlecruiser fall and join the wreckage below, crushing the trees that lay on the outskirts of Windsgate.

Solah was curious and looked at the falling husk, but after seeing people jump to their deaths while wailing from being lit aflame, he couldn't keep looking. They jumped so they could end their suffering faster, and his hands felt cold even as they gripped tighter around Rauliax's hair.

The *Reliant* moved on in formation to deposit more elves on the *Razor*, and Rauliax dove out to help the *Lightsworn*, which was taking fire from two frigates trying to blast through to the *Reliant* as they had, evidently, seen what they were doing.

Rauliax flew behind the pair of airships and prepared to burst their bubble, but he couldn't when the *Firestorm* was launching attacks at them.

Luckily, they had an angel in the sky watching. The admiral ordered all ships in the right flank to cease fire on the two frigates, and on her mark anyone with a clear shot behind them would give them everything they've got. Rauliax dove in when the guns stopped, and there was, as predicted, practically no resistance from the rear of the frigates. Rauliax was hit by a stray bolt of lightning once, but it fizzled harmlessly against his scales, and he proceeded to fly with an entire wing dipped down so that he could rub Solah against both of the ships' aft shields.

He felt the swish of air that marked the cancellation of their magic, and then he dove sharply down. Solah was held tautly by the harness, but Siwan needed to keep a heavy grip on the dragon's hair so he wouldn't start flinging around.

As soon as the dragon was out of the way, the *Firestorm* and the ships on its port side opened fire. Without any protection, the shots penetrated through into the hulls of both of the ships, and fire followed not long after. A cannonball smashed into the left frigate's propeller duct which caused the blades inside to chop out of its cage and cut into its neighboring engine.

The damage happened too quickly for the frigate to react, and it leaned towards the side lacking lift and crashed into the other frigate, causing both their shields to collapse. They fused into one body, and any remaining operational engines weren't enough to keep the mess aloft.

The *Reliant* finished transporting elves to the *Razor* and flew on, its three assigned ships reforming their protective stance. They had decided that it would be easiest to transfer elves to the capital ships in each main combat zone, and then they would transport to whichever satellite ship needed them.

Rauliax flew along the *Reliant*, looking for any vulnerable smaller ships along their path, but then Solah picked up his radio as he heard the admiral calling them again.

"Cavalry has arrived," she said. "Fly north and keep close to our ships, and don't hesitate to help out if you're sure it's safe to do so."

Solah told Rauliax that the dragon army had arrived, but he couldn't see them through the two fleets. They had to be coming from the north, he knew, but through the ships and the fireworks of spells he would have had no idea they had arrived.

Back on the *Corona*, Admiral Lina smiled when she saw the dragon army. Summing the size of the scaly mass, it looked as if they could've counted as two airships the size of hers, and though they were late they came before she had taken too many losses. All of the fleet's dreadnoughts were still holding steady, especially after the enemy's failure to take down the right flank, thanks to the *Reliant's* arrival, and gobble the rest of her fleet from there, but there were still a lot more Elemarian ships. She had counted the ones that had fallen, and from her count it was now her twenty-seven against their thirty-eight.

Rauliax's father was also glad that his army had arrived, and he had come up with a rather reasonable idea to keep his sons safe. "Keeper," he asked, "can you contact your elves?"

"Yes," Ellcadur replied, "in sort of the same way as the admiral is using her two officers."

"I need four of them on dragonback, three that are good at shielding and one good at lighting things on fire."

"Sure, what do you want to do with them?"

"Have them join with my sons, and arrange them like this. Two shield makers in front, the fire mage behind them, and another shielder right behind him."

"Will do." The Keeper clasped his hands together and seemed to focus, but he uttered no words. A few seconds later, he opened his mouth and said, "It is done."

Wyrst wasn't curious enough to ask how he had told them, and he was far more concerned with the safety of Rauliax and Solah to bother worrying about that. The admiral wanted to ask, but she ignored the desire and just said, "Keeper, tell the elves on dragonback to concentrate on cleaning up the northern flank. If they can clear up the opposition there, we can start loosening some pressure and move them southward."

The old elf nodded as he acknowledged her orders, and again he sent them silently to his elves who then conveyed the orders to their dragons.

And then they descended upon the fleets; a swarm of locusts to Elemar, but a host of angels to Wesar.

Chapter 26

Although the northern edge was not under heavy attack, the commanding ship there, the *Oblivion,* had few satellite ships to protect it. All the barriers around it were shining at least orange, and the crew was visibly relieved to see the dragons swooping in to take on the Elemarian crafts.

The *Oblivion* was the only ship that had not been embroiled with another dreadnought, but that minor advantage was offset by the sheer number of airships, most of them the smaller ones Elemar possessed while their larger ships were at more strategic positions, bombarding it, and there were only two large Wesarian ships that could effectively combat them.

The dragons swarmed in, a powerful stream of beating wings and scales, and they flew at the Elemarian airships. They pulled away to retreat, but that only left their backsides vulnerable: the mages flung everything they had, but the small ships didn't have many rear cannons. The dragons' scales shrugged off the unfocused magical attacks, and none were hit by the deadly cannons since the elves on their backs reacted fast enough to erect a barrier whenever they saw one shoot at them.

When the dragons closed in, they launched their breath weapons, each one having a favorite though they made sure to coordinate and not attack with opposing elements, and the elves assisted with their own spells.

Lightning twirled with water, fire spun around light, and ice echoed with sonic blasts towards separate ships. The dragons flew in a line, and when they had exhausted their breath they would dive to let the line behind them take charge, and the attacks were relentlessly efficient. Seven ships tried to flee, but only three escaped into the safety of the next enemy dreadnought's sphere of influence, and even then they were heavily damaged.

Free of burden, the *Oblivion* took a short moment's rest and began flying to help the next capital ship down the line, the *Aura*. The dragons gathered around the large ship like a beehive protecting its queen, and then they charged into the fray.

At that point, Rauliax had already managed to sneak his way north to the *Aura*. With Solah's power, they had managed to seriously maim several small ships all throughout the line, and he was staying close to the capital ship, waiting for the next allied ship to fly by so he could proceed to join with the dragon army. He couldn't find one, but there was almost no need: the army was coming to him.

The *Oblivion* came in guns blazing, forcing the enemy dreadnought to pull back, and four dragons swooped down to where Rauliax was holding on the port underside of the *Aura*, right outside its barrier by an engine. One of the great things about the duct design, Rauliax appreciated, was the lack of air displacement around it.

They had been expected since Siwan had conveyed the Keeper's orders to Solah and Rauliax, and Rauliax's father had come up with a formation for the five dragons that he thought might be effective.

Rauliax recognized one of the dragons; a red one by the name of Yurik. He settled behind him, and another black dragon settled behind the red. Two green dragons set themselves in front, and the elves in their harnesses gestured for them to follow.

They wasted no time testing the formation: the enemy dreadnought at the northern battle spot, its name labeled in black on the side of the light brown hull as the *Pulverizer,* moved back to stay away from the *Oblivion's* entry, but the *Aura* pressed the retreat and tailed the vessel, launching suppressing fire along its route.

The dragon army focused on the ships orbiting the *Pulverizer* since they dared not go against such a well-armed vessel. A few tried to sneak in from the underside, avoiding the crossfire between the two capital ships, but the only thing they accomplished was to teach the rest of the army to stay away from dense cannon fire. But facing the smaller ships was no guarantee of success, and a well placed shot would occasionally knock a dragon out of the sky.

Rauliax was sure he would do better, however. With Solah's ability and an actually organized formation, he was sure they'd be able to damage the dreadnought. They came in from under, the elves on the two dragons in front holding up a strong barrier, and went straight for the engines. Blasts came at them, but the shields held.

Rauliax shouted out, amplified further by dragon magic, "When we reach their barriers, dive immediately! Yurik, you and your elf fire everything you've got, flames will work best!"

"We got it!" the red dragon shouted back.

"By immediately, I mean immediately!"

The green dragons gave a thumb claw up, and they kept flying up towards the massive leviathan of a ship.

"Solah," Siwan said, "remember to stop me."

Solah turned around, slightly confused by what he meant, but then he saw the motion of his hands and the gathering flame, and he understood. The three taut ropes that Captain Dillan had installed into the harness to facilitate carrying Nama weren't very long, and he was well within arm's reach to work whatever Siwan needed.

They reached the edge of the barrier, cannons blasting down onto the barriers around the green dragons, and then they dove, hard. Rauliax had prepared his breath and fired a shaft of light as soon as he felt the gush of air that meant Solah had broken the ship's barrier, and the light carved a molten line into the interior of the ship, but there wasn't enough time to melt any of the engines off their connections even though his attack was supercharged by Solah's presence. At the very same time Rauliax fired his breath weapon, Siwan unleashed a devastating inferno, and the only command he gave it was to make it go up. And that it did, a jet of wild fire loosed in a cone shape from his two palms, facing upward with his arms raised. Barely a second and a half later, Solah grabbed onto an arm, cutting off the fire flowing out of the elf, and then Rauliax whipped his tail up and dove, following the green dragons.

Yurik and his elf were clearly surprised by the devastating amount of fire Siwan had put out, along with the suddenness of its departure, but they did not allow it to shy them from their attack. The red dragon let loose a stream of fire, aiming at the engines to hope to melt them out of their encasements, and the elf on top rapid-fired mini fireballs onto various sections of the ship not lit up by Siwan.

They dived after, and the black dragon behind them followed, his elf raising the rear barrier to protect them from any retaliation. Few shots came after them, however, as the ship's cannoneers clearly needed to focus on putting out the fires, especially since they had ravaged their way into the inside of the ship.

They flew out and away, and then they targeted a battlecruiser in much the same manner. The dragon army had taken care of most of the smaller ships around the *Pulverizer*, and the majority had already started flying towards the next battle spot.

Siwan heard another order, sent through the Keeper's mental link, telling the army to reinforce the *Oathshield*, and he tried to look through the chaos to see the airship. There was still another duel between two dense forces between them and the *Oathshield*, and he saw the massive airship freely taking hits from spells and cannonballs, its shields having completely failed.

Several dragons rushed through the next battle area to help the airship that had taken the spear of the delta formation attack, but it was too late. The *Oathshield* sunk before they could help, and Elemarian forces pushed the dragons back out.

On the other hand, the *Pulverizer* was also crumbling apart, and the fires they had spread had covered too much of the ship to put out. It began to sink, metal and wood falling like it was a ripped bag full of bolts and planks, and it fell with just a little more help from the *Aura*.

With the *Aura* and *Oblivion* pushing towards the middle of the line, and the *Firestorm* and *Razor* holding on the other edge, heavily reinforced with a large number of elves, the battle seemed to be turning towards Wesar's favor. They had seven dreadnoughts to their five now, another having been destroyed when the *Reliant* reinforced the position one south of the *Oathshield*. Regrettably, the *Oathshield* had been under far too much fire for the *Reliant* to transfer its remaining elves, and instead it chose to stay and fight alongside the *Thorn, Stoneholm,* and *Lightsworn* after empowering them with its remaining supply of elves.

The *Eclipse* gave in first. The massive flagship of Elemar fired up its rear engines and flew towards the middle of the line, hoping to join with its ships there to reinforce their position.

Admiral Lina smiled. It was an indication that they were winning, and she said to her signalers, "That's our cue. Have Holden take us in, let's help the *Firestorm* and the *Razor*."

Both of them waved their hands and sent her message along. Grayson told the Fleet Lieutenant to move the ship in, and Moreau told the fleet to expect them to join the fray.

Admiral Lina felt the gentle jolt as her ship began to move. The humming beneath her feet increased as the ship's fifteen engines charged to full power, and she saw the sails fully unfurl with the warp master and his crew up on top in the tallest platform on the mast. Elementalists poured out onto the deck, and the forward section no longer consisted of just Wyrst, Ellcadur, and herself.

She swung her arm in a small slow arc, and it felt as if the wind shifted. The sails became tight, and the ship moved faster.

"Interesting," Ellcadur said. "A wind elementalist?"

"You would be correct," she said, her focus still on her craft.

"I have never in my long life met one."

"And by all probability, I might be the last."

Wyrst coughed. "Are wind elementalists rare or something?"

Ellcadur, still watching the admiral swing her arm, replied, "Quite. Elves can't control the wind, much like how no human can learn the healing arts. It is a rare skill, and I should've guessed she was one from her uncanny appearance."

"Well, I sure appreciate that," she said.

"Sorry, I didn't mean to offend."

"And I," Wyrst said, "as a dragon, really had no idea you looked any significantly different until the Keeper pointed it out."

"It's fine," she said to Ellcadur, "I'm not troubled by it." Her eyes seemed to break focus for a moment to look at Wyrst, but it returned quickly to the front though she did say, "And I can see why Solah might be happy to stay in Noriath."

Ellcadur shifted his head a bit. "Is that why you gave him a chance?"

"A little bit of me can relate to him, yes."

"You have given all Valeria a chance."

"Well, he did just help take down a dreadnought, with just five dragons, and contributed to the destruction of several more enemy ships throughout the line."

"No, I don't mean that. He's the only one who will be able to stop King Arashal."

"What do you mean?"

"I've kept this information hidden from the crew of the *Reliant*, and I thought it would be best if I told you personally. The king has been dabbling in blood magic.

She furrowed her brows in disbelief. "Blood magic? That's just a fake story to scare children with."

"It's not fake, and I don't know what stories you have made of it, but it is dangerous and deadly. Only Solah, a spellbreaker, can stop him if he has learned the art."

"Keeper, I don't doubt your recollection of history, but in this matter, let's just say I'll believe it when I see it."

Ellcadur closed his eyes in resignation. Humans were always difficult to teach to, even when the subject was about their own history. "You will see if we win."

"And I plan to."

The *Corona* blasted its way between the *Firestorm* and the *Razor* much faster than the *Eclipse* could group up with its ships in the Elemar dominated section, and the enemy forces started retreating to the glob around the enemy flagship. The Elemarian ships caught between the *Corona* and the *Razor* had no chance against the massive leviathan, and another four hunks of wood were sent to the glowing forest below.

The *Eclipse* fortified its position as much as it could, and it was clear that Admiral Morit knew his failure in the southern flank caused their entire fleet to be surrounded. Their numbers were equalizing, and the dragons had tilted the numerical advantage over to Wesar.

With the Elemarian fleet now orbiting around the *Eclipse*, Admiral Lina ordered a double-pronged attack. Some of her ships had to retreat: they were too damaged to continue battle. The *Firestorm*, for instance, limped away with half her engines blown off, and her shields were on the verge of complete failure despite the elvish assistance.

The *Corona* joined the *Razor* and the *Lightning* on the southern side along with five remaining ships. On the northern side, the *Aura*, *Oblivion*, and *Paladin*, all much less damaged than their sister southern dreadnoughts, gathered their remaining nine ships and the dragon army, now only two-thirds the size it was before, to prepare for one final push.

"Open fleet channel," Admiral Lina said to signaler Moreau.

He spun his hand and opened his palm in front of her face. "Channel open, admiral."

"All ships, this is the admiral. The *Eclipse* has formed a heavily fortified sphere around itself, and we must break through. Do not hesitate to retreat if you take too much damage, and cover any retreating ships the best you can. The *Corona* will try to pierce their defenses, and then we'll try to board the *Eclipse* and capture their admiral, and hopefully they will surrender peacefully after. Godspeed, and I don't think I need to say this, but don't do anything stupid." She pushed the signalers hand away, and then she said to Ellcadur, "Repeat my message to the elves and the dragon army."

"Will comply," the old elf said.

Rauliax's father flexed his neck down and asked, "Are we allowed to participate in the battle now?"

The admiral nodded. "You'll be forced to anyway, especially if the tables turn against us again."

And so the separated Wesarian fleets began to converge, a dual-pronged strike that Admiral Lina hoped would result in the capture of Admiral Morit, and, more importantly, information about his king's madness.

Chapter 27

Rauliax regrouped with the dragon army, his squad still organized around him, and watched the formation. Three battlecruisers were in front of their dreadnoughts, the *Aura, Oblivion,* and *Paladin,* and there were four frigates, one armed with a long-range artillery cannon, along with two scouts on the outer circumference of the fleet. The dragon army flew between the battlecruisers and the dreadnoughts, split into two lines: one high above on the level of the highest airship's mast, and one below its lowest cannon so that they would have a clear line of fire between the two lines.

On the other side of the battle, the *Corona, Razor,* and *Lightning* flew with two battlecruisers in front of them, two frigates, and one scout. One of the frigates was the *Lightsworn,* which had stayed relatively safe while protecting the *Reliant,* the only scout ship still flying on the southern side since it was protected rather well and kept a small crew of elves to bolster their survivability. The *Reliant* was a dwarf under the shadow of the *Corona,* but the little ship followed it into battle nonetheless.

The admiral kept the wind flowing, increasing its area to affect all the ships on her side, and the two battlecruisers in front crashed into their first defense, a wall consisting of five middle-class ships including one artillery unit that had barely a chance to take advantage of its long range. The *Corona* penetrated through, all two hundred of its cannons bursting, until they were stopped by a blockade of ships protecting the *Eclipse.*

Six frigates broke their defensive stance and flew over to the less maneuverable *Corona,* but two dreadnoughts remained to protect their flagship. The *Razor* and *Lightning* fended off any ships trying to attack from the side, but the enemy instead flew overhead and began focusing attacks on one single quadrant of the sixteen quadrant barrier protecting the *Corona*.

Warp Master Benson, up on the crow's nest, knew what they were trying to do. The barrier section they were hitting was almost directly over him, and if the shield failed then he and his warp team would become unprotected targets. He huffed at the strategy and started rotating protectors to different shield circles on the ship to constantly switch the shields around and give tired out ones time to rest and recharge.

One man couldn't handle managing all sixteen shield circles on the *Corona*, of course, and his team was hard at work moving them around too, and transporters moved more than people too: cannonballs needed to be teleported up onto deck from their storage rooms.

Even when he was casting his teleportation spell, Benson would note the speed and precision that his apprentice, Ryson, possessed when casting, and he was proud to have trained such a fine young man to such a point that his skill could rival his own. The Lieutenant Warp Master was the only other transporter that knew the *Corona* inside and out, and he didn't need the shield circles to help him position the barrier mages.

The *Razor* and *Lightning* found it difficult to maneuver over to the top to fend off the frigates, especially since the dreadnoughts protecting the *Eclipse* had decided to move forward to keep them occupied. At the rear of the fight where they had entered, however, the *Reliant* and the *Lightsworn* noticed the pummeling the upper section of their flagship was taking, and they flew up to assist.

The Elemarian frigates almost paid the two ships no mind, especially to the *Reliant*. They focused on their bombardment of the *Corona* and only gave the small ship token resistance, but then the *Reliant* closed in to optimal range and *made* them notice it.

The scout's new rapid-firing dragon cannons surprised the first frigate they hit: with just one volley, they had already pierced through one side of their shields. Lieutenant Avery and some of the elves took the opportunity to toss a fine, semi-corporeal mist towards their engines before they could rotate their barriers. The mists solidified into ice once they were sucked into the propellers, and most of the engines came to a grinding halt despite the fact that the frost was relatively weak, aside from the block created by the lieutenant, since elven magic was not as powerful as human magic, and there were no human elementalists on board the *Reliant* since they had traded them for levimages before they departed for Noriath.

That only meant that Avery had more to boast about: he alone had frozen down two engines while several elves had to combine their spells to freeze another two. With only two operational, the opposing frigate began to lurch and descend, and though their levimages caught the ship from tumbling to the ground, they had to retreat out of the battle.

The fleeing ship didn't get very far, however, since it was surrounded by the two Wesarian dreadnoughts and were limping along on mostly magic. The *Lightning* made quick work of the disabled frigate, and it joined the mass of wood, metal, blood, and bodies below.

Meanwhile, the *Corona's* elementalists were blasting away with what they had. Kineticists ran up and down the deck to reload the cannons by floating iron balls into their top-loading feeding tubes, though ensigns that weren't busy helped load them by hand. The transporters up top were busy rotating the shields and teleporting stacks of cannonballs out from the storage deck, and Benson kept his attention on the state of the shield above them.

When the cannons were loaded, a cannoneer, most often a fire or lightning elementalist in training, would run down the deck and snap his fingers at each one to conjure up the small spark that ignited the Pyrucium powder mix inside and fired them. The frigates were already visibly having trouble handling the *Corona's* return fire, but they kept their attack on, hoping to break through.

And the *Eclipse* stopped sitting idle. Once Admiral Morit was sure the Wesarian forces were too entangled to group up and focus on his flagship, he ordered his ship in to help his frigates crush the *Corona*.

The *Reliant* and the *Lightsworn,* combined with the might of the *Corona,* were able to dispatch another two frigates before they were forced to flee from the enemy flagship, both their captains knowing they wouldn't stand two minutes sitting between the crossfire of the continent's two mightiest airships. They retreated back to assist their two friendly battlecruisers which had already destroyed two of the enemy ships in the back line by themselves, one frigate and the artillery ship.

The other three Elemarian middle-class ships were giving one of their battlecruisers, its shields completely gone, everything they had, and the *Lightsworn* rushed to place itself between them, but it was too late. The ship was torn by cannon and ice, and fell in nearly cut into two pieces. However, the other battlecruiser, the *Thunderbolt*, repaid in-kind and blew apart one of the ships so they joined the rubble together.

When the *Reliant* and *Lightsworn* caught up, the two remaining frigates went straight for the *Reliant*. Captain Dillan guessed that they knew they were trapped and that they might as well take down another ship, logically his since it was the smallest, but they probably weren't aware of his compliment of elves.

The pair of frigates came together and opened fire at once. Cannons smashed into the *Reliant's* barrier, and a mix of lightning, which drained the ship's barriers rather quickly, and fireballs blasted over. With its dragon cannons firing entire volley's worth of ammo each minute, the *Lightsworn* assisting, and the *Thunderbolt* approaching, the *Reliant's* crew went on the defensive: Lieutenant Avery along with several of the elves threw blocks of ice outward to cancel out fire attacks, and the extra levimages they had on board went out of their comfort zone and tried to at least alter the trajectory of incoming fringe cannonballs, something kineticists would be able to do much easier, so that they would not hit their shields or at least hit with less impact. Even Captain Dillan joined the fray, tossing out conjured rocks with the ship's naturalists to ground incoming lightning bolts.

The *Reliant* was more maneuverable and faster, but there wasn't exactly anywhere better to move. The ship's original four protectors had long been exhausted, and only elves held the shields around them now. In fact, more than half the crew, elf and human, had turned to cannon duty since magically exerting themselves.

Captain Dillan stayed on deck even after the barriers around his ship started glowing ominously red. One of the frigates was near destruction, thanks to the *Lightsworn* and the *Thunderbolt*, but there was no way they would hold much more against the last frigate. The elves on his ship had completely tired out, many of them lying down because their bodies demanded rest, and his crew was in no better condition. Everyone fought their very hardest, some even needed to be forced to stop before they fainted or died from blood loss, and even he felt a trickle leak down his earlobe. In fact, the only people still running the cannons were the ensigns and trainees since they weren't allowed to attack with their yet un-honed magic. Then there was a crash, and Captain Dillan saw part of the deck's floorboards shatter out, a cannonball having hammered down into it.

And then there was fire. The *Reliant* tried its hardest to move behind the *Thunderbolt*, but the enemy was relentless and pushed their levimages to keep up with the scout, and the *Lightsworn* was not quick enough to be able to stay between them to defend against their charge.

The fire spread rather slowly, thanks to Lieutenant Avery's attempt to control it with his conjured water, but he was tired too. When he tried to quell it, he overestimated his ability and only summoned up a gallon worth of water. A spark had hit his feather-tipped hat, both feathers burnt to a crisp in the time he took to react, and he cursed himself after putting out the small fire up there since it would be the second hat he'd have to replace this week alone. Still, the fire was under control, for the moment, but it would consume the ship if they didn't teleport in some more ice elementalists soon.

Captain Dillan used his radio, Signals Officer Donnovan having been killed by cannon shrapnel, to put in the request to the fleet, and he could only hope the *Lightsworn* or the *Thunderbolt* would send him the ice elementalists he needed. He would've asked for a protector too, but they were too precious a commodity to be transferred since they were so few in number, and those assigned to a ship were adept enough to create a barrier strong enough for that particular class of airship. He did wish he could have one of the *Corona's* protectors, however, since they were the best of the best: one probably could've been enough to reform the entire barrier around his ship and fend off a bombardment from a frigate for several minutes.

Even so, it would make no sense to ask any ship to leave a whole section unshielded, and such a transfer would've never been allowed. Instead, the good captain had to rely on the next best thing.

He positioned himself near the fire, which was still barely under control, and spread his arms in front of him over the ship's railings. Using what reserve power he had left, he willed into existence a wall, made of collected stone, to form a heavy slab in front of the line-of-fire, blocking further attacks from the merciless frigate that refused to give up its chase, even as its shields started to fail from the *Lightsworn* and the *Thunderbolt's* bombardment.

Ensign Frazer and Waters left their dragon cannons after the captain's wall formed in front of them, and they rushed to try and help Lieutenant Avery put out the fire. Waters ran into the ship to fill some buckets with the ship's drinking water, but Frazer went right up to the ship's lieutenant and looked at him continuously try to douse the flame, his arms swinging up as if he were jetting water up like a fountain.

Frazer pulled up his sleeve to reveal the bracelet given to him by Professor Faraday still on his wrist. He channeled electricity into it like the old dragon had told him to do when he was at Noriath, and from his right fist he shot out sparks of lightning. Just like during the experiment, the fire started to wither, encouraged by Avery's water, and it shrunk to non-dangerous levels before Waters came up and put it entirely out with his buckets.

"Thanks for the help," Avery said. "How did you do that?"

"Magic," Frazer replied.

"Very funny."

The ensign smiled. "I like to call it dragon magic."

Ensign Waters looked at his friend almost mockingly. "I believe the dragons like to call it science."

"Same thing," Frazer said.

Avery rolled his eyes. "Right."

Then the lieutenant noticed the stone wall in front of him, his attention previously completely consumed by the lethal fire, and he looked around to find his captain leaning over the railings struggling to maintain the wall's existence amidst the cannon impacts and spells slamming into it. It was impossible not to notice the thick crimson that seemed to stream out of his head like a pair of faucets, and he had to get him to stop before he killed himself.

The muffled booms against the stone wall had become uneven in their timing, and there was more and more time between the resounding sounds of impact. The captain's body was trembling, and Avery caught him before he collapsed onto his knees, but he kept holding his arms out, struggling as if he were pushing a boulder up a mountain. Blood was pooling on the hard floor, and Avery was afraid even if the captain stopped now he wouldn't survive.

Humans could die by *using* magic far beyond their mental strength. Magic was a tool, and Captain Dillan was tapping into the very energy that kept him alive to hold the stone wall, to make the magic stay. It was a tool that humans manipulated, and it also emphasized how differently dragons almost literally breathed magic. They could tire

227

themselves from wielding magic, sure, just like their physical body would tire from working, but it wasn't possible for them to kill themselves with it, just as it was impossible to die from breathing.

The captain knew this. But he didn't give up, and he held the wall until there were almost no more impacts. His lieutenant was shaking him, trying to get him to stop, but he couldn't. "The first duty," he said to him, his voice trembling, "of an officer is to his ship and his crew."

With the last of his life energy expended, the wall collapsed into dust that faded into nothingness as it fell, carried by the light wind. The captain collapsed too, but Avery caught him and gently set his still bleeding head onto the floor. He didn't care to notice, but Frazer and Waters was still behind them, and they did not move in fear, though they did see, after the captain's wall collapsed, that the enemy frigate that was targeting them had been destroyed, and the *Lightsworn* and the *Thunderbolt* was moving to help the *Corona*.

The lieutenant looked up and almost yelled at Frazer and Waters to go find an elvish healer, holding out for some hope yet, and they scurried off to ask any elf that wasn't recuperating their strength by sleeping if they knew the art. It was highly unlikely they would find one since healers were a rarity, and Avery knew.

"Captain," he said, almost like a restrained shout. "Captain, stay awake! Don't close your eyes, please."

Captain Dillan nearly coughed out, "Ship, safe?"

Avery looked up and saw their allies heading for the *Corona*, and the ship attacking them was gone. "Yes, sir."

"Good."

"Captain! Don't die on me, I'll find an elf!"

"Too late." He coughed out some blood. "Jonathan, do me one last favor."

Avery's voice was becoming strained and quiet. "Anything, captain, anything."

"Keep the ship safe. And be nicer, especially to," he said, coughs interrupting him more, "you know."

"I will. I will."

"And Jon, your hat is burnt."

The lieutenant managed a weak smile. "I know."

Captain Dillan reached for his own hat, his hands slow and quaking, and moved it to his chest. "Try not to wreck this one."

Avery weakly nodded, tossed his hat away, and put on the captain's. "I won't, I promise."

The captain coughed again, and then he was gone.

Chapter 28

The *Eclipse* had settled over the *Corona*, which had destroyed another one of the three frigates that was firing on it, and aimed all its weapons at the crow's nest. Benson and Ryson worked quickly to reinforce that particular section of shielding by warping two of the currently less vital lower protectors from the aft side of the ship to where they were needed. Two more layers of shields insulated the original one, and then the *Eclipse* opened fire while the topside crew of the *Corona* reloaded their cannons and retaliated in kind.

It was enough to last for a while, but they couldn't possibly defeat the *Eclipse* in their current position. Admiral Lina knew this too, and she ordered the ship to move the only way open to them, down. With her dreadnoughts engaged on both port and starboard, and no other ship capable of standing up to the massive flagship above them, they had to hold until the northern fleet broke through.

Unless, she thought, they board the *Eclipse* and capture Admiral Morit. And she had an idea of how to do it before her ship would become rubble.

"Keeper, Grayson, send an order through," she said. "Full speed through their defenses, I need Solah and at least a handful of dragons here as soon as possible. Do not stop unless it's to delay an enemy vessel, or to free one of ours."

They nodded, and carried on her orders.

"Moreau, tell Holden that once our sides are clear, try to move us laterally away from the *Eclipse*. On my mark, raise the ship with as much power as she has, and try to get us above them."

Signaler Moreau sent the order, but then the Fleet Lieutenant's voice came back, vibrating his palms, "Admiral, I don't think we'll be able to get over them, they already have the height advantage and they're forcing us down with their attacks."

230

"Just keep enough distance away so we have room to go over them," she said. "Trust me, I know what I'm doing. You're going to have command after the maneuver, Holden."

"What, why?"

"Regardless of whether my plan works or not, I'll probably be knocked out of commission for a while. Send a boarding party after, the dragons will be most helpful, then find and capture Admiral Morit and win this battle."

"How are we going to board them when we're not even close to punching through their shields?"

"The exile."

"Ah, I see."

"Expect mark when the dragons are here."

"Roger."

Rauliax, Solah, Siwan, and their squad had helped the northern fleet dominate over the Elemarian forces, and the only ships they had trouble with were the three commanding dreadnoughts which had figured, on the barest level of understanding, what they were doing and focused all fire on them when they tried to approach. The *Aura*, *Oblivion*, and *Paladin* let themselves tangle with them, minimizing losses to the dragon army, and when they received the admiral's orders to move for the *Eclipse*, they covered their fire so the dragons and faster ships could pass over unhindered.

Still, the dragon army was only half its original size now, but they moved fearlessly nonetheless. Many dragons couldn't tolerate leaving their allies behind, and many broke off from the group flying over the battle to the *Eclipse* to help.

Rauliax was no exception either. At the very least, he wanted to help nullify a barrier or two on their way south, and his squad did not protest when he suggested it. They followed a group of dragons, mixing in with the crowd, but dive bombed after flying over one of the dreadnoughts. However, one of the ship's signalers, standing in the second highest lookout point on the ship's mast, saw them dive and alerted the crew.

Shots came after them, and the green dragons in front of Rauliax kept their barriers on and blocked them. The cannon fire was focused, however, and arcs of lightning blasted at the shields, draining them faster. Less than ten feet away from the huge ship's rippling barrier, a dead-on shot hit the green dragon on Rauliax's left side and pierced through. The green dragon died on impact, and Rauliax, Yurik, and the black dragon behind them had to swerve hard to the right to avoid getting hit by the poor dragon's body. Rauliax had seen that the elf riding him was unconscious, but there was nothing he could do to help him, and another moment later he had to roll around to glide Solah onto the ship's barrier.

The other green dragon performed a sharp rebounding twist after bouncing onto the barrier, and then Rauliax followed. He rolled, felt the barrier dissolve, and fired a quick beam at the main mast while Siwan randomly shot out fire for barely a second before Solah canceled his attack. A spark of lightning had hit him on his tough belly scales, and though it did no damage it spooked the dragon since he had thought it was a cannonball.

Yurik followed after and fired another shaft of light to finish the job Rauliax had started. The main mast toppled over, cut near the middle, and dragged and ripped the sails down. Some of the transporters on the crow's nest were able to warp themselves off in time, but more than half fell to their deaths, and the signalers on the second platform below them were all killed. The red dragon's elf was nearly exhausted, but he managed to shoot a fireball at the tearing sails before Yurik dove up and away, and the black dragon behind shielded their rear.

After losing a dragon, Rauliax decided that was enough: the dreadnought had lost their barriers on one side and they had tore down the ship's mast and sent the crew into a panic, and he wasn't going to risk losing anyone else by diving for another attack run. Instead, they raced through the rest of the blockade and flew directly to the *Corona's* aid.

The dragons were approaching, Admiral Lina could see, and she had Ellcadur send a message to Siwan. "Tell them to break the *Eclipse's* shields from above. The deck will be clear when they are here, and then they can land after and join the boarding party."

Ellcadur didn't question how exactly she'd clear the enemy's deck and sent the command. Meanwhile, the warp team was busy playing cat and mouse with the *Eclipse*. The massive airship kept changing focal points over and over, and Benson had to keep up or they'd break through. His team was starting to get tired too, and he was surprised when the *Eclipse* started split-firing at three different spots, each bombardment equally powerful, though less so than if they were one.

Still, the break in the pattern caught the transporters off guard and mentally tripped them up. Benson was in the middle of rotating the shields when the *Eclipse* suddenly switched focus back to the barrier protecting the crow's nest above them while the other transporters were busy teleporting cannonballs up to the deck from the storage room.

The old warp master only noticed the change in target after he finished his previous spell, and by then the barrier above him was already glowing orange.

Admiral Lina was looking out and saw the dragon army approaching, and she looked up to prepare her mark. That was when she noticed the failing barrier, and she saw Benson frantically waving his hands to try and reinforce it in time.

She tugged at Ellcadur's arm and Wyrst's wing. "Up there! He's not going to make it in time, Keeper can you shield them for a few seconds?"

"I can, but I'm not a human. I need to get higher, and if I flash myself up there I won't have the strength to create a shield so quickly."

Rauliax's father turned his back to the elf and unfurled his wings. "Then what are you waiting for, hop on!"

Ellcadur did so with grace and haste, a mixture that seemed natural for an elf, and then the dragon leapt off the forward deck towards the main mast.

Time seemed to slow as the admiral watched on, and she wished she could do more. She saw the grey dragon approach the failing barrier, and Ellcadur was starting to wave his arms to cast another one above it. Benson was still motioning his hands to move another barrier mage into position, but it was rather clear that he wasn't going to make it in time, and she saw that Lieutenant Warp Master Ryson had stopped to stare fearfully at the barrage coming from above, though the other transporters seemed to be busy casting spells and didn't notice what was happening.

The barrier failed. It melted away, red filter removed, but it was almost immediately replaced with a fresh and clear barrier crafted by Ellcadur. Almost.

In the split-second that there was no protection, a single cannonball flew in and slammed right through the main mast. It burrowed through, cracking it into two, and rolled onto the deck before settling, and then there was a deep rumble that moaned through the ship's wood.

The mast began to tilt, and the upper part fell to the side, the entire post deciding to fall. It was auspicious that it wouldn't crush anyone on the deck, but its loss was not good to begin with. Shocked out of their spellcasting, the transporters were distraught and disoriented by their predicament, and almost none of them, not even Benson, could gather enough wits to think. Their bodies fell out of the boxed platform like ragdolls, and they fell faster towards the ground than the mast.

The admiral could do nothing but watch. And worry. She no longer had any well-trained transporters on her ship. "Confound it Benson," she muttered, "I told you not to put all your eggs in one basket."

The loss of the ship's transporters wouldn't hinder her plans too much, thankfully, though she was still saddened by the loss of her Warp Master. He was an old relic that should've retired a decade ago, but she couldn't dwell on it now. The dragons were approaching ever closer, and she had to concentrate for her plan to work.

But then there was a flash. She turned around to see what it was, and she saw Benson's apprentice lying flat on the deck. She ran up and knelt down to speak to him. "Ryson, are you alright?"

Lieutenant Warp Master Ryson was a middle-aged man, brown hair and average in all appearance, but he had a terrified look on him more fitting on the face of a teenager that just realized they were not invulnerable, and he was lying on the floor, arms reaching up and trembling. "I, I tried admiral, I tried! We were all falling, and I tried to catch all of them, but I couldn't, I couldn't focus. They were going everywhere, and in the end I could only find myself."

Blood was slightly drooling out of his ears, and the admiral comforted him. "You did fine, Warp Master. Better one than none. Take a moment's respite, I'm going to need you to send the boarding party over."

"Y-yes sir. I'm the only one?"

"Only one as far as I know. You teleported right behind me."

"Understood."

The admiral looked away and sighed. At the very least, Benson's legacy would live on in his apprentice. Some dragons had started circling the *Eclipse* already, most keeping their distance, and she had to call Solah via signaler and radio since the Keeper was occupied with the upper barrier.

"On my mark," she told him, "the *Corona* will rise above the *Eclipse,* and then you'll know when the top side is safe to break through."

"What exactly are you planning?" Solah asked.

"Don't worry," she replied, "there won't be any resistance if you come in from top, trust me. Just wait until we're over them."

"Okay, we'll watch."

The admiral looked out and saw the familiar silver dragon amidst a small formation of five, and then she gestured to one of her signalers. "Ready, Moreau?"

The officer held both his hands, palms facing up, in front of her, and then she yelled into his hands, "Mark!"

Her voice seemed to explode from his hands, not just through the ship but through the air and all around. The dragons heard, and they shuffled up, ready to strike.

The *Corona* started to rise, but the *Eclipse* matched its rate of climb. Admiral Lina stared at the ship above them, and then she hovered her arms in front of breasts, palms facing downward as if she were trying to shut a lid.

And then everyone felt the air shift. The dragons directly over the *Eclipse* moved away, sensing something was coming, and then a gale-force gust thrust itself on the ship, pressing it down and allowing the *Corona* to gain altitude over it.

Rauliax's father and Ellcadur could feel the residual blast of air from where they flew, right where the crow's nest used to be. The dragon had taken the opportunity to fly closer to the shield to breathe out pot shot fireballs at the ship, but he had stopped when he heard the admiral's voice and was now watching the microburst smash into the ship and tear apart the sails. He asked the Keeper, "How is it passing through the shields?"

"Barriers," Ellcadur replied, one hand grasping the grey dragon's hair, the other facing up towards the barrier he was holding, "all barriers, whether crafted by human or elf, have a property about them that a wind elementalist like the admiral can exploit. An apprentice protector cannot make barriers that only block things from coming in, but every protector, from the first barrier they ever make, unconsciously allows air to pass through both ways unhindered. Because, you know, otherwise they would suffocate."

"And that means, by extension, they must allow wind to pass as well."

"Correct."

The *Corona* soon overtook the *Eclipse*, and the admiral kept her spell working, her eyes glowing with a faint green light that made her look even more ghostly than normal. Once she deemed that they were significantly above them, she released her hands from their position in front of her breasts, and then she made heaving swipe as if she were knocking everything off a dinner table.

On the *Eclipse*, its torn sails completely flew off to the side as a hurricane gale smashed sideways against the ship, and nearly all of the flabbergasted crew were pushed over the railings to plummet to their deaths.

When the wind ended, Admiral Lina fell to her knees. The spell had tired her out, she knew it would, but it hadn't been as debilitating as she thought it would be. She shuffled back to her feet with small droplets of blood on the edge of her ears, and then she leaned onto Officer Moreau.

"Ryson," she called out, "are you well enough to teleport?"

"As ready as I can be," he said, his eyes still shut as he was recuperating his strength while lying on the floor.

"Grayson, get an offensive team over here so he can move us all at the same time. And tell Holden to send his party too, there's a clear line of sight so the less trained transporters should be able to handle it."

"Aye sir," the signaler said, and his hands started working right away.

While a group of crewmen organized themselves to the front of the ship to join the admiral on her boarding team, the dragons over the *Eclipse* took the wind as their cue to attack. With the deck nearly devoid of all life, there was little resistance as Rauliax and his squad descended to pass through the shield. Hovering over the shield, he gently rolled over, almost in a mocking manner, and let Solah's body shatter the barrier, and then they went down onto the deck as the crew inside the ship started rushing out to rearm the deck.

But they couldn't get to the cannons fast enough, and once the deck was full of dragons there was no way they could fight them off. It took three or four humans to hurt one, and even more to outright kill one with magic. And that didn't take into account the elves that were riding and helping them. Before long most of the major hatches and stairs were clogged with burning, fried, or frozen corpses, and nobody else dared to climb out to the deck.

Some of the dragons started crawling onto the side of the ship, their claws digging into the wooden hull to stick on, and the ship's cannons couldn't fire at them. They crawled over the ship like a colony of ants, and once they reached the bottom they started tearing apart the engines with their breath weapons.

Meanwhile, Rauliax flew up onto the platform in front of the bridge, designed similar to the *Corona's,* and there he let Solah and Siwan unbuckle off. A short while later, the admiral, signaler Moreau, and a group of mages appeared bunched around them in a great flash.

The inside of the bridge was in a clear state of panic, and most of them rushed out of the back door and fled to the waiting dragons on the other side. One man stayed inside, his hands raised, and Rauliax helped the admiral enter by bashing through the door so she could declare checkmate.

When she entered, Admiral William Morit looked at her with the eyes of a man that knew he had been bested, and he smiled. "Admiral Lina. I must say I'm not entirely surprised about your most unusual element. It was something our spies have not been able to discover, and I was most curious to know what magic the admiral of the Wesarian fleet wielded." His feigned smile faded, however, and he continued, "I must know what you've been doing to break right through my ship's shields."

"I'll tell you once you sit in a prison and your king is defeated."

The smile returned. "That is only fair, after all. I didn't count on the dragons joining your fight since my king told me he had reached an agreement with them."

Ellcadur said, "No, only with one dragon."

"Ah, and the elves. Didn't expect them either, strict isolationists from what our spies say of them."

The Keeper gave him a smirk. "Only in recent years, but that will change."

"Well, in any case you've defeated me and my fleet, Admiral Lina. I submit myself to your custody."

The admiral kept her eyes fixed on his, wary of any trickery. "I'm glad even an Elemarian is conscientious of proper etiquette. Very good." She turned to one of the mages in her company and said, "Bind him. We'll take him to the *Corona*, and keep your eyes on him."

The mage nodded, and he motioned his hands until vines sprouted on Admiral Morit's wrists and tightened them until they locked together.

Admiral Morit sighed. At the very least, his heart did not have to worry about the prince as he would've been safely back in Lokin by now.

"Admiral," Officer Moreau said, "I'm getting a message from Grayson. Apparently Holden's party has found out that Prince Rayleigh is on board. And, well, we'd better get to his chambers."

Will perked his ears at the message. The Wesarian admiral seemed like a reasonable woman, and there was no way she would've had the prince killed, would she? He'd find out soon enough as the mages around her dragged him along as she moved out of the bridge.

"Direct us to the prince's chambers," she said. She noticed his eyes appear almost pitiable, and she added, "I promise he will not be harmed."

Will found it difficult to look at her in the eyes, uncanny as they were, though he did so for the prince's sake. "Very well, this way."

When they arrived in the extravagant chamber, they saw Signals Officer Grayson and another man in a loose white coat standing over Prince Rayleigh's body.

Before Admiral Morit had a chance to speak, Admiral Lina asked, "Doctor, what happened here?"

The doctor was holding the clear blue bottle that Will had given to the prince before, and he sniffed at it. "This is a bottle of Death's Hand. He died before he even finished drinking half of it."

Will was stunned. He almost stumbled backward and fell, but the mages around him held him up. "I-impossible! That bottle was given to me directly from the king, and I personally handed it to the prince! H-how could this be?"

Admiral Lina glared at him, critically analyzing his facial expression. "You gave this poison to him personally?"

"What? No! It was supposed to be a transport potion that would take him back to the capital!"

She stared at his face and nodded. There was no deceit, and there was a deeper hurt that she could see. "He wasn't just your prince, was he?"

"I raised him in his father's place. He was a son to me."

"I see. If you're sure this bottle came from the king himself, then you must understand there is only one possible explanation."

The reasoning was undeniable, but Will couldn't accept it.

"Filicide is not unheard of amongst powerful men," she said, further driving the point home.

"B-but why?"

"Just another question I plan to ask your king when I get my hands on him."

Will couldn't fathom it. The king murdering his own son? Why? He couldn't bear to look at Prince Rayleigh's body, but he needed to know why. "Admiral," he pleaded, "I wish to defect."

She saw the look of a man who had been betrayed and she expected the question coming from a mile away, but she wasn't sure whether she could trust him or not. His eyes were sincere, but he was still the admiral of the Elemarian fleet. Was his loyalty to his prince greater than that to his king?

"If I allow you to join our fight, you will always be under watch by no less than three mages. What do you intend to do when we capture the king?"

"I understand. I would do the same, perhaps more." He paused for a moment. "When and if you capture him, I will ask him whether he murdered his son."

"And if he did?"

"Then I will let justice be done."

Chapter 29

The *Eclipse* started rumbling as the dragons under it wrecked enough engines for the ship to start to falter. The doctor wrapped Prince Rayleigh into a body bag so he could have a proper burial later, a gesture of goodwill to Admiral Morit, who did not resist in any fashion, and then the group ran out to teleport back to the *Corona*.

Rauliax picked up Solah and Siwan again, and then they flew over to the *Corona's* bridge platform. At about the same time, the admiral and her team of ten people reappeared outside the bridge, and they carried William Morit and his prince inside.

Afterwards, Rauliax's father flew down to greet his sons, and Ellcadur commended them on their performance in the battle. All the while, the dragons on the *Eclipse* finished tearing apart its propellers and engines, and without a single source of non-magical lift, the ship's levimages couldn't hold the massive leviathan afloat. It crashed, and every dragon, man, and elf in the fleet could hear its impact with the rubble below.

Solah sighed and set himself down next to Rauliax's side. "It's over?"

The dragon craned his neck over and smiled at him. "It's over."

"Yes," Wyrst said, "it looks like the battle has concluded in the other fronts as well."

"Oh? Let's take a look," Rauliax said.

Solah nodded, and he hopped back onto the silver dragon's back, not bothering with the harness this time. They flew up with *their*, the boy supposed he should think of now, father and took a quick look around, leaving Siwan with Ellcadur.

Wyrst guessed that less than a fifth of the dragon army made it through alive, and there were only a handful of airships still flying. There might've been dragons, and their elves for that matter, that were incapacitated and crashed down to the forest, however, and he needed to organize a rescue effort with Ellcadur before the fires in the forest consumed them all. The General sighed at all the devastation. Most of the bodies, dragon, elf, or human, would not receive a burial since they would be burned back into the dust that they were forged from.

Rauliax looked around too, and Solah was peering into the distance looking for a single ship. They saw that in the north, only the *Paladin* remained afloat, heavily damaged, and another smaller ship was heading down to Windsgate, probably for repairs. On the south side, there were only two ships left, and Rauliax knew both of them. The *Lightsworn* was also descending to Windsgate, and the dragon could feel Solah start jittering with joy as he saw the other ship approach: the *Reliant*. It was in far better shape than any of the others they had seen, and even the *Corona* looked like a bigger mess with its shattered mast.

"Son," Wyrst said, "get down to the wreckage. Try and find anyone still alive, and I'll send the rest of the army down to rescue them."

Rauliax nodded and, without another word, flew down to the demolished forest. He saw that only a few scraps had strayed far enough to actually hit a building or two inside the city, but he was most happy to see some dragons had crawled their way to the city's gates, marked by the openings in the city's wards, and people were scurrying to treat their wounds. Once he landed on top of the rubble, however, his disposition changed for the worse.

The forest was burning, assuredly, and there wouldn't be much time to recover the wounded. Even so, there were small pockets of fire on various slabs of splintered wood, and it was dangerous to tread through many areas. Rauliax chose a flatter area, devoid of any flames, to land on, and there were four dragon bodies for him to examine. Their harness straps had snapped, and their riders were nowhere to be found. He walked past them, pressing his paw against each one's hides before continuing to another, and after the last he lifted off to move to another place in silence.

He saw another larger group in on what appeared to be the front section of a dreadnought, and he landed through to take a quick summary glance.

Some of them had crushed their riders when they crashed, and bones were often sticking out in places that made Rauliax feel nauseous. Several more elves were lying dead, scattered randomly about the floorboards. This wasn't a job he should've accepted, and he wanted nothing more than to leave. But at the very least, he knew he had to try, at least until the remnants of the dragon army came down for a more thorough search.

After a cursory glance at the bodies, he approached a white one.

"I recognize some of these faces," Rauliax said. He placed a forepaw onto the top of a white dragon's muzzle. There was no life. He sighed, and then said, "This was Javic. I remember he was the only that dared to beat the General's son in a sparring match."

Solah said, "You mean-"

"Yes, everyone always let me win. Since I was the General's son and all. It was terribly boring, but I didn't really want to fight. I only spent a couple of years training in the military, and even then I was mostly only interested in the intellectual part of battle. You know, the tactics, strategy, command, that sort of stuff."

"But you fought Malyfar?"

"He was older and slower, but more experienced as a result of his age. Still, he was a council member, not another army-trained dragon. Javic would've wiped the floor with him. I only beat him because you helped."

Solah stayed silent, and Rauliax moved on past the white dragon to take a closer look at a blue one lying behind him past a pair of elves. He could tell there was no hope for the blue dragon either: a cannonball stuck out in a bloody hole through his chest.

Rauliax sighed again and looked at the fallen elves. "I lived. We lived because of them. We were more important, that's the only reason why we lived. We were given a squad to protect us, the rest of them were left to fight on their own." He curled a paw into a fist and pounded the ground. "And I chose to go against that dreadnought when we were told to just fly through. My decision killed that green dragon in front of us."

"That's not your fault, Raul. Your decision might be the reason the *Paladin* is still in one piece. Heavily damaged, sure, but at least they're not burning down here."

"I know, but still." The silver dragon brushed a paw down the front of his head. He looked up and saw the dragon army heading down, their eyes scanning through the rubble. "Let's get out of here.

There's more death than life here. Let's leave this job to real soldiers like Yurik."

Rauliax took his foster brother's silence as approval, so then he lifted off and flew back up to the *Corona.*

Admiral Lina fell into her chair in the bridge, exhaustion finally catching up to her. "How many ships do we have left, Holden?"

The Fleet Lieutenant looked at her grimly. "Less than half a dozen."

"How many are able to continue into Elemar?"

"None, admiral, unless you count the *Corona* and the *Reliant.* The *Paladin's* lost half her engines, her sails, and three quarters of her crew is dead. The *Firestorm's* lost more than half her engines, and Captain Fourier expects a week for repairs. We have two battlecruisers left, heavily damaged and already retreating to Nomel for repairs, and they expect two weeks downtime. Three frigates, two also retreating to Nomel, and one at Windsgate. They're out for a couple of days. We have no more scout ships left, except for the *Reliant,* and I haven't received any updates from them since their signals officer went silent, though they appear to be mostly undamaged."

She sighed. King Arashal had sent an all out force to take Wesar, but there had to have been ships that were undergoing maintenance or repairs that would put up a resistance. "Admiral Morit," she asked, "how many ships are left in Elemar that could be made battle-ready in one week?"

Will found no reason to lie, not after his king's treachery. "Five were left in Elemar only because they had difficulty installing the new engines from Noriath," he said. "Three frigates and two scouts. We went on without them, not worth waiting for five extra small ships when we had perfect weather."

Admiral Lina gave him a curt nod. "Very well. Five small ships should pose no threat to us."

"There is another dreadnought under construction," Will added, "and it's scheduled to finish in two months, but if you give them a week they might be pressured to make it operational by then."

She thought for a moment, and then she made her decision. She grabbed a nearby radio and switched it on, not bothering to use her signalers now that there was no need to a secure channel. "Admiral Lina to *Reliant*, respond."

She waited a while, and then a young voice came through the box. "Ensign Waters here, let me hand you off to the lieutenant. Standby."

"Roger," she replied, and then she waited.

A minute later, another voice flicked through the box. "This is Lieutenant Avery of the *Reliant*, receiving admiral."

"Lieutenant, I need to speak to the captain."

She unclicked the radio button, and then there was a rather long moment of silence. She heard a click as the lieutenant pressed the key to say something, but instead she just heard an audible sigh. Another moment later, she heard him say, "Admiral. Under Emergency Fleet Provisions, Article Two, I am now acting captain."

Then she understood the apprehension in his voice, but there was no time for sentiment. "Understood, Captain Avery. Your ship is needed beyond the call of duty once more."

"The *Reliant* is ready to serve, admiral."

"We're going straight to the capital. Take an hour's rest, and then be ready to move. I'll order personnel transfers to give you a fresh and well-trained compliment."

"Understood admiral, thank you. Permission to speak freely, sir?"

"Granted."

"Captain Dillan has family in Windsgate. Can I have two hours to," he paused a second, "to deliver their news? And to, you know, present his body, so umm, they can prepare him for whatever ceremonies they wish."

She understood what the lieutenant was feeling. She had never lost her captain when she was a ship's lieutenant, but losing Benson must have felt the same, only she didn't have a body to deal with. "I'll give you three, captain."

"Thank you, admiral."

She set the radio down so she could go about handling crew transfers. She would need transporters, of course, and she could transfer the protectors on the *Paladin* to give the *Reliant* absurdly powerful shields for its class. She needed the best for their expedition to Lokin, but before she could start sorting through crew lists, she was called back to the radio when a female voice transmitted through.

"Sorry for eavesdropping," the woman said, "but you've actually got another ship. Captain Pearce of the *Defiant*, reporting in."

Chapter 30

The admiral picked up the radio and called back, "Captain Pearce? Your ship is ready for duty?"

"Yes, Professor Reynolds signed off on everything but one of the guns this morning at Nomel. He said Professor Moonsilver would be more qualified, so we headed out. Looks like we just missed the fight?"

"A little late, but you're just in time for the after party."

"Good, haven't had a chance to test out the new cannons on live targets yet."

"Excellent, how far out are you from Windsgate?"

"Half an hour, tops."

"Very good. The *Defiant* and the *Reliant* will be the *Corona's* escorts."

There was a chuckle from the radio, and then Captain Pearce said, "That's rather ironic, don't you think?"

"What do you mean?"

"The names."

The admiral thought about it for a few seconds, and then she got it. "Ah! It is, isn't it?"

Wendy chuckled again and said, "Don't worry. You can *rely* on the both of us."

Afterwards, the admiral put the Fleet Lieutenant in charge of overseeing personnel transfers, and she went to bed. She was exhausted, not just from her spellcasting, but also from the fact that she barely slept the previous night. Before she went to bed, however, she had sent Admiral Morit to a guest room, shocking most of the crew that expected him to be thrown in the brig. His room was guarded by three elementalists at all times, however, and he was a known lightning elementalist so there wasn't really any way he could

Christopher Hwang

escape, and she was sure he wouldn't try either.

The man had been hurt, she knew, and that sort of betrayal only begot a pounding sense of vengeance. He would do everything in his power to find the opportunity to question King Arashal, and she would enable it. It remained a mystery, however, as to why the king would murder his own son, and she also wished to know the truth.

Madness was always a possible answer. Maybe he had a secret son that he would've preferred to succeed him? Despite Keeper Ellcadur's assurances, however, she did not believe blood magic was involved in any way.

She set herself down onto her bed in her quarters. The admiral's room had once been spartan and utilitarian, but after many renovations it had become an extravagant display of rank and she always felt awkward sleeping on the ridiculously large and showy bed. Even more ridiculous were the crystal ornaments hanging over the bed: every time she lay down on the bed she would note how a particularly heavy vibration from a cannon blast could knock the crystals down and shatter them all along the floor, but she was too exhausted to think about them this time.

Before she fell asleep, however, the Fleet Lieutenant knocked on her door.

"It's unlocked, come."

The Fleet Lieutenant opened her door and entered, and she turned onto her side so she could see him. He was an extraordinarily plain looking man: he had dark brown hair that was mostly flat, and he looked rather much like Ryson. She swore that if he didn't wear the sun-embroidered hat that every member of the senior crew of the *Corona* wore, herself included, then she would never be able to tell the man apart in a crowd.

"Holden," she said, "what do you need?"

"Sorry for the intrusion, admiral. I just wanted to know how much personnel we should take on since I'm not sure if you just wanted to cram the ship full of people or not."

"As many as two day's worth of supplies will allow."

"Two? That's only enough to get us to Lokin. Will we be looting the capital for supplies?"

"No, Holden. Lokin has a teleportation stone, remember?"

"Oh! That's right! We can just teleport people back to Farrain after we capture the king."

246

"Exactly."

"Alright, that makes sense. I'll go sort out the transfers now."

"Make it so, Holden. Move the ship eastward in three hours after the captain of the *Reliant* has returned to his ship."

"Yes, admiral." The Fleet Lieutenant left, shutting the door behind him. The admiral rolled around in her bed once more, and then she was fast asleep.

"Dad," Rauliax said, "are you sure about this?"

Rauliax's father, his wings sagging on the ship's floor, bore a frown on his face. "I'm sorry son, but we have too many wounded, and we're too few to continue on like this."

The lighter dragon whipped his tail in frustration, and Solah moved away from it to avoid getting slapped. "Fine, I understand. But I'm not leaving until this is done."

"Of course you aren't, Raul. I wouldn't expect anything otherwise from you."

"Thanks dad. When I get home, I promise I won't do anything potentially dangerous anymore."

Wyrst smiled, but he also shook his head. "Son, I know you. You can swear you won't, but you will. Curiosity is in your blood."

"I mean it this time, I really-"

"No, Raul. It's alright. Just promise you won't go off alone anymore."

"I...okay. That I can promise."

"Come home in one piece."

"I will."

"And not in a bag."

"Dad, I get it."

"You too, Solah."

The boy was pretending he wasn't listening to their conversation, but when his foster-father said that he had to reply, "We'll come home. To *our* home."

The older dragon nodded, and then he looked into the bridge's window. The Fleet Lieutenant had given them a moment to themselves, and now Wyrst had to, regrettably, repay the kindness with dreary news.

Holden came out and almost immediately asked, "You're sure you can't come?"

"No," Wyrst said, his chest flexing as he extended his neck upward to look like what a noble commander of an army should. "My sons will stay with you, however, and you go with the goodwill of all dragons."

Holden gave him a curt nod. "I'll take whatever I can get, and I thank you for the aid you have already rendered."

"I am happy we were able to fulfill our duty. Farewell."

Rauliax's father gave his sons a cursory glance, and then he leapt off the platform and flew down to Windsgate. Once he was gone, the Fleet Lieutenant turned to Rauliax.

"Sir," he said, "we'll be departing for Elemar's capital in three hours. It'll be a two days trip if we are unhindered, and we have several quarters that a dragon may fit in."

Rauliax's wings did ache and he was exceptionally tired, especially after Solah got off of him, and he would have liked to rest even though he had not even come close to how much he had exerted himself in his sortie with Malyfar. He thought about the *Corona's* accommodations, and though he appreciated the offer, there was nothing like familiarity for comfort. "Is the *Reliant* coming with us?" he asked.

"Yes, and one other ship that just finalized its last airworthiness tests. I believe you're acquainted with the ship's captain. Wendy Pearce."

Rauliax and Solah's face seemed to brighten at the news. "You mean," the dragon said, "she wasn't participating in the battle?"

"No," Holden said, "she was assigned to a new ship, but it wasn't ready in time. You should ask her for the details when she arrives."

"I believe I shall. I hope you'll excuse me, sir, but I will be resting on the *Reliant*."

"Very well. The captain is not on board right now, but I'll inform him of your arrangement when he returns."

"Thank you. We'll take our leave now."

The Fleet Lieutenant gave him a bow, and then he went back into the bridge. Solah crawled back onto Rauliax's back, and he looked down at the forward section of the *Corona* where Siwan and Ellcadur were looking out to the horizon. He wanted to ask Rauliax to see if Siwan wanted a ride, but he figured Ellcadur could send him over when he wanted to.

And then the dragon flew off to the *Reliant*. The ship was like the moon around the world, absolutely dwarfed by the colossus that was the *Corona*, but by now the little ship felt like home to the dragon, and he wouldn't mind being in the company of a familiar crew.

When he landed in front of the captain's cabin and let Solah off, he saw some of the crew on deck look at him, but he knew them and they knew him, and those that saw him while wearing a hat tipped it to him before he went inside.

He never had a chance to roll up the rug inside before they left for battle, and he was thankful he didn't have to bother putting it down now. Barely a minute after he laid himself down, he was snoozing peacefully, leaving Solah to his own devices.

Chapter 31

When Rauliax awoke several hours later, he felt and heard the familiar light rumbling that resonated through the ship in such a manner that indicated they were moving now instead of hovering in place. He looked around the room and saw Solah asleep, but there was also a tray with some pancakes and two glasses of orange juice, though he was sure he couldn't have slept all the way to the next morning already.

Nonetheless, it wasn't unheard of for him to sleep an entire day away, so he stepped outside the cabin after gobbling down a dragon bite-sized slice of the syrupy pancakes to make note of the time. Alas, the sun's position indicated that it was only late in the afternoon, and it was only visible because the *Reliant* was flying higher than the *Corona*. It was a rather majestic sight: even with its main mast shattered, it forged on, the flags of Wesar, blue and imprinted with a picture of a tower shield, flowing in the wind. It was a true emblem of spirit and strength, and it had done what it was most appointed to do: defend the realm that created it.

He watched the ship fly along for a while. The engines were mostly undamaged from the battle since the brunt of the attacks it bore came from above, and they hummed along at a hypnotic rate. The air distorted in such a way around the propellers that seemed a warning; if the *Reliant* approached too closely, then it would be destroyed by their wake. Even though the ship was a colossal giant, had only one rear engine to propel it forward, and had damaged sails, it had taken on several levimages from the rest of the surviving fleet and, along with the surviving elves enhancements, was moving at what appeared to be a nominal cruising rate, especially since the Ridgeback Mountains were already visible in the distance.

There also appeared to be another ship on the other side of the

Corona, but he could only see part of it. What he could see, however, seemed to be a pure reflection of the sunlight, and looking towards it hurt his eyes so that he turned his head away and looked at his own ship, the grogginess of his recent nap devouring any sense of curiosity he might have had about the shininess of the other ship.

The crew was still hustling along the deck, busy with whatever they were doing, and he still felt a certain weariness as he watched. He went back into the cabin and started drinking the sweet orange juice from the larger glass since it was obviously intended for him, being nearly thrice the size of the other, and the cool drink worked wonders at fighting off the lingering lethargy that remained after just awakening.

There was nothing to do now but wait until they reached Elemar, so he set up his folding table and started reading in a vain attempt to forget the faces of the fallen, the green dragon that was killed because of him, the piles of flesh and wood that burned outside of Windsgate, and the smell the poor citizens of the city would undoubtedly be weighed under for days after the fires starved themselves out.

In fact, the only thing that kept him calm was Solah's light snoring, an affirmation that his foster-brother was alive and well, and a symbol of what he was fighting for.

Solah woke up and saw a familiar elf talking to Rauliax.

"Sorry I was gone for a while," Siwan said. "Ellcadur wanted me to help him organize the elves that are still around."

"I'm just glad there are still some that stayed," Rauliax said.

"Most never let themselves exert themselves so that they wouldn't be able to flash to another ship if they needed to, though the ones on dragonback stuck with them to the very end."

"Ah," the dragon said, "I'll have my father give a ceremony of gratitude for that."

Solah sat up and interrupted their chat. "We're not done yet."

"Solah! You're awake," Rauliax said. "Here, Ensign Waters left us some food and refreshments."

Solah took the plate of pancakes and, unlike Rauliax, used the utensils to eat them properly. Not that he knew what proper meant to a dragon, however, it just seemed more proper since they were provided after all. When he finished eating, he asked, "So what's happening?"

"Nothing much," Rauliax replied. "Just flying to Elemar, going to capture King Arashal. You know, pretty boring stuff."

"Uh huh," Solah replied.

Rauliax reached into his mouth and pulled out his Algebra textbook. "Here, Solah. I find reading takes my mind off of certain things I don't want to think about."

He took the book from his paws. He wanted to object to returning to such a normal state of living, but there was a heaviness in the way the dragon handled the textbook and spoke that told him it was how he was coping with what he had seen. Without that sense of normalcy, there was no telling what Rauliax would be doing, and he himself understood and felt similarly enough to seek out what peace he could find.

But the peace he found in the world of parabolas and quadratic functions didn't last for long. Avery came in, and the first thing his eyes noticed was that he was wearing Captain Dillan's hat: the silver lining all around its edges was unmistakable.

"Lieutenant," Rauliax said, "it's good to see you. Ensign Waters has been most accommodating."

Avery's face seemed to scrunch up, and then he said, "I'm glad to hear that, but, well, it's Captain Avery now."

With the way his face appeared and how his eyes seemed to drag on the ground. It was rather clear to Rauliax what Avery meant. "I see," was all the dragon could say.

Solah was far less subtle. "You mean," he said, "the captain is...gone?"

"Yes. I'm sorry, but I can't keep the news away forever."

Solah shook his head in disbelief. "But the ship is almost undamaged, how did he die?"

Avery looked up and his face loosened. "He died a hero. He died so nobody else on the *Reliant* had to."

The boy stayed settled on the rug, completely speechless. He thought back to his conversation with Priscilla's father and remembered what he had said to the old dragon. He was in this war to keep his friends safe, and he had counted Captain Dillan as one of them. He had given him a chance after finding out about his power and his past, and he valued honesty as one of the best indicators of a man's goodness. And that belief made him a good man himself, a man that didn't deserve to die.

"W-why?" Solah whispered.

A hand gently held onto his shoulder, and he looked around to see it was Siwan's.

"I know it seems harsh," the elf said, "but we're in a war. People die. Friends die. We can do everything in our power to try and stop it from happening, but it still will."

Solah felt weak, and his stomach felt hurt. He could now truly emphasize with the pain Siwan must've felt when his best friend was killed. "I don't like this," he stammered, "I don't understand what people are dying for."

"I know one thing," Siwan said. "Everyone west of the mountains is dying to protect their homes. Everyone from the east is dying for the whims of some mad king. Once justice deals with him, we can go home and live in peace."

There was a long uncomfortable silence, and then Rauliax feigned a cough. "Lieutenant, err, captain, I think it would be best if we were left to quiet for a while."

Avery nodded rather quickly since he was quite eager to leave the dreary mood. "Of course," he said. "And all of you can call me by my first name, please. Jonathan Avery, Jon if you'd prefer."

Rauliax crossed a forearm across his heavily scaled chest and gave a slight bow. "Thank you, Jon."

Avery bowed too before turning around to leave, but before he stepped out of the cabin, he turned around. "One last thing," he said, "Captain Pearce would like to see you again, and Solah. She's on the ship on the other side of the *Corona*."

Rauliax smiled and looked at his foster-brother, and he saw the boy's face had become less burdened. "I would love to see her again as well. A visit would definitely take our minds off, well, yes."

And that was what they did. Although Solah wanted to introduce Siwan to Wendy, he declined for some business with the Keeper. When Rauliax lifted off with the boy on his back, the elf flashed over to the *Corona*, courtesy of a transporter. They flew over the leviathan, Rauliax needing to fly diagonally to keep up with the flow of the formation, and once they were over the top half, they saw Wendy's airship.

The first thing that caught both their eyes was how *small* the ship was. It was even smaller than the *Reliant*, and it looked like the *Corona* could swallow it like a whale a fish. The second thing that they noticed was how shiny it was; not just the rails or the decor or the engines, but the entire ship glimmered with a brilliance greater than that of even Rauliax's scales. They flew closer, and they saw that the ship was designed very differently from the airships they had seen before.

The *Defiant* had no sails, but it seemed to possess an extra large rudder attached to the rear, along with an elevator for pitch control. There were only two propellers holding the ship aloft, and another in the back, attached over the rudder and elevator, for propulsion. Rauliax flew around the ship to take note of its craftsmanship, and it appeared as if the ship had only one cannon on its sides, except for the front, and two on the bottom. Two dragon cannons were mounted on the deck, and the front had a massive pair of tubes sticking out along with what seemed to be two flat plates between the tubes. The reason for the *Defiant's* shininess was obvious now: the entire airship was plated in steel.

While the ship was small, there appeared to be a small building in the rear, the aft propeller mounted above it, and Rauliax guessed it was the bridge. The bridge had an uncharacteristically large door for its size, but he didn't need to go inside since he could see a lone woman standing on the forward deck, and he was sure that was the captain.

He landed and braced his paws and feet for cold, but the steel was apparently warmed up by the sun, and it was not at all uncomfortable to walk on. Solah hopped off shortly after he landed, and they cheerfully made their way to the captain.

Wendy gave Solah a quick nod as they approached, then she and Rauliax shared a mutual nod. Rauliax thought about how he should've expected her to be military: she was middle-aged for a human woman, but her face appeared tough, and he remembered how she looked a lot like the guard that blocked him from entering the Tourist District in Farrain. It really should've been unsurprising then that the humble innkeeper was former military.

Wendy was wearing a hat now, tipped with a single feather like Avery's old hat, but her dark hair was still visible and flowed gracefully to her shoulders. She greeted the dragon first. "So, *professor*, it seems you kept the truth about the boy hidden from me that night?"

He smiled. Her tone was nowhere near serious, so he replied, "Indeed, though I wish you understand how important it was to keep his true identity masked. Besides, it seems we both kept secrets, right *captain*?"

She smiled. "It's alright. I fully understand which is why I helped you get on the admiral's good side."

Rauliax craned his neck down in a bow and said, "And I haven't had the chance to thank you for that until now."

"Now now, no need for any of that," she said. "I've been told that you two are the only reason we won. If anything, I should be bowing to you!"

"Wendy," Solah said. "Instead of bowing, could you just do us one favor instead?"

"Sure, anything."

"Don't do anything that'll get you killed."

She looked at him oddly, and Rauliax raised his paw. "I'm sorry, we've just lost a friend."

She nodded after a slight pause. "I understand. Loss like that has to be expected in a war like this, but it's harsher on the young, I know."

The dragon didn't want to press her for what he was sure was a rather personal anecdote, but the silence that followed was long and uncomfortable. "So," he said, "what's with this airship? It looks completely different from any other."

The change of subject brought life back into their meeting, and she said, "Knew you'd ask! This ship is the result of a joint human-dragon initiative: a gesture of our two nation's friendship. The *Defiant* was mostly designed by someone who, he's told me, is quite familiar with you, professor."

"Oh?" the dragon asked, "who?"

"A Professor Reynolds."

"Ah! So that's why he was gone from Noriath."

"Yes, he spoke really highly of you, and he oversaw the installation of a rather special weapon he said you'd invented."

"Weapon? I'm not sure what he meant, the dragon cannons weren't invented by me."

"No, another weapon."

There was static coming from the inside of Solah's coat, and he reached inside to pull out the radio he had forgotten to give back to Rauliax. Admiral Lina's voice came through, and she said, "Rauliax? Solah? Either of you hear me?"

The boy clicked the radio's button and replied, "Solah here."

"Hey there," she said, "sorry, I just woke up. Does Rauliax mind helping out with some heavy-duty ship repairs?"

"Not at all," the dragon said, and the boy conveyed his response to the admiral.

"Thank him for me," the admiral replied.

Solah did so, and then Rauliax flexed his wings out, stretching the muscles a bit. "Well, Captain Pearce, it's a pleasure to see you again, and I'll be sure to visit again tomorrow, assuming the admiral's done having me haul stuff." His tail swished, gesturing Solah to hop on, and he did so.

"I look forward to your visit," Wendy said. "In fact, I'll actually have to put in an order for it to the admiral if she doesn't give you time."

"Really now? Well, I suppose it'll be for some business then, won't it?"

"The weapon you made, we'd like you to look it over."

"Ah. I'm still not sure what Reynolds would be referring to, but I'm sure I could assist anyway."

Before the dragon lifted off, Solah said, "You'll retire again and return to the *Flare*, right Wendy?"

She let out a boisterous laugh. "Of course I will! I have a friend running it right now, and I only left because the admiral practically begged me to."

"That's good. Not even the king's cook could make a steak as well as you could."

"Now that would be a flattering compliment, though I daresay it should go to my own cook. Of course, if word of it got out then the King Devran would be looking to take my chef away."

Rauliax was chuckling too, and he had to afford her a greater elaboration. "Really though," he said, "it was only the king's morning cook that tried to fill Solah's steak order, and there was no doubt the cook was flummoxed by the request."

Wendy let out a sigh of relief. "Oh good, I'm sure my cook will safely remain mine then. Silly boy, you should have waffles and pancakes for breakfast, not steak!"

"He couldn't have known any better anyway," Rauliax replied.

She chuckled. "Of course. I'll serve steak any time when we get back, okay?"

"That'd be great! Bye Wendy!" Solah called out as Rauliax's limbs flexed downward in preparation for flight.

"Until next time!" she called back.

Then they were up again, and they headed to the *Corona* for some much needed distracting busywork.

Chapter 32

Rauliax woke up and rubbed his eyes into focus. Solah was still asleep next to Siwan, so he took a step outside of the captain's cabin on the *Reliant* alone. The admiral had asked him to help move and handle a lot of heavy items yesterday, many that wouldn't fit into his mouth, and he was busy working well into the night. Rebuilding the main mast, after receiving one from Illum, the last major city before the Ridgeback Mountains, had been especially tiring although the *Corona's* kineticists had helped the best they could. Still, the admiral had told him that it would've normally been a week's repair job that he had helped finish in one day.

Thus with the *Corona's* sails repaired, the entire formation could continue at the fastest speed the leviathan could travel at. The work had kept him well past midnight, however, and it was not a surprise that Rauliax looked outside to see the sun already a little past noon. He had to move a little to the side since the cabin was blocking his rear vision, but sure enough the Ridgeback Mountains were already far behind them, its jagged peaks softened with the illusion of distance and the sun's light waves.

He remembered that Siwan hadn't returned yet when he and Solah had fallen asleep this morning, past midnight being morning, and if he was right then the elf wouldn't wake up until much later. The way to Lokin in front of them seemed to be plains for miles and miles, and only near the horizon did he see some resemblance of a forest.

The airships were flying high: the reduced air density increased their airspeed, and they were so high that not even a master fire elementalist could hurl a fireball and hit them, though they were nowhere past the limit of human comfort.

Without any further work from the admiral, Rauliax decided to fly over to the *Defiant* and see what Professor Reynolds had been doing in his spare time. The little steel ship was exceptionally solid, he noted, and Reynolds had designed the ship to be both utilitarian and aesthetically pleasing. He landed on the forward section of the deck and noticed the lines between the plates of steel that armored the ship, but what really caught his eye was the silver figurehead that faced out from the bow.

It was a sculpture of a dragon, and a female one at that. She was beautifully carved, and it was clear she was made by human hands with all the intricate details on her. The curves and etches in her horns were perfect, and her ears were sharp but unlike an elf's because they were also thick, somewhat like his own, and he walked up the railing to stretch his neck out as far as possible so he could look at her from the front. Though the statue's eyes were lifeless, they still exhumed a sense of determination, of strong will, and he couldn't help but think of Priscilla. The dragon's back, of course, melded in shape and color into the ship, but from the front her belly scales were fully carved out and detailed, and they ran down to the absolute lowest point of the bow. Her belly scales, however, were sharp and triangular, not like most dragons' round ones, but he knew the shape was chosen for more practical purposes like cutting wind resistance, and the odd shape did not detract from the dragon's beauty at all.

He started to think about how beautiful she would've been in the flesh, but then he stopped and felt a paw hit him on the snout, an invisible and imagined purple paw. The slap was a self-induced hallucination, of course, but it scared him nonetheless. He shook his head to clear the phantom pain away and imagined Priscilla's scorning face glaring down at him. No, he would not do anything that could possibly make her feel jealous. Even just admiring the statue of another female dragon could've been disastrous if he'd done it in front of her! He stepped back and looked away towards the horizon, but then he saw something else he had not noticed earlier. There were little brown dots that seemed to be growing slowly, and he wasn't sure whether or not he was just seeing things. He was fixated on them for about ten minutes before he was finally sure: they were incoming airships.

When he turned around to find Captain Pearce, he saw her standing right there and twitched his tail in surprise.

"Hey," she said, "I was in the bridge and saw that you've been staring at the figurehead for quite a while. I mean, I'm sure she's beautiful, but my chief of engineering has been most eager to meet you."

Rauliax's face flushed with scarlet, visible through his bright scales, but he had to set her straight. "No, no, you misunderstand! I was looking to the horizon, look over there." He pointed a claw right over the dragon statue's horns, and she peered in that direction. "Do you see them?"

Rauliax knew human eyes weren't as acute as dragon eyes, but she should've been able to see them by now. She seemed to squint her eyes a bit, and then she pulled out a small tube from inside her coat. Her fingers clicked something, and then she seemed to pull the tube apart, but then he realized it was a compactable telescope.

She looked through it for about ten seconds, and then she tucked the telescope back into her coat while pulling out a radio. She clicked onto it and said, "Captain Pearce to Admiral Lina."

Another ten seconds passed, and then he heard the admiral's voice call back through the black box. "Admiral Lina receiving, what is it?"

"Admiral, we've got five Elemar ships approaching. Just frigates and scouts by the look of it."

"Roger," the admiral replied, "my lookouts just reported them to me too. Prepare your ship for battle."

"Yes, admiral." Wendy put the radio back into her coat, and then she looked up at Rauliax. "Well, now's as good a time as any. Come with me."

He followed the captain down into the interior of the airship. He noticed that the ship really was designed by a dragon since it was most accommodating, and the stairs down into the hull were large and the interior was tall enough to give his horns plenty of clearance. Once down inside the spacious inside of the ship, he was greeted by an energetic middle-aged man.

"Ah," he said, "Professor Moonsilver, I assume? Chief Engineer Tresca, at your service."

Tresca held out his hand, and Rauliax held his paw over to shake it. "A pleasure to meet you," the dragon said.

Once they released their mutual handshake, the engineer asked him, "Are you related to Reuleaux Franz Moonsilver, by any chance?"

Rauliax was a little surprised to hear his namesake from a human, but he supposed it made sense if he had studied a bit of engineering in Noriath. "Yes," he said, "Reuleaux was my grandfather, on my mother's side. I suppose you know him from his polygons?"

"No," Tresca said, "actually from his work in kinematics."

"Ah yes, one of the best physicists of his time."

"Indeed." He pointed to another man sitting next to a massive pile of wood. "That is Lieutenant Engineer Mises."

"A pleasure," the other engineer grunted.

Rauliax nodded at him in response and then directed his attention back to Tresca. "I must say, this ship's design is really different. I know Reynolds designed it, but how did you manage to build it?"

"Yes, it is different," the engineer said. "Professor Reynolds designed the *Defiant*, yes. He came up with the idea of a highly maneuverable, nearly indestructible ship, and designed the steel armor around the hull along with the two massive cannons. They're specially constructed to hold twenty cannonballs each for rapid-fire."

The dragon chuckled a little. "I had wondered why the old professor had left Noriath. It's very unusual for a dragon to venture far, you might know."

The engineer nodded. "Indeed, it is a strange quality, though I can understand it."

Curious about the steel armor on the *Defiant*, Rauliax asked, "How did you apply the plates onto the ship? For that matter, wouldn't conductivity help lightning elementalists fry the crew?"

"Interesting," Tresca said, "that was a matter that Reynolds had overlooked, but you caught it rather quickly."

"I suppose it's because I've been around humans more often, so I can imagine the possible modes of assault."

The engineering chief smiled. "True, and yes, you are right. Though Reynolds created the idea of steel armor, we had to refine it since it would be difficult to just mold steel into an airship. Hence, we figured to stick plates to cover the *Defiant*. And actually, the plates are put right over a normal wooden hull so it would be easier to apply and it would result in a lighter weight."

"Makes sense, it explains the creases I saw between each block of steel. Is there an enchantment that reduces the conductivity of the steel?"

"Yes, but such an enchantment would take years to apply on every block of steel on the *Defiant*, so you can imagine that we had to come up with something different. We had to use a lot of steel stock just to put this ship together. It would take a year to make this much steel from transmutation, you know, and a couple of years to build this one ship wouldn't be feasible."

"What did you do?"

"Between each block, we put in a layer of industrial strength rubber. That way, any lightning attacks that come through will only conduct around the particular section it hits."

"Oh, I see. That's rather ingenious!"

Tresca nodded, and then he gestured the dragon to follow him further into the ship. "Now professor," he said, "Reynolds, on his last visit, also sent me your railgun design. He showed me your prototype, and I must say I was impressed. Come with me."

Rauliax was slightly taken aback: he had been told that Reynolds had taken his little model railgun in Noriath, but surely Wendy didn't mean that was a weapon on the *Defiant*? He followed the engineer a couple of steps to the center-forward section of the ship, and then he saw it: a scaled up version of his original prototype jutted straight out between the twin cannons out the front of the ship. Another man sat on a stool at the edge of the rails and was looking over in a large box full of the special ammunition forged for the weapon.

"Behold," Tresca said, "your railgun."

Rauliax walked up and down the magnetic cannon and remarked, "My, this is marvelous! Have you tested it? How did you scale up the power without a power source, and how did you account for structural integrity and heat failure?"

"Unfortunately," the engineer said, "We have not had time to test it. This is the *Defiant's* maiden voyage, and we were hoping to test it in battle, but we were late for the party. Soon, we'll see if it works."

Wendy had not partaken in the two's trade of technobabble, but she did say, "Very soon. Five ships are coming to us, chief."

He nodded, and then he tapped at one of the rails and continued, "Your other questions are easily answered if you consider the effect of magic. That's always the issue with dragon research. You guys never account for the benefits that human magic can provide. Not that I'm complaining, of course. A strong independent design is always better and less exhausting to maintain."

Rauliax scanned his eyes down the railgun and tapped at his chin. Now he remembered why the name Tresca sounded familiar: he had seen it on one of the engineering books in Malyfar's library. "Do explain," he said.

"Well, the rails were constructed from transmutated silver mixed with other hardening materials. The great thing about being a transmutator and an engineer is that you can make your own metals, so I can guarantee you that my rails are free from imperfections. I also checked the mounts myself, and I can tell you that they will hold well beyond the magnetic force that will be applied."

"Interesting," Rauliax said, "And how about the friction from the projectile? How does the metal keep from melting?"

"A good question. See, while transmutating the conductive metal for the rails, I also had an enchanter and a frost elementalist at hand. We imbued a freezing enchantment at the atomic level during creation of the metal so that the atoms themselves will not move from heat, or at least will not increase in motion, and naturally friction will do nothing. I swear the structure will not fail."

"Wow," Rauliax said, "that's an ingenious mix of several schools of magic and engineering."

The chief engineer grinned in pleasure. "As for the power source, the battery device you had on yours was obviously woefully inadequate for this sort of size, so we called back one of our best lightning elementalists into service." He gestured at the man at the edge of the rails. "May I present Master Elementalist Onthraey."

Onthraey came up to Rauliax and shook his paw. "A pleasure, professor. You may not know me, but you know my son."

"Oh? I'm afraid I cannot guess who," the silver dragon said.

"I retired and worked at a power plant in Noriath," Onthraey said. "He visited me for a short while to deliver a request from the admiral to return to service. Ensign Frazer, of the *Reliant*?"

The dragon smiled. "Ah, yes, now I see the resemblance."

"Aye, I left for the capital as soon as I received the summons. Left on the last merchant ship departing before the Second Fleet formed up, too."

"Oh," Rauliax said, "I believe I remember seeing that ship before the *Reliant* departed for the Sylvan Forest."

"That was the one. I'm glad you were able to get the Council to send aid, professor. And the elves."

Rauliax started to reply, but then a voice boomed through the ship. The signals officer's voice resounded through and said, "Attention, all crew to battle stations. Enemy inbound, three frigates and two scouts. Captain Pearce, the Elemarian ships are not on an attack course. They're on a suicide course."

Captain Wendy was watching Tresca introduce Rauliax to his weapon, but she ran up to the bridge when she heard her signals officer and pulled out her radio to call the admiral.

"They're on a suicide run?" Admiral Lina asked to Admiral Morit.

"The king must be desperate," Will said, "and Elemarians will do what their king wants them to do. Even give up their lives."

"You're the admiral of the Elemarian fleet, can you try to call them off, maybe turn them to our side?"

"I can try, but it's very unlikely I'll be able to sway any of them while I'm under the custody of their enemy."

She handed him a radio. "Try."

Will nodded, and then he adjusted the frequency on the radio to display the one most commonly used by his fleet. He clicked it, and then he said, "Airships about to engage the Wesarian fleet, stand down. This is Admiral Morit, verification code alpha bravo one six, repeat, stand down in the name of Prince Rayleigh."

There was a minute of silence, and then another voice came through the radio. "Admiral Morit, you have failed your king by accepting capture instead of death. You have been stripped of command, and the king knows you have also failed to protect the prince. You will surrender yourselves to us, or you will die aboard the enemy's ship."

Will's face seemed visibly annoyed and perturbed, and he said nothing for some time.

"Well?" Admiral Lina said.

"They said that Arashal knows the prince is dead. How could he possibly know that? I'm the only living Elemarian that saw."

She raised an eyebrow at him. "I think you found your proof."

"And I promised that justice would be delivered. I am at your disposal, Admiral Lina."

Chapter 33

There were two windows in front of the *Defiant*, one over each of the main cannons. The enemy ships were planning on ramming into the *Corona*, but that didn't mean they were unarmed. The *Reliant* and *Defiant* had to take the five ships down before they hit the *Corona* while avoiding getting destroyed themselves from their attacks.

Destruction was more of a concern for the *Reliant*, however. Rauliax was sure the *Defiant* could handle scouts and frigates like he could handle taking magic attacks. And he probably didn't have to worry about the *Reliant* either since it had taken on more and better protectors.

He had noticed too that the *Defiant* only had two protectors, one for the top and one for the bottom shields. He supposed that the ship would do fine without shields: the armor could handle cannon blasts, ice elementalists would do nothing unless they could freeze cold enough to make the steel very brittle, lightning elementalists would no nothing with the rubber dividers, fire elementalists wouldn't be able to melt the steel unless they joined together to conjure an extremely hot flame, and he supposed the only danger was a boarding party. But he was also sure they were trying to destroy them, not capture them, and he could help handle them if they tried. The engines were a weakness, but the ship had four levimages that could hold it up without any engines assisting for some time.

Tresca's grin grew wider as the incoming ships grew larger through the pair of windows. "Time to test out our new toy. Professor, if you would load the projectile?"

Rauliax nodded and picked up one of the heavy metal balls that were to be loaded onto the magnetic accelerator cannon.

"It can shoot four at a time," Tresca said. "Just put them in the loading area."

The dragon heard him and placed three more onto the gun.

"I'll head back to the main cannons," the engineer said. "Look straight down the gun and you can see outside. Professor, you judge when we are within range to fire and then tell Onthraey to charge the rails."

"Got it," the dragon said.

Tresca left, and then Rauliax felt the *Defiant* start to move to the very front of the *Corona.* He supposed it would've looked almost humorous for such a small ship to be protecting such a colossus behind it, but he kept his focus on the weapon. He stared down out of the hole that the railgun jutted out of and saw one of the ships, a frigate, was already directly in front of them.

The sight of the ship grew larger and larger until at last the dragon waived at Onthraey. "I'd say now is a good time to shoot." He backed off and let the mage stand in front of the rails.

"So as strong a constant current as I can keep up, right?" the lightning elementalist asked.

"Affirmative," Rauliax said with a nod, "Go for it!"

Onthraey's hands danced with sparks as he made some casting motions and then released the charge onto the railgun. The four magnetically charged cannonballs flew straight out the ship faster than a blur.

The first one rammed into the first frigate's barrier and tore a hole into the invisible force field before resting in the ship's hull. The second shot flew straight through one end of the frigate and came out the other before being deflected by the barrier of the scout ship behind it. The third iron ball flew through the passage carved by the second one and hit the scout ship's shields with nearly full power. It pierced the barrier and embedded itself into the scout's hull. There was no time for either of the ships to react, and the fourth ball shot clean through the frigate and the scout before being stopped by the next scout's barrier.

"Holy heck, do that again!" the *Defiant's* signaler shouted through the ship.

"Hold on," Onthraey said, "I need to regain my focus. I need a minute." He took a deep breath and sat down on the floor.

Tresca took out his radio and told the captain that Onthraey needed to rest a bit before firing the railgun again.

Meanwhile, the *Defiant* had closed in, leaving the *Reliant* in the dust, and was doing perfectly fine with her regular cannons. She blasted through the vulnerable forward section of the frigate before diving down, and then she started shooting down the engines, its non-stop rapid-firing capability destroying everything under it.

Rauliax was watching the elementalist in charge of firing one of the cannons. His arms danced as if he was a conductor of a symphony, and every wave resulted in another deafening boom as the cannon fired. It was a rhythmic force of destruction, and the man was controlling it with his sparks of fire.

He also noticed Mises, the Lieutenant Engineer, start waving his hands around the pile of wood he was next to. Some of the wood started turning black, and his hands seemed to press it into a ball. And then the dragon realized that Mises had created another iron ball sized for the main cannons.

Evidently, the *Defiant* had a warp master in addition to a transmutator since more piles of splintered wood started appearing next to the engineer. The wood was broken, messy, and mixed with metal pieces, and it was obviously teleported from the devastation of the enemy ship.

Rauliax looked back to the front windows, and he saw that all the engines were already broken. The *Defiant* tilted a little and fired another shot from its main cannons, and evidently that shot had found the levimages' room because the frigate dropped like a rock after barely three seconds.

Then Rauliax heard Wendy's voice boom through the ship, relayed through her signals officer. "Hey Raul," she said, "When you get back to Noriath tell Reynolds that he gets to stay in my inn for free, for life!"

Rauliax chuckled. He wanted to ask Tresca if he could borrow his radio, but he decided to wait until after the battle to ask Wendy if that offer could be extended to himself too. Not that he meant to freeload; he only wanted to ask jokingly.

The *Defiant* moved back behind the *Reliant* to reload its main cannons, and Rauliax saw the crewmen carry out more of the cannon balls carried out from a storage room, so he did wonder why Mises was making more. He supposed that the room didn't appear large enough to hold a lot, so perhaps the transmutator was just making more for good measure.

In any case, it was clear the *Reliant* was not doing enough damage.

The scouts flew faster ahead, taking potshots at Captain Avery's ship, and the *Reliant* had barely damaged their remaining shields, but they kept their speed matched so they could continue firing as they approached the *Corona*.

Meanwhile, the flagship was accelerating to full reverse, a slow feat for the leviathan, and had stuffed the forward sections of the ship with as many elementalists as they could fit.

Back in the *Defiant*, Onthraey got up from the floor and said, "I'm ready for another."

The ships had changed formation so that they weren't lined in single file, but the two frigates were still flying side-to-side so the *Defiant* maneuvered past the scouts and lined up with them on their port side.

The master lightning elementalist wasted no time and fired another four ferromagnetic balls from the railgun the moment they were lined up. Both their shields had broken, and the last ball had actually shot clean through the second frigate and flew on into the distance, far into the north and out of sight.

Again, the *Defiant* dove straight in, its main cannons blaring in a melody of destruction, and it flew straight through whatever engines it had destroyed so it could hit the other frigate before they managed to rotate their shields.

They didn't make it in time, so the fast little ship turned around to blast through the first frigate's levimages, and they only moved away once they were sure the ship was going down.

The *Defiant's* main cannons were down to half capacity, with some more crew trying to drag the large ammunition of the storage closet as quickly as possible, but there seemed to be no stopping the armored airship. The other frigate had rotated the hole in their barriers to the opposite side, but the *Defiant* flew right under and turned on a dime. Rauliax had to hold onto a railing embedded in the wall just to keep from falling over from the inertia, and even he was surprised by how quick the ship was.

Before the frigate could even open fire, the *Defiant* had crossed to the unshielded side of the ship and blasted away again. One of the frigate's protectors implemented a better strategy of shrinking his barrier to shield an engine directly, but the other protectors hadn't followed suit and the frigate couldn't just fly on one engine.

And they didn't. The *Defiant* had single-handedly wrecked three frigates by itself, and now it sped on through to take care of the scouts. Rauliax just sat there on his haunches, dumbfounded and still gripping onto the railing, and he simply stopped worrying about what threat could come to the ship he was on, and instead he placed it all on the *Corona*.

The scouts were small, sure, but if they collided at full speed into the *Corona,* then the flagship would be crippled and possibly even seriously damaged if both hit. Kinetic energy was delivered by mass times velocity *squared*, after all, and they had to be stopped.

With the engines rumbling at full speed, they caught up to the lagging scout, but Onthraey was simply too tired to fire another volley from the railgun. It already had a hole in its shields thanks to the first volley, however, and the *Defiant* tried to maneuver to the hole faster than the enemy could rotate it away. It proved more difficult with the scout than the frigate, however, since its speed was faster, but they caught the opening eventually and blasted them with the little ammunition they still had loaded in the main cannons.

Not that it wasn't enough: the scout tore like paper from the massive ship-length cannons, and it fell without much of a hassle. The cat and mouse game it played with its shields, however, guaranteed that the *Defiant* wouldn't be able to catch up with the leading scout ship.

Briefed on what Captain Dillan had done by Avery, Admiral Lina ordered the forward barriers reinforced with extra layers of protectors, and stone walls would be erected by the ship's few naturalists if the *Corona's* attacks failed to destroy the scout by the time it approached too closely. Even Ellcadur was at the front, ready to help. It would be enough, she hoped.

The *Reliant* stayed alongside the last scout, the hole that the railgun burrowed through seemingly unaffecting it, the entire time, firing what it could, but it wouldn't have the ship's shields down in time for the *Corona* to make short work of it. It approached firing range, and then the *Corona's* crew rained down everything they had.

The scout had directed all its shielding to the front and allowed the *Reliant* to attack it. With the first volley from the *Corona*, the scout had already lost one layer of shielding, but it kept returning fire to weaken it's target's shields.

And then the scout caught on fire. Admiral Lina realized what a terrible idea it was to assail the ship with fire elementalists, and if they collided then it would light the *Corona* on fire too. She used one more asset to slow the ship down: herself.

She balled her hands and started flicking out her fingers repetitively at the scout, and a wave of wind formed in front of them that pushed the scout back. She willed it to become stronger, and it was enough: the *Defiant* caught up, flew in, and blasted the scout into oblivion.

Without any hesitation, the admiral ordered her ships to continue forward as fast as possible, now, assured by William Morit, unhindered by any further resistance.

Chapter 34

The three Wesarian ships had to finally descend to teleport teams into Lokin after their two days of restless flying. They arrived late in the afternoon, blatantly visible and alerting the capital, but Elemar had no more ships to fight them with.

Rauliax had Solah and Siwan harnessed in when they approached, and together they stood on the edge of the *Reliant* in an area without a dragon cannon blocking the view. Looking down while they descended, they saw that Lokin was very much different from Farrain. Whereas the Wesarian capital was arranged in a circular fashion, Lokin seemed to be tiered linearly; the lowest and poorest buildings started from the west and grew taller and better-looking as the city grew eastward. Near the eastern edge was the king's castle, and indeed it could be described as a castle since that was how it appeared. Unlike King Devran's palace, King Arashal's was made of stone masonry in the classic square shape, with turrets at each corner, like a more primitive version of the University of Noriath. Inside the walls was the keep, the tallest building in the city, and there were some cannons placed on the highest points of the keep and the turrets.

They were pointed up, of course, and the castle walls were lined with elementalists ready to fire. Some of the turrets were protected with small barriers, but Admiral Morit had assured that Elemar's best soldiers had been assigned to the fleet, and the soldiers below would be pushovers.

And he was proven correct. When their cannons came within range of the castle, they started firing down, enemy cannons a priority. The shielded ones took a bit longer to demolish, but their protectors failed extremely quickly, especially considering how small an area they needed to shield compared to a whole side of an airship. The men below fled into the safety of the keep and holed up when it was clear that staying outside was suicide.

Admiral Lina had created a plan after William had drawn up the castle's schematic. The king's chamber was protected by protectors, the only strong ones still remaining in the kingdom, and they would have to break through them before they could warp more troops in. However, there were many soldiers inside the keep, and though they were not as well-trained as a ship's crew, their number would prove problematic.

In answer, the admiral had put together a diversion team consisting of no less than a hundred elementalists and elves. The *Defiant* would use her railgun to blast a hole on the level below the king's chamber, and the diversion team would warp in and fight. Hopefully, they would draw most of the troops away from the level above. Afterwards, they'd blast another smaller hole with the *Defiant's* main cannons on the same level of the king's chamber, and then Rauliax, Solah, and Siwan would fly in followed by a smaller team consisting of five elementalists, a protector, Signals Officers Grayson and Moreau, Admiral Morit, and herself.

And so they were ready to bring an end to this war.

The *Defiant* performed brilliantly and shattered the wall so powerfully that the magnetic ammunition flew straight through the castle, creating a hole on both sides, and effectively drove hordes of soldiers to that level while the Wesarian transporters beamed in their own troops and fought for the opening.

Meanwhile, Captain Avery maneuvered his airship around the castle, shooting down any straggling cannons, and Rauliax stood on the edge with Solah and Siwan harnessed on his back. He waited, blood thumping through his heart, for the *Defiant* to open their path.

He expected there would still be a modicum of resistance, even if the majority were below them dealing with the diversion. After dealing with it, they'd have to rush in and Solah would have to break the barriers in the main chamber to capture the king.

"I'm scared," Solah said. "All this time, I've been distanced from killing. Everyone else has been doing most of the fighting, I just support with my power. All the people on those airships, well, I could sort of handle it because I didn't have to look at their faces. But now." He looked down on the floor. "We're going straight in this time, Raul, and I don't know if I'll be able to, you know, when I have to."

"Don't worry," Rauliax replied. "You don't have to kill anyone. They can fling everything they have at you and do nothing, so just soak up their attention, break their barriers, and I'll handle the rest."

"Me too," Siwan said.

The *Defiant* moved up and blasted apart the stone wall in the level above, and they had to move in a few seconds. Solah looked at the hole the *Defiant* had blown through, afraid of what they'd face inside. "Okay, thank you Raul. And you too, Siwan."

And then the *Defiant* moved away to blast away the other cannons in the capital. Men and women, even children, dressed in plain clothes, came in droves to the castle and started flinging spells at the *Corona*.

Admiral Lina was ready for Warp Master Ryson to send her covert team over after Rauliax flew into the opening, but then Holden, communicating through Grayson, told her about the civilians attacking the ship.

Admiral Morit flicked his wrist at the news. "I'm afraid," he said, "there is no notion of innocent civilians here, Admiral Lina. Everyone will die for their king, and you will have to fire on them unless you want them to slowly strip away your ship's defenses."

She pressed her palm to her forehead and sighed. It was distasteful, but he was right: she couldn't consider anyone firing at them willfully to be a civilian. "Grayson, tell Holden that he has permission to fire."

"Aye," the signaler said.

She turned back to look at the opening the *Defiant* had created, and when the dust settled, she saw Rauliax fly in. "Now, Moreau!"

The Signals Officer sent a mental message to Warp Master Ryson, and a moment later the team was away.

When Admiral Lina reappeared behind Rauliax, she saw that the rest of her team made it without a hitch along with Admiral Morit, and then her eyes were drawn to what was happening in front of her through the translucent barrier her protector had erected around them.

Solah had run up the hall, and he was being attacked by all sorts of magic. They did nothing, of course, and he just walked through fire and ice like they were nothing. Fire wrapped around him and dissipated, lightning arced around him, and he walked forward, his eyes shut, and he looked like nothing short of an angel wreathed in the flames of justice.

Will said, "That boy was your secret weapon, wasn't he?"

Admiral Lina nodded. "I don't suppose you have recorded people with such ability in Elemar?"

"Never."

"We do. We exiled them into the wilds, really a death sentence, because we were afraid of them."

"I don't blame you though, look at how he's just strolling through a whole contingent of soldiers."

She glared at the former admiral. "Ignorance. All they have to do is toss a rock at him."

"Lucky there's no kineticists here, they were all transferred to work on building the dreadnought."

"See how quickly you figured out a weakness? Unfortunate that the general public can't think like that."

Will sighed, the prince's last conversation echoing with Lina's words. "Indeed. He's like the Evoscar embodied."

Solah walked backwards now, luring the elementalists out into the hallway. He fell flat onto the floor, and then Rauliax shot out a beam of light that carved its way through the flesh of the mages, killing some of them and burning others. The dragon still wasn't sure what his magic attacks would do to Solah, and he wasn't about to try here, so he carefully aimed high to avoid firing anywhere near him.

After watching the enemy troops burn by light, Admiral Lina thought the five elementalists she had brought were overkill, although three were still meant to keep watch on Morit. She trusted him, however, and she believed his honor would have kept him to his word even if his prince hadn't been murdered.

The attacks on Solah stopped, and she presumed that everyone had simply fled from fear, especially if they were not disciplined soldiers. They were ready to proceed, and she asked to her signaler, "Moreau, are you having any trouble disrupting communications?"

"No, admiral. The diversionary team reports that they have taken control of most of the ways up to this level, and the enemy signalers aren't offering any great attempt at sending communications out of the keep."

Will added, "Why would they? Everyone knows it's under attack."

"They don't know that we'll be breaking into the king's chamber in a minute," the admiral replied.

Another voice came from behind them. "Best keep that advantage."

Lina turned around and saw Ellcadur. "Keeper, you didn't have to come here."

"On the contrary," the old elf said, "you will have questions. Some questions that only I can answer. The Elemarian admiral too."

"What are you talking about?" both admirals asked.

"That is not one of the questions I am here to answer," Ellcadur replied with a smirk. "Hurry."

The admirals nodded at him, their faces slightly confused, and then they moved up behind Rauliax and moved to the main chamber, the barrier around them following as they progressed. There was no more resistance along the way, however, and at the end of the hallway there was a heavy wooden door and a lone man holding a barrier that blocked their way.

Solah approached the man who glared at him with determined eyes. "Sir," he said, "put down the shield and we won't have to hurt you. Please."

"You will not enter this chamber while I breathe, Wesarian scum."

The boy sighed. He was reluctant to do what he had to do: this man wasn't trying to kill him, after all. He was just trying to protect his king. An evil king, but that was because he was only taught to obey him.

But alas, he was the last obstacle to stop the mad king, and Solah didn't need to look back to Rauliax or the admiral to know what he had to do. He lifted his hand to the barrier, its creator's face clearly in a state of confusion, and then he pressed on it.

There was a whirl of air, and then it was gone.

"Sorry," Solah said. He pressed himself against the wall, giving Rauliax a clear shot, and the man was too stunned to dodge the attack.

The man burned away, and when all was done only his shoes were left, some smoke rising from his seared feet. The door had been hit too, though it was a thick and heavy door that only melted halfway. Solah felt disgusted when he looked at the shoes, and his stomach churned at the man's fate. He had no choice. He had to stop the king so people could stop dying. Rauliax sensed the boy's discomfort, so he came up to the boy and quickly brushed the smoldering shoes away with a paw, and everyone else followed behind him.

"Don't kill him unless necessary," Admiral Lina said. "Remember, we want to capture him. Grayson, head downstairs and join the diversionary team. Moreau, I want you, the three elementalists, and the protector to stay behind and cover the door, signal Grayson if you're having trouble."

"Yes admiral," the soldiers said.

"Keeper, you might actually be needed after all. I'll need you to bind Arashal if he proves to be too difficult." Ellcadur nodded, and then she said, "Let's head in and finish this."

Solah grasped the handle of the door, and then he pushed. It wouldn't budge, however, and he pushed harder.

"Pull to open," Will said.

"Oh," the boy replied, mildly embarrassed. He pulled the handle and the door opened easily, despite the half molten wood melding at the bottom of it. He stepped forward into the king's chamber, but there was no elite guard or any final guardians that he expected would be there.

William Morit looked in too, and the chamber had been transformed from what he remembered of it. The throne was still up a small fanning stairway, and the paths to the king's chamber on were still on both sides behind it. However, directly in front of it, in the middle of the room, there was a great circle carved in the stone floor, its lines thick and bold, and there were four lines that went to the center of the circle, but they did not cross because there was a pedestal there blocking the lines from intersecting. On top of the pedestal, there was the only man in the entire room. His eyes traveled from the pedestal up, noting the royal robes he wore: red, trimmed with wool cloth and streaked with lines of gold string. But when he saw the man's face, he let out an audible gasp.

It was King Arashal, but he looked no older than twenty-five, nothing like the fifty-year old man with greying hair that he was the last time he saw him.

"Impossible," Will muttered.

"What is?" Lina asked.

"That's King Arashal."

She furrowed her eyes at the young man and rubbed them to make sure she wasn't hallucinating. The man wore a golden crown, sure, but the king was supposed to be an older man, nothing like the young black-haired man that stood on the pedestal before them.

"I'll take your questions now or later," Ellcadur said.

"Later," Lina said. "I don't care if it's an illusion or not, the king must be captured *now*. Solah, move aside."

The boy moved to the side of the room, and she walked in with Admiral Morit, two elementalists, Rauliax, and Ellcadur, and they shut the door behind them, but the king seemed to pay them only the barest of attention.

Admiral Lina shouted, "King Arashal! You are hereby taken into the custody of the Wesarian Air Fleet. Surrender yourself peacefully, and this doesn't have to get bloody."

The king's mouth grew into a grin on his unnaturally smooth face. "Surrender? But I do so want this to become bloody, as you say."

Chapter 35

The two elementalists in their group raised their arms as soon as the king expressed his refusal to surrender, and they were ready to attack because of the threatening undertone in his words.

"Don't be a fool, Arashal," Admiral Lina said. "We have you outnumbered and outgunned."

The king started chuckling as the circle beneath him filled with a red liquid. "You have me outnumbered, but you do not have me outgunned. Not even with a dragon."

"Be careful," Ellcadur said. "He is wielding a power none have seen in centuries."

The king seemed to ignore the Keeper and stared right at Rauliax. "I take it that Malyfar failed to keep his end of the contract. That is why my fleet was defeated, wasn't it admiral?"

King Arashal shifted his eyes to his former most trusted servant, Admiral Morit, and waited for a reply, but he did not move. "The entire dragon army came."

The king's grin did not fade. "Good. I had prepared for both possibilities, admiral, but I did not expect you to survive and join the enemy."

There was an undertone in his voice that insinuated that he knew. "Tell me," Will said, "did you murder Prince Rayleigh? Did you kill your own son?"

"My son. Progeny. A weak attempt at imitating immortality. Tell me, admiral, what does a god need with a son?"

"A god? You've gone off the deep end, my *king*!"

"On the contrary. His death was part of my plans, in case you failed to defeat the Wesarian fleet."

Will's blood was boiling now: he didn't want to believe the king had done it, but now there was no denying it when it came straight from the horse's mouth. "I've heard enough!" He raised his hands and threw everything he had into a fan of lightning.

The red liquid in the circle around the pedestal turned into a fine red mist, and then the king reflexively raised his arm in defense. A red translucent barrier appeared around him, and the lightning did nothing but dance around it.

Will didn't stop throwing everything he could put out, however, and let out all his strength and fury into a relentless attack. But it was all to no effect: the king's barrier was undamaged, and he slumped onto his knees after tiring himself out. "What is this? You're not a barrier mage."

"I am a god," Arashal replied.

Ellcadur interrupted their conversation. "You are using blood magic. I hope everyone believes now. He's been using it to rejuvenate his life force, and he has taken the blood of others to restore his youth."

"Smart," the king said. "Too bad humans don't believe in the old tales of elves."

"You cannot win here today," the Keeper replied. "I suggest you surrender before you get hurt."

"Not even the elves can stop me now."

Ellcadur sighed. It was actually sort of funny how the king had remarked on other people's ignorance when he himself was ignoring his most prudent warning. He tried not to glance at Solah, however. "I'm not the one that will stop you."

The king barked out in laughter and looked back at Rauliax. "You know, dragon, Malyfar's contract would've protected Noriath from me. Now that he's dead, the Blood Oath no longer applies, which means I'm free to feast upon your life."

Rauliax narrowed his eyes at him. "What are you talking about?"

"Malyfar's contract would've prevented me from stealing the essence of any dragon. Now I can." The king licked his lips. "I do so wonder how powerful it'll taste."

"Dragons are resistant to magic," Rauliax said. "I'm not afraid of you."

"Not blood magic." Arashal raised his arms and shot out a tendril of red and black lightning, and it wrapped around Rauliax's neck, tightening around it and holding him down.

Siwan seethed with anger and hurt as he saw the dragon forced down. He wanted to just unleash everything he had and completely obliterate the one responsible for causing his best friend's death, but a firm hand grasped his shoulder.

"Not now," Ellcadur whispered to him, "you cannot defeat him. Let justice be dealt by the hand that fate has designated."

The two elementalists, one an ice elementalist and the other lightning, retaliated for the attack on Rauliax by hurling their respective forces of nature at the king, but his shield held firm.

"The blood," Ellcadur said aloud, "the blood in the circle is his source of power."

"Smart and perceptive," the king said. "And thus too dangerous to leave alive. Elven blood must be like dragon blood, if their long lives are anything to compare with." He shot another tendril at the Keeper, and though he tried to dodge it homed in on him and wrapped tightly around his arms so that he could not cast any spells. The tendril felt like a heavy metal chain too, and it dragged his hands down until he fell to the ground, much like how Rauliax was being grappled down.

However much Siwan wanted to fight, he knew he could just as well kill almost everyone else in the room if he failed to control his rage. He held back, even as the Keeper fell, and then he was forced to lie passive when the king tossed another binding onto him.

Admiral Lina joined with the elementalists and started swishing her arms around to generate a micro-tornado where Arashal stood, but unlike a protector's barrier, the blood barrier seemed to be impervious to her attempt to subvert it.

"Oh?" King Arashal said, "A wind elementalist? No wonder you have such an otherworldly beauty."

"Shove it," the admiral said, rather disgusted that her uncanny appearance was being complimented by a monster.

"And feisty too. I simply can't let such a treasure pass through my fingers. You can be my queen, think about it. Wife of a god."

"Shut up!" She tried to will a stronger tornado to tear through his shield.

"Well, I'll just keep you here until you think better of it then." There was a black shadow that passed from his fingers and flew towards the admiral. When it hit her, she fell limp to the ground.

The king then shifted his eyes to the two elementalists who were still flinging spells at him, and he chuckled. "I think I'll have you two as appetizers before my main course," he said, taking a side glance at

Rauliax. "I'll save the elves for dinner."

The elementalists were unfazed by the king's words; true soldiers of the Air Fleet. But they were rewarded with a line of thick black string that erupted from the king's palm, one for each of time, and they latched onto their chests. The elementalists tried to pull them off, but to no avail.

And then Solah saw one of the most frightening things he had seen in his life. The black line turned red, and the two elementalists screamed in horror. Their skin wrinkled as their life was drained away, and their hair grayed as their bodies became frail and old. Barely thirty seconds later, they were lying on the ground as nothing but skin and bones, rotted and dead.

Will forced himself off his knees. "You have gone mad."

"It is an odd thing," the king said. "I planned for all of this, you know. Either my fleet would destroy Wesar's and claim Valeria as mine, simple as that, or the enemy's fleet would come to me. And here, Wesar will provide the power for what I need to destroy its fleet."

"How so?"

The king grinned even wider. "Their ships are firing on our people as we speak. Blood is being spilled, soaked into the very ground." He looked up. "Ground that has been enchanted to destroy everything in the sky, once fully powered. And once the citizenry find out, it will be too late for them to do anything to stop me. And many would help me, anyway."

Ellcadur managed to speak even with the fizzling rope binding him down. "This is your last chance to surrender peacefully."

Arashal barked out again with laughter, sharp and shrill. "And now for the main course," the king said. Solah had seen him glance at him, so he knew he was there, but he was ignoring him for the moment.

He shot out another black line at Rauliax, and Solah feared for his foster-brother's life. He wouldn't have it; he wouldn't leave the dragon to the same fate as the elementalists, and he leapt at the line before it turned red.

His touch broke the line, and it disappeared. King Arashal was visibly distraught and scrunched his face up to look at the boy, angered by his foolish heroics. "And how long do you, boy, think you can hold a barrier against me?"

Solah raised an eyebrow. Arashal thought he was a barrier mage? He had to work the presumption to his advantage, so he did not touch the binding around Rauliax's chest. "Forever," he said.

The boy moved forward, his hands splayed in front of him, and pretended to cautiously approach the king. Arashal let loose another splash of bloodied lightning, but it too dissipated against the boy's palms. Solah acted as if there was force behind the attack, and he jolted back to feign being hit.

"You're stronger than I thought," the mad king said. "Brave, but foolish. Admirable, even. Unfortunate." More of the blood in the circle beneath him turned into a mist of crimson. From the clouds erupted more lightning, red and black, and they blasted at the boy.

Solah was the spellbreaker, the blood hunter. And Ellcadur was happy to see that of all the infinite possibilities that his visions showed him, this was the one to come to pass.

Nothing the blood mage threw at Solah even fazed him, but the boy did pretend to struggle against the undeniably powerful attacks. However, the acting only drove Arashal mad with fury: the boy was supposed to be dead, his life added to his own, and he shouldn't have even been able to resist a second of his magic, let alone a minute. And the way he blocked his attacks didn't seem to be like that of a common barrier, but since Solah seemed to be weakening, though he did not know he was only pretending, the king spurred on his assault, nearly draining the blood in his circle at a rate faster than it could replenish from stores unseen.

The attempt to kill Solah was very flashy, that much he had to admit. The boy inched ever closer, and once he was at a distance close enough that he believed the king wouldn't be able to react to, he made his play, the very last one that he hoped would end the conflict once and for all.

He leapt at the king, his right hand gripped around Rauliax's tooth dagger, and crashed through his attacks, his mists, and his blood barrier. King Arashal looked back at him wide-eyed, and Solah felt his right hand become wet as he pushed the dagger into the blood mage's stomach, his left hand holding his back so his limp body wouldn't topple over.

Arashal gasped, and he reached out his arms in a vain attempt to heal his wound by taking the power of the blood of everyone in the room. There was no magic he could reach, however, and he could not even force a weak light to spark at the tip of his finger.

"What are you?" the dying king asked.

"A blood hunter."

Arashal had shut his eyes and did not reply.

Chapter 36

It was done.

King Arashal was defeated, his power unmasked and subsequently countered with the counterbalance that nature had crafted, all as the true Keeper of the Sylvan Forest had said.

Solah let the king topple backwards, more blood not of his own body splashing onto him, though he kept the grip on his dagger as it slid out of the king's body. He had managed to do it after all, he had managed to kill someone himself, but he did not take any pleasure in it, only relief from the assurance that he would not have to do it again. He dispelled the chains still grappling down his friends using his left hand, the right being smothered with blood, and Admiral Lina awoke as soon as the boy tapped her shoulder. He tried to touch one of the elementalist's bodies in the hope that it would restore them, but there was no effect aside from how his skin crumbled into dust. The elementalist's life was already stolen, and it was lost when he killed the king.

Everyone was content to just rest. They wanted to just take a moment of respite before dealing with the aftermath of the, admittedly relatively short, war.

Admiral Lina thought about how she was to rebuild the fleet, the number of ships of each class, and how many more of ships like the *Defiant* she should ask the dragons to help build. Simple matters often had complicated logistics, and though she knew she should've been issuing some commands right now, she simply didn't want to move, not for a while anyway. The Fleet Lieutenant could handle anything else that came up, anyway.

"What of this enchantment he said he placed on the city?" Solah asked. "Will that be a danger?"

Ellcadur shook his head. "There is no blood mage left to activate the spell. All is done. Except for one thing."

"What?"

"You can come with me, spellbreaker. Raul and Siwan may come too, but the rest of you must stay here."

The admirals didn't complain. Will was still tired from exhausting himself; though not to the point of suicide, he still didn't feel well enough to stand up. Lina kept herself on the floor too, still tired and lost in thought.

Ellcadur led the three into the king's bedroom. The pathway behind the throne was extravagantly large, as royal abodes tended to be, and the king's room was large enough for the dragon to walk through with his wings fully extended. Dark purple tapestries and cloth hung elegantly around Arashal's, naturally, king-sized bed, and there was a single podium next to his bed-table that bore a single book.

The Keeper opened the book once to make sure it was what it seemed, and then he backed away from it. "The source of Arashal's knowledge," he said. With a snap of his fingers, the entire podium was lit aflame, and the fire burned the tome away. "But where he obtained it from, I do not know. Let us hope it was the only one left from that age so long ago."

"Why did you only let us see it?" Solah asked.

"You three cannot use it. Power corrupts. Absolute power corrupts absolutely. I do not trust a sliver of this knowledge to be read by Admiral Lina, even despite her benevolent nature. She, along with everyone else, cannot even know it existed. What Arashal knew died with him, and where he learned it from will remain a mystery."

"Understood," they replied.

Solah couldn't understand it. Everything after King Arashal's defeat had been a blur. There was no celebration, no declaration of victory. Admiral Lina left a contingent of troops garrisoned in Lokin, but she had handed over rule to William Morit. The people of Elemar resisted, of course, but when their former admiral told them what had happened, verified by the prince's body, which had been kept preserved in ice on the entire journey to the capital, the population was quelled for the most part, especially after the former king's own surgeons verified the toxin that killed Prince Rayleigh.

The *Corona* had departed after sending the extra crew it had picked up back to Farrain via Lokin's teleportation stone. Many of the elves were sent back that way too, Ellcadur included, and in the west King Devran arranged ground transportation to send them back to the Sylvan Forest.

While there was no celebration on board the last three combat-worthy ships of Wesar and only a quiet acknowledgement of victory, there had been plenty in Farrain. After all, there was no reason not too: the citizens there had won a war, but they had not faced the adversity the people that fought for them had.

Admiral Lina and the *Corona* returned to Windsgate to deal with salvaging and cleaning the aftermath of the battle there, but more importantly to return as a symbol of hope for the future. But while the fleets could be rebuilt, there was no way to bring back the dead to the realm of the living.

And so it was with an unsettling sense of tranquility, forged from the silence of the ships' crews, that Rauliax, Solah, and Siwan rested in their cabin on the *Reliant*. They had splintered off from the other two ships to head straight to Noriath to drop them off. The *Reliant* had also taken on elves that were injured so they could be taken straight home instead of having to wait for weeks to travel there from Farrain.

Solah was back to studying Algebra under Rauliax's guidance, and he smiled as he thought about how the conflict was over. He could finally live a life, with his *family*, and he thought about how he would visit Wendy and all his friends.

Siwan had elected to return to the Sylvan Forest since the Keeper had revoked his banishment, which was unwarranted anyway, and offered to train him to control his magic himself. While Noriath had been his home for much of his life, he felt like he could not return to it for a long while. It just didn't feel right to be in the city without Ozzari. Besides, with his return and the Keeper's grace, his own family would take him back in without question: they had been torn from him when Nameron banished him, and his mother had been most to suffer. She had very nearly been banished herself for refusing to let him go, and he did wish to return to her arms, though nobody but Ozzari knew of it.

Which was why Solah was surprised when the elf said he would not return with him to the dragon realm. The boy understood, however, and with Keeper Ellcadur restored to his role there would be no problem visiting.

And so they made the best of their remaining time on the *Reliant*. Captain Avery would share a dinner every night, and they enjoyed chatting with him about everything besides the war. He really did end up being a pleasant fellow, in the end, despite his initial attitude towards Solah.

In fact, everyone in Farrain had learned of Solah's status, and the reaction to his existence was completely the opposite of what Avery would have expected. The population hailed him as a hero, undoubtedly supported by the soldiers that saw how he, along with Rauliax, had fought and worked so hard, both in battle and in politics, to turn the tide of the war. By the king's word, he was welcome to visit any land belonging to Wesar, though Solah had already started planning a visit to Farrain anyhow.

But first, he would go home. Rauliax's home. His home.

Chapter 37

"Her telomeres have returned to a length characteristic of a human in her thirties," Priscilla said, her light purple wing swatting aside an annoying fly that had flown into her lab. "And I've a hypothesis for her age reversal."

Rauliax waited a few seconds for her to continue, but she didn't. "Go on," he said.

"What, you're not impressed I was able to run a DNA analysis in just a few days?"

"Go on."

She rolled her eyes and flicked her wings at him. "Fine. I think, just as she and Solah restores our natural magic to its most powerful state, we give them something back. Their power resonates with our magic, and in return they share in our long lifespan. Probably not as long as ours, from what I can guess, but at least as long as an elf's."

"You're not kidding? You're saying she could live another four hundred years?"

"Why would I be kidding? That would a horrible joke to play on someone as pleasant as Solah."

The boy was standing in her lab. He had been listening, but he couldn't understand most of her technical biology jargon, though he did understand the last part. Most importantly, however, he had heard Rauliax's question. "So she has time? Time to make up for everything she's missed? Oh, I do want to show her Farrain, the mountains, the elves, and everything!"

Rauliax smiled. "Yes, Solah. We'll have plenty of time. Plenty."

The boy smiled with an intensity he had never seen before. "That's great, that's fantastic!"

"Indeed," the silver dragon replied. "Now go on, Priscilla wants to test your cells too."

"Yesss," she said, "I wantsss your delicccious blood sssamplesss."

She had not been told about King Arashal's affiliation with that forbidden magic, so she was confused when her attempt at humoring the boy only garnered a sad frown.

Rauliax knew it, however, and he tried to play on the joke. He leapt between them and clawed at Priscilla playfully. "Back, back you filthy snake!"

While that did lighten Solah's mood, it seemed to earn a glare from Priscilla. "Did you just call me a filthy snake?" she asked.

"That's what you are!"

"I'm going to refrain from giving you the satisfaction."

"Uh huh."

"Go get ready, your presentation is tonight, isn't it?"

"Yeah, yeah, I'll go."

Rauliax hadn't forgotten about her deal with him after all. She promised she'd help him earn a grant for his research into atoms, and she was delivering on it tonight. Though really, he would've let her go back on it after feeling her hug him when he came back, but she didn't try backing out anyway.

In any case, he started walking back to his laboratory, three levels below Priscilla's and on the opposite side of the University. He'd probably ask for a room swap next to hers soon, however, since they were, in a sense, together now. Not that it changed much of their demeanor towards each other; it only meant that their arguments could be solved with a kiss instead of with a contest of insults.

He strolled out onto the tower and flew over to the other one, passing by all the windows of the University's library, and settled down onto the opening platform for his desired level. He was walking casually and slowly, a mistake: as soon as he passed by the double doors of a large classroom, a dragon popped out and shouted at him. "Professor! Professor Moonsilver!"

The silver dragon sighed and turned around, there being plenty of space in the dragon designed building to do so. He looked and saw it was a bright blue dragon who seemed to be jittering his hind legs like ants were crawling all over them. "Good day to you, Professor Priestley."

"Yes yes, good day, could you please watch my class for a minute or two? I really, terribly, really need to go to the bathroom."

"Err, okay?"

"Thank you so much!" he yelled, already running away from him.

Rauliax sighed and went inside the classroom. It was pretty large, clearly a lower-division class, and there were wide rows where dragons sat on their haunches, their front paws settled on their notebooks and writing utensils. He walked in front of the chalkboard and noticed several empty glasses on Priestley's table. "Umm," he said, "good day everybody. I'll be your substitute teacher for a minute, I guess. What are you fellows learning?"

"Integration techniques," one dragon called out. "We're on integration by parts right now."

Definitely a lower-division Calculus course, he thought. Professor Priestley was a very old teacher and he hadn't adapted well to modern sciences, so it wasn't entirely unexpected. "Oh, that's simple. Just memorize the formula and you'll be fine. Well, if anyone has any questions, feel free to ask."

Five minutes passed while the students worked on whatever assignment they had been given, and Priestley still hadn't returned. Rauliax just sat in front of the chalkboard, his tail gently swishing, as he kept waiting.

And then a purple dragon, her shade rather close to Priscilla but entirely unlike her because of her horn shape and black hair, raised a wing. "I have a question," she asked.

"Go ahead."

"How do I find the integral of the natural log of x? I'm not sure how the formula works here."

"Oh, that's simple," Rauliax replied. "The key is to know that dv can be set to equal to dx. Try putting it into the formula while I show you the solution on the board."

The purple dragon nodded, and then she started scribbling onto her notepad. Meanwhile, Rauliax picked up a piece of chalk and started writing on the board while standing in front of it on his two legs. "In truth," he said, "it's really one of those integrals you should remember, but let's work it out the first time." He wrote down the steps to the solution, writing words and arrows onto the chalkboard, and looked back to see if the purple dragon was done. Once she had stopped writing, he wrote down the answer and said, "There you have it, x times the natural log of x minus x."

"That's exactly what I got!" the purple dragon said. "But what about the-"

Before she could finish, Rauliax caught his error and scribbled on the missing part of his solution. "Plus constant," he yelled. He nearly hit himself in the face again after he said it. If Priscilla knew he had almost forgotten to add the constant of integration again, he would never hear the end of it.

And then Priestley returned. With a cup of orange juice too, it seemed, and if he offered it to him then he wouldn't have minded him being gone for so long.

"Sorry," the light blue dragon said. "I've discovered the most delicious thing, and I've been drinking so much the past week to find the best balance of taste."

"What, is that orange juice a special mix?"

"Not precisely. I've discovered a method for mass-producing carbonated water."

Rauliax raised an eye ridge at him. Carbonated water wasn't as good as orange juice or tea, but it was fine when nothing better offered itself. "Have you now?"

"Yes," he said. "Enough that I can try mixing it with other things. Professor, I think you'll like this." Priestley offered the glass of bubbling orange fluid to him, and Rauliax drank out of it.

And the silver dragon went nearly delirious with taste-budding pleasure! Without any coaxing from the other professor, he drank it all down, savoring the fizzling sweetness on his tongue, and immediately wanted more.

Professor Priestley smiled at Rauliax's obvious affection for the drink. "I call it orange soda."

"I simply must have more!"

"Excellent! I plan on selling it for a bronze bar a gallon, or a pewter bar per glass."

Rauliax shook the other dragon's shoulders with his paws, somewhat frightening the poor professor. "I'll take a silver bar's worth! As soon as possible!"

The blue dragon laughed. "That's a tall order! I'll try and get it out to your lab or your home if you'd prefer, by tomorrow!"

"Lab, probably, and make it so!"

"Alright, I'm glad I finally found the best mixture ratio. Anyway, back to my class."

Rauliax never relaxed his smile. "I look forward to seeing you tomorrow, professor."

"I can't believe they agreed so easily!" Rauliax said.

"I told you it's easy once you make your presentation interesting," Priscilla replied. She was still wearing a pink ribbon on her forehead, between her horns, and another one tightened around the middle of her tail. She was also wearing a pearl necklace, and all in all he thought her accessories made her look most ridiculous. He himself wore only his standard business horn rings to look professional, and he thought she looked like some schoolgirl instead of a professor of the University.

The board didn't seem to mind, however. They actually seemed *more* interested in what she had to say about *his* research. The board agreed to the grant after she simplified it to some silly metaphor about steamed buns.

"Relating it to food always works," she said. "I told you to trust me, and look at how it turned out!"

He mocked her voice and repeated what she had said in the meeting. "Take a steamed bun, for example. When you break it open or bite into it, there's all that heat inside that comes out! Imagine harnessing that sort of energy from atoms!" He glared at her. "I can't believe *that* worked, no wonder I've barely ever been able to get any grants. I've been doing it all wrong this entire time."

"You sure were."

"Well, no need to be so brutal."

"Aww, but I want to!"

Rauliax smiled and nuzzled his head against hers. "Okay, dear."

"You're allowed to call me that now."

"Why, thank you for such a gracious allowance. Shall we head off to the library now?" He needed to refresh his memory on atomic physics, and he had invited her to study with him since she was interested and, unusually, not as familiar with the subject as he was. And he supposed that, well, it counted as a date, and was thankful that she had carried Solah back to his home before coming back for the presentation.

"It's rather busy at this hour though," she replied. "Do you think there'll be a place to sit in the library?"

"You can sit anywhere in the library."

"No, I meant do you think there will be tables?"

"Of course there will be tables there, what good is a library without tables?"

Priscilla almost wanted to slap the silver dragon. "Curse you, I meant will we be able sit at the tables?"

"Tables aren't meant to be sat on."

The urge to slap him was reaching critical levels. "For the love of - I meant are you sure there will be enough tables for us to use and sit in front of at this busy hour?"

"Oh, well why didn't you just ask that first?"

Priscilla frowned, her restraint almost broken. "Just answer me, you ridiculous beast!"

He nuzzled his wing along hers and replied, "Yes, dear. There will be tables for us to use and sit in front of."

"Thank you."

Rauliax didn't come home until midnight, and his mother had worried that he had flew off again without telling anyone. Her worries were unfounded, however, when he showed up at the door, his scales lit up by the moon, next to Priscilla.

Once he came in and said his farewell to her, she scolded him about wandering off again.

Rauliax shook his head at her accusation, though. "No, mom, I won't go off leaving Noriath without telling you anymore. And if I do, I assure you it'll be with good reason, and Solah will probably be gone with me."

She looked at him and saw his face didn't contort as it usually did when lying. "Okay, I believe you this time."

He wanted to check in on his father. The dragon army had returned to Noriath a fourth of its original size, and he knew his father had lots of memorials, dedications, and letters to write. His father was already asleep in his parents' room, so he moved on and found Solah with Nama in the guest room. They were going to build new rooms for them, but for now the guest room was for her.

"Tomorrow, or rather, today," he said, noting it was past midnight, "before I go to my studies, I'll fly you to see the ocean, alright?"

Nama was, as Priscilla had said, a woman again. She wore new clothes his parents had bought for her, made from elven tailors, and looked very graceful. Her hair was luscious and dark, and she had not even a hint of the frailty that she would have in another four hundred years again. "Thank you, never in my wildest dreams could I have believed this was possible."

"Priscilla believes it's a mutual share of power. Just as you can make me feel invigorated like a young dragon, so too have I given you, both of you, a longer life."

She smiled. "Remember your offer?"

"Yes."

"I'd like to see everything. Oceans, cities, maybe even other continents."

Rauliax smiled. "That last one might not be possible on my back alone."

Solah jumped up. "Maybe Captain Avery could take us if we asked!"

"Maybe, dear boy. But we can hardly ask him now when the *Reliant* is one of the only three airships in workable condition."

"Well, not now. We have plenty of time now, right?"

"Plenty."

The next morning, Solah had woken up early and found Rauliax's parents in the kitchen having a nice breakfast conversation while lying across each other from the wooden board they ate over.

"When do you think they'll marry?" he heard Rauliax's mother ask.

"They took a hundred years just to admit they like each other, it'll probably be another hundred years before they marry. And probably another hundred for them to have-" Wyrst paused when he noticed that Solah had come in the room. "Another hundred for us to have grandchildren."

Solah heard them but pretended not too. It still didn't make sense to him since he held on to his belief that only people who liked each other should marry, and Rauliax and Priscilla didn't exactly seem to fit that ideal.

Wyrst had become more distant to his friends, but closer to his family after his return to Noriath. The Dragon Council heard the tales from the soldiers of the army that returned, of the valor and sacrifice that all races took part in to stop the invasion of Elemar. In turn, the Council found no reason to seek reparation from anyone, and the Eldest, along with Wyrst, had convinced them that Elemar's people would be best left unpunished so that they would not resent the western kingdoms in the future. And now that they understood the danger that humanity could present, the Council ordered the expansion of Noriath's dragon army to three times the size it was before, and many young and impoverished dragons from the lower parts of the mountain base, like Ozzari had been, answered the call.

While his father was busy with the Council and the army, Rauliax's life returned to a sort of relaxed state. He was free in the morning after he awoke, and he did take Nama and Solah flying, harnessed of course, to the oceans north of Noriath. The mountain was already close to the coast, and the flight barely lasted a few minutes. Nama didn't mind the flight; on the contrary, she seemed to enjoy the air rushing by her very much, just as Solah did, and the view of the sparkling water nearly brought tears to her eyes.

But she seemed to enjoy the ocean's water much more. She waded into the tides, afraid of going too deep, but she reveled in its rhythmic waves anyway. She laughed when she let a tall one crash into her, the water splashing everywhere, and then she walked back to just sit on the beach sand. There was so much time now to see everything, and she was in no rush to do anything else just now.

Chapter 38

A month later, Solah had still not visited Farrain or Sylvanis as he had wanted to. Rauliax had been busy with his work, but he had promised to take Nama and him by the end of the month.

And then the *Reliant* came. Captain Avery found Rauliax in his lab at the University, much to the dragon's surprise, and gave him a heartwarming hug, wings and all when he saw him.

"Jon! How's everything been?"

Avery was slightly taken aback by the hug, but it was not entirely unwelcome as he bore a smile after. "Pretty alright, all things considered. I'm here to hire some dragon laborers to help reconstruct the fleet now that our remaining ships have been repaired."

"Oh? I can't imagine the *Reliant* will be able to carry many dragons."

"Nope, just here to hire them. Captain Fourier will be here in a few more days with the *Firestorm* to take them to Farrain."

"Ah, I see."

"I'm also authorized to grant you first-class accommodations on our flight back to the capital, if you wanted to. We're stopping by Sator to make sure all the elves made it back okay, and I know I want to thank our former enchanter too. What do you say?"

"Of course I'd like to! I'll find Solah right away, he's been wanting to go to the capital and visit the elves for some time."

"Great! I'll be moving the ship down to the lower docks, so find us there."

"Will do."

Rauliax rushed home to find his foster-brother, and he was ecstatic to hear that Captain Avery was here. He missed everyone: Siwan, Wendy, Waters, the admiral, and even the nameless crew of the *Reliant* that had become so familiar to him.

They set off at once, and Nama came too. He told Priscilla that they were going, and to his surprise, she asked if she could go with them.

"After all, I have always wondered what you found so fascinating about traveling. And you'll need someone with brains so you don't entangle yourself into another war, right?"

The addition of another dragon made the captain's cabin of the *Reliant* less first-class than Rauliax would've liked, but it wasn't a terrible thing since Nama agreed to sleep in another room on the airship.

The first thing Solah and Rauliax saw when they went into the cabin was the plaque that hung from the middle of the back wall. It was silver molded into the shape of Captain Dillan's face, and he even wore his hat that Avery now wore. Below it was a dedication, and his name was embossed in gold. Captain Robert Dillan, it said, and Solah and Rauliax were ashamed that they had not known his first name. They realized that they hadn't asked the admiral for hers either, and they vowed to ask her when they reached Farrain.

Siwan choked as his tears continued to flow. He coughed, and then he kneeled down to caress the sapling that stood over the fresh dirt. Ozzari's body had been properly treated in Noriath, but here, in his home, Siwan created a symbolic grave for his best friend. "Goodbye," he said. "Though the sun will still rise without you, the days will never look the same to me."

Rauliax and Solah dipped their heads in respect, and they stayed silent for a long time.

Later, Ellcadur met with them. "Thank you for all your help," he said. "Valeria is safe, and I have my kingdom back. The elves live in cooperation with the trees again, not to exploit them, and surely the best possible outcome has come to pass."

"And thank you," Solah replied, "for your role in helping us."

"I hope that I was a fine enough teacher. The rest was up to you."

"You were."

"Thank you."

As a matter of fact, Rauliax and Solah didn't have to look for Admiral Lina at all. When they had dinner in the *Corona's Flare*, Wendy had already returned to ownership since they found a replacement captain for the *Defiant,* and everyone that Solah and Rauliax knew from the *Reliant* was there. Even King Devran appeared, and there was all sorts of merriment: the true celebration after their victory.

Except there was one missing. The man that had given Solah a chance, and during the meal he had to rise and praise him. "I want to thank Captain Robert Dillan. He believed that honesty was an indicator of a person's integrity, and I am proud to be an exemplar of his belief. Thank you, captain, for giving me the chance to prove myself."

"Hear, hear," everyone in the establishment echoed back.

During the feast, Ensign Waters and Frazer came up to Solah, and the fire mage said first, "Scared stupid, but now made to know."

The former exile, now hero, nodded at him. "It's good to be able to walk inside a city in peace."

Frazer laughed. "I doubt it! Instead of flaming torches, you'll be followed around by pen and paper!"

"What do you mean?"

The young lightning elementalist found it difficult to contain his laughter. "People will be coming after you for interviews and autographs, Solah! Be careful out there."

Solah laughed back too. "Oh dear, I do suppose I will!"

Afterwards, he learned the two ensigns first names. Raymond Waters and Charles Frazer.

And he didn't forget about Admiral Lina. After the meal, when nearly everyone had gone home, Rauliax and Solah asked her for her first name.

"Rachel," she said. "Rachel Lina."

"I want to thank you too, Rachel," Solah said. "Captain Dillan was the first to trust me, but you were the one that had the final say in my fate."

"And I daresay I chose well, Solah Moonsilver."

"I'm happy I lived to not disappoint."

She smiled. "Not one bit."

When night fell, Rauliax, Solah, Priscilla, and Nama went outside to look around the capital while Wendy cleaned up the aftermath of the party. They looked to the center of the city, and there was only the *Corona* and the *Reliant* docked, the *Defiant* and other newly repaired ships gone to repair the damage they had done at Lokin. The skies of Farrain were nowhere near as crowded as they had seen on their previous visit, but at least its crown jewel was still there, towering over its city.

With Elemar under the stewardship of William Morit, the continent became mostly free of conflict. The pressure of war had bonded the western realms together stronger than ever before, and free trade and tourism thrived throughout Valeria.

More importantly, the ideas that he instilled based on Prince Rayleigh's philosophy changed his people for the better, encouraging critical thought and to question everything, and when he opened his land to trade with Wesarian airships, these ideas fostered and grew amongst his people until King Arashal's influence was finally gone.

Rauliax and Solah never stayed idle in Noriath for longer than a month. They would always go somewhere, sometimes close by like Sylvanis, sometimes farther. They would go with Nama, and Priscilla had taken a liking to traveling with them so she would often go too. They flew all over the western continent, both by airship and by dragon flight, and when Captain Avery came to Noriath again a year later to ask if they wanted to fly to Aveen, a whole different continent that was a week away by air, to pick up a package in a job contracted by one of the merchant guilds in Farrain, all of them went aboard.

And once more, Rauliax and Solah watched the sunset while leaving Noriath on the deck of the *Reliant* with the wind at their back, except now they were with Nama and Priscilla, though without Siwan. But unlike all the other times they had done so, there was no sense of dread, no fear. They would return, and their home would still be there.

Of course, Priscilla had developed a total insensibility to such beautiful moments, and she asked, "Raul, do you think they'll have jewelry with rare gems and such in Aveen?"

Rauliax turned away from the sunset with a frown. "Really?"

It was only then that she realized everyone else was enjoying the sunset instead of looking out because they were simply bored. "Wait, never mind, ignore what I said."

"What did you just say?"

"Ignore me!"

"What did you just say?"

"Oh for the love of-"

Whatever else Priscilla had to say was drowned out by Rauliax's laughter. She was about to yell something at him, but then he stopped laughing and wrapped a wing over hers. Then he pressed his muzzle alongside hers, forcing her to feel his face and watch the horizon, and they were well. She kept her tongue, and they stayed next to each other well after darkness fell, their tails and wings entwined, and they were lit only by the moon and the flame posts that Ensign Waters was walking around and lighting up. Solah took Nama under the ship for dinner, and the only sound that remained on top was that of the ship's gentle humming as it flew along.

ABOUT THE AUTHOR

Christopher Hwang is currently studying Aerospace Engineering at the University of California, Irvine. He was born and raised in the suburbs of Los Angeles.

He didn't truly love to read until he found J.R.R. Tolkien's *Lord of the Rings* series. After reading the series, he went on to read *The Hobbit* and *The Silmarillion*, becoming a trivia master of Middle-Earth, and loved reading thereafter.

It wasn't until his first fiction writing class at UCI did he start loving to write too. Ideas always flew through his head, but he never found himself capable of putting thought to paper until taking that first introductory class.

In his spare time, Chris likes to read or play video games like normal college students.